ANCIENT
ECHOES

with stories of
Ninja Girl and Lavender Jade

Elizabeth Snyder Reed

Ancient Echoes
Published by Kick a Pebble Enterprises, LLC

Interior Book Design and Layout by
www.integrativeink.com

ISBN: 978-0-9890497-0-2

"As the ages slip away, the man passes into and out of all signs. His particular sign being determined by the nature of the personality ray which itself changes, as you know, from life to life…."

Alice A. Bailey, "Esoteric Astrology"

"Throughout time, there have always been troubadours, wandering minstrels and storytellers singing their songs, telling stories of battles, other countries, customs and traditions – encouraged wanderlust in some…faraway lands and new ways."

Cayce Foundation
Numerology Profile

For Craig, my beloved son,
without you my life would be unfulfilled.

Contents

Preface

IF DESTINY KNOCKS AT your door and you open it, you could be shocked and surprised. It's likely to change your universe and shake you out of your comfort zone. This happened to me. It caused turmoil in the otherwise stable life that I had crafted for myself. It wasn't an easy time. It manifested like a big balloon that burst with all its pent up force, releasing a magical mist in a rather well defined trajectory. Creative energy was unleashed, and with it a new direction for me. I'll look at life differently forevermore.

When a person has an overwhelming feeling of familiarity with someplace, something—or someone—totally unfamiliar, it's called déjà vu. It happened to me. It started as "a someone" and metastasized from there. I tried to dismiss the synchronistic barrage of odd events that bombarded me. Friends passed them off as coincidences, but so many highly peculiar experiences happened that I could not dismiss or deny them. I felt compelled to confront and examine them. I am now of the opinion that destiny can be a good thing, but you must grasp it and engage.

Great and small wheels and gears of life are continuously moving, and every once in a while they meet at exactly the right place. Pow! Things happen. Good things. Bad things. Things that make you think, ask questions, and make adjustments. These are well documented as pivotal points in history; they also happen in every person's life. Most ignore such occurrences.

I know that I'm not alone in wondering why am I here and what this world is really about. When those questions, provoked by the confluence of déjà vu and "a someone" crossed my mind, I became a seeker after the mysteries of life. In doing so, I got a glimpse of the beyond; or as they say, "behind the veil." I learned that sooner or later we are all going to die, and that people don't want to hear that; they prefer to ignore it until the last moments of their lives. It's just this simple; if you were born you are going to die. I've learned the beauty of that, and I am good with that. I mean, I'm really comfortable with that, because now life has new and real meaning.

What happens in between counts. My friends and I agree to the physical evolution of mankind and, further, that each of us is as unique as our fingerprint. Is it simply genetics that accounts for our differences? I say there is a spiritual evolution simultaneously carried on individually and collectively that goes on relatively unnoticed. About this we may differ, have conflicting views, and may part company. This is poked at through philosophy and religion, but it's so subtle it's largely overlooked by all of us as we go wildly about life chasing our aspirations in pursuit of happiness.

I'm saying at the outset, there is more unseen about life than there is seen. The spiritual evolution aspect of us is easy to overlook. To see it you must open your heart and your mind to possibilities. Luckily for me, I did not dismiss my circumstance and simultaneously, the universe provided me with another coincidence—some rare time, space, silence, and solitude to consider the body-mind connection. I'd say a bridge to universal consciousness was found, a veil was lifted, and I was able to tap into my universal self. Secrets were revealed that give me reason to believe that somewhere before my birth, life's parameters and objectives were likely set; and one day, when I shed this Skylar body and personality, my vital essence will continue its progression.

The Sanskrit word *samsara* means "passing through intensely." I'll call it reincarnation, but a few words are precious little to explain that our vital essence follows us through hundreds of lifetimes, giving us countless opportunities through eons of time to conquer our fears and learn valuable lessons. It seems I've had failures, and I'm inclined to say, backslid, but now I realize that my actions, deeds, and my intentions are of utmost importance.

Could a person I knew in a past life play a pivotal role in this one? Do I carry engrams of people and places from my past lifetimes? Does some vital energy, called *prana* in other cultures, leave

2

my body at death and flow on? Are my actions toward others or theirs towards me important? Are future lifetimes contingent on past and present actions? Must I atone for misdeeds? Could a near fatal war wound in the past affect me now? In my dreams, can I tap into some continuous flow of consciousness? Am I, Skylar, the sum total of aspects of this continuum? I conclude, yes.

I felt it before, but now I know for sure—something is pulling me forward, inching me toward my destiny. Not only me but also every spec of humanity.

1
Pioneer Woman

As a matter of habit, I checked my watch when I left the highway and pulled on to the access road. There were a few pickup trucks on the road this morning, but the traffic was light. It was Monday, and the several museums in the area were closed. This was a good thing. Only one staff meeting and one appointment, and then my calendar would be cleared to finish the five-year program and financial plan.

Slowing the Lexus, I turned right on to the street at the sign with an arrow indicating, "Museum Parking." I followed the arrows, passing the chained off visitor's parking lot, and then the delivery zone. Continuing on the driveway brought me around the back of the building to the end of the paving. Slowly, I drove into the gravel and the area designated "employee parking."

It crossed my mind that it had taken me three years to convince the Board to have this employee parking lot built, and it would probably take another three to get it paved. We were making progress.

Except for a shiny new red pickup, I recognized all four of the vehicles and, at a glance, knew who was at work—or more likely getting caught up with the local news over a cup of coffee. The red pickup was a puzzle.

I pulled into the space marked "Director," which was my parking space. Turning off the ignition, I sat back for a moment. This convenience honed a bit off the time it took me to go from my office at home to my desk here. Some argued that it was unnecessary, but I felt no guilt. Staff parking in the back made it more convenient for the staff, I argued back. I justified the expense and made a case for it. More efficiency. We were making steady, consistent progress. Increased gifts and grants were due, in large part, to my credentials and the quality of my initiatives. The Board was pleased, and I felt positive momentum. It had been building, and it showed in the growth and expansion of the museum. The outreach program needed more attention. The docent program needed more attention. But we had made big progress in recent months.

In other words, this parking space had been earned. Thirty years in college, research, and professional experience had brought me to the top of my career. I had gotten here on my own merit. I had gotten here by being extra careful, businesslike, even fastidious—the type of person who checked and double checked, had an organized clothes closet with all garments facing the same direction, locked the doors at night, and locked the car after getting in. I was probably a pain in the ass to people not like me. What all this care and concern added up to was a rather average salary for a person in my profession, a marked parking place, and, of course, a stellar reputation in the field. No one ever said there was money to be made in the arts and humanities; the compensation was "job satisfaction."

This was the fifth of such projects I had tackled—of lifting small, private, and failing museums out of the ashes. In just over four years, this one was all but turned around. Resources were coming in, small facility improvements had led to a building project, and I couldn't have been more pleased with the programs and calendar approved for next year. The important thing was that participation was up, and I had gained the support of the community. This was vital in order to propel this project higher.

Some things tend to get easier as we get older, and some things tend to get more difficult, I think. Thirty years of commitment and focus had paid off, and now I had my own marked parking place to show for it. Big deal!

When in college, I had thought those were the difficult years— struggling to scrape together money for tuition. A few skirts, a few sweaters, a couple blouses, one coat, and stretched out elastic and worn thin underwear was all I had to my name. Replacing underwear was out of the question in those years. My clothes were so few they would hardly classify as a wardrobe. Then there was the wholesome and varied diet of peanut butter or baloney sandwiches.

Don't go there, Skylar, I cautioned myself. That was so long ago and so far away, it doesn't matter. You've got a drawer full of underwear now, and you eat red raspberries out of season. Such extravagance. Justify it this way: you never got hooked on cigarettes because you never had enough money to buy a pack.

My mind wouldn't let it go. *Don't allow yourself some kind of a pity party,* I thought. *You don't have time for it this morning. Staff meeting—yes, focus on the staff meeting agenda.* But no, the first few years of my marriage flashed through my mind: expenses of a baby, then a new house with seemingly endless expenses. *Oh yes, and car payments. We had a lot of cars over the years. How many? Think back on that someday when you have more time. Don't even go there,* I told myself again. Then I asked myself, *Where is all this babble coming from, today?*

I grabbed the thin notepad from the visor over the passenger side seat, my grocery list. I added mayo, lower sodium deli ham, Swiss cheese. Hmmmm, it seemed there were two more things. But what were they?

Now, just when everything should have been getting easier for me—although in many respects, they were—the wheels were falling off. Divorce. Shit. Why was I complicating things, and why couldn't grown-up, adult children understand? Becka was the bigger problem. She was more difficult than her dad. How do you split a marriage in half? Or by the time the attorneys finish taking their half, well, I guess it would be half split in half. What little we were able to accumulate seemed destined to be generously disbursed to attorneys. Their law offices sure were plush. I wondered how much their leather chairs had cost.

We needed to be smart about this. It was going to have to be talked over. This was not an easy thing. We hadn't communicated well in thirty years. Nothing about that fact was going to change.

I told myself to stop thinking about it. I could only deal with so much at one time. I knew that I had to keep moving forward with this new exhibition.

I slipped the grocery list back up under the visor. There were a couple more things for the list, but they wouldn't come to mind. Maybe it would come to me later.

I returned the pencil to its holder and removed the key from the ignition. It was downright amazing how much stuff, junk, and important information ran through your mind in a matter of seconds. What the memory conjures up, what problems the mind solves—it's fantastic. Today, it was something like a computer run amok. The creative part of my mind put a positive spin on the chatter going on inside my head. It was phenomenal. I felt certain one's entire life really could pass in front of you at the moment of death.

I flipped down my visor with my left hand as I glanced into the mirror on the back of it, checking my lipstick. Then I jammed the car keys down into the side pocket of my purse and simultaneously felt around there for a tube of lipstick. Once I found it, I opened it, looked back up into the mirror, refreshed my lipstick, checked my teeth for smudges, and snapped the visor back in place. Slipping the tube back in the side pocket I pressed the switch to unlock the car door.

My mind was back on the divorce. Life is about choices. On the surface, it was a difficult situation, but to me it was also a no-brainer—done, finished, kaput, through, and at this point, it was just that simple. Something I was finally getting around to, but long overdue. Why I felt obligated to explain myself to others, I didn't understand, exactly.

I cautioned myself again. *Skylar, you need to be careful how you express your feelings about this when curious people ask.* A cavalier attitude expressed publicly is not acceptable. Divorce was a serious issue to people, particularly in this area of the country. It was a God-thing for them. If mentioned, some people get all sad, mushy, and apologetic. In some ways, your reputation is at stake. But this was about us—between me and Stan, not them; I'd had to move on with my life.

I opened the car door and finished the lesson with myself, efficiently collecting my Coach purse and Gucci attaché case in one fell swoop with my right hand. At the same time, my peripheral vision caught sight of a man squatting under a tree, the only shady spot in this area of the campus. Hmmm, so that accounted for the red pickup. I wondered what he wanted.

While walking on the gravel to a path that connected me to the employee entrance, I tried to avoid scratching the heels of my new Anne Klein shoes and deleted further thoughts of divorce. Job requirements were about to press in on me. It had always been an easy matter to transition from home to work. Priorities of the job were my main focus. My professional life was so much a part of me that little else interested me.

As I approached the stranger, I did a casual survey of the grounds, visually checking the grass and shrubbery, the landscaping, and flowering plants in the distance. The new contractor was doing a much better job. It was a smart move not renewing the contract with the previous one. Convincing a Board was never easy; getting consensus to change old, unproductive habits and procedures took time and patience. Why were people so resistant to change? They stayed stuck in their comfort zone. *Because it's easier,* I thought, answering my own question.

The stranger closed the paperback he was reading and shoved it into his backpack. Lying next to him on the ground was a black daypack, a camera bag with a Nikon camera strap, and a bottle of water wrapped snugly in a gee whiz shiny lime green and purple bottle holder. Now that was something you could never forget and leave behind! The morning light through the small tree speckled him all over with faint shadows. Three more hours, and this sapling would provide no shade whatsoever in the powerful Oklahoma sunshine.

I greeted the guy with, "Good mornin'" and a halfway quizzical look. "What brings you here?" I asked, pausing to shift my purse and attaché case to the other hand.

As the speckled stranger smoothly rose to his feet from a squat position, he vigorously swiped the seat of his pants.

Whoa, he was quite a big guy. Tall, wearing new hiking boots, well built, broad shoulders, fair skin, clean cut, easy to look at, maybe even handsome. I gathered all that in before he had time to reply with, "Good morning, ma'am." His face broke into a very pleasant smile.

Like everyone in his generation, he was wearing a ball cap. This one was old, well used, faded, a burgundy color Phillies ball cap with a stylized "P" in white. Some indistinct reminder of something—a thought I didn't have time to capture. Something about home and my childhood careened through my mind. The center of the bill on his ball cap was creased, evidence it had been folded a lot.

"Is there something I can help you with?" I asked.

"I saw a classified ad in the newspaper some time ago, and I'm wondering if the job's been filled." He went on, apologetically. "I didn't realize the museum was closed on Monday. I should have checked in advance." His smile widened. "Would you happen to know if there is still an opening?"

My mind went in search of recent job vacancies, advertised statewide. Nothing came to mind. "Perhaps I do," I said. "What job was it? You say it was published in a local paper?"

"It was for an exhibits builder; it specified three-dimensional design and woodworking skills." Then he added, "I have some design and woodworking skills."

"Gee, that is an old ad, published maybe four or more months ago," I said. I was being polite. I didn't a want to insult him, but I'd run that ad well over six months ago. Although the position was not filled, I was noncommittal.

"Well, at the time I saw it, I was on active duty, you know, in the Army. I tore it out of the paper and put it in my wallet. I thought I'd follow up on it when I got out and well, ma'am, I just got out." He ran his hand up the back of his neck, pushing his cap forward and revealing the close, tight haircut on the back of his neck. "Well, I just thought there might be a chance the job's still open. Or maybe you have something else?"

Actually, the job had been vacant for eight months and had not been filled, but I didn't tell him that. I allowed him go on talking about himself, while I assessed the situation and analyzed his suitability for the job from what he was telling me.

Having made several errors in hiring over the years, I knew that hiring people was probably the hardest part of any administrative management job. It had taken a while, but over the last year, my team had finally started to pull together. I was not in a hurry to make a selection that might jeopardize our current situation. A wild card in the deck could ruin the team. People were not always what they appeared to be on paper. Today, even references were not necessarily reliable—former employers were afraid they would get sued for telling the truth. Furthermore, some employers outright lied to get rid of poor performers, effectively moving their problem worker to someone else's payroll. I learned my hiring lessons by experience.

In this particular job situation, I felt those who had applied weren't a "good fit." There were skilled cabinetmakers, carpenters, construction workers, and artists that applied. Maybe I'd missed something, but none truly indicated an affinity for museum work. I was searching for a particular amalgam of skills and abilities. Construction workers didn't have the fine-tuning to handle collections; the artists were usually deficient in the use of power tools for woodworking.

A discussion of this vacancy had come up in the last meeting of the Board of Directors, and there was pressure on me to find someone and fill the position. We were making do.

He bent down and pushed aside the camera bag, turned over the daypack, and handily retrieved a white envelope from a side pocket. Neat, tidy, muscular, tall, good posture, shoulders back, a military bearing—his words all rang true and accounted for his demeanor and courtesy.

"I put together this resume," he said. "In case the job is still open, or, if not, maybe there is something else. I did go to college to study art after high school."

"Photography?" I asked, pointing to the camera case on the ground.

"No, actually, pottery. That's really what I do. That's really what I love to do. It's a long story, but in a nutshell, you can't make a living as a potter. I tried. I really tried. I've been in the Army for eight years."

He'd skillfully brought the conversation back to the job vacancy. "I couldn't tell by the ad exactly what you are looking for, but if it's a matter of building shipping crates and packing boxes,

I'm sure I can do that. I know my way around a wood shop. The ad specifies three-dimensional design," he reiterated.

"Do you have a BFA?"

He said, no, he didn't finish college, but he hoped to someday. He went on to say he had some industrial arts training, did sculpture, and built furniture.

I concluded he was yet another example of an under-financed college education. In his case, he'd bowed out midstream and joined the Army. Sheer conjecture on my part, of course, but I'd heard that scenario so often before, and I'd bet it's true of him.

"At this moment photography is my interest, my main focus you might say." He laughed at his joke and added, "Forgive the pun."

"I'll forgive you," I said, with a raised eyebrow.

"I'm sorry to hold you up this morning," he said, extending the envelope to me. "Could I leave this resume with you? Maybe you can look it over or get it into the hands of the hiring person. I noted my buddy's phone number on the back. He knows how to reach me. If nothing works out here, I'll be heading back east. I should be in the area for a few more weeks."

"Yes," I said, "I have a meeting this morning. So I must be going. But, listen, you stay in touch. In fact, check back with me in a few days. I mean I may have other questions and since you don't have a phone, that could present a problem." I took his resume.

He gave a respectful nod of his head, said thank you, and collected his belongings up off the grass. He moved fast, and his long strides got him to the pickup before I could unlock the door and look back.

As I turned the handle, I thought, there was something almost vaguely familiar about him, some kind of easy, casual familiarity. I was sure I had never met him before, but there was something peculiar, something I couldn't put my finger on. There was also something just shy of flirty about him. He sure was handsome.

I dismissed that thought, went inside, and concluded that I had just conducted a job interview under a tree. Maybe he was the right one for the job.

Our strange encounter hung in my mind. References for Jacob "Jake" Byron Wolfe checked out, and within three weeks, I'd hired him. I revised his job description, tailoring it to include photography of the permanent collection, recent accessions, and work on a catalog I wanted to develop.

After handling the prerequisite personnel matters, I introduced Jake to Lloyd Redfeather. Then, I sent them off to get acquainted with the facilities and begin training in the wood shop. Lloyd was a valued employee who was approaching retirement; he knew museum operations inside and out. Jake was in good hands.

The week following, Lloyd came to my office, tapped lightly with one knuckle on the side of the doorjamb, peered in, and asked, "Got a moment?"

"Sure, just working on the budget," I said. "Have a seat."

He said, "You know, Skylar, I think you've hired a good one there."

I looked at him quizzically.

He followed with, "You know, that 'easy guy' you just hired. The packing cases for the traveling exhibition are finished. He squared those away real fast. He got right on it; he has some good ideas, and his woodworking skills are better than anyone else we've ever had in here. He's even done a fair amount of well overdue organizing down there. You know he's a potter, right? I'm no judge, but I saw some pictures of his work, and it's mighty impressive for a Yankee," he added.

Lloyd liked to rib me about being a Yankee from the north; we do some good-natured sparing.

"Lloyd, you're showing your ethnic bias," I said. "The American Indian may have been the first potters, but they certainly aren't the only potters in America."

Lloyd shook his head. "Speaking of that, have you seen that ceramic mold stuff the Acoma are doing? That's really disgusting. Tourist junk. What have we come to?"

"It sells. It's cheap. That's why they do it. It puts food on the table. You know there is stellar work still being done, but its cost is out of the reach of average folk who just want a souvenir." Changing the subject, I looked at him and asked in a serious tone, "Lloyd, have I ever told you the story of the Blue Whale Bag?"

Taking a moment to search his memory, he shook his head. "No, I don't think you have."

"Well, sit down; this is going to take a minute."

He was still standing in the doorway. Lloyd is knowledgeable and professional; he is also a bit of a character. He has a laid-back demeanor, and the polite manners and charm of a cowboy with a dash of Will Rodgers humor. He made me laugh and left me puzzled at the same time. He liked to "pull my leg," so to speak. Whenever he left the office, I was left wondering whether he'd just told me a tall tale, a yarn, or a true story.

After a recent dream, I had decided I needed to take a bit more time with and be more relaxed with my staff, to get to know them better and find a better balance for my focused, all business, keep-pushing-forward attitude. Lloyd was really my right hand man, but we rarely sat down over a cup of coffee for idle conversation. We were always working on museum objectives. We seldom took a moment to relax.

Lloyd sat down and reared back, giving me a "this better be good" look.

"Lloyd, I was working with Eskimo and Indian artists in Alaska. They were expert carvers of ivory and soapstone, the crème de la crème. There was a good market for their work. One day, I received a notice in the mail from a major east coast museum. They were planning an exhibition of 'all manner of bags,' as they put it."

Lloyd wrinkled his forehead and cocked his head without saying anything.

"Yes," I said, "all manner of bags, any kind of bag, such as, hand bags or shopping bags, for example."

"Okay, I got it," he said.

"Well, my right hand man on that job was a King Island Eskimo named Paul. He was a really great guy—talented, original, and, conscientious—a teacher. He helped others. Art history will record him among the best. His work is in the National Gallery and many private collections. He died too young, never having reached his thirty-third birthday." I shook my head. "Sorry for that digression," I said. "It makes me sad. Anyway, he was a really great guy, and I loved him dearly. One day I sat down with him to explain the bag request, to brainstorm and maybe come up with a novel idea."

"He thought about it for a while, then told me that when he was a little kid, his dad would tie a rope around his waist and lower him out over the rookeries of King Island. King Island is about as remote as you can get. It's between Russia and Alaska. Even though at one time all the King Island Eskimo's lived out there, the BIA moved them to Nome years earlier. The weather was so bad there they were marooned most of the year, which they didn't mind, but the BIA did. They couldn't receive mail or get medical attention except briefly, for a few weeks in the summer. Anyway, Paul went on to say that all parts of the whale, the seal, and the walrus were used—nothing but nothing, was ever lost or thrown away. If not eaten or used for making parkas, mukluks, and mittens, then, well, it was used for something, for example the bladder was used for drums. You've seen those drums, I expect?"

Lloyd said, "Not really, but I can imagine." Then he added, "Oh, yeah, I do remember. We had a collection of northwest coast art and artifacts in here about ten years back."

Lloyd was with me on this, so I went on. "So, Paul described how his dad hung him out over the rookeries to collect eggs in a bag made with the intestine of a seal. Can't you just see this very little kid dangling over those steep cliffs? Even the bird eggs are shaped differently on those rookeries. Really, Lloyd, I have seen them; they are almost pear shaped. It happened over eons of time. Regular eggs would have rolled around and fallen off those shelf-like rookeries, but mur and puffin eggs won't roll off because of the shape. I guess it's an adaptive evolution or survival of the species thing.

"So I asked Paul, 'Weren't you scared?' and he said, 'Are you shitin' me? Of course I was! Most of the time I peed my pants, if I had any on.'"

15

I was just breaking up inside remembering the visual picture Paul had painted for me, which I was now recounting for Lloyd, of a little kid with a seal intestine bag collecting eggs in mid-air.

Lloyd was listening intently, so I continued. "Paul got very quiet and rather thoughtful, then looking directly at me, he said, 'There was the Blue Whale bag.' As I recall, there was a dramatic pause before he asked me if I knew about that.

"Well, Lloyd, Paul had me totally absorbed by then, and I was thinking we might have a good response for the museum back East. I told him, 'No, I don't. I never hear of it.' 'Well, you should,' he quickly retorted. 'That's the one we put missionaries and the earliest settlers in.'"

I paused, waiting a moment until it sunk in with Lloyd. Then he groaned, smiled, got up, and said, "If that's the best ya got fer me, I'm goin' back ta work."

"Lloyd, it's a true story. Really," I finished.

After Lloyd left, I attempted to return to the budget, but the Alaska experience pushed into my consciousness with a vengeance.

I thought about Paul. He was a master carver, whose ivory work looked much like Henri Moore's sculpture in miniature; he died of natural causes, a weak heart. I was greatly saddened by his death. I thought about all the sculpture he had yet to create. What a great loss to the world. But I was profoundly affected when it occurred to me that all his dreams went with him. For three years we had worked together almost every day. He talked of his dreams, and I was committed to helping him further his life plan. Among that entire group of King Islander's, Paul had a real chance of lifting his wife and four children out of poverty with his talent and skill as an artist. Knowing that his wife was illiterate and unskilled, I wondered how they faired without him.

The figures on the page blurred as tears welled up in my eyes. I regretted that I'd let life get so busy that I hadn't stayed in touch. Over the years, a note on the back of a friends' Christmas card read, "I thought you'd want to know that..." another of the carvers had passed, or someone had gone to work on the pipeline and was no longer carving. I thought about the word "survival" as the watchword of the Eskimo. The difficulty of making money as an artist, the harshness of life in a rural village, the struggle of an Alaskan Native American at this point in time. Sociologists called it acculturation; that's a tidy word. Acculturation. It was nothing less than an on-going massive socio-economic catastrophe that affected real people. For three and a half years, I tried to come to grips with what I saw and felt.

Sitting there with my head in my hands, I found myself still troubled by the experience. I could only hope that my work and my relationship with those carvers had done something to improve the circumstances of the guys with whom I worked. If so, it would be a fair exchange, because I'd learned a lot from them.

I remembered my dad's response when I'd cheerfully told him I'd gotten a job in Alaska working with Eskimo and Indian artists. A small town guy, Dad always went straight to the heart of any matter. He said only one thing: "What do you want to go and bother those people for?" I went anyhow.

It didn't take me long to learn that over time, the whalers had come, the missionaries had come, the military had come, and faced with the encroaching western world, the traditions of the Eskimo were being obliterated. The struggle was evident. Little by little, this generation of men were losing their identity. They were torn, some intent on holding to tradition, others attempting to embrace the new. They were faced with tough, no-win choices. Upon reflection, they were in limbo, or free fall. Their forefathers, who were skilled hunters and fishermen, fed their families in the traditional way. But traditional skills were on the wane, and they were poorly educated and prepared to cope in our society; they didn't have the skills or means to earn money, thus, to shop in the grocery store. At the very least it was demoralizing. Many turned to alcohol.

The impact on this generation was not a pretty picture. The Inupiat were a gentle people caught in the downdraft of the fast moving current of time. Because Paul and I had worked so closely, I'd developed a real understanding of their predicament. I've always been empathetic, and after a while, I found myself with one foot in their culture and one in my own. Understanding their plight and feeling their pain, if there was a solution, I wanted to be part of it. At the very least, *do no harm.*

The experience still evoked strong emotions within me. I liked things well done and finished up in neat packages, no loose ends. But in this matter, there was no right answer then, and I doubt there is one today. It will take years. No, generations. Born at this moment in time, they were destined to be ground up in the wheels of acculturation.

I felt angry and restless. I couldn't get my head back into my work, and anyhow, it was almost quitting time. I collected up the loose pages of the budget, slid them into a folder, and crammed the pens and pencils into over-filled tray of the middle drawer. For an instant, I considered that maybe this was simply how social evolution worked and that most people called it progress. By whatever name, it was damaging and hurtful.

I decided to quit for the day; I couldn't focus. On my way out, passing Jake in the corridor, I asked him how things were going. He said, "Great, couldn't be better." It crossed my mind that he always had a great attitude, was pleasant, and for an instant, I wondered if anything ever troubled him. He lifted my spirits with a glance.

Without any forethought, I stopped, put my stuff down on a bench, and said, "I've been meaning to catch up with you. I have to drive to Ponca City tomorrow to photograph 'Prairie Woman' for a presentation I'll be doing. I don't know if you're familiar with that sculpture, but it's a 17-foot bronze by Bryant Baker. Over 30 foot from the base to the top."

"I know of it, but I never made it to Ponca City. I've only seen it in pictures," he said.

"Well, since you're living in Oklahoma, it's probably in the 'must see category' for a person like yourself," I said. "I'll tell you what, if you'd like to go, I'll speak to Lloyd. We'll have to leave here at 7 a.m.; you know, the sunlight and all. If you can go, I can use the help. Meet me back where we park the van at seven. You might be interested to know that Baker was a sergeant in the Army in the early nineteen hundreds."

"I'd like to go," he responded eagerly. "Seven's not a problem for me; in fact, in my former life as a soldier by that hour the day was half over. I'll be here on time."

"Okay then, I'll see you in the morning," I told him.

The Alaska experience shared with Redfeather earlier in the day stirred memories and a sort of nervous dissatisfaction. A kind of melancholy came over me. Once I got home, I tried to work. I microwaved a frozen dinner for supper. That didn't interest me. I thought I was hungry but didn't know what I wanted. The sadness worsened. If I had been a drinking person, I might have found a bottle.

Instead, I laid the annual budget segment of the five-year plan on my desk and halfheartedly extended a few numbers in the columns. In less than ten minutes, I realized I couldn't focus on it, and I was not going to be able to work my way out of this state. Paul and thoughts of others crowded in to my space. Old memories of the Eskimo struggle for survival refused to go away. Paul's energy surrounded and clung to me.

I glanced at the TV schedule and found nothing of interest. I decided I needed something creative to do and found a needlepoint project I stitched on occasionally. I didn't invest much time in it before I realized I needed something more than filling squares with threads to get me through this; I needed something creative that would totally engage my mind.

I picked up a pen and began to write. The words practically wrote themselves. Surprised, I wondered how long they had been pent up, waiting to be said. When I finished the piece, the distress of the day was gone. I had gained a feeling of satisfaction, and I was finally calm and in control. I went to bed.

2
Survival

MY NAME IS KALILUKTUK. We are approximately between what is today known as Nome and Kotzebue, Alaska. I say approximately because the land we are traveling across no longer exists. It was lost eons ago as the ice cap melted and covered the place I know as home.

It is a joyful time for us; winter will be over soon. After the long dark nights, brief, twilight days, and the general malaise and doldrums of winter, I look forward to the work of spring, when the round-the-clock daylight cycle of summer begins. Then men are out fishing and hunting, socializing with friends, and the women pick fresh tundra greens to preserve. Late summer will bring the pleasures of storing greens in seal oil, smoking salmon, drying game, tanning leather, collecting driftwood, gathering grasses for my basket weaving, and preparing bone and ivory for my companions' winter carving.

Angalgaq, my partner in life, my *aipaq*, and I are traveling to my village. I have been looking forward to this for months. We have our first baby, and because we live with Angalgaq's family, mine has never seen our child. Although the message of his birth could have reached them by now, our arrival will be a surprise.

Now is the time. He and I have chosen to travel by dog sled the few hundred miles between communities. His father, an elder, is opposed to this and has cautioned us against leaving at this time. He sees the ice moving ever so slightly in the vast distance beyond, signaling breakup has begun. In youthful anticipation, we are skeptical. I want to go. The blinding, glistening snow indicates no such movement to us. As we watch and wait, his father acquiesces and I prevail.

Angalgaq is proud of his first son and understands the loneliness I have for my family, and so, we set out by sled with three of the best dogs. We travel two days and know that in the next day we will reach my home. I am euphoric. We make good time; the dogs are fast.

Whenever we settle down to rest for the night, the dogs seem restless. My *aipaq*, the baby, and I are curled together, partially buried in the snow. Periodically, the dogs disturb our sleep. The lead dog has not settled this night. He is now pacing back and forth not far from us. I wish he would stop agitating the others. Under the starry night and the dark coldness, I fall back into my dreams until the baby or the barking dogs pull me into reality.

We are joyful but exhausted from two days' travel. Angalgaq sleeps heavily. I nurse the baby, then I fall back into a deep sleep. Together he and I, barely fifteen and fourteen, respectively, lie together. Drifting and dreaming together, we are awakened by the cracking, splitting sound of ice breaking.

Movement far beneath us indicates we are separating from the main mass. There is the sensation, then the realization, that we are moving. Startled, Angalgaq practically tramples the baby and me when he jumps to his feet. Looking at me with concern, he follows the noisy dogs.

For three days, he and the dogs search for a way back to the main mass. Each day the currents grow stronger. At first, it is imperceptible. Our provisions are depleted. We eat snow to stop the rumbling in our stomachs. He releases the dogs on the forth day. They may be able to find their way back. In the next five days, the ice flow reaches the open sea.

By this time, there are many spirits around us. Some I recognize. The first to appear is Nukallpiaq, an old shaman. He was the last person from our village to die. He is the great hunter for whom our child is named. He comes and takes our child with him. Angalgaq thought I didn't notice in my frozen delirium, but I felt his spirit leave this world with my child, and some of me went with them.

Then placing his nose to mine, we knowingly breathed our final kiss in this world, with full assurance that our spirits will soon join and travel with the great spirit of the north, and, eventually, the icy waters will consume our bodies.

Survival is the watchword of the Inupiat. Death comes quickly in the icy winds of the north, and no one survives into old age.

3
Dream Catcher

THE LONG SUMMER HAD been a season full of active tornados. Then fall turned to a bitter cold winter. I heard the wind whipping around outside. A shiver ran through me. Then I smiled. A letter had come from a consortium in Japan inviting me to do a lecture series. It was an attractive offer. I thought possibly the opportunity of a lifetime. I didn't mention it to anyone. I needed time to think it over before responding.

As I worked late in the still, darkened museum, I knew I had to brave the weather and go home, so I neatly ordered the stacks of papers on my desk, put my scarf around my neck, wrapped myself into a black wool cape, pulled the collar up, picked up my purse and gloves, and turned off the light. As I passed the staff room, I was reaching in to flip the light switch off when I noticed that someone had forgotten to clock out. Jake's card had not been punched out. I made a mental note to remind him.

The unobstructed cold prairie wind hit me as I stepped outside. I was about to pull the door closed behind me when I noticed his red pick-up and stray light under the overhead door of the loading dock. I retreated into the building and down the dimly lit corridor to the workshop.

Crates were stacked nearly to the ceiling. I stood in the doorway and called, "Jake, are you there?" The room was nearly dark except for ceiling lights near the overhead door. His voice, muffled by the crates, sounded far away. I said, "You're working awfully late tonight, aren't you?"

He responded, "I'm almost finished. I just need to double-check the markings on these crates, yet. I need to make certain the paperwork matches the labels, exactly. You know how the freight line is, and they'll be picking these up early tomorrow morning before I come in."

As he stepped from behind the crates, he was backlit, a shadowy dark figure in an even more shadowy space. The breath was sucked out of me. I gulped and stepped back. I somehow managed to say, "I saw your pickup out back and just wanted to say goodnight. Don't be too long; if we have any precipitation tonight, the roads will get slippery. Also, I turned the lights off in the staff room, so please see the night watchman before you let yourself out."

I fled. I don't remember driving home. Some sort of instantaneous recollection had occurred. It was vague and dream-like, and I was shaken to the core. When I got home, I turned up the thermostat, made a cup of hot chocolate, slipped into my recliner, and pulled my afghan around me for warmth. *Jake must think I am crazy,* I thought, *bolting like that.* I closed my eyes to think over the incident. As I warmed up, I dozed off and dreamt.

> *It is dark. It is night. There is a rainy fog. The picture is obscured by the conditions. There is a large rock cliff facing in this dark place. He is walking among the boulders. I see him vanishing and reappearing. It seems a hiding place of sorts. There is a dream-like state in this misty fog. The scene is troubling, just falling short of ominous. I appear as a shadowy figure in a hooded dark cloak. He appears from the darkness and comes to me. This is all vague and mysterious, yet real. Just a dream-like impression, an embrace, and lovemaking, fading in and out in the darkness of the crags and moving mist. There is never a clear or total image shown. I can't identify the person.*

Awakening, I thought there was a bit of kabuki in that dream, some floating world quality. Then immediately I fell asleep again, surrendering to the dream state.

This time I appear to be in Edinburgh, Scotland. There is a man. This is not the man from the previous dream. He is slim and tall, dressed in a suit and waistcoat in the style of the day. He could be the proprietor of a business. That changes. It seems he is a teacher, a musician, and a professor. He is prosperous with the air of total confidence. It is late in the evening; he walks along the cobblestone street in darkness, not far from Holyrude House, in the shadow of the castle that not long ago imprisoned Mary Queen of Scots.

He passes the dark mahogany-colored stonewalls of the row houses. All the houses are attached and identical except for an occasional break, opening into a narrow alleyway. Each house has a stoop. The front of each house has two front windows and one wooden door. He reaches a house with freshly white-washed window trim and a framed door. He walks up the step and, taking the key from his vest pocket, he unlocks the door and lets himself in.

I watch him remove his hat and place it where he always does. Somehow I know this is not where he lives, but he owns the house. The scene is hazy, vignette-like, and fading out around the edges. Like someone or something seen in an old photograph.

There is a clock, a candle, and a few pretty things on a lace-covered fireplace mantle. He walks into the room, saying nothing; he lays his key on the mantle. He begins to remove his coat, but first he picks up the iron poker and stirs the coals, causing them to flare up.

The room is furnished with a highly polished piano, piano stool, a straight-backed chair, and two upholstered chairs. Everything is immaculate and in its place, but too ridged to be comfortable.

I appear to be nearly twenty years of age. I am wearing neatly laced, high leather boots with pointed toes, and a long dress with a dark floral pattern. The neck and the bodice are made of cotton lace. I am corseted, small, and delicate with a shawl covering my shoulders.

Modestly, I hold a child as he suckles. The infant is very beautiful, fair, and angelic. He has fine blonde hair. He is peaceful in my arms. With the palm of my hand and fingertips, I lightly caress his head. My fingers lovingly touch his cheeks and tiny ears. I bend slightly to kiss him on the forehead, an instinctive action that automatically follows my caress. I adore him. And now, even though separated from him by birth, he remains as attached to me as he once was in my womb.

I want to continue holding him; however, the man's abrupt attitude indicates that I should finish with the child. I want him to appreciate us, but he has his own selfish needs. No words are exchanged, but his manner implies dissatisfaction. He seems jealous of his own child, or he is short of time—perhaps both. Quickly, I button my dress and gently place the baby in the cradle nearby. Then, I turn to face my piano teacher.

I awoke when the hall clock chimed twelve. I had dozed off while reading in the recliner, and now I had a stiff neck. I wondered briefly what the dreams had been about. They'd seemed like moving pictures, with images of two different lifetimes in the Scottish highlands or some remote crags of Wales.

I was tired, but I was alert enough to realize that this had all been provoked by my encounter with Jake—even though he hadn't done anything out of the norm. There was something attractive about him, something dangerously attractive about him. I'd have to sort it out in the morning.

For now, I turned off the downstairs lights and went upstairs to bed, but the dreaming continued.

A fair young man with sandy red hair is sitting on bare ground, very near the summit. From here, there is a splendid view of the highlands. Majestic mountain ranges are seen overlapping one another, retreating in the distance. He is looking across the moors toward the village that is our home.

I'm coming up the mountainside and may appear to be meandering, but I am picking my way around the spikey gorse

26

and clumps of prickly heather, taking care not to catch my skirt.

With evident pleasure, he is watching me approach. A thin fellow with clear blue eyes who works in his father's mill, he already knows I will marry him when I am old enough. Although, we haven't said.

Only two more steps. He reaches out for me, and I alight next to him.

We lie back on our elbows, talking and enjoying the summer day while watching racing clouds cast shadows across the valley and produce cloud-capped mountains far beyond. He occasionally points something out to me so that I have to turn my head from side to side to see what he sees. I'm comfortable with him and attracted to his easy way of being.

The afternoon passes, with the sky providing a constantly changing panorama of images. Clouds form and rearrange, heavy rain is seen pounding the distant high country, while cones of sunlight stream through elsewhere. Then a rapidly moving dark cloud casts a shadow over us; I draw closer to him for protection from a sprinkling.

After a while I get up, the earth and sky are spinning and the wind catches my billowing skirt. Joyfully I run down the hillside, pausing from time to time to look back at him and wave—all the way to the bottom.

He sits motionless, with his slim arms draped effortlessly around his knees, just watching me and thinking how things will be someday.

I was awakened slowly by bright sunshine forcing its way into the room through the closed shutters, throwing vertical lines across the comforter. Barely opening my eyes, I reached for my dream journal on the other side of the bed, knowing I must write as much as I could before I moved around and broke the moment. The dream could be lost—gone forever, forgotten. That's how it was with dreams. Now that I didn't have to jump up to make family breakfast, I could take time to write. Pressing on me was the decision about Japan, but since it was Sunday, I knew I could take all day to write if I wanted.

As I poured my morning coffee, I realized that I had stumbled into a situation I couldn't explain. Several déjà vu events and the weird dreams had unhinged me, creating an increasingly uncomfortable situation between Jake and me. There seemed to be some strange recognition I'd never before experienced, a shared commonality between us that triggered instant flashbacks that were at once disturbing and intriguing.

I wanted to know what was happening here. I needed some understanding. Whatever was going on? I resolved to document as many of the incidents as possible and analyze them. Hopefully I could sort it out and make some sense of it, because uncomfortable or not, what choice did I have? Life goes on, and we have to work together.

The Ponca City episode was the first of many; however, I recalled a weird experience with some samurai armor a year before Jake came into the picture. I attributed that to overwork and dismissed it, but what was happening now could not be easily dismissed. I felt that an odyssey of sorts seemed to be unfolding.

Most unnerving had been the incident when an insurance claim had to be filed, and I was called to the woodshop to see broken pottery in a shipment. Jake had two broken pieces cupped between both hands. As I took them from him, our fingers touched. To me it was like an electrical current. I can't be certain, but it seemed he registered something, too. It could not have been avoided, and for me there was an instant recollection of a scene from the distant past in which two young American Indians were working in clay. This is a scene I can't shake from my mind.

Fortunately, I had been interrupted by the pager system and had to take a phone call, so I returned the pieces to him, being ultra careful not to touch him. A similar incident had occurred when he and I examined a pottery collection at the Gilcrease Museum in Tulsa.

4
Time Passageways

A THREE-INCH CANDLE SURROUNDED by some large chunks of amethyst crystal glowed in the middle of an otherwise dimly lit room. The low chatter of the women seated on folding chairs around a large table diminished as Janis interrupted their intimacy by saying, "Let's begin by having a few moments of meditation." Sinking onto a chair, she immediately struck a Tibetan singing bowl. We lapsed into silence and followed the vibration.

About three minutes later, Janis quietly disturbed the silence by saying, "Thank you for coming tonight, and I especially thank you for being on time." She went on, saying, "As you know this is our last session, and I want to tell you all I have thoroughly enjoyed this group. I have been impressed by each of you, your interest, commitment, and your sensitivity to one another. Let me say that if you would like to delve deeper and continue your inquiry, I have scheduled a follow-up. This will be a six-week segment to begin three weeks from tonight. If you are interested, register afterwards in the store. The course title is DreamWorks II. Class size will be limited to nine. I would enjoy seeing you again."

She went on. "There are two things I want to remind you of. First is that because of the nature of dream works, what is said in this room stays in this room. Every dream is a personal story about your inner self and therefore, by now, you all realize that privacy and confidentiality is essential, a necessity, and to be expected. Please do not discuss what you hear in this room, outside of this room. Be particularly mindful of this when two or more of you might happen to be with other people in another setting. Second, let me remind you again that you are the best interpreter of your dreams. I can't say this often enough. If this is the only thing you take away from this group, please remember—you are the best interpreter of your own dreams."

Janis simultaneously gathered up the pen and sign-in sheet and distributed two handouts.

One was a two-page bibliography related to dreams and dreaming. The other was entitled "Symbols and Colors in Dreams."

"We have a lot to do this evening, so I want to move along. According to my notes, Skylar and Cynthia are contributing this evening. Everyone else has had the opportunity to read us a dream from your journal. Right?" Everyone nodded to the affirmative. "In that case, let's start with Skylar. Would you like to go first?"

"Sure," I said. "I chose this dream from my journal because it is sort of typical, I'd say, 'classic' Skylar. There are elements or themes in this dream that frequently recur in my dreams. The first of which is the classroom. In recent years, I've had many dreams that include spaces that I'd define as a classroom, hallways in schools, or the university.

"The second has to do with the people or my relationship to them in the dream. Rarely can I identify a person as someone I recognize; yet I feel I am very well acquainted with them. Maybe you all might have some insight on this aspect after I read it to you. I seem to be moving past 'people' in my dreams, engaging and disengaging quickly. This shows up in this dream big time, and I think you will see that this vexes me, the dreamer. Also, I seem to be questioning myself, dropping things and moving on. Maybe this is because I have moved on a lot in life, certainly more than the vast majority of people, many of who are born and live in the same town throughout their lives. For me, there is a lot in this dream to contemplate.

"One other thing before I begin: I don't think this dream took very long to dream. Probably, it took less time to dream than it took me to write it out. For the last year, I have been experimenting with lucid dreaming after reading *Lucid Dreaming, the Power of Being Awake and Aware in Your Dreams*, by Stephen LaBerge. Having some success with this, I am able to 'take a look around' at the details while in the dream state. I hasten to add that Ray Grasse in

The Waking Dream seems to caution against tampering with one's dream. Now when I'm dreaming, I am often aware that I am.

"Another thing I am keen to know is how an acquaintance from years ago can just show up. Like the opening scene in this dream is about my high school band bus, which is something I haven't thought about for over twenty years and has no relevance today. So this is the dream:

"I was getting off the school band bus; I was thinking we are going to play a concert. More buses arrived, and the scene was orderly chaos as one after another we piled off and milled around, laughing, talking, and waving to friends disembarking from the other buses. Amid piles of bags, luggage, and musical instrument cases, there was a feeling of expectation and the unknown, combined with the high-spirited pandemonium of youth. We linked up with kids from other buses and waited as the bus driver unlocked the luggage compartment and unloaded the instrument cases.

"The driver pulled out the small and medium-sized instruments first. Some were handed directly to the students, who dodged the others, grabbed their belongings, and moved out of the way. More black instrument cases and luggage were pulled from the underbelly of the buses; they lay unclaimed, as items pile up in heaps.

"I was waiting with several friends when my saxophone case was taken out and put on the ground. There were too many people in the way, and too much stuff was between it and me, so I didn't go pick it up. Soon, it was buried under other pieces.

"Some kids were now heading toward two revolving doors and multiple sets of double glass doors. These presented a problem for kids carrying bulky musical instrument cases that caused a back-up at the doors. I left my sax and followed my friends though the glass doors. Once through and inside, I was swallowed up in a sea of people. There are four more sets of double doors off to the right, probably leading to an auditorium. The kids I was with crowded up ten or twelve deep, talking loudly, waving at friends, and waiting impatiently to go through. I avoided the congestion and moved into the flow of another group.

"I found myself in a deluge of people coming and going in all directions. I noticed what seemed to be a check-in counter and thought I was in a hotel lobby. There was a crowd of people between the counter and me. I had the feeling I was supposed to go check-in. Not sure. It occurred to me that I'd left my luggage and instrument case next to the bus. There was so much that was new, exciting, and fascinating to see that I just kept moving along in the flow of the crowd. I lost sight of my friends.

"I came upon massive, gold-gilded mirrors, ornate wall sconces, and scenic Aubusson tapestries. I simply kept walking and looking. As I got further from the entrance, the crowd thinned out, and I paused to study furniture, elaborate tables, and chairs in various styles from different periods. There was so much to see that this took a while.

"When I looked around, I didn't recognize anyone. The fact that I had been separated from my friends didn't daunt me. The surroundings were alluring, and I was caught up and engrossed in all of it. I tried to take it all in—the paintings, and fabrics, and textures. I wandered into room after room. Every alcove and anteroom was more enticing than the previous one. Something more than desire and natural curiosity beckoned me onward; it was as though I followed an invisible cord.

"The dream shifted focus from interior decor and fine arts to handcrafts and artifacts. I found myself in various wings of a museum-like space containing Egyptian scarabs, pre-Columbian gold jewelry, Korean celadon, Mexican polychromes, *ikat* fragments, and precious ivory carvings; later, the items I saw evolved into specimens of minerals, fossils, and butterflies. People were scant.

"I came around a corner next to a large mirrored column, which initially dominated the space. At first, it appeared that I was in the china and crystal section of a department store. I advanced a few steps, and it changed into a sparkling hall of crystal and mirrors, until I was standing in the center of a spectacular crystal gallery. I was alone. The space and light in it was stunning. It had a lucid shimmering transparency, with a glint of color. I was spellbound as radiant, glittering refracted rays of light and waves of energy surrounded me. It was otherworldly, and I had an indescribable feeling of awe. Everything was brilliant and shining. Sparkling, glittering light falling everywhere was further reflected in mirrors; it was incredibly glorious. Sublime. I was rapt in wonder.

At that moment, I knew that I was dreaming and that I very much wanted to remember this part. I also felt that my memory of this place, at least in part, would be forgotten, blocked, or too remote to be accessed when I awake. This was troublesome. There were no words to adequately describe this experience. I wondered whether I was in a crystal, enveloped in a colossal prism. I stood there just basking in the dazzling space. My dreaming self was overcome by the splendor of it all. Then again, I was aware that I was dreaming and had a strong instinct to examine this place—or remember the feeling—so I could recall it and make some reality out of it when I woke up.

"When I left this place, I was carrying some parcels. Time was distorted, and I was confused. I thought hours had passed, but then maybe only a few minutes. I considered that I hadn't seen my band friends and that my luggage was back there somewhere. Puzzled as to where I was supposed to go, there was no one to ask; everyone I came across seemed busy with his or her own agenda.

"To make matters more confusing, somehow the situation morphed from large, open, lavish circumstances to smaller compartments. The people were fewer. The corridors were reduced to cramped passageways. I was bumped and jostled around when people met and had to pass in the narrow hallways. The folks I met were pleasant, friendly, and good-natured; the earlier ones had been an impersonal mass. These people were engaging and passionate about whatever it was they were doing. The elaborate glitz and glamour of highly embellished rooms had changed to plain, unadorned classrooms, stark with wooden desks, chairs, tables, and a chalkboard. I continued along, down a dimly lit inauspicious corridor that kept narrowing. The ceiling was getting lower and lower. In the distance, the corridor appeared to end.

"When I reached what I expected to be a dead end, I found that the hallway continued to the right. To the left was a small doorway framed in wood. I noticed that it had last been painted a greenish-blue, a long time ago. The wood of the doorframe was now shrunken with age, and the paint was flaking off in long strips.

The layers of peeling paint indicated that the doorway had once been painted red, then white, then yellow, and several other colors before its current faded greenish-blue.

Somehow, I recognized that this was a doorway into a pottery studio, but for the moment I was drawn to the stories in the layers of paint on the doorframe. I realized that each color told a different story—stories about the many craftspeople who had walked through this doorway and worked and created here. By the age and paint colors, I judged there to be forty years of history layered there. The stories of numerous persons who did pottery and painted the door-frame—and the others who repainted it—with a color of their liking.

"This particular location was a very tight squeeze, a dead end, or a T-intersection with a very low ceiling. I met several people right there. This juncture seemed to be a strange confluence of time and space and strangers. I asked them if they had seen my friends. They told me that earlier in the day, they'd seen the people I'd described. Then they continued on. I didn't know what earlier in the day meant. 'Time' was so confusing.

"Initially, I stood there and peered in; the unpainted plastered walls had clay splatters everywhere. Unmistakably, it was a pottery studio. I smiled and went through the painted doorway. I ducked low to enter, being careful not to brush up against history and knock off any more of the old layers of paint and time.

"Immediately, I recognized the craftspeople working there. It was like a joyful reunion. They were all friends of mine whom I hadn't seen for a long time—like years. They were happy to see me, truly happy. With few exceptions, their hair was long, unkempt, pulled back in a ponytail, and fastened with a rubber band. Like the surroundings, they were dust-covered. Their shirts, jeans, and shorts had been worn soft and thin with age; they looked older than I remembered them. They continued to work while we reminisced. They wanted me to stay. I was very comfortable among them and in the familiarity of this workshop—the potter's wheels, the vats and buckets of clay, the dust, the dusty bottles, the boxes and bags of glaze compounds and the dusty glaze test tiles on the wall.

"I liked the physicality and earthy easiness of the creative clay work underway inside and in the adjacent outdoor workspace. The familiarity of the equipment, materials, and the people added to the ease. I realized that the heat and flame of the gas kiln and the sweat was a part of who I was, or who I am. In that moment, there was genuine warmth and friendliness among us all. They wanted me to stay. I wanted me to stay. We chatted away the time amicably while in my mind, I quietly considered getting involved.

"I was not sure why I left. I was ambivalent. There was a strong inclination to stay. I liked working in clay, and I really wanted to get my hands back into it again, but I didn't. There was a vague feeling of reluctance. Maybe I felt this was no longer my place. There was a more compelling urge to continue on. I didn't know how to explain to them that I was leaving. I don't think I did. I slipped out while they were absorbed in their work.

"Again, I was walking along a very wide, long corridor. On one side was a grand exhibition of massive, mural-like canvases, primarily Gauguin, Rivera, and Rousseau paintings. Strangely, I deliberately avoided looking directly at these paintings. Peculiar. I just felt them. The powerful energy of the line and motion and vivid color of the Diego Rivera paintings registered with me. The Rousseau's beguiled and intrigued me; they captured the mysteries of nature. I somehow knew others as I passed by without even looking. Intermingled were Gauguin's; his masterful use of raw color and shape, sensuous human figures—the primitive qualities telepathically conveyed an invitation to distant and exotic places. They all spoke of cultures other than my own. Inherent in each were many dichotomies. Oppression and the courage to overcome; youth and vitality juxtapose foreboding and death; statements of a bold, adventurous spirit and the simplicity and reality of life— slammed up against life's mysterious nature—if we cared to look.

The huge canvases were interspersed with delightful maps created by unknown cartographers with vivid imaginations. The scale was distorted; some were mural size. Others were minuscule, note-book-size; these were mostly ochre in color, with dark blue-black ink markings. Some were fanciful, and others reeked of importance in highly carved gold leaf frames. I walked up closely to examine the detail. I needed a magnifying glass. I couldn't determine the place or period in which they had been drawn. I knew they were quite old; rendered hundreds of years ago on parchment or handmade paper from the South Seas, Java, Italy, the Mediterranean, and the Sea of Japan, I thought. These seemed unlike the coastline of current world maps; but the boundaries were different. Maybe they depicted ancient civilizations. There were pictographs. I deciphered a few words; they were in incomprehensible foreign languages and scripts. I wondered whether there was a message here for me. The maps really intrigued me. Both the map-making process and the locations piqued my curiosity.

"The gallery remained on my right, but on the opposite side, floor to ceiling windows stretched the complete length of the corridor. I looked out across a rolling lawn. In the distance, I saw an ultramodern glass and steel building in pastel pinkish, bluish-gray. The color softened the stark, austere, industrial look of it. I was curious, but I made a conscious decision not to go there, to stick to my present course.

"The corridor somehow changed. There were numerous doors, including doors to stairwells. I peered into little windows in several of the solid, core maple doors. These were labs and classrooms. Mostly empty. Thoughts of my missing friends returned. The missing musical instrument no longer concerned me. There were small groups of people working together. I passed them by—there was no one I recognized. Everyone was engrossed in conversation and their interests. I continued down more corridors and hallways. I wanted someone to tell me where I was supposed to go. Eventually, I got the attention of a young man who tried to help me, but I got distracted and wandered off.

"The tenor changed, and I was meeting and greeting many more people now. Our pathways converged briefly, then diverged. It seemed like we coalesced then vaporized; our desires and interests collided for a moment. Then we moved off in different directions. Nonetheless, I had the feeling something important had been accomplished. The thought occurred to me that we could all be spokes and sprockets in a great wheel of time.

"I felt really bad about the guy who'd attempted to help me. He was a pleasant and considerate person. It was rude and inconsiderate of me just to wander away. Again, I attempted to get help from a passerby. Again, people rallied to my aid. Again, I wandered away intrigued or distracted by something. When I checked back, they were gone. The matter dissipated, and I went through an opening and found myself in a big room standing next to a tablesaw. I was in a woodworking shop. I had several bundles but no idea what was in them. Except I knew I'd had them since the crystal place. I attempted to reinforce my objective to remember that place when I woke up.

"The equipment in this wood shop was covered with sawdust, indicating that it had been in a state of disrepair for a long time. Parts, along with hoses from the disabled dust collection system, lay on top of the saw. I lay aside my packages, picked up, and examined the pieces with the intent of repairing the saw; but something was missing, and a part had to be ordered.

"Across the room, three guys, waving wildly, called out my name. There were hugs all around; we were glad to see each other. I laid the parts back down on the saw and started to pick up my stuff. Now I had even more bags, more than I alone could carry and more than I'd came in with. One guy went off to get more help; the other two stayed with me. One was dressed in a madras shirt and khaki pants, the other in a T-shirt and jeans. They picked up my considerable luggage, and off we started.

"As quickly as my bags had morphed from a few to many, my friends were transfigured into baggage handlers, appearing much like the Philip Morris man of the '40s. They now wore cute little pillbox hats, white gloves, and spiffy blue, tight fitting bellhop outfits of the type worn at posh New York hotels in that era. They promptly stacked the suitcases and packages on their shoulders and rushed off, with me hurrying along behind.

"Someone else showed up to show us the way. It got quite amusing. He, too, was dressed as a door attendant, but he wore a bluish gray hat, about eighteen inches high, with a wide band; it was cone-shaped, but flat at the top. I thought this bizarre. I laughed, wondering whether he'd gotten it from the "Cat in the Hat." I lost sight of the guys and my luggage when they went through a pair of swinging doors, resembling those seen in an Old West saloon."

I finally looked up from my dream journal at Janis and said, "I guess I decided to follow them because at the end of the dream, I was pushing open those swinging doors."

Janis smiled. "Okay, Skylar. You first, what are your thoughts about your dream?"

"Come to think of it, it has an *Alice in Wonderland* feel to it. Well, to the dream, I don't understand why my adolescence band bus experience pops up after all these years. That's bizarre. I totally understand much of the art part, and about the classrooms; after all, I've been a student, a teacher, or an administrator of art all my life. The corridor thing, I think symbolizes my journey through life. When I read back through my journal, I'm struck by how I leave or drop people, which I guess is to be expected if you move or change jobs, but that part is disturbing. It's evident in the dream that at some point, I am moving on and no longer giving attention to personal relationships. I mean, at first I was concerned for my band buddies. Maybe the message is that I should have stayed in touch.

"About the crystal part of the dream, I think there is something very important about this. I think I am supposed to gain some insight, but I don't know what. The spectacle of the light and the awesome feeling, I can't describe. I don't know what to think about all of that. It was sensational. Maybe I tapped into something special here. It was in the center of the dream. Maybe I'm not supposed to remember it. This may be the only part of the dream that's worthy of mentioning. If only I could verbalize what I saw and felt. It was sublime. I wonder whether the rest of the dream was just to distract me from remembering this segment. I was struggling so hard to remember it while I was in the dream. Of course, that could be simply because of the dream work we're doing."

Others in the group asked me questions and made comments, and then we heard Cynthia's dream. Afterward, some of us exchanged phone numbers. We said our goodnights and left the room. I was still wondering what, aside from dreaming, gets done while in the sleep state, which is about one third of the day/night cycle. Maybe we travel to different planes or realms. The crystal dream had been otherworldly and beyond my comprehension.

5
Rae

SOME OF US STOOD in line next to the counter waiting to sign up for DreamWorks II. I was last. Meanwhile, I saw a friend, not in the class, across the room in the books section. I had been meaning to call her and thought it a coincidence that she was out at this late hour. The store was about to close.

I caught her eye and waved. As I was finishing my transaction, she came over to me.

With a light hug, I said, "Hey, it's good to see you. How are you doing? What are you doing out at this late hour?"

Rae gave me a quick scan and said, "I was in the house all day and just needed to get out. What's going on with you, Skylar?"

I casually responded, "Nothing."

"Yes there is," she said. "It seems like you're wearing a hair shirt, Skylar. This is Rae you're speaking to."

I said, "Yes, well, I didn't realize I was that transparent!"

"Well, you are to me," she said. "There's obviously something going on with you. Is it Stan?"

"No, it's not, Stan," I said. "Rae, I really need to talk to you. I should call and make an appointment, but I don't see any time I can get away for the next two weeks. We're installing a new exhibition. Two crates were mislabeled, went awry, and arrived late. I'll be lucky to pull this off. I really should not have come here tonight, but it was my turn for 'show and tell,' and I didn't want to renege on that.

"Listen Rae, do you have time for quick cup of coffee? We could run right down the street to Berta's Café; they don't close until ten. I hate to do this to you, but I have an issue I just have to run by you." As if to bribe her, I added, "My treat, and I'll even spring for dessert." I teased her, looking for an affirmative answer.

Rae said, "Sure, I'll meet you there in a few—soon as I finish up here."

I waited for her in the parking lot, and we walked together into the quiet mom and pop café, empty except for three customers. One lost soul sat alone gazing into his coffee cup; two lovers, oblivious to the world, gazed into each other's eyes. We walked past them to the back booth.

A waitress named Sylvia came over immediately to take our order. I read the look on her face as, *"You're not going to mess up the kitchen at this hour, are you? I'm tired, been on my feet all day, and I'm ready to go home."*

We pleased her when we both ordered hot tea and pie. I ordered chocolate; Rae ordered lemon, then Rae said, "Let's get to it. Spill it. I wouldn't want you to combust right here. What's your burning question?"

I waited to respond, as Sylvia returned, laying forks, napkins, the pie, teapots, cups, and the check on the table. She left without asking the perfunctory but polite question, "Will there be anything else?"

"Rae, there is this guy I hired recently—and there is something strange about him. I mean he's normal and all, so maybe I'm the strange one. But I'll tell you there is something definitely different going on. Nothing I have ever experienced before. First of all, we were going through some camera lenses and filters the other week, and I looked up at him while we were talking and noticed that he had one blue eye and one brown eye." I said to him, 'Did you lose one of your contact lenses?' He said, 'No, I don't wear contacts.'

"It was a very awkward moment. I had this peculiar, vague feeling of nausea. I can't explain the feeling. I mean I wasn't actually sick, but I had a very sick feeling. I guess that doesn't make sense. Anyhow, he looked at me and smiled in some kind of charming, almost flirtatious way. Then he said, 'Oh, the blue eye, brown eye thing? It's in the genes. We've got it in the family.' Well, Rae it doesn't sound like much when I tell you that, but it really was weird. If I give you a name, can you pick up on him?"

"Well, maybe. Would you happen to know his birth date?" she asked.

"Yeah, he was born in May. The name is Jacob Byron Wolfe. He goes by Jake."

I noticed an almost imperceptible change in her demeanor, a slight adjustment somehow when I gave her this information. She put down her cup. Inhaling, she leaned her head to the right, as if listening to or for something. Her eyes were partially closed. It semed she immediately took on the pleasant attitude or aura of Jake, whom she had never met.

"Hmm. Hmm. You can always count on him to be pleasant," she said slowly. Then pausing for a moment, she added, "You two have fought many wars together. You've had many lives together—back to Biblical times."

With an overwhelming sigh of relief, I said, "Oh, Rae, that explains everything. I feel so much better." At that moment, the words "war" and "Biblical times" did not register with me.

Rae looked as if she had just stepped into something. "Gosh, Skylar, of the many clients I've seen, all the readings I've done, I have never told anybody anything about previous lives before." She seemed apologetic.

"Rae, it makes perfect sense to me. It's the only logical explanation. I mean really! I was wondering what the heck was going on between the two of us. Wars? Biblical days? That's weird. But everything has been totally weird. Squirrelly things have been happening. I mean, there have been so many synchronistic things I've lost count. You know, déjà vu-like stuff occurring. I was about to ask you about my sanity. I mean I start a sentence and he finishes it, or vice versa. We think of the same thing at the same time. It's like he's reading my mind. So if you say I 'knew him before,' that makes perfect sense." I exhaled.

"I never had this sort of open, easy communication with anybody, not even after more than twenty years of marriage to Stan. Rae, I tell you, I am totally relieved."

"I can see that," she said, somewhat surprised at my reaction. "This type of communication is extremely rare." Maybe she didn't want to further explain because she changed the subject. "So, Skylar, are you going to eat that pie or has he taken your appetite, too?"

"Very funny, Rae," I said, as I picked up the fork. "I'll tell you, the fact that we have so much in common, like the arts for example, I can hardly explain all the so-called 'coincidences' that keep happening. Also, there is some sort of sizzle factor there, too. Sometimes I wonder if he is flirting with me. I am almost old enough to be his mother. Heck, he's not much older than Bradley."

Rae put her hand up to stop me. "Skylar, get over it. You're not that old. And I've told you before, life is not all about work. Lighten up, for heaven's sake."

Then, with her quirky, mischievous grin, she said, "I can tell you this—he is very well endowed."

I feigned shock. My jaw dropped open in phony, righteous indignation. "Shame on you," I teased. "Shame on you, Rae. I don't believe you just said that. You should be ashamed of yourself." We both had a good laugh.

"Well, Skylar, I'll tell you this: every other client of mine asks that question first." Then she gave me her shy little wry smile and said, "Besides, I just took a little peak."

I came back in jest with, "Rae, I am just not believing what you said!"

"Well, you can believe that, and you can believe what I have been telling you for as long as I've known you. You need to lighten up. Screw all that professional stuff and all your lofty standards. You work too much. What are you getting out of it? You need to have more fun. As I see it, you're a little out of your comfort zone, and that's a good thing."

"Actually, it's worse than that," I said. "I mean, after all there is a professional relationship and professional boundaries that have to be maintained."

Rae interjected, "Phooey."

"Rae, listen. I have been having these deja vu, strange, vision-like experiences as a result of him. The first two happened in the workshop, which at the time was sort of dark. Only half the lights were on, and later I had this vague, kind of misty, cloudy recollection of us in the Scottish highlands, and another flashback that seemed to be in Edinburgh. I wrote this stuff down because it's just so bizarre. I don't understand it.

"Furthermore, I wrote a whole series of poems that seem to have come out of nowhere. These poems are about ancient times, and they are about wars. I mean, Rae, what do I know about wars? Nothing. I've never written anything like this and, as you just said, we fought wars together. Do you think they are about us?

"I almost can't handle pottery when he's present. And this is a real problem because we must handle pottery all the time. One of the reasons I hired him was because he studied pottery, and he is a very good potter. I mean I come from the art history direction, and he from working with clay, but the experiences mesh. One time, when he was unpacking some new pieces we received for the collection, I saw or felt the two of us in what seemed to be an American Indian setting, and the next morning, I woke up with this vivid memory of being a young woman who had been kidnapped from a wagon train. It was so vivid I had to avoid him for a few days."

I shook my head. "Rae, all this defies reality. And we don't have time to discuss it tonight. Sylvia is about to boot us out of here. Except that I must tell you about this, because this is what really started it all.

"Recently we drove to Ponca City. I needed to photograph 'Prairie Woman' for a project. He'd never been there. I invited him to come with me, on company time, of course. I figured he could drive the van, carry the gear, and set up the tripod. Further, I wanted to check out what he knew about photography. He carries around a Nikon. He told me that he'd never been there, and I think it's sort of sad to miss a bronze sculpture like that if you happen to be in Oklahoma.

"We had a great conversation on the way, talked art and life experiences, that sort of thing. But try to envision this: We were setting up for a shot. Actually, he was doing the tripod, camera thing, and I was walking around. There was no one else there. We were discussing the light and shadow, the angle, exposure, and all those details.

"I walked around to the opposite side. You might say Prairie Woman was in the middle of this thing. I looked over at him working, sort of in the distance, when I saw and felt the most bizarre thing. It was like I *became* prairie woman for a moment, except that there were two children, a boy and a girl, tugging at my skirt—not just one boy, like the actual sculpture. It was weird but weirder still when Jake morphed into a rider, a stereotypical cowboy on horseback in the distance, whipping the horse with his hat and coming toward us at a very fast pace, as if he were happy to be getting home. And we, the children and me, were waving and happy to see him. I raised my hand to my forehead to block the blinding sun from my eyes. It was like an image frozen in time."

I paused for a moment, then said, "Rae, I was really shaken by this. I could hardly regain my composure. When I went back to check the shot, apparently he noticed something was amiss because he asked me if I was okay. I said sure, why? He didn't say anything, but I am not at all certain that he did not intuit something himself. I just blew it off—for the moment. I mean, I was rattled and haven't forgotten it, and I'm not likely to.

"On the way back to OKC, he asked why I was so quiet; after all, we had had a lively conversation on the way to Ponca City. I blew it off causally by saying I had a lot on my mind; that I was tired just thinking about all that had to be done in the next week.

"Surreptitiously, I put a bit more physical space between us after that. I thanked him for his help but was thinking, *What the shit is going on?*

"So, when you say we had previous lives together, frankly that explains it all. From my point of view, it's really been awkward between us. It's knocked me off balance."

Rae looked at me contemplatively, making no comment.

"Thanks," I said. "I really feel so much better having talked to you. Yeah, other lives, that's logical."

Then something else occurred to me, and I went on. "When I got to thinking back over things, something else may have happened before Jake, that I brushed off. I never mentioned it to you before because, as I said, I brushed it off. It was spooky, too. Last year, we were installing the Japanese Expo; I bent down to adjust the placard in front of this samurai armor. Well, the darn thing came to life, just for an instant. I mean I felt light headed, and the room was spinning, but just for that moment it came to life. Really, I mean that samurai armor came to life. I backed away in awe and fell on my ass. At that moment no one else was there, and I never mentioned it. I mean, who would believe me?

"After that, I never got too close to those Japanese artifacts. Even though they are inanimate objects. I was glad when that collection was packed up and shipped off my premises. So I am thinking, that was last year, and Jake wasn't working at the museum at that point. The Pioneer Woman sculpture event was much the same. Do you think I'm going nuts?"

Rae shook her head. "No, I've always told you to pay attention to your synchronicities. Now, maybe you will." She smiled and added, "I think this is a good thing. Let's get out of here. I've got to get home. I should have fed the cat before I left the house."

Rae was a friend, as I saw it; she would probably say she was an advisor. She was clairvoyant. I met her in a calligraphy workshop I'd conducted in conjunction with a show at the museum when I first came to OKC. We sometimes attended Poet's Corner, an informal, loosely knit group of would-be poets who got together at a small bookstore once a month. I enjoyed her company a lot. She probably preferred other company, and I suspect that to her, I was just another client.

She lived in a quaint little house on what appeared to be a dusty country road in Oklahoma City. As she explained to me, she'd grown up in that house and would probably die in that house. She said that about thirty years earlier, a tornado set down in her neighborhood and, except for hers, wiped every house off the face of the earth. Her family was inexplicably untouched. Even their garden, the plants, and vines had gone unscathed. Only two families rebuilt, and they were some distance further down the road. Parts of old foundations could be seen in the winter, but they were otherwise overgrown with weeds. The toll of lives lost from the powerful storm that struck Oklahoma City that year was from her neighborhood. The families and all her childhood friends were swept away. Tumbleweeds now populated the area.

Rae had no visible means of support. She wrote poetry, did handcrafts occasionally, and tended her garden. Daily there was a steady stream of people coming to her house. She was a psychic. Her reputation evidently drew a clientele from Tulsa to Wichita Falls, Texas. One time, she confided in me that I would be surprised by the number of public figures, whose names I would recognize, who came to her for readings. So as not to be found out, they did not come in their own cars, she said.

She told me that as a child, her mother forbade her to use her sixth sight, but as she grew into adulthood, there was nothing she could do about it. Her mother and later her children raged against it, but she said it could not be denied. She told me her grandmother had the gift also and had been a predictor of weather and natural phenomenon, which her mother also denied to her dying day. "It is what it is," she'd said. "It's something I have to deal with. I may as well embrace it."

I always felt Rae preferred to be alone. She told me that giving a "reading" took a lot out of her. She said that sometimes after a reading, she was totally spent.

I was not exactly what you would call a believer in psychic stuff. But I was not the skeptic most people were either, because I respected her ability. I thought of myself more as an inquisitive. There was something about what she did that I wanted to understand. She wanted her clients to accept her advice *cart blanc*, but I didn't buy into the "advisor" concept. She enlightened me on some matters, but I used my own judgment, and in the end, I did as I pleased. I felt in my gut that "free will" was an essential factor in life and that it trumped destiny.

6
Lavender Jade

As I reached the monastery complex, I was becoming weary. The sun was high, and it had been hours since I'd passed through the Jade Gate of the Blazing Beacon. The poplars were a refreshing sight, shimmering silvery as the sunlight caught the underside of the leaves. The light breeze and the sight of the saffron robes of young monks lifted my spirits. They scurried away instead of toward me, a sure sign tea would be waiting.

I flung my leg and the fullness of my long skirt up over the hump and slipped off the camel, which had obediently knelt at my command. I stretched and flexed to loosen up my muscles and then walked across a grand expanse of well-swept courtyard to a walkway elaborately painted primarily in red and teal. The corridor would take me to one of many pavilions. The corridors were covered and offered protection from sun and the elements. The ceiling of the roof was highly ornate; large, painted timbers not procured locally, supported it. Wave upon wave of spandrels overhead marked my way.

Near a pavilion, I stepped tentatively through a moon gate. After laying several small packages on an altar table with upturned ends, I settled myself on a ceramic garden drum and sat silently, enjoying the tea a monk had set for me. It was very hot, and the fragrance was inviting. There was also a steaming bowl of egg drop soup with cabbage, pieces of tomato, and bits of vegetables and sprouts. This was my welcome, fit for a princess.

Although my visit had been anticipated, it would not be intrusive. I sat silently in meditation or enjoying each vista through the round openings on three sides of the pavilion. The grounds were quiet, but somewhere within I heard the monks' susurrations. Working in the kitchen and in the garden was a normal part of their day. I knew a young monk would gather up the parcels from my father and take them to the living quarters as soon as I departed. I inhaled and exhaled deeply, fully relaxed, satiated, and happy to be unburdened from this detail and grateful for the nourishment.

As soon as was respectable, I retraced my steps along the covered corridors and went toward the temple. I slowed my pace so as to approach reverently. At the entrance, I pulled hard on the rope to ring the bell, then clapped three times while bowing my head. The coins I dropped in the wooden offering box tumbled through the bars, hitting the bottom with a thud. This sound indicated to me that the box had either been recently emptied or that there had been no visiting pilgrims. I thought the latter. The monks would be grateful for the packages I had delivered, which were sure to contain prayer requests and money.

After placing an offering of fruit on the altar, I lit several candles as an expression of my gratitude for this life and in respect for my ancestors.

My prayers were as stipulated by my father. I asked for the safe passage of caravans traveling to and from the east through the Taklamakan, those caravans leaving China to the west, and all those traversing the vast and dangerous Gobi Desert. I asked that the caravans be safe from marauders and bandits, and that sand storms not place the lives of my father's friends and business associates in peril. I added my prayers that the animals cooperate lest they be beaten by a mean spirited driver, that the camels were not bothered by pestilence, and that any snakes on their path might move out of their way as they trudge along. I knew that creatures needed our prayers, too. All too often, the camels were taken for granted. People forgot that without camels, we would be walking, or worse yet, carrying our load.

I concluded my prayers and hurried across the courtyard to my camels. I alerted a monk in the distance that I was leaving the camel there, and that the supplies for the monastery would be on the ground. It was better that I off loaded him. He was finicky about who handled him, and he was quite likely to spit on the monk. He knew me; we spoke the same language. I fancied myself a cameleer, the best in Dunhuang.

Without giving voice to my words, I apologized to this beast for not unburdening him before taking care of the deliveries and prayer requirements. He responded by blinking his eyes. He seemed to understand but indicated to me that he felt he was due his rest. I ran my hand over his velvet-like snout and smoothed the fuzz across his broad nose. He motioned me on by wrinkling his nose, curling his lip in a snarky smile, and turned his head away. I walked around him to the other side. When I untied the thongs, the strapped together bundles fell to the ground. He rolled his eyes closed and continued to chew.

Lounge here until I return, I conveyed to him. Other handlers avoided this camel, but he and I had a mutual understanding, and he knew better than to cross me up or it was back to the other handlers for him. He knew with me he had it good. Hearing my thoughts, he humpffed and shifted on his haunches, as he prepared to enjoy his respite from the morning's work.

I sorted through the bundles on the ground. Grabbing several, I settled the largest on my head and started off at a near run. After ten minutes, I slowed down. As I ascended, the climb became arduous. I hiked for a considerable time. Then I treaded carefully through deeper and shifting sand on the narrowing trail, which led around the honeycombed cliff on the eastward facing slope of Mount Mingsha. I had to focus carefully now, being mindful of my footing and balance, lest I slip and topple down the incline, or drop the supplies over the edge. Eventually, the path tapered into nonexistence.

I struggled to reach a small opening on the third tier, where I ducked low and nimbly wedged myself through the entrance into a dark, cavernous space. Taking a moment for my eyes to adjust, I was about to announce my arrival by quietly calling out, as is my custom, when I realized Yonji was at work above my head, out of my sight line. He was on a rickety, crudely built scaffolding. It hadn't been there previously. He likely had dragged the timbers from another cave. I saw that he had painted a lot since I'd last visited, and had made great progress.

49

When my father sanctioned my visit here today, it was because he had too much business to permit travel at this time. Sometimes he allowed me to come here, unbeknownst to my mother. He trusted me to give him a reliable report. Looking around, I knew he would be happy to hear from me that a great deal had been accomplished—much more than I had anticipated.

My father sponsored this artist and several others from Dunhuang. This particular project in the Mogao Caves was a very large commission from a wealthy family far to the east. They wanted to honor the Buddha while simultaneously glorifying their own good work in this lifetime. They had sent my father drawings and paintings depicting their life, and fine renderings of each family member so our artist would have a true likeness with which to record their life accurately. They probably would never see the cave, but word of their generosity would spread throughout the land.

There were many sculptors and painters involved in this commission. Back in Dunhuang, several clay sculptures were in production. Several had already been installed on a raised platforms carved out of the rock cave.

As my eyes adjusted to the dim light, I scanned the cave and marveled at the flying *apsaras*, chimerical and superbly painted. These incredible images left me awestruck. The colors were at once poignant and vivid. Strikingly, one after the other caught my eye and carried me on to the next. Each was unique in appearance, having different, meticulously painted faces and seemingly different personalities. They were elegant in gossamer gowns, beautiful of body and face, their hands and arms graceful. Their long, flowing sleeves undulated across the ceiling and down the cave walls. Some played musical instruments, flutes, or lutes; they were indeed angels of fragrance and music. The sensitivity of each ethereal entity radiated waves of rhapsodic energy.

Their energy caught me up. Just for the moment, they took on a life of their own and briefly I was one with their lyric. In my imagination, I was in a sheer yellow gown playing the Chinese four-stringed lute, a *pipa*, moving gracefully along with the *apsaras*.

Something rolled off the scaffold, hit the cave floor, and snapped me out of my reverie. A wide, bamboo-handled brush landed near me.

I thought he must be working day and night. The oil lamps had burned out and yet he persisted in his work with the light of only one candle. He looked disheveled and was oblivious to my presence, not uncommon when he was painting. If ever I arrived when he was grinding and mixing color, he might be talkative. At that time, he was coherent and gave me a comprehensive list of supplies and materials needed. Other times I was invisible to him. Sometimes he seemed agitated. Then frenzy-like, his moods cascaded into long periods of rapid work, day and night, with little or nothing to eat or drink. Then he collapsed, sitting silent and motionless, in a stupor or meditation or deep thought. At that point I was not certain if he saw me even when I stood directly in front of him. He appeared to look right through me; his sight seemed focused somewhere behind or beyond me. Nor am I sure what he was seeing. Not wanting to intrude, I didn't ask.

Having prodded the camel and rushed through the rituals, there was now time to wander from cave to cave enjoying the day and indulging my curiosity. If I came upon a former monk whose soiree had left him crazed in an opium delirium, I quietly stepped around him and kept that sort of encounter to myself. If I were to tell someone and it got back to my father, he'd curtail or halt my visits here all together.

I entered the cave of a colossal Buddha carved out of the sand-stone hillside. This Buddha soared three stories above my head. Light streamed in from a lofty opening. The effect was that high above my head, his massive outstretched hands reigned over me, palms down, showering blessings upon me. The comfort radiating from His hands was palpable. The warmth encapsulated me, and I knelt down in meditation. After a time, I asked for health, safety, and protection for my family and myself.

Upon the altar in front of the Buddha were gifts from previous pilgrims. Some were so fragile they'd deteriorated to dust. With-ered flowers in small brass receptacles, dried apricots, kumquats, and a decayed peach were on several plates. I took a small packet from my pocket, carefully untied the vine around the wrapped leaf, and peeled out a small delicacy I'd made with pounded rice flour, almond paste, nuts, and dried fruits. I placed it on the altar reverently, bowed, and backed away.

The work in the Mogao caves had been going on for many generations. There was more than one colossal Buddha. Most of the caves had been inhabited to some extent over the generations. The soot and grime from cook fires was beginning to have a deleterious effect on some of the cave paintings. A few of the caves had chimneys. Over the centuries, these cliffs had become shelter for itinerant monks and pilgrims. A labyrinth of cells, hundreds of chapels and grottoes, had been carved out of the mountainside over time. I had walked through many unoccupied ones and tried to be careful not to step into someone's the living quarters, if there was a current occupant.

The caves were adorned with magnificent carvings and wall paintings, including priceless sculptures of the Bodhisattvas, the Buddha, and Anada, among others. Some had been created on site and others had been brought here. There were niches containing rare manuscripts and scrolls, finely rendered spinach jade carvings of life in China, others of Suchou jade brought across the silk road from Xian. Still more figures in wood and terra cotta were on altars and recesses honed out of the rock wall.

Pilgrim monks, who brought Buddhism to China from India and Tibet, rendered the earliest wall paintings. The wall paintings and scrolls depicted Tibet and Hindustan, and for some inexplicable reason, I was intrigued by the Hindu religion. Exquisitely stitched wild animals, frightening tigers, spirit winds, and clouds captured my imagination.

Having allowed extra time to explore, I was free to wander in and out at will—viewing the colossal imagery of Maitreya; exquisite royal ladies and their attendants of the High Tang Dynasty; and scenes of everyday life of holy men, pilgrims, hunters, trappers, farmers, and traders. Many altars held prayer books and rare sutras. I looked closely at the script; it was not Chinese. I had heard about Sanskrit from my father, but I had no understanding of it. I thought this was Sanskrit. The characters were like nothing I had seen in town or among my father's records.

I wandered from cave to cave in awe, mesmerized, half dazed, at once immersed in history, religions, and the arts. This was *ming-oi*, rock temple complex of Buddhas.

I squeezed into a small chamber off to the side of a glorious, cavernous room populated by the Buddha, Anada, and numerous Bodhisattvas. My candle cast a shadowy, rather mystical glow, as I peered around the walls and ceiling at paintings of ethereal, diaphanous beings. Commanding my attention was a magnificent banner of fine silk, with a pointed top and colorful streamers; it was heavily embroidered with exotic birds, various animals, mountains, rivers, clouds, and characters that were beyond my understanding. Except for fine sand dust, this centuries old shrine appeared as though someone had recently left and would return momentarily. Several texts and sutras laid open on a silk altar cloth. I placed my candle on the altar, where its wax would mingle with the ancient candle drippings.

Stacked in the recesses behind the altar were bundles of tablets and manuscripts. They were very dusty, and some were wrapped in cloth, probably undisturbed for over a hundred years. It was a library of sorts, I ventured. I had time to investigate some that were lying loose. Turning the leaves, keeping the pages in order, I could see these were not in Chinese characters. It was some other language I couldn't read. I could only admire the exquisite calligraphy and paintings. I felt convinced it was Sanskrit.

My grandfather read Sanskrit and had Sanskrit books in his library. From his studies as a young man in Beijing, he could read and write many foreign languages. Grandfather was a very learned man. I had heard him translate books with pictures of medicinal plants to Su Lin and Ana Wei. My father was not versant in other languages, but he spoke in many Chinese dialects, which sounded like different languages to me. My father learned to communicate with people from a diversity of backgrounds. Even when he didn't understand the language of a person, somehow he knew what they wanted or needed. He was very considerate, never rude to them simply because they couldn't speak our language. I heard townspeople ridicule foreigners. Father told me that it was because they themselves were ignorant, and if they were ever to travel beyond

Dunhuang, they would gain some respect. I was sure he was right about that. Even if I were never to travel beyond Dunhuang, I would not be unkind to a visitor to our town.

An unexpected draft, in this closed-in cave of a room, fluttered the flame of my candle, which almost went out. At the same time, as if struck I dropped to my knees and fell into a deep meditation. It was as if I was in a dream. A window opened in my mind and images of Mohenjo Daro and other ancient cities streamed toward me in fast-moving clouds. They seemed to fold in on top of one another, toppling over. The demise of one civilization after another was shown, being swept away in front of my eyes, covered with the sands of time. The vision moved before me rapidly, too quickly for me to grasp all the flickering images that passed. I wanted it to stop. I wanted the images to slow down enough for me to see what was transpiring. All the accoutrements in these grottos were just as they were today, but waves of sand swept in and over them, just like the vanished Mohenjo Daro. Just like the blowing sands that covered the remains of Mohenjo Daro, my *ming-oi* was buried by sand.

I was immediately lifted out of my sadness as the clouds reversed, and I was rapidly transported far into what could be the future of these very caves. I got a glimpse of people trampling through the grottos. The sand had been dug out, the sculptures uncovered, the monk was not protecting the art, and it was being defaced by a parade of unknowns, strangers, foreigners, and soldiers from other lands. I saw waves of plundering, pillaging, and the destruction of *ming-oi*.

The window snapped shut. Nothing more was shown to me. I was back, not quite sure what had happened, where I'd gone, or momentarily where I was. Had I been dreaming? I felt stunned and like I needed to touch something tangible.

I got to my feet shook up, confused, and dizzy. Mindlessly, I busied myself dusting the altar. Then I reached down and picked up the gritty prayer rug upon which I had knelt. I took it outside into the light to shake out the fine sand. My not too rational mind was thinking perhaps I could change what seemed to be a prophecy, deter the eventuality, and protect the Mogao Caves from the sand and time.

An unusual breeze tugged on the rug; the wind increased, pulling with a vengeance. The ledge I was standing on was narrow, and the wind pulled me toward the precipice. It seemed to want to carry me out beyond the cliff face. There was an inclination to let go of the rug, but with all my strength, I held and pulled back. A final vision was revealed.

The scenes kept changing in a slow moving cloud of dust that was speaking. An unknown but sweet voice whispered, "Always a camel, and always a caravan." One caravan, then another was presented. The locations changed. The locations were unfamiliar to me. I was in the picture, but I was older. No, I was old and I was astride a camel. It was the lead camel in a string of heavily laden camels. We were on the leeward face of the dunes. The camels were struggling in sand more than ankle deep. Instead of moving forward, we seemed to be sliding away. My first thought was that these were the dunes of Crescent Lake not far from here, but before I could clearly see the image, it had morphed into a place I did not recognize. I was faced with a vast panorama of sand dunes that had to be scaled. The vision snapped shut.

Immediately I was in an outer courtyard of the monastery. It was a rapid descent, the details of which I don't recall. As I rode home, I thought about the phantasmagoria of the caves and the visions. It seemed that I had stepped through a window. I recalled shaking an ancient prayer rug, but I had no recollection of returning it to its place or descending the cliffs.

My father was a merchant, and I was one of his several children. All girls. Now in early adolescence, arrangements were being made for my marriage. At the behest of my mother, who constantly affirmed I was "too high-spirited," father kept a watchful eye over me. Mother's tone was disparaging, and I was not certain what she meant by "too high-spirited." I was only being myself.

My name was Jade. I was Han. I had the classic features of the Han people. My eyes were dark brown, nearly black, and my skin was naturally yellowish. Much to my mother's displeasure, my skin had been further darkened by the wind and sun. I was average in height and weight for a girl in this era. My health was robust, much better than others, owing to good care, plentiful exercise, and healthy foods. In comparison to most in this town, I had a life of abundance—sheltered and protected. I had always been athletically inclined and loved being in the outdoors. Until recently, playing outdoors had been encouraged and was not a problem.

We lived in the oasis town of Dunhuang at the edge of the Taklamakan Desert. It was a major stopping place and thriving business center at the confluence of trade routes. Depending on your approach, Dunhuang was either the beginning or the end of your leg of travel before entering or leaving the Taklamakan. Any westward travel out of China on routes to India or Persia passed through Dunhuang. From any direction across the desert, the traders and the animals of the caravans will have lost their strength and vigor by the time they reach Dunhuang, the Blazing Beacon.

Traders, pilgrims, and other travelers who had survived the rigors of the Taklamakan coming east into China stopped here to trade and transfer goods, rest, and prepare for travel onward to Lanchou or Urumqui or northward into the Gobi, Mongolia, and beyond. This then was known as the Silk Road. It covered a long distance and joined China with many foreign lands. I was told that it began in Chiang Xi (Xian) and ended at the banks of the Tigris River.

My father was very prosperous; he had many associates and was well respected for his knowledge of the trade routes. He knew the needs and provisions required for caravans to successfully cross the desert in the various seasons. He outfitted caravans and arranged for food, clothing, animals, carts, and camels—among other necessities—for the grueling overland passage. He was a spiritual person, revered for his generosity and wise counsel.

Father told me Dunhuang links China with our friends in the West. He gave sound advice to travelers and others who sought him out. He was intelligent and well versed in goods that were needed and traded throughout the world, some of which were life sustaining, others simply rare, exotic, and luxurious. I enjoyed being in his presence and wanted to learn everything he knew.

In his childhood and youth, my father traveled some of these routes in the shadow of his grandfather. My ancestors were legendary in Dunhuang as merchants and traders, except for my paternal grandfather, who was a learned scholar and a doctor. They had initially settled this place and established a way station, building it up over successive generations. Many of the old timers told of my great-grandfather's exploits and how he expanded the marketplace into a thriving community. He was highly respected because he made stalls available to others to sell their fresh fruits, vegetables, chicken, eggs, and other items. Even in winter the place was bustling and burgeoning with heaps and stacks of goods.

I was fortunate in this life because of the work of my ancestors. I vowed that I would never forget and this I always expressed in my devotions.

My mother was a poor match for my father, in my opinion. She was parsimonious and pious. In private, she was critical and vindictive. She had always been nasty to me and sometimes pulled my hair. She had a jealous nature, which I could not understand, because my father gave her everything she asked for. She had only to whine. She was not a common townswoman; she was blessed beyond measure. Yet her moods and qualms made for an uneasy household.

Normally older girls helped to some extent with the smaller children and the myriad of household duties, but since infancy and early childhood, I had been permitted to stay in the care of the Two Ladies much of the day. Ana Wei and Su Lin were related to me on my father's side of the family. They had a lovely home and gardens. They cared for me as an infant, and during early childhood I stayed most of the day with them. They came for me early in the morning and brought me back home later in the evening. Probably because of this I had a greater bond with them than with my mother and sisters. I grew up playing among their many plants and vines. I watched them as they dried plants and made little round pills for my grandfather, the doctor. I helped.

Only later in life did I realize that this was at the behest of my mother, who it seemed suffered greatly during my birth and was not able to care for me initially. Both of the aunties were unmarried, very gentle women. They were naturalists and understood a great deal about medicinal plants, most of which they'd learned from my paternal grandfather, who practiced medicine and animal husbandry into old age.

My father told me that in my grandfather's youth, his father had taken my grandfather to the east by to study medicine. Revered by the townspeople, he was now elderly and frail. He was no longer out and about. Su Lin and Ana took care of him. I helped.

Later, in my childhood I was permitted to stay much of the day with my father. This happened quite by accident and then became routine. One afternoon I was in the marketplace with my aunties, who were delivering herbs to a vendor. We were nearby my father's compound of stables and warerooms and stopped to visit. As we were about to depart, my father told his sisters, "You can leave Jade with me. I will be going home soon."

I always remembered walking home with my father that day. I was so proud. Some sort of natural transition took place after that, and I went to his business with him. I brewed tea and served it to his business associates; also I made myself useful tidying up after his guests and friends. I was most careful not to annoy him or interrupt him when he was thinking or having a discussion. As I got older, he allowed me to carry messages for him, and so I learned my way around the marketplace. The vendors of the marketplace came to know me well, and ultimately I was allowed to ride out to the monastery and the grottos delivering supplies and materials to the artists and the monks. But that happened long after I got acquainted with the camels.

My father made it clear from the beginning that camels were not pets, like the puppies we had at home. Of course I knew that. I had always known that. I had a "very deep knowing" about it. Perhaps my father told me this at an early age because it was easy to accept. Some things required learning and practice, other things one simply knows. It was simply a matter of "knowingness." I believed "knowingness" included things we already knew when we were born. I had decided we all were born into this world with "knowingness" about one thing or another. Mine was about camels.

Camels behaved for me. Frequently, when a driver could not make a camel obey, I could. I must tell you candidly that this was a quite remarkable "gift," especially for a girl. Most girls my age preferred not to be near camels. Actually, I much preferred working the camels than doing embroidery. My skills were naturally acquired from spending time in the company of my father and other men who worked for him and from my grandfather, who treated many camels and other sick animals.

Of course my mother and father were now at odds over this entire matter, and he was losing ground. In recent days, I was being kept at home more and more. I knew this was a great loss to my father. I was being occupied with "women's work" according to my mother. Not that my mother knew much about "women's work," because as I saw it, she never did any of it; she had household help. She was indulged, and as far as I saw the only thing she did was give orders to people around us. This was a very difficult time for me. The problem was compounded because I had little in common with my siblings, who had grown up together, while I had been mostly with the aunties.

My mother was winning the conflict about what sort of training and activities were appropriate for a girl of my age. I saw that life, as I had known it, was falling apart in front of me. Some of the change was due to an impending marriage. My marriage. Two of my sisters had already been married off. I was next. Mine had been prearranged, as was our custom, and negotiations were taking place between my father and another merchant family. This was no concern of mine.

One afternoon, I overheard a conversation between my mother and father, in which my father told my mother that I was very useful to him, helping with many aspects of the business. With as many caravans as there had been lately, I would be useful. According to her, his business kept him too involved and occupied to watch over me to the extent she thought necessary. Although she agreed that maybe I was useful to him, there were other factors to consider, she said. It was not proper; it simply was not proper for me to be among "those" men in the workplace. She told him emphatically, "Jade's no cameleer."

When I heard her say this, I was crushed, and I thought I would cry. She was taking everything away from me. I left the house and ran to the orchard, kicking a fallen apple as far as I could. I scuffed around in the leaves, and only then did I recall what Auntie Su Lin had told me once. She said, "Whenever someone says things that are not nice, not fair, that you are not pretty, or you are this, or you are that—forget it and strike it out of your mind. Only you can say what you are. Only you can say, 'I am.'" Su Lin looked me straight in the eyes and told me this was something she wanted me always to remember. She said, "Do not permit anyone to tell you who you are. They may try, but do not accept their words." And so I said, right out loud, "I am a cameleer. Mother may say what she wants, but I know who I am."

My father taught me how to ride a horse and how to handle a bow. If I were a boy, given time, I could become a skilled horseman or a cameleer. I saw now that my mother was going to stop this from happening.

This was going to be a difficult summer for me. My father was becoming more remote as my mother exerted more control over me. I wanted to go out, but I had to stay in the house helping with food preparation and caring for my two youngest siblings. Mother was having a relative come in daily to teach me embroidery and sewing. I missed the daily interaction with the men at the stables. My feelings were hurt. I felt like I was being penalized, and I wasn't sure why. I needed to get out of the house and back to what I knew. Mother tried to convince me that the marketplace and the stable were not suitable for a girl of my standing. She said she had regrets for permitting me, as a young child, to go with my father in the first place.

This women's world thing was not the place for me. This I knew. My place was among the people and activities of the marketplace, preparing the camels for the caravan, and running errands for my father. My mother didn't know that I went alone to the Mogao Caves and the monastery. I never told her, and it appears no one else did, either. My secret.

Talking to her only incurred her wrath. I never told her that I preferred the company of the country people at market, the shopkeepers, the camel drivers, and my father's friends. It was easier to capitulate than suffer her ire—this I learned early in life. She had no interest in me ever, nor has she cared what I think.

It would be good if we could come to some understanding. I attempted to explain to her how I felt, but my words fell on deaf ears. I told her that I was proud to be a trader-merchant's daughter. That it ran in my blood. The skill of the deal was more important to me than babies, needlework, and kitchen chores. To which she replied, derisively, "What do you know about the skill of a deal?"

When she wasn't looking, I made tassels for the camels with my embroidery threads. When I was with my father, I started tassel making. He gave me a variety of cords and yarns and beads of every color. I cut and wrapped the cords, added bells, and threaded beads of different colors on the ends. He and the aunties encouraged me by finding special materials for my project. I wanted every camel setting off from Dunhuang to have at least one tassel.

I never told my mother about this and, because I was confined, getting the tassels to the camels was a problem. If one of my father's workers appeared in the courtyard, delivering something for the household, I found an excuse to go outside—like taking the little ones out to play. There I passed the finished tassels to the worker, who gave me a knowing wink as he stashed them in his pocket. But I did not have sufficient materials to make very many.

My needlework improved, and the summer droned on. I thought about the banners in the Mogao Caves, exquisitely stitched, emblazoned with symbols and wild animals. The caves were now out of reach for me. My enthusiasm for life had been squelched, and I was just waiting for the next thing to happen. I responded willingly to what I was asked to do because it was easier that way. No longer a person of action, with my own thoughts, I was getting increasingly more like the lifeless woman of the household and less like my father, a person with purpose.

There were several harvests throughout the year celebrated in our region. Harvest and the changes of season equate with festival times. Some were religious in nature; some were more special than others. My family was preparing for a very large festival that would happen soon. These were special days of celebration, which included many social gatherings at our compound, with relatives and close family friends.

Caravans were larger and more frequent at this time of year, with many pilgrims coming to worship at the shrines and visiting the monastery. According to my father, the towns' people were thriving and doing particularly well that year. They were convivial and neighborly. The town was flourishing. There were throngs of men briefly stopping for a rest, changing camels, and buying provisions for the next leg of their journey. Some left one caravan to join another; still others returned, retracing the route they had just taken.

I knew my father was extremely busy with the requirements for the caravans and providing support to the townspeople for the festival. I wanted to help him. I believed he needed my help, but he didn't intercede on my behalf. I approached the subject several times, but no, my mother was adamantly against my being involved in his work.

Failing that, I had begged my mother for days to allow me to go with some other girls and their family to a festival where, I was told, there was to be much celebrating with good food, music, and dancing. My mother said she would talk to my father about it. I knew my father, and I was rather certain he would not agree to this, so my mother would have to be very convincing to win him over.

When she told me he was not in favor of this idea, I became persistent, finding one reason after another that she could use in persuading him. After a number of discussions, she had finally convinced him, and so he called me to him in order to lay down some strict rules.

The rules were that I must stay with my group at all times and not wander off, that I would not befriend foreigners, that I would not drink intoxicants, that I would only eat and drink from my host's family and what I contributed, and that I would accept nothing from strangers, particularly food and drink. I listened to him intently. He made me repeat the rules to him several times. I told him I understood what he meant, and I promised to obey.

The whole household had been enlivened with preparations for these festivities. I had sewn a long red skirt, embellished with colorful embroidery. My mother was a bit puffed up and pleased that I had achieved this level of skill in needlework. She had hopes for me.

Mother helped me with my hair and used her jade roller on my face. It was cool to the touch, and I felt favored by her this once. She found some of her jewelry for me to wear. She fastened a large silver necklace around my neck. It was beautiful and lay against my chest lightly and perfectly. The silver was embellished with a chased design of flowers and humming birds. Tiny bells hung all along the lower edge. The earrings were of shiny smooth cut out flowers, a humming bird, and tiny bells that jingled as I walked.

Dressing for the festival, with the long dangling earrings and the fanciful skirt and mother's under skirts, made me somehow transformed and very special. I was grateful to her for making this work out so well.

For a moment, I thought my father would change his mind when my friends arrived. He looked rather hesitant, then he shook his head and took a deep breath. I could not tell what he was thinking, but I went to him and gave a quick bow. He pressed a few coins into my hand and whispered, "Don't forget the rules." I shook my head, affirming this, and jumped aboard the cart with my friends.

The festival grounds were pulsating with activity—milling crowds socializing, drumming, drinking, and dancing to the rhythms of local musicians. People were everywhere, jostling and bumping into one another. Some were camping and had set up tents. Most of the people were strangers to me, except for some people from the marketplace, who waved enthusiastically at me. Many families from Dunhuang were picnicking and enjoying the day. Others from out of town seemed to be mostly men. Cook fires were set ablaze, and the embers soon wafted forth with smoke and mixed aromas. The men and women enjoyed each other's company as they stirred cooking pots, and dipped and poured samples for passersby. Every manner of food and drink was available. Some of the women appeared to be tipsy. I remembered my father's rule not to eat food other than what we brought. It smelled so good, I was tempted but managed to resist.

As daylight faded, fires glowed, crackled, and sometimes shot sparks into the darkness. Babies and little children worn out from the exhausting day were sound asleep. Some men were getting boisterous; they talked and laughed together, bragging, and exchanging stories as men do. Some men, exhausted from their work, travel, and the heat, and satiated from the food and drink, curled up and fell asleep. Others staggered or toppled over from intoxicants right where they were sitting.

Even though I didn't know how to dance, the music and the firelight made me want to move like the others. My friends and I danced around in a group. I was given some finger cymbals and experimented with a tambourine someone tossed to me. Tonight I felt very different somehow. I was aware of the eyes of men watching me. Maybe my judgment was overcome by the pulsating music and excitement. Normally shy in social situations, I was easily coaxed into the merrymaking. All my friends had joined in and were dancing with abandon. The music was crowding out my father's rules.

One particular group of men sitting together appeared to be ruffians. From time to time, I was aware that they were looking at me. Observing the movements of the dancing women, I pretended not to notice that one of the men was flirting with me, beckoning for me to come closer. Feeling the rhythm of the dance and the exuberance, I was caught up in the moment and found my eyes meeting his more than once.

Somehow my body felt different. My blouse loosened and was off my shoulders, my skirt was swirling, showing the colors of my underskirts. My hair had fallen loose, and I felt disheveled from the heat and exertion. I kicked off my boots and danced barefoot.

A man lounging with his group motioned for me to come closer, and he put a bracelet of bells around my ankle. This was bold of me. It was out of character for me to permit a man, and a stranger at that, to touch me or to do such a thing. His friends were drunk and lunged at me, attempting to grab my skirt. I cleverly swayed out of their reach, moving away quickly. I danced into the crowd, hoping to be out of his sight and out of his reach.

But their eyes followed me into the crowd, and they started laughing, pushing, shoving, and elbowing each other. Except for the swarthy one, who had given me the ankle bracelet, his friends were all bawdy, ruckus, and in their cups, or sullen, in a stupor. Either way they were all drunk. He was not, or so it appeared. He poked them with his elbow and hushed them up, as he set his mind on beguiling me.

I stayed in rhythm with the music as I combed through the crowd looking for my friends. They seemed to have vanished. I couldn't find anyone I knew. I was lost among throngs of unknowns, dizzy in the darkness and firelight. The drums and music continued to pulsate as I searched faces in the crowd for someone I knew.

Somewhat later, I neared the group of ruffians again. They seemed more subdued. With a slight motion of his head and eyes, one indicated that he wanted to see the bells he had put on my ankle earlier. The bells were delightful. I really liked them and in appreciation, I twirled around with my arms raised. My skirt swirled out widely, revealing the ankle bracelet. He liked that: he clapped his hands lightly and nodded approval. I touched my castanets with some hesitation. He indicated that he wanted me to sit down beside him by patting on the ground next to him. I shook my head "no" and danced away.

Although there was something that attracted me to him that caused me to find his eyes many times that evening, I was not inclined to join him and his troupe. I could tell from their un-kempt clothing and demeanor that these were strangers just passing through.

His gift came at a cost. I cannot tell you how it happened. I have a hazy remembrance that we were talking; he said he had one blue and one brown eye. He said that, just like my name, he traded in jade. He said his cargo was jade of various colors, including lavender jade from Siam. I told him he was just saying that, and I didn't believe him. I did not recognize the thoroughly inimical situation I was in because my life had provided me no frame of reference. He wanted to show me his jade cargo.

My father's cautionary remarks were forgotten for the moment. No doubt, overcome by my natural willfulness, determination, spirit, and curiosity, having a look at trade goods was an everyday occurrence, nothing unusual for me. Siam jade would be interest-ing, and so I went with him to see it. The last I remember was walking into the darkness with him. And that he had one blue eye and one brown eye.

Fading in and out of consciousness, I was aware of the familiar rocking motion that is only felt atop a camel. That part seemed clear to me. I fell in and out of sleep synchronized with the rhythm of the camel's steps. Dozing intermittently, I realized I was terribly uncomfortable; it was prickly and rough against my skin, and I could hardly breathe. I tried to stretch out, but I couldn't. I was inside a basket, a hamper of some sort. I could see daylight through the weave.

I needed water; my lips were swollen, and my tongue was stuck to the roof of my mouth. I wanted out, but I had no strength. I was dreaming. I passed out repeatedly. Images of my father faded and vanished. He spoke to me, but I couldn't understand what he said. I wanted my mother.

The image of a drugged, wayward monk curled up in the Mogao Caves settled on me. He was in the basket, in the basket with me, and I was frightened and quivered and pushed him away. I tried hard to think. The Buddha. He had one blue eye and one brown eye. Cave paintings circled around in my foggy mind. I had to pee. I was peeing. Oh, no.

The caravan came to a halt. My camel pitched forward, and then backward, then he heaved forward again, before settling to ground. I tried to call out. I was parched, confused, and it seemed as if I could not be heard. I saw someone through the weave of the basket. "Water, I need water." My words were uttered weakly. Someone was outside; the lid to my prison was slightly raised, just high enough for someone to reach in cautiously with a skin of water. There wasn't enough space to sit upright. I barely drank. Some water trickled down my throat; mostly it slopped over my face and down my neck. The opiate brought sleep. The caravan moved on.

The sleep was welcome. My dreams were not. We were climbing a mountain. The basket was sliding sideways, scratching, and scraping me. The path was rough, and I was jostled around. The top of my head hurt. The full weight of my body pressed my head and shoulder against the basket, but I was helpless and without strength. From time to time I almost regained consciousness. The camel was climbing, and I realized we were no longer in loose sand. The pain and stink caused me to cry out, but nobody listened. My inaudible words just echoed somewhere inside my head.

I slept. We stopped once again. I moaned in an attempt to attract some help from those outside. The voices were rough, and the language, unfamiliar. Eventually someone raised the lid and poured water in the general direction of my mouth. Most was spilled, but the drug was induced. Unbeknown to me, the caravan continued on.

At mid-morning, an avalanche interrupted the moving caravan. By Divine intervention, three camels near the middle of the chain were inexplicably broken free. If anyone had been there to witness this event, they would have called it a miracle. Others would tell you it was a coincidence, that the rope was old and frayed specifically in two places.

As the entire caravan cascaded down the mountainside, three camels remained standing at the edge of a precipice. Before and behind the three of them, the face of the mountain had broken away in several places. Earth, trees, camels, men, supplies, trade goods, gear, and cargo, slid, careened, and tumbled end over end and rolled up into dirt balls, debris, rocks, and boulders at the bottom. Some would say it was the result of changing environmental conditions brought on by excess rain and a period of draught. Others would say it was the hand of God that loosed the mountainside at that precise location to rid the world of evil.

No outside observer ever saw it, and no one reported the incident, but it happened nonetheless. Interestingly, except for the three heavily laden camels, there was not one witness to attest to what happened that day. Further, there was no indication, not one shred of evidence at the foot of the mountain, that anyone or anything was buried there.

The event was quick and blinding. Then for hours, the dust billowed up and settled. The three camels hunkered down and gently closed their eyelids over their eyes to protect themselves. Much, much later, they sat blinking as the sky cleared of dust. Rocks, boulders, and earth had collected below. There was no sign of life or remnants of the caravan. The trail was gone.

When the earth stopped shaking and all unnatural underground movement ceased, the camels stopped blinking and chewing. Heads held high in the air, seemingly on cue, they majestically arose in a ripple effect with the first camel leading the chain of action. They each seemed to know they had precious cargo and began a precipitous descent.

Attached to one another, they appeared nonchalant as they picked their way over the clumps of soil and boulders that had never before seen the light of day. If it was treacherous, and it was, they didn't register it. But they moved unerringly and deftly without panic because they knew their job and were masters of it, carefully searching out stable ground, circling around and knowingly avoiding unstable earth. They nimbly balanced their heavy loads. Before nightfall, they reached an old, unused yet somehow familiar caravan trail. They continued on it at a steady pace through a dark but starlit night.

Sitting silent, deep in meditation, Ochi had left his lithe body sitting erect on the ground while his spirit in another "body" traveled the universe. Day had turned to night, and night to day, repeatedly. The dew and dust collected and intermingled on his body. Like anything else that remained out in the weather, he was blotched with spots and rivulets. Neither cold nights nor intense sun affected his concentration. Unmoving, he retained the lotus position.

A concatenation of visual and sensory experience disturbed him and interrupted the moment so that sounds and smells combined to create a vision of animals, specifically camels, picking their way across rocky terrain. As the vision continued, it seemed to indicate they were on a trajectory that would cross his path.

Ochi had a gift of clairvoyance, but to him this power was more of a problem and less a gift, often troublesome and seldom helpful.

Was this an omen, a warning, or nothing? Sometimes he failed to properly interpret what he saw, but then, after all this was a new gift, recently received.

Ochi sat silently and waited. Being perfectly honest, he realized that knowing the future had advantages, particularly in the advent of danger, but this vision did not seem to forecast danger; however, there was some element about it that was more perplexing than just the three animals. He could not ascertain what that was. This information was not given to him, and answers did not come. The morning sun rose higher until it was nearly directly overhead, and just as in the vision, he saw three camels, heavily laden caravan camels, not wild camels, coming through a narrow, distant clearing. He blinked in disbelief.

He found his predicament particularly disconcerting, intrusive. Much to his chagrin, these camels had somehow found him in this vast wilderness. Was this providence, some altered state of reality, or maybe he'd stepped into a parallel universe? *Perhaps,* he thought, *I am still dreaming. That's it, I am still inside my dream.* The thought pleased him. Ochi knew about lucid dreaming. He had practiced it for years. He was quite adept at changing his dream content or elements in his dreams, while he was dreaming. In fact, Ochi was a masterful dreamer. He realized that if he were dreaming right now, he could make any number of changes. He could change their trajectory or better yet transform the camels into three rabbits. The problem was that this situation had him wide-awake and slightly agitated, as the camels kept walking toward him.

If this was real, maybe it was providence. Ah so, he quickly concluded, they were lost and want to be found! He felt he was loosing his composure; a possible encounter with humans and animals had not fully trickled down from his subconscious mind.

Life in the monastery and his superiors had earnestly endeavored to expunge his sense of humor. As a child, he saw humor in many situations. The monks worked tirelessly to drive into obscurity the "little trickster" part of him so that eventually, Ochi seemed serious minded among his peers. But his sense of humor and creativity had not been drubbed out entirely; it was only driven underground.

Privately he saw the funny side of things, and although unspoken, the playful little boy in him was alive and well.

His solitary conversation went like this:

If this is a dream, it is rather humorous. If this is a premonition, it is ridiculous. It could be synchronistic. Could three camels leave a caravan route somewhere in time and space with the deliberate intention of passing directly in front of me, a human being, sitting alone in the wilderness in a stream of sunlight on an earthen outcropping at the edge of some woods?

Ochi inhaled deeply and slipped into a light meditative state so that the vision picked up where it left off, but it had nothing new to offer. Aware of possible danger from dishonest and desperate travelers, Ochi decided the best course of action would be to use his other gift: his ability to make himself invisible. This was a skill he possessed from years of training and practice with an ancient Hindu holy man. In the blink of an eye, he blended into nature and watched and waited. Highly sensitive, he felt low-level earth vibration and the internal noises of the camels, but nothing he felt or heard indicated that their master accompanied the camels. Strangely, he felt there was something in this vision that was extraordinary but that had not been revealed to him.

As if in a mirage, the camels continued to amble toward him. As they got nearer, he saw that indeed they had no driver and, furthermore, there was no sound indicating there was anyone or any more camels to follow. *It would seem they are on their own,* he thought. Ochi remained silent and invisible, keenly listening and patiently waiting.

Sensing a human presence, the camels slowed and milled around. They were nonplussed. They came to a complete standstill, and just like him, they waited. Erring on the side of caution, Ochi stayed in place, unseen to the human eye. Although he picked up no vibrations of an approaching caravan, he expected the owners would be searching for them and the cargo—or else this dream would end.

The camels waited patiently, too, until finally the lead camel dropped to his knees, then the second, followed by the third. They dipped back and lunged forward, then settled on the ground in an open space very near to Ochi. Their heads held high and their sleepy looking eyes alerted to any movement.

The monk calmly slipped into a meditative state again as the camels remained unmoving. No one arrived to claim the animals, and they seemed disinclined to move on. After he called on his extrasensory perception once again, Ochi concluded that no one would be coming. After a while, he decided he had no choice but to investigate.

As an itinerant monk, Ochi traveled with only the clothes he wore and very nearly no provisions, quite capable of living off the land. He provided for himself and survived with little or no food or water for extended periods. He was lithe and lean; smooth muscles covered his small and fine frame, belying his physical strength and endurance. His smooth skin was darkened by exposure to the sun and elements, and his wispy hair was sparse and fine with some gray or colorless chin whiskers. Fine wrinkles populated a delicate and kindly face. Ochi was a scrupulously clean person, owing to a combination of his ultra concern for personal hygiene and spiritual purification rites.

It would have been difficult to guess the age of this limber, spry, and acutely alert little monk. He carried a walking stick, rarely needed for walking but essential. It was useful for carrying provisions, self-defense, or balancing a bundle or a bucket on his shoulder, when necessary.

Ochi appeared in his body at the tree line, arose slowly, and picked up his stick, prepared to see what the day had wrought. The camels turned their heads toward him and blinked their eyes as if to say, *We knew you were here.*

With some reluctance, and at some distance, the monk walked around the animals. Hesitantly, he approached them. Ochi was an empath. He felt the weight of their heavy burden. Without touching, he looked at their ropes and concluded they had broken free from a caravan. It seemed they had been attached both in front and back where ropes now hung free. He crept cautiously around the animals, three large heaps fully relaxed and waiting patiently, blinking, chewing, and proudly seated, their noses in the air.

71

Confronting the fact that they had lost their owner, he grew concerned that he bore some responsibility to return them to their rightful owner. This thought flitted through his mind, and then loomed largely. The thought was daunting. The wilderness was vast, and he had chosen this path because it was not a likely one a caravan would follow. Where would one look in this vast wilderness? The thought that he had just become the owner of three camels and bountiful provisions—of who knows what—did not occur to him. He had no thought or cares for personal possessions, materials goods, and the associated problems they bring.

Now camels have remarkably good memories, and all have experienced a mean spirited handler. These were not unduly concerned about this monk, but they respectfully eyed his walking stick. A stick had meaning to a camel. There was a slight, mutually felt apprehension, but they all seemed to realize they had no alternative but to trust one another.

Ochi, who had been in total isolation for several months, was now abruptly jerked out of his peace and solitude by the situation that confronted him. His difficulty in coping was furthermore exacerbated by his having no particular fondness for camels. The last hour had been a shock to his system, a huge leap from meditation to the reality of three camels. He turned and gazed around, carefully surveying the immediate vicinity, then off in the distance from which they had come. His eyes rolled skyward, as if asking for help from a higher power.

Just three camels. No driver. Not a soul in sight. A feeling passed through him that no one was going to appear. "What do I know about camels?" *Nothing,* he thought, answering his own question. They needed a cameleer. They needed food and water and someone to tend to their injuries. There was dried blood on the nose and injuries to the legs of the lead camel. The last one had many scrapes, lacerations, and a serous gash that could become infected.

This unexpected gift of camels posed a dilemma. He rubbed his long, fine-boned fingers over his chin, stroking his few soft scraggly whiskers in contemplation. With a deep sigh of resignation, he wiped his hands across his forehead and then up over his practically baldhead contemplating his onerous duties.

The camels shifted on their haunches as if to say, "Get on with it," wanting to encourage some action on his part. *They look worn out, tired, and ready to be unburdened,* he thought, as he inspected and considered the number of straps and the methods by which the loads were tied down.

The entire caboodle seemed extraordinarily dusty. He wondered how long they had been wandering alone. He vaguely remembered someone told him that domesticated camels released into the wild become wild. These were domesticated camels after all. He considered just how well they would fare if released into the desert wilderness. Perhaps they needed people. Perhaps they would not do well, or survive on their own. After all, they had found him, and it was his perception that they were giving him a blatant request for help. He had the distinct feeling they were not likely to leave him.

If he simply walked away—and that would be unkind and irresponsible—likely they would follow him. He circumnavigated them once more, casually looking at the attached cargo. They had two humps, indicating that their origin was China—his destination. They had been coming from China.

He reconsidered how the loads had been strapped down. The loads on the first and last camel seemed to be heavier, with lighter bundles strapped on the top, maybe rugs or textiles. He approached the middle camel, which, unlike the others, carried barrels, water skins, a huge lidded basket, shovels, and some smaller containers. The lidded basket was stained and reeked with an offensive odor. The smell was revolting and caused him to draw back. Whew. He held his hand over his nose. *This is a problem of another kind. Probably a load of dead animals,* he thought.

He took his walking stick and prodded the outside of the basket. He saw no movement nor heard anything, not a sound, just the nasty acrid stench. He covered his nose again. As he drew back to poke his stick in the basket forcefully, the camel shifted just out of reach.

With his walking stick firmly in his hand, he raised it above his head with the intent of hitting the basket. When he was about to land the blow, the camel moved again, just enough to miss his strike. With great force, his stick jabbed into the ground. Three times the camel moved as he swung. Three times he missed. He looked at the camel and quizzically thought, *This animal seems to be playing a game.* At the very least, the animal did not want the basket to be struck. The monk was at once curious and perplexed about the camel's behavior.

He moved on to the other two, which seemed more cooperative. He had to climb up on them to reach and release the top most bundles, which were bulky but light in weight. Once he figured out the knotting methods, the pieces fell away easily, tumbling and rolling down. Caravans carried trade goods, but they also carried foodstuffs, medicine, and gear for a long journey.

Beneath the top-most layers were some sort of heavy blocks wrapped in woven mats and tied artfully with plaited and twisted vine rope. These were extremely heavy; they fell with an obtuse thud. They did not roll or bounce. He had to be careful so that they did not fall on him; sometimes he had to jump out of the way. Working at a steady pace, he had unleashed all the straps and ropes, and everything was strewn on the ground. The two camels seemed relieved to be free of their burden.

Ochi sat on a pile of stuff and surveyed the situation. He realized that he could never reload the animals. If their owners did not appear, the stuff would lie on the ground for eternity. He had worked for almost two hours in the heat, and his fingers were sore from handling the ropes.

Second-guessing himself, he wondered whether he had created a bigger problem for himself by off-loading everything. He was having further thoughts when he saw the last camel roll his eyes closed. Maybe it was his imagination, but the two with no loads seemed content in spite of their injuries.

He pulled the blankets off those two and shook them vigorously. Dust flew everywhere. Then he threw the blankets and mats used for padding over the stuff on the ground. He picked up a broom that had been bundled together with some tools and, careful to avoid their injuries, he went to work sweeping the camels. The amount of dust, dirt, and coarse rock particles embedded in their coats seemed unusual enough to hold a secret.

It was mid-afternoon when he turned his attention to the middle, uncooperative camel. His curiosity had been aroused; it certainly seemed the camel was protecting the basket, but he was avoiding this onerous task. No doubt something alive had been stowed in the basket, fresh meat or fowl, maybe exotic birds for trade.

He searched his memory for live animals that the Chinese might be sending to India. Or vice versa. Puppies or ducks crossed his mind. The basket was securely fastened, and he couldn't get to its ropes. Also, it smelled foul, and he didn't want to go near it.

The uncooperative camel watched as he removed the smaller baskets of foodstuffs and skins that appeared to contain water and oil. He carefully laid those aside. A basket fell off the top and scattered dates and figs on the ground. He gathered them up and set them aside to wash later. So far so good. The camel was amenable, so maybe they'd had a truce.

He looked around for a place to drag the large lidded basket in anticipation of getting it off. He needed a place to bury or burn the contents. He didn't want it in his campsite, and it might attract wild animals. He hoped it wasn't so heavy because he did not want to touch the contents, and emptying it was out of the question.

Ochi decided to have a conversation with the camel. So, he started speaking aloud, saying, "Well, you see I have put my walking stick way over there. And you see I have helped your buddies here. I did not hurt them, and I will treat your wounds as soon as we can finish here. I helped them, and I would be happy to help you. They are both dozing, and we could be, too. We could finish here promptly. We could be done here in no time at all if you'll let me drop this last basket to the ground. What do you say to that?" he ended.

While looking eye to eye with the camel, he approached the basket. As he reached for one of the O-rings, the camel moved ever so slightly, almost reluctantly. "That's not going to work. You have to sit still so I can undo these buckles," Ochi said aloud, continuing with, "You're not being helpful, and rightfully this is not my problem. It's yours. You should be happy to get rid of this load. It's not healthy."

"I'll give you one more chance. Be still. You have tested my patience, and I am about to run you off," he said, as he stood next to the basket and took up a handful of loose straps. At which time he heard a moan. He looked at the camel and then looked at the soiled basket in disbelief. The second moan came from inside the basket. Wide eyed and frightened, he jumped back so quickly he fell over the heaps of stuff on the ground and landed on his rump.

Ochi was shaken, the moaning started again, and it seemed the basket moved. He drew back and listened. His eyes and ears keenly focused on the basket. Many things flashed through his mind, including ghosts and headless spirits. The moan continued. Finally he ventured a weak, "Hello?" There was no response, but the basket moved again. So he said, "Hello, hello?" There was a definite moan, and the basket moved even more.

Ochi had a healthy respect for ghosts, but he got to his feet and somehow managed to traverse the few meters to the camel. He heard himself say, "Hello, is anybody in there?" A weak moan came in response.

This was quite unbelievable, and he wasn't quite certain what to do or what he was expected to do. "Was today some sort of test? First, I have the camels and now this. Something fate has contrived perhaps?"

Standing in the wilderness with three hunkered down camels, he felt a bit foolish calling out, "Who's there?" There seemed to be an incoherent human response. The basket moved ever so slightly. Walking closer, he leaned his ear toward the soiled surface, wrinkling up his nose. It seemed to be a child's voice.

He braced himself and mustered all his courage as he fumbled with the variety of leather straps, buckles, and hardware. If there was a human being in the basket, he could not drop the basket to the ground like any old cargo. He would have to get the lid off in order to get the person out. He worked feverishly, and the camel cooperated fully.

Ochi was small, and his reach was short, so he found himself climbing right up onto the animal's back. He lay across the camel, pulling and prying. The lid seemed designed not to come off.

By the time Ochi got the basket opened, he was frantic. The real work of the day lay before him. He realized my vital essence was ebbing, along with daylight. He knew he had to act quickly. With hands palm down above my body, he did a scan, detecting that I was severely dehydrated, had no lesions or broken bones, but that my organs and nervous system were closing down. It was questionable whether I could be snatched from the throes of death. I had been deprived of water and nutrients for a very long time. It was necessary to keep me warm and make me comfortable. He needed herbs and hot water and somehow he needed to cleanse me. Ochi was a man of few words, but he was a capable man of action; he knew precisely what to do, even under austere conditions.

Throughout the night, he cradled me for warmth, soothed me in my delirium, and comforted me from tremors that appeared to him to be drug induced. All the while he maintained a state of prayerful mediation.

During the first day, he brought me through one crisis after another. As if feeding a sick little bird, he gave me liquid a drop at a time. On the evening of the second day, I improved enough to swallow on my own. Ochi was able to find dried figs and apricots among the caravan stuff. He soaked and mashed the dried fruit, blending it into a thin liquid, then administered it a drop at a time. My shivering stopped. Little by little I improved. Days later, I regained consciousness.

Once I was stabilized, Ochi turned his attention to the camels' injuries. Brushing the gravel and dirt from their coats, carefully he exposed their cuts and treated them. They were free to go or do as they wished. He thought it uncanny that they never ran off or wandered far from us. He did not tether them, and when they left the immediate area, they returned at nightfall.

I was frightened being with a stranger, and trembled when Ochi approached. The camels instinctively moved closer to me, forming a protective barrier. At night, they drew even closer. Ochi wasn't fond of animal smells, and his inclination was to run them off, but he observed that the camels and I had a peculiar bond. They calmed me. From a practical point of view, Ochi realized they provided welcome warmth and protection from the cold night.

The fact that the camels had brought me to Ochi was nothing less than providence, for he had the caring, knowledge, and patience to help me through this critical point in life. As I regained some strength, Ochi was faced with the dilemma of what to do next. We two could hardly communicate; I spoke a Chinese dialect that he barely understood. I was frightened, involuntarily shaking when he came too near. I cried a lot. Despite my anguish, fundamentally I was in good heath, and my age helped me recover my vital essence. Ochi knew something grave had happened to me but knew not what.

Ochi did not know how far ahead into China he might have to travel to find help for me, and after several weeks he came to the conclusion that he would not be finding the rest of the caravan. Some mild earth tremors reminded him of some earlier stronger tremors he had felt, and he wondered whether earthquakes could have played a part in how this situation had unfolded in his life.

When I was healthy enough to travel, by signs and gestures I instructed him how to reload the camels. It seemed strange to him that I knew how to do this. He was trying to put together a picture of who I was and where I had come from. I had these skills, but he saw that I was too refined to be a worker from the caravan. I seemed to be lost and couldn't tell him where I had come from or where I was going. I had no sense of direction. I cried uncontrollably when he asked where I was going. While there were major frustrations due to language barriers, it seemed to Ochi that there might be issues that I was unwilling to or unable to reveal.

He decided to abandon his pilgrimage to China and return over the same route he had just travelled, where he was assured he could find help for me. Proceeding into unchartered territory with winter approaching would not be wise.

Then, like a caravan, life moved on—this time, toward a valley of Buddhist monasteries in Bamiyan.

Under the care of many female Buddhist practitioners, my physical health improved. Unfortunately, the connection of the body to the emotional and spiritual aspects of my life had been broken. Although much was applied, no amount of nutrition and nurturing could heal the damage from my kidnapping—damage caused from tearing me away from my beloved home and family and from my guilt over not having heeded my father's words.

Merely enduring the motions of living, I helped with accounts and contributed by preparing the altar and the service. In the monastery gardens, I found a strange peace, planting, weeding, and hoeing. For some reason, I was never set to floor scrubbing like other girls my age.

Beyond doing my fair share, I was unable to reach out to those who were doing so much to help me. Being withdrawn, I was sure they felt nothing could be done to help me overcome my trauma. Whatever it was that had happened to me was not known by anybody. To be sure there were language barriers; but it was apparent to the monks that there was something, some deep hurt, some blockage that prevented my being reached and which would not free me from bad dreams. Bouts of crying eventually diminished, but after a year, tears were still plenty and unpredictable, occurring as if for no apparent reason. Overwhelming sorrow would not permit me to move ahead.

Ochi visited daily while I was in the infirmary. He came less frequently once I moved into the girls' dormitory. When he did visit, we walked mostly in silence, just as we had after he'd found me. I had no idea how long our journey here had taken because I'd lost track of time and place, and we never speak of it.

After we arrived in Bamiyan, I never left the confines of the monastery unless Ochi came for me. I felt safe there and I felt safe with Ochi. Several times he took me to the work sites of the massive Buddha's. This I enjoyed immensely. The work of the artisans interested me, and their methods piqued my curiosity. Ochi saw that; he discovered a key to my recovery. This project somehow engaged me with the world, whereas nothing else had before. On these outings, Ochi tired of climbing the cliff paths long before I did. He commented that I seemed to be in my comfort zone. He asked me whether I had some acquaintance or knowledge about the process and projects underway. He said he thought he saw an almost imperceptible smile across my face and a glimmer in my eyes while looking at some of the niche paintings.

He saw too the moment my mind snapped shut and the almost-smile disappeared. Then tears slid down my cheeks, reminding us of the weeks we'd travelled together, when I was inconsolable. Now, two years had passed.

The healing of the body had been relatively quick, yet my spirit had been crushed, and Ochi wondered what more he and the nuns could do. I never explained to him how I happened to be in a basket with three camels on the Silk Road, and he never asked. He would not pry. Maybe in time I would explain, then maybe not. It didn't matter. All things change.

Three nights after our first visit to the Bamiyan Buddhas, I had a vivid dream.

I saw two monks sitting at a long, low writing table in front of me. A younger monk, who is to the right of the older one, has some materials in a pile in front to him. It's not apparent to me at first what these materials were—fragments of textiles maybe? Looking at the older monk, I notice he is writing with my father's preferred writing brush; father's brush basin and ink stone are also on the table. I am about to ask him how this could be when he lifts the brush and points it toward his assistant. The assistant reaches into the pile of threads and withdraws a tassel. It is one of my tassels. Then he fastens it onto the end of my father's brush. I am surprised and about to say something about my tassel when the older monk points the brush with the dangling tassel directly at me. Practically nose to nose, looking straight into my eyes, I hear my father's voice clearly saying to me, "Thrive."

I awoke, shocked and wide-eyed in amazement. I was frightened and shaking at first, but after a time I regained my composure, grew reassured and drew some comfort from it. I heard my father's voice. It was real. I heard his instructions. I never had a dream experience like this before; it was a powerful. I knew nothing about dreams or there meaning. I wondered about the meaning of this one and pondered each element. I was preoccupied with it throughout the day and the weeks ahead. I considered discussing it with Ochi, or one of the *samaneras* closest to me, but decided against it. I felt no one would understand. For, after all, they knew nothing of my life in Dunhuang.

I remembered hearing grandfather tell Su Lin that we were the best interpreters of our own dreams, and he talked to her about prophetic dreams. Thus, I began to reflect and questioned whether I had had a prophetic dream—for it had been so vivid. It was exactly father's voice. But I did not recognize the monks. It had been almost two years since I had seen my father's writing instruments, but they had been vivid and very real in the dream. As had been the tassel, for I clearly recall that specific tassel, and saw every single strand I'd put in it the day I'd made it. It was the last one I'd made.

Thinking about the items in the dream occupied my thoughts. But what of the monks I hadn't recognized? I considered the dream and my circumstances, past and present, but could not shake it, particularly the word "thrive." I was confronted by the message, for truly I was not doing well. I was living but not thriving. I concluded that my father, whom I loved and missed most of all, had sent me a message, and I would be wise to heed his word.

It was several weeks after my dream that Ochi came to meet me for a walkabout. The abbess told me he was coming, and that I should be prepared to spend the entire day with him. In great anticipation, I packed my knapsack with extra food and hoped we would visit the grottos near the colossal Buddhas.

But Ochi had other plans. When I approached him, he said he detected a subtle change in my demeanor. I knew he harbored a silent hope that I would be healed.

We walked up the valley, passing many monks and busy monasteries, and some smaller quiet ones almost hidden away in dense vegetation. After more than an hour of walking, seeing fewer monks, and more distance between monasteries and homes, we sat down to rest in a shrine grove, across the pathway from a small, recessed Buddhist shrine, which was meant for travelers. The shrine and the surrounding area, including where we sat, was well tended.

As Ochi sat in silence, I opened the small bundle, a packet that included some dried fruits and nuts and rice cakes wrapped in leaves. Selecting a choice one, I walked across to the shrine, bowed, and placed it on a small plate. After a moment of gratefulness for the beautiful day, and appreciation for the *samanera* in the kitchen, who had thoughtfully tucked in extra food, I turned and walked back to Ochi, but I didn't see him. So I turned back toward the shrine, wondering where he had gone. I looked back around to where he had been seated. There he was! I didn't say anything to him. He had a way of doing this to me. First, he was there. I turned away. He was gone. I looked back; he was there again. Some day, I intended to ask about this disappearing act, but not today, as he seemed to have something weighing heavily on his mind.

We sat together eating and silently observing the birds and plants. It was a lovely place to rest and simply enjoy nature. My thoughts turned to the day's agenda, which was at best puzzling. Although the sandstone cliffs and the Bamiyan Buddhas could be seen in the distance, clearly we had been walking away from them.

Ochi inhaled deeply. I thought he was preparing to meditate, but he exhaled, blowing out through his nose, and giving a strange sort of sigh. I smiled. He was a special person, who had done so much for me. Why had I never told him?

Ochi interrupted my thought, saying, "Jade, I have things I must discuss with you. How are you feeling? You seem somehow stronger today." He breathed deeply again and continued. His tone was serious, and his body heaved with his breaths. "Jade, you have been at the monastery for two years or more." He did not know the exact period because he did not count time. "Do you see yourself entering the order?"

I was about to respond, when he said, "No, I didn't think so. Neither do I. This is not to say you would not be welcomed. I am sure the abbess would be happy to recommend you. You have been very helpful and indeed very useful to the monastery. She tells me. But in this direction I have not encouraged her, nor you."

He paused but did not seem to want an answer from me. Finally, he went on. "Jade, there are things I must tell you. To be perfectly truthful, I have been less than candid with you; in fact, I have deliberately withheld information from you since we came to Bamiyan. I felt it was in your best interest. Primarily because of regaining your strength from that arduous travel and because of your age, of course."

Shifting positions slightly, he went on. "The travel was taxing on your body and also your mind and spirit. Your body seems mended. With more work on your part, and given time, I believe all will heal." Ochi seemed to be working up to saying something. He was not his usual direct and to the point self. I considered his words as he was cogitating.

Yes, what he said was so. I was feeling much better, especially since I'd made a personal commitment to thrive. But at this time I could not and did not want to discuss my inner feelings, the abduction, nor my family and my former life with anyone. My emotions were still too close to the surface. When I tried to verbalize it, I always choked up. I wanted to tell Ochi about my family and how I'd gotten kidnapped. Many people had helped me, but Ochi had been faithful to me, protecting and looking out after me, as a kindly father would have done. I owed him my life. Truly, I was and have been dependent on the kindness of strangers.

I shuddered at the thought of being left in a basket somewhere in the wilderness. I would be dead, if not for Ochi. Surely it was providence that had brought me to him.

Ochi finally continued. "Jade, things are not always as they appear to be."

I nodded, knowingly.

"Yes, we've discussed 'illusion' a dozen times before. But, no, 'illusion' is not what I am talking about." He said, "Jade, some things need resolution." He paused again and left me hanging there.

I took a bite of a tasty ripe apricot and studied him. Although he seemed to me unchanged, there seemed to be something troubling him. Every once in a while he sighed. I was about to speak up when he said, "I'm not getting any younger."

I was beginning to think he was going to tell me he was ill or that he was leaving Bamiyan to restart his pilgrimage. After all, he had sacrificed his own plans to secure my recovery. Although he never said it, I knew he had given up his life's goal for me.

He took a deep breath and went on. "About the monastery, Jade, you have skills and a high spiritual nature, and I know you well enough to know that the sacrifice involved in living a monastic life would be easily attainable for you. Nonetheless, I think there are skills and knowledge unique to you. I don't know how you came by them, but the abbess has told me you have knowledge of Sanskrit, and she frequently comments how useful you are to her in managing the business of running the monastery."

"I don't see the monastic life as befitting you. Well, maybe it would be a choice, but I think something else might be a better fit. Let's say a more perfect fit. To be honest, I think the monastic life could become tedious for you, the very routine of it boring. Oh, I think you should continue your dharma studies. I am trying to tell you, you could have something more fitting, in addition to dharma studies.

"The Buddha never said one had to become a *bhikkhuni*. Ordination is not really so important to living as it may appear here in Bamiyan. The abbess and I both feel you need something that engages your mind—let's say, differently. You are very creative, and excellent at problem solving. You should know she is most impressed with how you reorganized and managed the gardens. Yes, you are an excellent manager. She told me how much more productive the gardens are now than they were before you came, how carefully you keep records, how you have increased the yield in the herb gardens and all you have taught her about the medicinal properties of herbs. As I said before, I know she would be happy to have you in the Order, but maybe, well, I want you to consider an alternative."

Throughout his discourse, my monkey brain flew from one thing to another. My emotions ran rampant. Was I to leave the monastery? This was the only home I had now. I was beset with fear, panic, and dread. Had I overstepped in making changes, improvements in the gardens? I questioned myself, and my behavior. Was I a problem for the abbess?

Finally, I snapped out of it when he said, "Jade, we are going to visit an old friend of mine. I want you to know a bit about him before we arrive. We can see his orchards from here." He pointed to a beautiful swath of color further across the valley. There an orchard was just coming into bloom. I had looked at it admiringly, as he talked.

"He's a very wealthy man who has given much in support of my monastery. Without his money, the monastery where you stay likely would not exist. Indirectly, he has helped many women over the years, the young and the elderly alike, and their training has helped build up this vibrant community. He is patron of many of the cultural ventures in Bamiyan—like work on the colossal Buddhas that you love so much. And, he provides support for many of the artists and artisans that live in the cliffs, to whom I have introduced you. He is a very good man, as indeed was his wife, but she passed away several years ago. I'm sorry to say, it seems the light in his life went out when she died."

My monkey brain came to an abrupt halt as Ochi drew me into the story.

"He needs help, and I thought, well, it occurred to me that you both have similar interests. I know what made his eyes sparkle for many years, and the same things seem to light up your eyes. I am speaking about gardening and the artists. This is not the kind of thing I know much about, Jade. But I hate to see his orchards and the vineyard go into decline."

Ochi shook his head. "Last year, his harvest was very poor. Previously he provided fruits and vegetables to the monastery daily—with plenty left to sell in the marketplace."

I was listening intently.

He reflected momentarily, and then started again. "Part of the problem is the loss of his wife, another part is his age, but it's even more complicated than that. They never had children. He has no living relatives and no overseer. His workers need direction and instruction. He feeds and shelters them and they grow idle. I hate to say it, but the place appears more and more neglected every time I visit. Sometimes his workers can't be found. Less and less is getting done. I hope I'm wrong, but I feel his workers are taking advantage of his good nature. Now I'm growing concerned over his personal welfare and struggling over a solution.

"My point is that I think you know what needs to be done, and I think you could be of immense help to him. That is, if you are interested. He has household help and a cook, but they need firm direction." Then, he added, "Jade, maybe this would be an opportunity for you, maybe you would be a perfect fit. Maybe it would give you breathing space, a place to sort out the future."

I was about to speak when he said, "Jade, don't say 'yes' and don't say 'no.' I only want you to meet each other. I'd like you to meet him, to see the place, and think it over. You are under no obligation.

"We are not far from the place now." He stood and pointed toward the ribbon of color that defined the orchard and then, with his finger in the air, traced the property outline. Such a big place! As we walked, I could see several structures and what was probably the main house. My interest was piqued.

When we reached the path leading to the farmhouse, Ochi said he would go alone to find the master of the house and told me to continue walking on the trail for about four minutes, saying that if I encountered any of the workmen to tell them he would be coming along soon. He described a shed, and told me he would meet me there, and that we would talk further, because there was more he had yet to reveal.

The path was well trodden; the soil compacted from years of daily usage. It was quite overgrown on either side, and there was every indication that the entire area had once been cultivated, maybe as recently as last year. Fast growing weeds can take over quickly.

As I walked, thoughts of Su Lin and Ana Wei in their garden and their cautionary tales about the nature of weeds came to me. Weeds disguise themselves and grow next to the good herbs, they told me. They grow so close to the good herbs that it is difficult to tell them apart. The counterfeit cozies up to the good herb, hoping to pass for the other. Look closely for the counterfeits; sometimes they are nearly identical.

Bad weeds can be toxic, they said. Good herbs and bad weeds. The counterfeit wanted to be next to the good herb. I thought the story took a strange turn when Ana Wei added, "It's like choosing companions—bad ones cozy up to the good." A shiver ran through me and in a flash, I understood how I had learned that lesson the hard way.

Sure enough, just as Ochi said, in less than four minutes I arrived at a long shed. It was somewhat rickety, and the roof was in need of repair at one end. It was quite dilapidated, beyond repair at the other. I went around the other side and saw it was three-sided. One end was used for storage—three were stalls piled with bales and sacks of feed, tools, and who knows what all.

I smiled at the sight of six camels, two of which were not very old, frisky, and fortunately tethered. I approached them gently, but the youngest skittered to the protection of a mare, which was obviously his mother. The other one, more than a year old and more independent, seemed to want to take off. He pulled hard against the rope.

The two older males alerted. Picking up their majestic heads to have a look around, with their proud noses in the air, they gave me a condescending look and benign blink. I recognized them immediately and hurried to them. Camels have remarkable memories. They remember a stick, but they also remember a friend. They remembered me.

It was such a wonderful moment. I felt so happy to see them. Overjoyed. I walked around them, talking to them, touching their noses, patting their flanks, rubbing them, half just enjoying them, half checking out their condition. Like the gardens, they were neglected and in need of a brushing.

I felt as though something washed over me, as if the gloom had lifted, like my vital energy was restored. I felt like myself again, for I had not touched or talked to a camel in two years. If only this day could last, I thought, as I searched around for a brush. By the time Ochi arrived, something wonderful, like a miraculous change, had taken place within me.

"Aha! I see you have found your friends!" he said. "And, I must say, as long as I have known you, I have never seen a smile on your face, like you have now." He stood back and watched me joyfully talking to and caring for the camels.

Pointing to the older male camel, I said, "I see his leg has healed." Then I rubbed it.

Getting to the crux of the matter, Ochi said, "Jade, as we were coming to Bamiyan, my foremost concern was about your health, and if we survived, your welfare. But these camels have posed a major problem for me. Since I have no knowledge of animal husbandry, I had a lot to learn. This has turned out to be the biggest dilemma for me. These camels are what needs resolution."

I smiled at him. "They look like no problem at all to me."

"I hoped you'd say that." He went on, "No one ever enquired about these camels, and I made many enquires myself as to their ownership, but to no avail. The law says they are yours. When we first arrived in Bamiyan, I asked my friend if he would stable them until you were able to make some decisions. That time has come. Things around here were better then. Now, well, you know the situation.

"Jade, I apologize. As you can see, one camel is missing. It was the biggest and probably the best of the lot. But it was suggested that I trade one for a female. Well, I got two females for the big one. I was advised they would be useful for producing milk. There was mutual agreement between us that there would be no charge for stabling the animals, in exchange for the milk they produced. Being damaged, the shed had fallen into disuse, so, it worked out well all around. Except of course, for the loss of the male camel. He's long gone and no telling where he's been. So, you're short the biggest male camel. I hope you don't mind."

A smile came across my face. I almost laughed out loud. "So Ochi, all this time I thought you were a monk, and you were a camel trader?"

"Not really. All this camel business has been troublesome. Very troublesome." He was so serious I thought I'd laugh out loud.

"Well," I said. "Ochi, perhaps you should have talked to me about this sooner. I don't want to criticize, but your math skills seem to be lacking. You started out with three camels, and you now have six. One more, and you'll have the auspicious number of seven. Which will be soon by the looks of that mare. And just in case you ever get into this predicament again, let me share some advice from my father. Camels are not pets, Ochi! I am not criticizing your stewardship. Don't get me wrong. But these two older male camels we came with should have been traded, too. They are not worth as much today as they were two years ago."

With a twinkle in his eye, Ochi said, "I'm glad you are feeling better. There is much for you to do. Before we go to the house to meet my friend, there is one more thing you need to see. Come over here to the far end of the shed. There, you see, in that corner. That is yours. That is the cargo these camels were carrying the day I met you—you all. When I arrived in Bamiyan, I had no place to go with the animals and all this.

"Thus, while we were on the road, it occurred to me that my friend and patron here, might store this for me, or rather you, and thankfully he was amenable. Jade, under all that dust and debris, well, that's all jade—blocks and boulders of it. And it's not just any old jade—this is quite valuable. I am sure that if someone was expecting it, he was mightily disappointed. I asked my friend to examine it, and he estimated its value. I must tell you, you are a wealthy woman. My friend believes some to be from China, but most originated in Siam. He made a written inventory of it and rewrapped it. It is all here."

Totally shocked, my mind raced in many directions, formulating questions, but before I could speak, Ochi went on.

"Well, it's all there except for a few small caskets of polished gemstones he has at the house because they were too valuable to leave here. It would fetch a king's ransom."

My eyes lifted to his. Hearing these words, my facial expression changed from one of pleasant surprise to one of a person who had just been shot. "A king's ransom." The words penetrated my heart and cut me deeply because more than once in the last year it had crossed my mind that I might have been held for ransom—or sold to a stranger in some foreign land. As it turned out, I hadn't been sold, and I hadn't been ransomed, but I was far from home and in a foreign land. If not for Ochi, if not for—as Ochi would say—providence, I shuddered to think where I might be.

Ochi saw my face change. He saw me visibly begin to crumble. He reached out, thinking I was about to faint.

"Jade, what is it? What is it? Did I say something wrong?"

Tears were welling up, and I struggled to control my emotions. "No, it was nothing you said. I mean, nothing you've done. Maybe we should go now," I said, moving forward toward the house.

He said, "I know this is a lot for one day. I don't want you to feel hurried. There is opportunity for you here. There are things to consider and choices to be made. But there is no rush. Let's go meet my patron. He is a kindly man, but unwell, today. We won't stay too long. I wouldn't want to tire him, and we need to get back before nightfall."

I had not moved into the main house, I did not feel it appropriate. I did, however, immediately set things straight there, establishing a routine and assuring Ochi's patron the care and nutrition he needed. I found comfort in a run-down herb-drying house the owner's wife had used at the back of the property. I rejuvenated the herb gardens and transformed the drying house into a cottage. I managed his workers well, and in two years, restored the farm to its former levels of production. The vineyards and orchards were revitalized with careful maintenance and pruning. The owner regained his strength. Although not physically involved, he was always eager to answer my questions. He was impressed with my talent and nurtured my natural curiosity; he encouraged me, providing resources whenever necessary to keep things moving forward. Most evenings we sat talking and drinking tea.

With winter approaching, he was concerned about the lack of heat in my cottage. One evening, he mentioned that I must come to the main house during the winter. In the course of the conversation, I explained to him how a *kang* was built and used for heating and cooking in China. He was intrigued. The next week, three workmen appeared with materials, and under my direction, they removed the back wall, built a *kang* nearly the length of the cottage, replaced the back wall, and extended the roof on the front and back, doubling the size of the old drying house.

Ochi had been right about our mutual interests. We were a team. Ochi visited from time to time, the two discussing the needs of the monastery, as well as requirements for the Bamiyan Buddhas. Over time, I was drawn into the owner's many philanthropic interests and was able to carry out his wishes.

By the time Ochi's patron passed away, we had forged a very deep bond. He had no family, and he left the main house and his property to me, along with much of his considerable, accumulated wealth. It was his wishes that I continue his work in support of the Bamiyan Buddhas. There were bequeaths to Ochi's monastery and a generous sum set aside for women and orphans, specifying that I use those resources as I saw fit.

The door was ajar, so he tapped lightly on the rough-hewn doorframe. Hearing nothing, he called out, "Hullo, hullo?" The anxious man of middle-age sensed there was no one inside, so he knocked harder and called louder, "Hullo, hullo?" After a few minutes, he peered into the cottage, which seemed deserted but open to the world.

The cottage was an unusual structure for this area—one could say, foreign, not like anything he had seen before. Standing at the threshold, he leaned in and glanced around the room. No one was there. Dried plants tied in bundles hung upside down from the ceiling beams, or stood upright in canisters, vases, and buckets on the floor and on the window ledges. A trestle table with a polished plank of hard wood surface dominated the room. Scrolls and books were on a shelf; parchment and seeds in small dishes populated smoothly polished table made from one slab of a tree. It appeared there was work in progress from which someone had just stepped away.

A splendid exotic folding screen, like nothing he had ever seen before, stood behind the table near the back of the room. It probably separated the living space from the herb business. A glimpse of a raised sleeping platform, the hearth, and unused fireplace revealed more small bundles lying out to dry.

He remembered the monk had said, if you don't see her at the main house, follow the path around back, then follow the trail. He felt sure he was in the right place. He called out several times more, but hearing no response, he looked around the front garden amid the raised beds of plants to find a narrow path leading through the garden.

She was wearing a long, narrow dress with slits at the side, and leggings. The dress was too fine for garden work. Colorful needlework of birds, butterflies, plants, and vines embellished the neck and hemlines. The bodice opened on a diagonal and had frog closures with a mandarin collar. It seemed she was in deep communication with the plants, and he hesitated to interrupt, unwilling to dispel her reverie. He approached but kept ample distance away. He observed her collecting the seeds from a flower pod and carefully placing them in a folded parchment.

She must have sensed his arrival at the cottage door and knew exactly where he was at all times and where he now stood in the garden. He was shy and uncertain how to begin. She said, "How can I help you?"

The monk had indicated the woman he was going to meet was a wise older woman, but the woman he was looking at appeared to be a young woman. He thought perhaps this was the daughter of the person he was seeking, although the monk hadn't said she had a family. As he came closer, he thought how odd and unusual her dress and shoes were. Not like those of local people.

The monk had not said whether or not she was a local person, but when she turned her face toward him, he quickly determined by her facial features and the process of elimination, she was not local—not from Hindus-tan, not from Tibet, not from the Caucuses... he decided she was a Chinese woman. But she spoke his dialect.

When I looked at him, he lowered his head and diverted his eyes. Speaking rapidly, he explained that his wife was ill, and he had gone to the monastery to seek help. "There, a monk named Ochi suggested you might be able to help us. So I have come in search of you," he said.

"Oh yes, my dearest, dearest Ochi. How is he?" I inquired.

"It's the first time I ever met him, but for a very old man he seemed quite well," the man said.

"Oh, yes, of course. I think Ochi has always been a very old man. I have known him for many years, and I thought him to be very old when we first met. Maybe some people are born old. Don't you think? And what is the age of your wife, if I might ask? And what sort of health problem is she having? Where do you live? Who is caring for her now? How long will it take us to walk to your house?" I sought the answers I needed one after another before we reached the cottage. Then I said, "Have a seat here in the garden while I make preparations."

Before changing and gathering some materials together for the journey, I brewed an unusually fragrant tea that tasted wonderful. I served it to him, along with some berries, nuts, and two perfect apricots.

I was ready by the time he had finished the small meal. I was no longer in the dress I had worn in the garden. I wore naturally dyed linen pants bloused at the ankle, a tunic that covered me down to my knees, and sturdy leather sandals with turned up toes. Unlike the Chinese dress, this attire had elements of the Hindu-kush. Any vestige of feminine grace was now transformed. I adjusted the two satchels slung on my shoulders; the belted webbing crisscrossed my chest, and a small water skin was belted at my side. My head was wrapped, concealing my hair, and I left the tail of the scarf hanging. It was wide enough to protect me from dust or serve as a veil. I had taken on the characteristics and appearance, indeed the disguise, of a trader or a cameleer or a foreigner of a different sort.

He offered to carry my bags, but I declined his help; I felt in balance and quite comfortable. I felt urgency and set a fast pace. As we walked, he told me that he had left his wife in the care of his brother's family while he had come in search of help. They lived alone; having had no children of their own, they shared the duties of a communal family farm. They grew mostly vegetables but had a small orchard and vineyard. He expressed sadness that they were childless. He said life had somehow passed them by in this regard, but he rallied, "My brothers have enough to share."

I queried him further about the length and symptoms of his wife's illness. I let him talk. The problem was very recent. Sever pains in the back and abdomen. I asked again about a possible pregnancy. He said sorrowfully, "My wife is too old and a doctor told her many years ago she would not have children." I let the issue drop, not wanting to bring on his melancholy again.

Later that day, with my help, his wife delivered a tiny baby girl.

The weather and the rainfall were precisely as needed to turn the springtime swaths of color into a busy harvest. I was in the orchard picking when I noticed a stranger on the cart path waving wildly. There was something about his dress that set off alerts, and I asked my headman to "go see what he wants."

He returned saying, "He is asking for the master."

There was a quality about the man that cautioned me, something that flashed back to the kidnapping. Naturally, I had become guarded and leery of strangers ever since. I told the headman, "Stay here. If you finish, take a break, but wait for me. Do not leave me."

As I approached a disheveled older man, who was probably from a caravan passing through Bamiyan, he advanced toward me, asking about the master. "Why do you ask?" I said.

"I have a message for him," he retorted.

My defensed soften, and I said, "I'm sorry to tell you, but he is no longer with us."

He looked perplexed. "Well, where is he, and how soon will he return? I have dealings with him. I'm passing through, and I don't have a lot of time."

For certain he was from a caravan. I was apprehensive and looked back to assure myself the headman was nearby. He was, so I stepped a little closer and said reverently, "The master passed from this life. More than a year ago."

He didn't respond immediately. He seemed overwrought and in a quandary. After a few moments, with head bowed, he seemed weakened and he slipped to the ground. He was an old man hardened by work and the elements, shaken by this news.

I asked, "Would you like some water?"

At first he didn't reply, then he nodded and said, "Yes."

My attitude toward him changed, and I called to the headman to bring water and some food.

He looked at the peach as if it were a foreign object, turning it over and over, looking, but not seeing. Then he brought it to his mouth and took a big bite out of it. Juice dripped off his frizzled gray beard. He devoured it in three bites, stood up, wiped his mouth and beard on a tail from his headwrap, and said, "Well then, sister, who is in charge, here?"

I lied, pointing vaguely to some workers in a distant field, I said, "The manager is yonder."

The stranger put his hand up to shade his eyes, squinting and blinking. I don't think he could see well. He made no effort to leave and seemed to be mulling something over.

Despite my compassion, I backed up, putting a little more distance between us. Then he said, "And who might you be?"

Reluctant to engage in talk with a stranger, I said, "A friend of the master."

To which he replied, "Well then, might I have a word with you? I was bringing a message to him." I could see he retreated into his memory for an instant. Then he continued, not waiting for my reply. "Sadly, he did not fair well after his wife died. I saw that. But he would be happy to see these orchards thriving, as they did when he was a young man." He smiled and looked at me. "Were you related to him?" I could tell he knew those who peopled this region and distant places and could readily see and hear that I was not local, and not likely related by blood.

I replied, "No." At this point, I knew he was a camel driver and this is what had instinctively caused me to go on alert. I glanced at my headman and workers, who were resting nearby. They hadn't left me.

"Please, little sister," he said, pointing, "could we sit over there in the shade?"

We kept our distance but sat, and he began. "I knew the master over this property since we were young boys. He stayed here in Bamiyan. I struck out early. Having wanderlust, I was a natural to work the caravans. I'm not young anymore, but I know the trade routes blindfolded. The last time I saw him, he asked me to deliver a message." He pulled a crumpled, sweat-stained, sealed paper from his shirt. He sighed heavily. "I am just getting back here, although I have crossed the Taklamakan and the Gobi several times since I saw him last. Until now, I never could get back this way. At the time I accepted this message, I told him I didn't know when I would return. He understood that. But I was headed to Dunhuang at that time, and this message was for a man in Dunhuang."

My heart sank, but I remained stoic.

He went on. "Since then the caravans took me through Dunhuang several times. I searched for this person. But in vain. Maybe the master was mistaken or maybe there is some mystery about this man. I found a locked, fenced compound I believed to be his former residence. If so, it is now run down and falling into disrepair. No one lives there, and there was no caretaker to ask.

"Even if there were a caretaker, probably he wouldn't talk to me. I enquired around town, but people looked away like they hadn't heard me. In the marketplace, they shook their heads 'no' or they gave me the 'stink eye.' Maybe the man died, or maybe there was a scandal. I think there was something mighty peculiar because people were so reluctant to talk to me.

"The last time I was through Dunhuang, I again made inquires in the marketplace. That time, one woman followed me, and when we were out of ear shot of the others, she pulled me aside and directed me to another fine house. There a woman was raking in her garden. I told her who I was enquiring after, and she ran me off with a rake." He ended the story with, "Some people are hostile to strangers." He looked defeated.

I couldn't say anything.

"So, I've come back to talk to the master and tell him what I found. I want to return his letter, which I couldn't deliver, so I can put this matter to rest. Everything has come to a bad end." He hung his head. "I'm sorry to learn of his death. He was a good man. I have lost a trusted friend. We were raised like brothers."

We sat quietly for a few moments. Then I found myself saying, "How would you describe this woman, who ran you off with the rake?" He described an older Ana Wei.

"Well, little sister, I have thought about this a great deal. Now mind you, I am not a learned man. I am a simple man, but because I have no wife or responsibilities of a family, I have time to ruminate on matters of life." He spoke painfully slow, like somewhere inside himself he was selecting each word. I got the impression he indulged in thinking about life often but never verbalized his thoughts to anyone. Then after a deep inhalation, he heaved forth, "From what I know of this matter, I believe this is an example of 'changing fortunes.'"

After a while he went on. "I've seen it before. Something happens, and in the wink of an eye, everything is changed. I'm certain there was such a man living in Dunhuang. I'm certain I found the family compound, and I believe they were extremely prosperous— but something happened. What? I have no idea. I think everyone in the marketplace knew him and maybe out of respect for him, they would not talk to me, a stranger. I'm relatively certain he is deceased. Beyond that, anything I say would only be speculation. Your guess is as good as mine.

"I'd like to set my mind free of this. I can't do anything more. Anyway, my good friend is gone. Kindly let me leave this letter with you. I need to unburden myself. I can't carry it any further." He stood up and pressed it into my hand; I put it in my pocket.

I gathered some fruit for him, wished him well and he went on his way. Then taking another path out of the orchard, I went to my cottage to sit in the garden and read the letter that had been signed and sealed by my benefactor.

It said, "Sir, your daughter is safe and well in Bamiyan. A monk on pilgrimage found her along the Silk Road near Khotan with three camels. He brought her to a monastery here, where she recovered. She is well taken care of. Trust that she will be provided for. You can find her here."

That evening I sat alone in the fragrance of my garden with a cup of tea. I was wrapped in thought. The man from the caravan had seen Ana Wei. I felt in my heart that my father, Su Lin, and grandfather were deceased. I wondered whatever happened to my mother and siblings, and my feeling was that I would never know. I pondered the stranger's words, "changing fortunes."

Through all the vicissitudes of the life times of Lavender Jade, including the pivotal kidnapping in this one, Jade survived and thrived, her vital essence greater than anything that came against her.

7
Poet's Group

I'D STAYED TOO LATE at work, and now I was not at all certain whether I could get to my poetry workshop on time. I was also hungry, but there wasn't even enough time to pick up something at a drive-thru.

The electronic garage door went up; I drove in, parked the car, and dashed into the house, tossing my purse and attaché case on a kitchen chair, then piled on my coat and scarf. There was no time to change, but I needed to find my bag with the writing.

As I passed through the kitchen, I opened the refrigerator door, then the meat keeper, and found no cold cuts or cheese. I stood there a moment, thinking, *Not much here; I must get to the grocery store this weekend.* Meanwhile, I shoved around the assorted Tupperware containers and found some meatballs in spaghetti sauce. That would do. No need to heat it.

I pulled off the lid, opened a drawer, found a knife and fork, and cut the meatballs into smaller pieces.

I took the first mouth full while walking into the den. A rule I'd always enforced with the kids came to mind: sit down at the table and no walking around the house eating food. My eyes searched the den as I took another mouth full. Although there was no one to hear me, I said aloud, "Rats! Where did I have that stuff last?" While still chewing the first bite, I was reminded of the "no talking with your mouth full rule." Finally, I spied the tapestry bag I used for poetry leaning against the desk and said, "Thank you, God." I took another bite.

I realized there was a folder missing from the bag, and laid the Tupperware container and fork on the desk. Sorting through a stack of papers, I found it. I scanned through the contents of the folder and realized that the latest version of the poem I needed was not there. I took another mouthful while trying to remember where I'd last worked on it.

Yes, I had been working on it in my recliner. Stan had taken his recliner, and the room didn't look balanced without it. I needed to rearrange the room. That was something else to do this weekend.

I searched through several annotated pages next to my chair and was relieved to find the one I was looking for. Glancing over it, I was satisfied. I tucked it into the bag and carried it and the remaining meatballs to the kitchen. Pressing the lid on the container while putting it back in the fridge, I took the milk from the door and poured some. After drinking a few swigs, I set the glass in the sink. I wished I had time to brush my teeth. Then, I did everything in reverse—coat, scarf, purse, electronic garage opener, and backed the car out, while feeling around for gum in the bottom of my purse. I really had to rush now, but random thoughts of my married life forced their way to the surface.

As I drove, I thought about how, since the kids were gone and Stan wasn't there, it seemed I didn't have any incentive to keep the house in order. It was really getting out of hand, and there was no one else to blame. The sink and the kitchen counter was a disaster and I hadn't put that glass in the dishwasher. I left clothes hanging over the backs of chairs, and there were books, papers, and pens left in every room—scraps of paper with jottings and dream journals in the bedroom, loose pages proliferating and floating around everywhere. When Stanley had been there, I'd kept everything picked up, his stuff, my stuff, and the kids' stuff. Why was that my job? Or had I just assumed those chores? No wonder I now had so much time for this writing thing. I wasn't doing housework.

I was smiling with some satisfaction about how the "writing thing" was going when I arrived at the location of the meeting. My pleasant thoughts quickly turned into the reality of finding a place in the filled parking lot. I drove around and around and then decided to park off the paved surface. Always mindful of my personal safety, I was now farther from the building than I wanted be. I was paying the penalty for tardiness.

Hurrying into the building, I barely had enough time to slip into a seat when the group leader called upon me. I wished he had started with someone else, first. He was a published poet. He was well-respected, and surely I had something to learn from him, but there was something prickly about our relationship. He took his eyeglasses off and said, "Skylar, what do you have for us, tonight?"

I managed to find the appropriate folder and paper while pulling my jacket off and said, "I've been working on several poems along the same lines. They have a reincarnation theme, like, well, how we lived and how we died. I titled them, 'Ancient Echoes.'" Then I began:

Ancient echoes of chants and drums
Sweep through my mind.
Bring thoughts of riding high on wind-swept plains
Bring images I can't explain.
We two were dragon slayers so to speak
We gave our lives, were slain in ancient fights.
Battle lines drawn, down we came
Slew them one by one.
Us two against the wind and rain
Our skin rough, taut, hardened to leather
Etched by a blazing sun.
Spirits united, obstacles overcome, struggling
Breathing free, kindling a burn for life.
Forged in ancient flames
Souls enrolled, deeds recorded in the ancient book.
Survival plans written chartering us through.
We rode through canyons dark and steep
Eating if and when we could
Living together, surviving together
Drinking from ancient streams.
Walking in wild-flower high country
On moors and heather-clustered mountains
Sat and rested under pleasant skies

Before we followed streams through ancient passageways.
Traveling silently through time and space
When in danger we moved in time warp motion
Your sign, a nod, a glance, in sync
To deeper grasses or forests musky.
We knew our roles honed by years of traveling
Instinctively meeting each other's needs.
Bonded from youth we painted our story on walls
While traveling through eternity.

The last word was barely out of my mouth when he practically shouted, "Stop, Skylar, just stop! Your words are powerful, but you're going to have to 'deliver' them. It's just not good enough to read the words. And this is true for each of you. As for you, Skylar, I suggest you find a voice coach to work with you on diction and enunciation. You just read that poem, and you read it entirely too fast. It has to be *delivered*, not read, and I mean *delivered*—presented well." Looking around the table at us, he said, "Each of you should prepare at least two pieces of your work that you can present well. Elocution is critical."

I felt dejected as I drove home through the darkness. I had liked my poem, but I felt that I had received no positive feedback from him. Very discouraging. If you asked me, he had a strange way of coaching, or teaching, or whatever he did. No warm fuzzy feeling from him. I considered that maybe poetry writing wasn't my thing. When I passed the expressway exit to Rae's house, I thought, *If I called her, she'd tell me how to deal with him.*

Biblical times, she said. Many battles. Hmmm.

8
A Hero's End

IT WAS AS SIMPLE as this: I was not expected to recover. All the doctors and all the gods in Egypt had not rallied to my cause. Alexander's doctors were convinced my toe should be removed. They chafed to hack it off. I protested with a resounding roar—a belligerent refusal. I admonished them to go. Leave me.

We had a lengthy discussion over the root of the problem. I explained it was a thorn or perhaps several thorns in the toe, which had gone unattended too long. I justified this to myself because I was too busy, too involved mapping out the new city of Alexandria and planning the multitude of public works projects necessary to support it. The toe was getting to be a major distraction. They said it was a scorpion sting. I retorted firmly that it was a thorn that wounded me—compounded by their bungled attempt to treat it. After all, I knew about my own toe. I had little respect for these doctors.

It was painful; it looked worse. The toenail was blue and black, with striations in shades of red. It didn't look good at all. Despite this, I was still quite able to navigate. I rode my horse, led my men, and did my job. It seemed better during the day. At night, it interrupted my sleep.

As days went by, I looked for signs of improvement, but at some point I realized I must admit that I was only fooling myself. It was bluer and blacker than ever. *Give it time to grow out,* I was thinking. Alexander indulged me and suggested that since I had no tolerance for his doctors, we find a local healer to treat it. He said it looked worse than yesterday and told me to reassign others to some of my projects and get off my feet. He said he had discussed my condition with a priest, who would send his best to have a look.

At this point, my foot was swollen and my foot and ankle felt stiff. I needed more exercise, but the injury was working against me. I propped my foot up to relieve the throbbing, and so they could better take a look. Maybe it was my imagination, but it seemed to me the priest and healers drew back in unison when they saw it.

Their examination was straightforward and perfunctory. It culminated in an application of ointment, prayers, and rituals, and a strong dose of some herbal concoction, which I willingly ingested, hoping for relief.

After another day there was no improvement, and the pain grew worse. I assigned some subordinates to handle some of my on-going work on the water works. I was not thinking too clearly, so cancelled some scheduled meetings with my top staff, putting several critical projects on hold. I realized this would delay things, causing havoc with logistics and interfering with the timetable that was, at least to some extent, contingent upon the change of seasons. The level of pain impeded my ability to function, and doing any design or creative work was getting impossible. I wasn't clear headed.

The healers came back and reapplied the ointment, some unpleasant smelling unguent made in this land, not Greek. One shook his head sadly as they respectfully backed out of the room. I took this as a bad sign. Word came back to me that the priest and healers, too, recommended the toe be removed—and perhaps the foot or maybe the limb up to the knee—without delay. The healers apologized profusely for the failure of their treatment and incantations.

The priest was of the opinion that my life was in jeopardy. There was little hope without amputation, and amputation was not a sure thing. I emphatically and steadfastly refused amputation. I had seen too much of it in my lifetime, mostly without success.

The only alternative he suggested was the temple in Thebes, where, he said, the High Priest and His Initiates had exceptional powers of healing. Travel required several days at this time of year, and it would be a difficult and strenuous journey, given my condition. There was that risk to consider. He felt that the heat and dust would exacerbate the condition. He told me my situation would likely decline rapidly in the desert, probably before I reached Thebes.

This information about my condition was relayed to Alexander, before I could think through the situation. I had work to do—many public works projects at various stages of planning and all this toe business was interfering with my progress. I seemed more scatter-brained and not up to my self-imposed, required level of efficiency. I could not tolerate inefficiency in others, or myself. It seemed my staff was dithering and hovering around me.

When Alexander arrived, there was a moment of embarrassment as I clumsily attempted to get out of the chair. My aid-de-camp swooped in to pick up the stool as it toppled over, and I gingerly placed my foot on the floor. Alexander indicated that I should stay seated and for the aid-de-camp to put my foot back on the stool. He seemed all business. Realizing I was recalcitrant, Alexander said nothing to me in the presence of others. After a few pleasantries, he dismissed them all and privately communicated to me that this was a grave matter. He said he would not allow one of his advisors and leaders to be butchered—his word—without their consent. He went on to say that if there was any other way, we should try it. He and I agreed that the best hope was the temples in Thebes—if it could be reached in time. We mutually acknowledged there was a risk and that in fact I may or may not reach Thebes in time. He knew that nothing, not even death, would convince me that surgery was the right course of action, although the situation was now desperate.

Alexander was his usual decisive self, commanding others to action. He ordered a boat, a crew, and provisions to take me down the Nile. He commanded the men to make hast. Despite the heat, everyone immediately stopped dithering and flew into action. A palanquin was brought, and I was directed not to move unnecessarily. I was not in a position to argue, but having men lifting and carrying me was something I found humiliating. The incompetent healers and one of Alexander's surgeons were to escort me, along with several of my aids de camp, closest and oldest companions. He was considerate and mindful of my comfort, and advised others to be of the same mindset. He conversed privately with several of his administrators, who were summoned and who, I learned later, were ordered to accompany the party.

Alexander had been short on words, but precise with directions. He dispatched a messenger immediately. Within hours, my small entourage and I were en route to Thebes. When we pushed off, we were twenty in number, and I could not walk without support.

I was embarrassed by all this fuss over me and—over a thorn. It was beyond comprehension that a battle-hardened soldier from the legions of the great Alexander could be brought low by a thorn—or a scorpion—or both. My feet were hard and calloused. I could not say for sure which it was. What was evident was that blue and red streaks were now flaming up the inside of my leg, and the healers were wringing their hands, lamenting and looking forlorn. This was not a fitting end for a soldier.

I had this vague recollection that when we departed, Alexander placed his newest medal for distinguished service around my neck. Under his breath, he said to me, "Take care old man and take as much time as needed to recover." He told me not to be concerned about the work. "The work has a way of getting done," he said. I knew he didn't believe that! He said, "Be assured that arrangements have been made for you." We separated on a jovial note, with him suggesting I take a wife or find some lovely women to attend me.

I was self-involved, distracted by the pain and my condition, with an overriding concern for the continuation of the works in progress, so I had not fully realized what he was telling me—that if somehow I survived, I would not be reporting back to him in military service. How events in our lives would transpire was unforeseen. That I was seeing him for the last time was unknowable.

I should explain. I was a family friend. I knew his mother well. As a young man, I soldiered for the young Alexander's father. I was decorated for valor many times. I had been in service to his family and my county all my life. Most importantly, I had years of valuable military experience. I knew what was required to run an army and wage a successful campaign. I mean, after all, I was a part of his parents' generation.

I had known Alexander since childhood. I taught him many skills. We had a close bond, quite different from what he had with his other companions. Our personal relationship was unspoken, a matter of place. He knew he could always rely on me, even in war—especially in war. My "can do attitude" was backed up with knowledge, experience, and action. I had a passion for life and my objectives were in sync with his. One word from him, and the job was as good as done. For us, milestones were marked with measurable achievement. While I surely admired the young Alexander, his youth, his drive and ambition, I was with him at the behest of his mother. This was known by us but never stated. Although he called upon me less and less, as he gained more experienced, he knew I was always looking out for his interests.

My name was Perseus, but ever since childhood, Alexander called me "old man"—never in front of his mother and never in the company of the companions, only when we were alone. I was nearly twenty years his senior. The "old man" reference slipped off his tongue when he was less than five years old. We were setting rabbit traps. As I explained the trap, the mechanism slipped from my grasp and snapped my fingers. He laughed, puffed up and said, "Move aside old man; let me show you how it works."

More recently, I was an administrator in logistics. My engineering skills and the recent conquest set me to designing grain storage houses and developing support strategies for the building of the City of Alexander. This type of work took me off the battlefields and out of major assaults. Although I felt useful, one could say the "old man" name was beginning to fit.

By the time we neared Thebes, I was lapsing in and out of consciousness. I had a vague feeling that Alexander was standing next to me saying, "Get some rest, old man, old man, old man…" The pain was unbearable. I was fading away. *There is a rabbit in a snare. Oh, I have arrived back in Macedonia. My wife is here. I am back home with my wife. My wife is alive? I'm confused. Get my aid-de-camp. It seems word came last year that my wife died. Where is my aid-de-camp? I have no need to go back to Macedonia. I have only to advance. I will not retreat. It's very hot. I need water. The eye of Horus is everywhere, coming and going, fading in, then out, then back again.*

My body was at war with itself. The pain was no longer excruciating. I went into a world of dreams and delirium. Lifted out of my physical self, I spent days in dreams and other realms.

All my battles are relived and fought again. *My fellow soldiers fall in front of me, one by one. Wave upon wave of advancing enemy soldiers sweep over us. The breath is knocked out of me. I'm falling, and I'm ground down by advancing forces. The life is sucked out of me. I'm overcome with darkness.* I rally, awaking in time to revisit each battlefield and count the dead—my brother, trampled to death; my friends lie amongst the blood and limbs of the enemy. Cut down. Unrecognizable. *My screams bring the eye of Horus, which swirls and careens around me. My leaden arms cannot be lifted to bat away either a fly, or "those troubling eyes." Alexander speaks to me, but I cannot reply. There was this fading in and out. Alexander was there, then not there. I must find him. I am accountable to Olympia. The "Eyes of Horus" watch me.*

I was powerless to move. Over and over I tried to get up. I had to get up. I had to find him. I had work to do. I wanted to mount up and leave this situation. It seemed I was tethered. Riveted in place, I mustered all my strength to break the hold.

I exert all my strength but fall back, again and again. "Old man" is ringing in my ears. *This time falling down and down, fighting the old battles, seeing comrades of past campaigns, the siege of Tyre, old warriors, young boys, those who had not survived battles past. They circled, came forward, and receded one after another. Their bloodied bodies and injuries miraculously vanish in front of my eyes. They're young and whole and vital again.*

I reach for them and attempt to follow. The pain has diminished. I rise above and view a body. Myself lying there. I am tied down—no wonder I can't move. I am tethered and confounded as to why and where I am and whether I am here or there.

Three women were attending a body, my body. My aid-de-camp stood nearby talking quietly with one of Alexander's administrators.

I wanted to get their attention, but they ignored me. Their murmurs created a din. Sound was distorted. I couldn't communicate my distress. They needed to cut me loose so I could get up.

A younger woman, possibly an assistant, clad in natural linen, held a bowl for the other, who with utmost delicacy applied something to the surgically open wound in my leg. Black and swollen, the right leg and foot were beyond use and hardly recognizable as a foot and leg. Another woman bathed my head and brow with lightly fragrant water.

I came to the realization that it was I lying there on the cot. And if it was so, then I was looking at me. Strangely, I seemed to be in two places. How peculiar. I watched her touching my leg—and I see it, why then didn't I feel it? I saw her touching my forehead—see it, why then didn't I feel it? The question remained—was I on the cot or somewhere else? I thought the answer was somewhere else.

A surgeon and a boy entered the room and conversed with my men. I saw their mouths moving and from some far off place I heard my aid-de-camp's garbled voice telling the surgeon forcefully that I did not want the foot removed. Not the foot, not the toe, and not the leg. I looked at the blue and red streaks of color radiating up my leg, now nearing the groin. The surgeon said it was the only chance he had to save my life. The older woman dressed in white linen waved them away.

I was thinking maybe I needed to reassess my situation, reconsider my stance with regard to removing my foot. They couldn't hear my words. The woman with the unguent was my only hope. However, it seemed she couldn't hear me either. If only I could move my body, touch her, or signal her in some way.

She placed the gauze in the bowl and covered my leg with fine linen, then passed an unspoken glance of defiance to the surgeon.

A woman dressed in a brilliant silvery-white fabric, the radiance of which blinded me, was here. She was attending me. I couldn't see her face. She placed the palm of one hand lightly above my solar plexus and the other over my head; leaning forward, she studied my face. I couldn't make out her features. She was so close, her light was blinding. Her radiance gave off heat. I felt my floating self reunite with my physical body. I registered a sort of silent thud as I reentered. Apparently, she noticed a difference, too. I felt heat from her palm above my solar plexus, her breath in my nostrils, and a cool gentle breeze passed over my feverish face.

Apparently the woman in linen noticed a difference, too, or felt the thud. She looked up, somewhat startled at her assistant, who hadn't noticed. There was a reticent exchange of glances among all those present, and the boy and the surgeon left the room. My soldiers moved to the doorway.

The woman in linen placed her left hand above my solar plexus. Bending nearer, she looked closely into my eyes, examining my pallor, hoping for a response. My rigid body relaxed as her healing hands scanned me. Engrossed and focused, she worked slowly and methodically, passing over my entire body.

The shining one was no longer here. The eyes of Horus replaced her. The two remaining women realized that a change in my condition had taken place. Their dark eyes, strongly lined with kohl and heavily painted an intoxicated green with ground malachite, carefully observed me. The three had brought me back from death's portal. I stood in front of a false door like one I had seen in Egyptian tombs; the jackal had been poised to lead the way through it. I collapsed into sleep.

I awakened on a leather bed wrapped in filaments of fine linen. I was outside under a colorful striped awning protected from the bright sunlight. The fly was attached to the house and staked into the ground. In the distance, I saw several women sitting on the ground. They were weaving, and little children played around them. Laundry that had been spread over bushes was drying in the bright sunshine. I wondered where I was and where my companions had gone. Despite the sun, there was a soft breeze. I realized a young boy was fanning air over me.

My head was elevated, and as my eyes opened, I saw a large, enameled *wedjat*-eye lying on my chest, a symbol of protection and health to the Pharaonic people. Also, around my neck was a medal depicting Alexander. Instantly, I regained my senses and glanced toward my lower extremities. In relief, I fell back against the pillow. My leg was there. An ugly incision was neatly sewn from below the knee to the ankle. My foot was there, my toe was there, swollen and strange in color. Lifting my hand to touch the amulet, my movement surprised the boy, who dropped his fan and ran away.

I recovered my wits, but I did not recover my mobility. Day after day, I was forced to remain prone, with my leg elevated. A great deal of attention had been paid to my comfort. It was embarrassing. Men carried me outside during the day, and boys showed up on schedule to fan me like royalty.

There were a number of different people who brought me food and juices throughout the day. Beginning the day with a diluted cooked porridge made of meal and minced figs and dates, I regained my strength in increments. Recovery seemed directly proportional to the consistency of the morning concoction, which increasingly got thicker. There was coconut water, kimmon juice, hibiscus juice, and various fruits to eat intermittently throughout the day.

As my health improved, my attitude deteriorated. I made several attempts to leave the confines of my bed. I found it humiliating to have men carry me in and out of doors. As the days passed, my frustration with my situation increased. I resisted the help of Nefer and Shoshan, the two women from the operating room, who now attended me daily.

One day, I asked Nefer, "Where is the other lady? I haven't seen her."

Nefer replied, "Do you mean Shoshan?"

I said, "No, I'm not referring to Shoshan. I'm talking about the other lady, the older lady, the one dressed in brilliant, silvery-white. You know, the one who was with you and Shoshan during the surgery on my leg. She wore a dazzling dress. Radiant, I'd say."

Nefer looked at me strangely. "Only Shoshan, the surgeon, and I attended you."

I looked at her in disbelief, but before I could pose another question, she realized by my tone of voice that she had not answered the question to my satisfaction. She said, "I don't recall any other woman being there. Your aid and one other soldier, Shoshan, the surgeon, and me, that's all. Perhaps a young boy came from the temple from time to time. But there were no visitors. You were gravely ill," she ended.

"But, Nefer, I saw another lady. I think she was older than you; she was wearing a shining white dress. I'd never seen linen or a fabric like that before. I can't quite describe it." I'd said the dress was silvery-white, but truthfully, I had never before seen a color like that, either. It was exquisitely beautiful. I went on. "Nefer, I took her to be quite a bit older than you and Shoshan. Although," I paused, "come to think of it, I am not sure she was older, and I'm not sure I'd recognize her if I saw her again. It's the blinding, radiant dress I remember quite well." I started to say otherworldly but something stopped me.

Nefer, looked at me rather perplexed, then realized that I was serious. She said respectfully that she thought I had been confused. Perhaps it was the effects of the depth of my condition and that really there had been no other woman present and that certainly she would have remembered a woman dressed as I described. When I pressed her further, she stated firmly that I was mistaken. I could tell she was finished with the matter.

Everyone I spoke to was vague and evasive whenever I asked questions. Any question brought evasive silence. It seemed I was totally at the mercy of other people, and the circumstances were unnerving. I gathered the facts of the matter slowly. Apparently I had been unconscious for more than a month. I questioned my aids about our location and the circumstances and when we were expected back to join Alexander's forces.

We were near Thebes and the Temple of Karnak. They were not forthcoming about anything else. When I expressed my concerns, my aid-de-camp assured me the people assisting me were being more than fairly compensated. He said that for now, Alexander's strategy was that everything and everybody should be focused on my wellness, and that I should be also. He said, furthermore, I should have no concerns about matters of logistics. Everything was going smoothly.

For weeks, my aid-de-camp and staff were vague about when we would return to our duties. When asked, my aid gave me no encouragement and simply stated that he was told that upon my recovery it would be fully discussed. When I wanted to talk about our return to Alexandria and the work undone there, he said only that he wanted me to rest and recover. The situation was awkward. I had little physical strength, and many times I lapsed into a deep sleep while we were talking. My lack of information, mobility, and my dependency left me in no position to debate him or give him orders.

One morning, I was dozing and considering that I must be recovering well now because the morning porridge was a heavier consistency and topped with chopped almonds. I had just finished eating when my aid-de-camp announced that two of Alexander's staff were approaching. He busied himself adjusting the bed to elevate me and arranging my garments, then came to attention when they approached.

They greeted me with a salute. My aid left momentarily and came back with two boys carrying leather sling chairs and more boys with fans. I asked the officers to be seated. They carried papers and obviously had business on their minds. They were not there to inquire about my health, except in a perfunctory way. I had a fleeting remembrance of these two men on the day I last saw Alexander, and maybe they were with us on the barge.

I was not expecting them, and there was a surprise element and awkwardness on my part. Although I outranked them, they were administrative officers that worked directly for Alexander, not part of my staff. I said, "You'll excuse me for not standing. What brings you to my bedside this morning?"

They were succinct, being direct and to the point. They respectfully reminded me that they traveled with me under Alexander's orders and had never been far away during my recovery. I said, "Yes, I do recall." They said that their duties here in Thebes were now complete, and they would be returning directly to Memphis, then Alexandria, then on to join Alexander.

One officer handed me a lightly rolled parchment affixed with Alexander's seal. The other handed me a fine leather pouch, dyed Tyrian purple. It was drawn together with extraordinarily fine strands of gold wire that, even when plaited and twisted together, laid as lightly as a silk ribbon. Quite exquisite. He took two sheaves of paper from under his arm and laid them at the foot of my leather bed.

The officers paused and respectfully remained quiet as I took the pouch in my hand, carefully opened the bag, and removed a gold coin with the engraved image of Alexander. This was a coin I had never seen before. My first thought was that it was one of a kind, a single strike. Alexander ordered that sort of thing on rare occasions. I was familiar with all Alexander's medals and coinage; it was my responsibility to approve all designs and direct the casting. I had not seen this one, but I recognized the work of the artist who designed it.

They started by stating they were under orders and were instructed directly by Alexander himself. They said that, per Alexander, *if* or when I recovered, they were to verbally advise me that my circumstances were as follows: I was retired with honors and distinction. They went on to say that the estate upon which I had been living during my convalescence was mine in total. Mine to do with as I wished. All the buildings and structures, inhabitants, grounds, gardens, vineyards, and a vast amount of money to administer the schools and various works on the property, which was thus and so many hectors to the north and thus and so many hectors to the south, etc, etc. The proceeds from thus and so many hectors of this and thus and so many hectors of that, including granaries, mineral stores, animals, equipment and transports were now mine. This extended to all regional public works and the oversight of these peoples, trades, and professions.

They also stated that inventories of goods and materials, maps, temple layouts, property inventories, and lists of key personnel and priests had been completed and records of transactions had been turned over to my staff. They were placing highlights, summaries, and official documentation of transactions in my hands now.

They further stated that if upon full recovery I chose instead to return to Macedonia, my wish would be generously accommodated. That was entirely at my discretion. A sealed letter containing alternate plans for this land was contained among the papers they were leaving. They stated that this letter was from Alexander for me personally, and they were not privileged to know the contents. They were directed to put this communiqué directly into my hands. If I had failed to recover, they had been further directed to return it to Alexander, so they stated. Then one handed me the letter.

The two said that the soldiers who had traveled with us to Thebes, including my aid-de-camp and the others, would remain with me under the orders of Alexander, unless and until I ordered them released. This was entirely at my discretion, too. Also, there was something about more soldiers and an envoy from Alexandria.

I really did not hear much that they said after the words "retired with distinction." I recalled that they'd asked me if I had any questions, and I responded "No." I was in shock.

They rose to their feet abruptly and in unison. They stated they had discharged all their duties at the order of Alexander, and they had fully briefed my staff and were now prepared to depart. One bowed respectfully and said my wise council would be greatly missed by Alexander, his cohorts, and to the many Macedonians who had served me. They saluted and departed.

I leaned back against the pillow. I felt I had been cut off from my future. I tried to control the trembling and compose myself. My aid returned after escorting them across the garden to their horses. He was gone only a few minutes. When he returned, he had a broad smile on his face, which I felt was inappropriate given the circumstances.

He said, "Sir, may I have permission to speak?"

I nodded in the affirmative. Although, I felt he should have had the good judgment to remain silent.

"Before you say anything, I want you to know your staff and I have been fully briefed. I have walked every segment of these grounds, and when you are up and around, I feel certain that you will find this a project you can enjoy—forever."

He went on. "I apologize for not being forthcoming. I have been under orders not to say or do anything that might impede your recovery." He seemed to know what I was thinking. "Believe me when I say every one of your staff realizes that you, that we, could have died on the battlefield. We are grateful for your leadership. And every one of your staff is hoping that you will accept this assignment, so to speak. If you do, I would be speaking for your entire staff in saying, we feel that this is an oasis, a place beyond anything we could have hoped for." After a moment, he said, "Sir. Incidentally, several of us have all been retired or discharged; nevertheless, we serve at your pleasure."

He shook his head. "Sir, I want to tell you there is something magical or mystical about this place. I've wanted to tell you for the longest time. It is something I can hardly describe. I have found this place and the Pharaonic people who inhabit it to be, well…" He searched for a word. "I think it is all together enchanting," he concluded. "Yes, enchanting."

I wondered how all of this could have happened without my knowledge. My first reaction was to be angry with him, but I quelled that impulse. He had been with me for years, and he was loyal to me, above all else. He would have died for me. That aside, I needed time alone. I needed time to think this through.

I was about to dismiss him when he went on to suggest I reserve my judgment until I had the opportunity to fully survey the situation by exploring the place. He said that the staff had constructed a palanquin, and we could begin discovering the estate tomorrow, if I chose to do so.

"Sir," he said, as he glanced around the area, assuring himself that everything was in order, "may I be dismissed?" I nodded to the affirmative. He saluted and backed out, low and respectfully.

He returned immediately. "Sir, I beg your pardon, but the day's routine has been scrambled, so I took the liberty of asking Nefer to come later in the afternoon." I nodded my approval, he saluted again, turned on his heel, and left.

My head was swimming, awash in thoughts.

Maybe it was my health, maybe it was the news, but for the first time in my life I felt terribly old and unable to cope. My hands were trembling; I yanked the pillows from behind my back and sagged against the leather. I closed my eyes, clenching my retirement papers in my hand.

I spent yet another day in some altered state of reality, sometimes asleep and dreaming, and sometimes daydreaming, falling asleep in mid-thought. I found myself in an untenable situation. The slow pace of my healing frustrated me. I felt captured and confined. I replayed my life on several levels, examining events long passed.

I confronted the fact that by the time Alexander's forces had reached Egypt, I was feeling every bit my age. Conquering new territories and war fighting was for young men. I conceded that the rigors of this tour with Alexander had caught up to me both physically and mentally. This was hard for me to admit to myself, but the journey from Tyre had been grueling. Part of it was because of the intense heat and limited fresh water. A bigger part of my problem had been the residue I carried in my mind from the siege of Tyre. In seven months, we'd lost four hundred and many more had been injured or maimed there. Two of the lost were battle-hardened officers, who had been with me since the beginning of the campaign. They were Macedonians. We had lost many along the way, but these were different. I knew them well and I knew their families. The image of them falling off the tower and into the water was emblazoned on my mind. I couldn't shake it off.

Both were seasoned war fighters; neither were strong swimmers. The Tyrians had thrown down a wide swath of fire, and as flames licked the base of the tower, it fell into the bay. I leaped into the water on the opposite side of the causeway as a barge hit it, and the tower crashed, splintered, and went into the water. I wondered whether they were dead when they went into the water. I didn't know. I sorted through many scenarios. I just didn't know.

The situation had been total bedlam. The bay was full of men. Some died immediately, hit by falling timbers; others drowned. I went unscathed. Despite the chaos, I managed to pull several to safety. The causeway had been heavily damaged and required total rebuilding.

I wanted to reflect on our accomplishment with some pride because the causeway had been an incredible engineering fete. Instead, I stayed in a deep morose state that tormented my dreams and plagued me even a year after the events. I tried to pull myself out of it. I had too much time on my hands. That was the problem; I was cut off from my work. This confinement was not good. Every day, I accomplished nothing. In my mind, I tried to work out a script of what I could say to their wives if someday we should come face to face in Macedonia. That is, if I recovered from this.

Somewhere in the back of my mind the question, "Why me?" was churning. Why had I survived while others had not? I had seen hundreds die in this campaign, but the effect of these two deaths gnawed at me, begging an answer.

Demetrios had been near my age. He had a wry sense of humor that quickly turned a dismal situation around. Fearless, I always felt that he easily summoned courage one battle after another, while I had to dig deep. When word came that my wife died, he was there for me. In every battle, he had my back or I had his. His body washed ashore in Tyre, along with so many others. I felt like a part of myself had been left in Tyre. The only good thing about his death was that he didn't have to endure the aftermath, the miserable march from Tyre into Egypt. We rode side by side for years, so even now I sensed his spirit presence. It was he who frequently handed me a skin of fresh water to slake my thirst.

On the short march from Sidon to Tyre, I privately urged Alexander to release some of the men, particularly those who had been among the original infantry phalanx from Macedonia. They served him and Macedonia well. Odds weighed heavily against the survival of pikesmen but miraculously some survived. Certainly they wondered just how much longer their luck would hold out. Many wanted to return home to their wives. Some of the young unmarried ones dreamt of finding a wife.

On that matter, talk increased before I developed a viable plan for some to be released and convinced Alexander of its merit. Others on his staff reported that there was dissention working its way through the ranks. Alexander responded by having several crucified. The problem was silenced, but festered. Some felt they'd accomplished their mission and resented their present situation. They felt the only end to this tour with Alexander for them would be death. One pikesman went mad and killed his self. Others silently acknowledged that they were not likely to see their families ever again and resolutely soldiered on.

Alexander rebuffed my advice and, influenced by his companions, he followed a misguided course of action. I had an overwhelming visceral response to those crucifixions—carried with me to this day. It was a tragic situation. And a turning point that caused me to lose respect for him. I felt our relationship deteriorating. Alexander had sought my point of view and conferred with me before and after engagements, but we never spoke of the travesty regarding the crucifixions of his own men. He was changed. He relied on the opinions of his cohorts.

Day after day, I lay on the couch immobile, in forced silence and inaction with the Siege of Tyre burning in my mind. Rethinking the loss of Demetrios and the others, I began counting back the cavalrymen and warriors lost along the way. I concluded that I had become increasingly hardened to the deaths as the campaign continued, accepting them more easily as time progressed. I realized that I had lost some of my humanity along the way, and that I was no more surprised to lose a comrade than I would have been to be counted among the dead. But I had survived. Why me?

Why me and, what if? What if the city fathers of Tyre had simply allowed Alexander to sacrifice at the Temple of Hercules? What if the barge had not struck precisely where it did? What if the Tyrians had capitulated, as they had at Sidon, a month earlier? What if Alexander had released some of his war fighters? What if I had continued to present that idea to him? I rationalized that I was consumed by the incident of the causeway. What if I had not neglected this toe?

Retracing these events manifested in violent dreams at night, irritability, and frustration with the generous people who attended me day and night. My mind raged against the death of Demetrios and Philippos and the pikesman who took his life. I blamed the gods, while intermittently I called upon Apollo, god of health and wellness. Privately my loyalty to Alexander cracked, specifically in regard to the crucifixion of our fighters. Again, I wondered whether this had been his decision or that of an intoxicated young advisor, some of whom I considered dangerous. I just lay there, refusing to let it go, questioning this issue and other decisions he'd made more recently.

There was a sense that I had reached the end, the finale, and I was done. There was also blame—the blame of myself. The knowledge that I had neglected my physical body, and a wound easily treated if I had acted immediately. Yes, I blamed myself. My life was over, and I was at fault. The new city of Alexandria would be built without my input. The plans on the drawing board would be changed, and I would not be there to further my ideas. My work was my life, and my life was my work. Now what?

Weeks passed. My sleep remained fitful, but I stopped railing-over and raking-over the damages of the last eleven years. While I was not at peace with myself, I came to the conclusion that perhaps this time, separated from my military duties and cohorts and virtually alone, was valuable in some way. Certainly it afforded me time to examine my life, to contemplate both loss and achievement, and to charter a path forward. And, something seemed to be pulling me forward.

With my hands I lifted my leg over the side of the bed and sat there, preparing to stand. I experienced pain, but it really was nothing I couldn't endure. I was determined to get back on my feet, and I resolved to start today. I'd accomplished much in my lifetime through sheer force of will, and I was determined to do this, now. At that very moment, Nefer arrived; she began preparing oil of the castor bean, ignoring that I was about to get out of bed.

There was a slight throbbing in my foot, and from my shin up to my knee, my leg hung down like dead weight. The sutures had been removed two weeks ago. There was still swelling, but the intense pain had subsided. I was sleeping better and thinking better.

As I groped around, I wished I had something to lean on.

Nefer spoke up. "You have made extraordinary progress, given the magnitude of the infection and the fact that the wound had gone untreated for so long. When you arrived, the prognosis was not good. Now I see that the outcome is likely to be even better than I'd expected. I hoped you would regain full use of your foot and leg." She continued to speak, preparing the oils. "If you put that foot on the ground, you will set back the healing process. Quite possibly, you will reopen the wound and cause re-infection."

"I don't have any feeling in it," I replied. "Maybe if I set it down, I will," I foolishly offered.

She turned, came over to me, and firmly stated, "Not now, and not for some time."

Normally she kept her eyes averted, but she looked directly at me. "We have all been focused on your wellness and saving your leg. I personally have a great deal at stake in this. Many told me that your foot and leg should not be saved. I believed otherwise. I went against the priests and I claimed for you full usage. I fought the priests and the surgeons on your behalf. Though you were delirious, I knew you had a strong will to keep this limb; no one else I know could have endured such intense pain. You have come a long way, but your recovery is far from complete. Until this wound is totally healed, the danger of re-infection remains. You have fought to keep this leg, and you must decide if you are going to stay the course, because from now on the healing is mostly up to you."

With no resistance, she lifted my leg back up on the couch. Once I settled back and the foot and leg were elevated to her satisfaction, I released an unintended deep sigh. She examined the limb, cleansed it, and applied the healing oil.

This one-sided conversation marked a turning point. Afterward, I was far more compliant, and she was far more forthcoming, giving instructions and explanations and sharing some of the practices of the healers.

One day, while applying the oil, she said, "You are getting a lot of help now. You need to avail yourself of this help. You know you need to be working with the unseen forces."

"What do you mean?" I asked.

"I simply mean there is more unseen than seen. I would have thought you knew that," she said, in a mildly questioning manner.

"Well, maybe I do," I said. "Or maybe I did."

I was very careful not to mention "the shining one," although my remembrance of her was still quite vivid, and my curiosity had not abated. To me, she was clearly an unseen force if ever there was one. Probing about this was met with silence. I felt it likely Nefer and Shoshan had discussed it. I pressed Nefer to explain what she meant by "unseen forces," since she seemed willing.

She started slowly. "Well, as you know, we are more spirit than we are physical. Most people are so wrapped up in their day-to-day lives that they are tending more and more to forget. Surprisingly my people, the Pharaonic people of Egypt, are increasingly forgetting this important premise of life." She went on gingerly. "At one time, we were entirely spirit—and we were with God. You know that. We were with God, and we were in spirit. Understand?"

"Well, sort of, I suppose. I haven't thought about such matters for years," I said.

"Well, perhaps it is time for you to give it more thought, because healing requires integration of body and spirit. It is more than the physical matter of a wound and a scar. A healing is in great part a matter of the spirit, also. This would entail the interactions of your spirit and that of unseen forces, as well."

She went on, saying, "I know your life path has been a highly physical one. You have seen a great deal of violence and, if I may say, inflicted violence yourself. It's in your muscles, as well as your spirit. All your experiences, all your memories, whether conscious or subconscious, including all the violent acts, are stored in your tissues and mind center. This affects your state of health. This is about subtle energies."

"Is that why you have that tuning fork; and, is that why you brought me these color tablets?" I asked.

"Yes, I had the tablet made especially for you." She smiled. "There is hope. Stored negative energies can be released and, as I said, you are getting a lot of help. I can feel a marked change in your vibrations since you've been here. Perhaps you have noticed this on a dream level. You can work with the higher power on this in the dream state. And I am asking you to do just that. As I told you, I can help, but this healing will be in great part up to you. As much as possible, I will work with you on this."

She explained the use of her tuning fork, discussed atonement, and attunement to color. She suggested visualization techniques for me to practice, daily.

I told her how we Greeks have sanctuaries used expressly for healing. I told her about our belief that healing is done through the dream with the help of an oracle. She was keenly interested in our methods, and we discussed similarities and differences.

She summed it up by saying, "From what you have told me, I think you could create your own dream temple, right here. Knowing what you do, I think you have the capacity to heal yourself. Consider yourself the sanctuary. Consider the sanctuary of self. Consider the self, your self, the sanctuary."

I said, "I would need to consult an oracle."

To which she said, "Maybe you could simply listen to your inner self. Although an oracle or the priests might not agree, my private belief is that we are able to heal ourselves, and we can interpret our own dreams."

After she left, I thought about our exchange. She was a very wise woman. I recalled my countryman Socrates, who had a voice within. He called it his divine voice, his Daimon.

At the very moment Nefer suggested interpreting my own dreams, a thought had flashed through my mind. I didn't say anything to her at the time, but I remembered that when I was very, very sick I saw our Greek god Asclepius, and I actually felt his animal assistant *cerberius* lick my wound. I felt relatively certain this happened but because of my condition, I could have mistaken his *cerberius* for a local dog. Things were somewhat confused in my mind. I knew I hadn't been well then, but after this event, my health started to improve.

I felt very far from home and all things Greek. If Asclepius, the son of Apollo, came to invoke my healing, I accept with gratitude the help of the subterranean spirits, those of the underworld, his chthonic deities and Olympian deities, the hydra or the serpent, and the dog. It then occurred to me that the Asclepius dog had an amazing resemblance to the jackal-headed Anubis of these people. What I was sure of was that for Greeks, a dog was always connected with births and deaths, and perhaps I'd been pulled back from the grave.

I allowed my retirement papers and the letter from Alexander to lie on the couch next to me for several days. I was rather certain I knew what was contained therein. I had written many letters of the same sort on his behalf. So there was no rush.

Without referring directly to the letter, my aide-de-camp inquired of me several times, "Are you all right?" He noticed the unopened letter, and he knew that allowing a letter, particularly one from Alexander, to go unread was quite out of character for me. He knew my rule was always to expedite all correspondence. I could have read the letter. It's not as though I had anything else to do.

It was a personal letter written by him. The crux of it was this: The odds are against it, but in my heart I know you will survive and thrive. You have served Macedonia and me beyond all others. My hero since childhood, you are a man of great courage and wisdom. I am forever in debt to you for your wise council. Nothing I can say or do could adequately express my gratitude. You and I have led a life of action. It was you who impressed upon me very early never to look back but to keep moving forward. Let us both continue to move forward. (This statement gave me pause.) He mentioned his mother, Olympias.

He wrote that he fully expected the Temples of Karnak and my Thebes estate to forever peak my intellectual curiosity and fascination with other cultures. He said unlimited resources, including manpower, were at my disposal to create and support public works projects to the extent I desired. He ended by adding, "Old man" yours is to linger and live a full life. He suggested I take a new woman.

I considered that every beginning had an ending and every ending was a beginning. I found that thought uplifting at this stage of my recovery. Exploring this place called Egypt would be a new beginning. I smiled at Alexander's suggestion.

9
Shadowy Memories

THE DATE FOR THE next poetry group meeting loomed ahead. I considered not going. My confidence had eroded. On second thought, I decided not to let the coach beat me up or beat me down, whatever the case might be. I conceded that he had a valid point. I had read it too fast, and my diction was not the best, but he could have taken a different tone. Generally, I had more than enough courage and confidence to face the world, but this poetry thing was something altogether different, reading a poem aloud to a group is exposing one's inner self in public!

Then there were the troublesome telephone conversations with Becka. I was about at my wits end with her. I tried to explain myself to her satisfaction, but she just wouldn't or couldn't understand. I struggled to help her see why her dad and I were not together, but nothing I said was enough for her. Either I faced a barrage of angry questions, or I faced a stony-cold wall. It was very frustrating when she went silent and refused to engage in conversation. I wanted to find an amicable resolution. She did not.

Becka and Bradley were adults, and I fully understood that they loved their dad. I did, too. I mean, there had been nothing abusive in our more than twenty-year marriage and, as far as marriages went, it had been a good one. I guess that sounded stupid. As Becka said, "If you love him, why did you divorce him?"

I should stop saying that I love her father, I thought. Even if it was true, because it just complicated the issue. There were all kinds of love. I'm exhausted with it all. Even though I need to keep the dialog open with her, she was wearing me down. If I said, "Your father is a good man," she countered with, "But not good enough for you?"

The truth was that I just didn't want to be married to him any longer. In my eyes, it was just that simple. It was over. The marriage had run its course. There was nothing there for me emotionally and, as Rae said, it had been that way for a good many years. True enough, but that shouldn't be said aloud because it sounded callous and unfeeling.

Why couldn't Becka be more supportive, like her brother? He may or may not have agreed with me, but somehow he was okay with it. He was okay with me doing what I felt needed to be done in my life, but Becka hadn't accepted that. She wanted things back the way they had been. Well, sorry about that! Things couldn't be, and she had to accept that. Or not. I had certainly learned that a divorce was not between the two people who were married. Everybody had an opinion, and everybody got into it.

Going to the poetry group and the dream workshop—and my work—helped me deal with all this stress and tension. In my heart of hearts, I realized that getting beyond my cerebral self was a good thing for me. I was out of touch with myself. It was strange that it hadn't occurred to me before. Over the years, I seemed to have lost my true and creative self—while on the way to becoming me, the professional museum director.

"So, Skylar," he started with me, in the same tone he'd finished with last month. "Would you like to deliver that poem again? Or do you have something else for us?"

"I have another one. It's from the same ancient echoes series. You'll have to pardon me, I haven't found a voice coach," I said, trying not to be sarcastic. "I feel these poems would be better delivered in a male voice. If is okay with you, maybe one of the guys might volunteer."

"Okay," he said, breaking his cardinal rule, that the writer must present his or her own words. "Is there a volunteer?" He looked around the circle. John and Chad both volunteered, so I gratefully handed the pages to Chad, who was sitting nearer. He started:

there were wars
throughout the ages
sometimes we were only friends
sometimes we fought
side by side
'til one of us fell
'til one of us died
life went on
battles raged
we rose to
fight again
valiant in defeat
victory for noble purposes
brave and gallant
to liberate
to hold the ground
our standard placed
we stood the test
there was blood shed
we always died
then rushed back in
to save the day
to place the standard
to lead the crusade
all for one and one for all
down the ages
the standard bearer
we knew the call of bugles
trumpets
pounding drums
cannons at the ready
chainmail, armor,
clubs, shields, and such
we knew earth's element
acquainted like family
knew the wind
we recognized drifts

we found our way over glacial ice
learning skills for future times
tides rose
boats took us there
or we found our way
half starved
we survived to live another day
another battle set to win
we fought together
lived together
died together
harsh nights
misery by day
you sheltered me from storms of life
encountered along the way
our spirits moved on
through eons of time
gathering pieces
shadowy memories
of the mind

The room was quiet and sober. Chad broke the silence by clearing his throat and saying, "I wish that I had had a chance to read through it before I read it to ya'll." He returned the pages, and I thanked him.

Without comment, the group leader went on, saying, "Who wants to go next?"

After the class, an acquaintance and I walked out to the parking lot together. In casual conversation, I said, "I'm thinking about dropping out. I'm so rushed with work and all. I'm just not sure I'm getting much out of this. I'm not sure I relate to our leader and doubt he relates to me—or women, in general." She agreed but said she really hoped I'd continue because she liked what I wrote. I told her, "Well, you know how life and things are constantly evolving. Somehow, my poems are morphing into short stories, and I feel my time is best used writing instead of talking about it."

As I drove away, I wondered whether I would see her again.

I thought about my poems a great deal. More important than the construction of the poem, I wondered about the words and the source of the information. Was it as simple as the workings of the imagination in the hypnagogic state, or was there something highly remarkable going on? It seemed clear they weren't going to bring public acclaim, but I felt a satisfying sense of accomplishment. It was like an innermost part of me had been laid out on paper. On one hand, the words seemed to be irrelevant to my life; on the other hand, there were amazingly familiar elements that pricked a need for continued inquiry. In the process, I had learned what Rumi meant when he said, "The morning breeze has secrets to tell, do not go back to sleep."

I analyzed where the Scottish Highland dreams had come from. I could think of nothing else except that the dark and shadowy crates had triggered them. There had been no mention of Scotland. It had been fifteen years since I'd toured England, Scotland, and Wales. There had been a passing reference to the work of Mackintosh in a staff meeting, but that had been last year. I even considered that some traces of blood and DNA of the Scot's ran through my veins, but clearly it was Jake, the crates, and the shadowy darkness that had triggered those dreams.

For certain Jake was the cause of all this. The dreams, numerous synchronicities, and reincarnation made for interesting conversation with Rae, but beyond that things seemed to confirm the fact that Jake and I had previous lives together in various roles. Sometimes I though he had similar feelings but felt it would be too awkward to ask. He'd never mentioned his beliefs.

I read that under hypnosis, people recalled their previous lives; also, during deep meditation. Could it happen in the dream state, too? I found a little window in time just before being totally awake and just as I fell asleep that could be important. Maybe I tapped into how to bring my subconscious thoughts into consciousness. It seemed to me there was a "creative space or window in time," immediately before waking. Stories, images of people, and the words to describe them "materialized," then.

The poems contained aspects of my present day persona. Aha! Was I dreaming it, or was it dreaming me? I considered that I was the dreamer, and I was in the dream. It was all about me. I read that it's believed the Greeks didn't separate time into day and night as we do. It was all a continuum.

Before Jake, I didn't give a wit about the concept of reincarnation, and I never considered previous lives. The incident of Jake and I handling the piece of broken pottery released engrams, memories of time passed. That night, two lifetimes came back to me. It was difficult, but I retained the thoughts. I forced myself to awaken long enough to record them. My journal read:

I was a young Indian girl, and you were a trapper—you captured me. Because you took me away from my family, I could never love you.

Although you were sensitive and gentle, you were never able to undo what had been done—in just one moment in time. I was a proud person and never wanted to show my fear, but I was afraid and whenever you touched me, I trembled.

It was much like a scene in the Russian-born artist Nicolai Fechin's drawing, whereby an Indian girl is shown in an everyday Pueblo village scene carrying a water jug on her head. It was as if she walked out of the painting and into my dream.

I saw myself walking along a wide but shallow stream with an earthenware jug. The water was clear. The picture I saw was very much like the stream that runs through New Mexico's Taos Pueblo. Walking upstream, I eventually came to a place where the water flowed over large rocks into a deep pool. I was filling the jug when I was attracted by nearby blackberry bushes, covered with plump, ripened berries.

I laid the half-filled jug aside, gathered a handful, and tasted a few. They were plentiful and more luscious than they looked. I gathered more and placed them into a woven sack. Intent on the task, I moved deeper into the bushes, engrossed in selecting the best.

I was unaware of the danger, but you had been observing me for some time. You came for water that day, too. It was not your intention to capture me. You were simply watching and waiting your turn for water. Inadvertently, I got so close that you could not leave or move without revealing your location and causing danger to yourself. It was a predicament that could only be described as fate.

So intent was I on berry picking, I came face to face with you before realizing the danger. In that instant, you were not sure what to do, because you, too, were in danger. You had no choice but to reach out your arms as I passed by, and you did, putting your hand over my mouth and drawing me tightly up next to you. Immobilized, it was only in that moment that I realized I was in danger.

Once you nabbed me, there was no alternative but to take me with you. Although there were regrets on your part, there had been no safe recourse.

Your life took a different direction, changed forever.

As was mine.

It was a moment in time.

It was a choice not thought through.

An impulse of yours, an impulse of mine.

A certain place.

A moment in time.

Sometime during the same night, I had multiple dreams, variations on the same theme. I had several about being captured in the early American west. This particular dream caused me to think carefully about the significance of a moment in time. It seemed to have a message that provoked questions. Was every single moment of our lives significant or just certain ones—like this one?

Some time later, an elderly Native American woman came to the museum to discuss some items she wanted to bequeath to the museum. She said they were treasured heirlooms, passed from one generation to another, but she had no living kin and she wanted to assure herself of their care and handling after she was gone. Although I had never met the woman, she said she knew me. She said that she was the great-great-granddaughter of the persons who made the pot and amulets that she brought.

Later, as I was accessioning this gift to the museum, I reflected on my interaction with the kindly gentle person who had brought these pieces. Serenely beautiful in old age, there was something strikingly understated but powerful about this tiny, graceful woman. Her black dress was worn gray and smooth as silk; it frayed at the edges and looked like it may not last another season. Unadorned, except for a discreet amulet with feathers fitted around her neck, she was herself a work of art. She had no knowledge of pottery, yet she treasured these and had a sacred mission with these pots. She trusted me with them. She had a mystical quality about her that seemed familiar.

Four months earlier, tired from the nonstop events of the day, I left work a six o'clock, picked up take-out at a drive-thru, and was soon home in my study reading and relaxing. I dozed off. Fortunately, I had documented this dream in my journal, and I went back to read it.

There was a wagon train. I was traveling west with my family in a Conestoga wagon. My father cautioned me several times not to stray, not to wander away. I was an inquisitive child and somewhat the dreamer—young, spirited, and oblivious to danger and the ramifications of walking off alone. I liked nature and plants above all.

When the wagons were circled for the night, attracted to the natural beauty of the land and the wildflowers, I went to collect a few flowers to press into a book. In the dream, I saw myself picking and examining the blossoms, sometimes drawing them in my book. I was focused and intent on the task of preserving them between the pages.

Unaware that a young Indian male rode out that day with two friends, I hadn't seen them crouched and disguised behind the tall, thick grasses. The three grabbed me and dragged me into the brush, where two were attempting to rape me. The third male was distraught and bewildered by the actions of his friends. He tried pulling the two of them off me. He saved me, but the ruckas left me bruised, bloody, dazed, and in a state of shock. As the two would-be rapists were kicked and pelted by their friend, they fled. He grabbed up my things, my bag, my books, and me.

He realized that he would not escape being ostracized by his friends and somehow he accepted responsibility for himself and me.

My father and the men from the wagon train searched in vain for me until nightfall, but we were already far away. The next morning, they found the place where I had been attacked. Fearing the worst, they returned to the wagons. In the distance, I saw the wagon train moving on, as though nothing had happened.

The young Indian boy spent a lot of time looking at me. Mostly as a curiosity. I did not look at him; I kept my face turned away. He examined the color and texture of my blond hair. The color and texture of my skin, which was not as smooth as his. The freckles on my cheeks and nose interested him. The locket that was torn from my neck in the struggle. He noticed the tiny drawings of a bearded man and pretty lady inside the locket, which made me cry. Whenever I looked at the quilting pieces, my mother's sewing needle, the pressed flowers, and the little testament in the bag of things that he recovered, I cried.

I had no survival skills, and his were limited. We were both alone. At one point I saw him bring me wildflowers. I didn't understand that it was an act of kindness and that he wanted me to put them in my book with the others. Words were of no use for communication, and there was a vast cultural divide. I walked away from him. I saw him bring me flowers another time. An act of kindness, but again I rejected the overture. Since he could not make himself understood, he found the book and put the flowers in with the others. I observed what he did, he observed what I did, and through this type of interaction, we learned to communicate.

In this dream, I was a forlorn young girl-child abandoned on the prairie gives who gave birth to the child of an outcast. He was seen attempting to deliver our baby while I was hemorrhaging and near death. He was exasperated, so young and inexperienced. He floundered as he faced the needs of a newborn and a dying girl, bleeding to death. My eyes showed that I was near death and had lost the will to live.

He was chanting. He bathed the baby in a stream and wrapped him in my apron. He laid the baby next to me. I had no strength nor desire to hold the infant. He tucked the baby in next to me and left.

I saw him chanting and desperately searching through the woodlands. He found what he was looking for. When he returned, the baby was lying on the ground crying; he knew I was near death, life was spilling out of me, the ground was saturated with my blood. He began a mournful lament.

He made tea from what he'd found and moved us into a naturally sheltered place. He gathered brush and made a lean-to. Carefully, he administered his herb tea medicine. He appeared to be composed, but inside he was frantic. It was almost nightfall, and he saw no change in my condition.

Settling himself on the ground under the lean-to, he gently cradled me in his arms. He slowly rocked me and the baby back and forth and mournfully chanted. He had confused feelings for saving me from his friends, on one hand, and guilt and regret because he had taken me from my family, on the other. He was isolated and missed his own. He was exhausted by his efforts to save me. I hadn't responded to his efforts. I saw exhaustion wash over him, and he fell asleep. He slept fitfully, and his dreams were filled with scenarios in which he faced the unanticipated consequences of his actions.

An elderly Indian woman shaking a rattle, dressed in shabby, blackened buckskin emerged from the woods. She dusted the three of us with a powder as we slept. She attempted to chant and dance, but her voice and movements were feeble. She placed three pebbles in a small nest of bird feathers. The rattle sounds remained long after she disappeared.

His body was warm. Like a vessel, he held me. He moved the child inside his shirt. In the morning, the hemorrhaging had stopped; the medicine had been effective. I survived but was weakened by giving birth at such a young age and being exposed in the wild.

With no common language, words were useless. The two of us communicated with our eyes and hands. He had primary care of the infant because I couldn't move without pain. He encouraged and taught me to nurse the baby and directed his efforts to restoring my health.

The dream showed that we survived because of his skills in the outdoors, his perseverance, and his prayers conveyed through chanting. Despite his efforts to save the child, and me I remained cold and aloof. I saw him as a person living a solitary life of introspection, doing what needed to be done in isolation. Frequently, he rode off to hunt or fish or search for food. My wilderness survival skills were nonexistent. I appeared to be unfeeling. He took responsibility for food preparation and maintenance of our camp.

Gradually, I observed and learned from him. We had another child. This time, I knew better what to expect. I saw us living together, without talking. As the children got older, I talked and read to them from the little testament. He listened. He thought reading was fairly useless, but he liked to hear my voice.

It seemed years passed, and he taught me how to survive in the wilderness. I was grateful for that. I came to realize how much work he had put into our survival. I respected him for that. I was not without feeling, although I appeared distant and remote. It was that at a very deep level, I felt alone. Our relationship strengthened as we aged.

He taught me essential things, cooking, and crafts. How to make pottery from special clay he dug out of the riverbank when he found it. How to fire and burnish pottery so it held water, how to weave and lash items together. I was good and fast at lashing, weaving, and knotting. This was important because we were frequently on the move, wandering. In this dream, I was shown bundling and tying our meager belongings together.

As time passed, my natural abilities in handicrafts were manifest. I knew by his expressions that he was proud of me, but language skills escaped him. He enjoyed watching me at work. He taught me what he recalled of his mother's methods with leather. I always embellished garments with some deco-

rative materials, some frivolous touches; he questioned these appurtenances. Why feathers attached to a basket? What use are clay beads? Later, he came to enjoy this part of me. I added beads and feathers to his leggings. Sometimes I added letters of the alphabet.

When he went hunting and was away, the attached beads and feathers reminded him of me. In the dream, he rubbed them for good luck. It became a ritual to ensure his accuracy with the arrow.

In the dream we were burnishing pottery, incising designs of stylized birds and feathers.

Collaboration in crafts became a bridge for us. He made the practical and essential and I added beauty and grace to existence. Working together pleased him. His joy was most apparent when we undertook projects together.

When he taught me to sew buckskin with a bone needle, our hands and fingers were working together. He touched my hands, remembering a time when they had been soft and white. He collected herbs and rubbed them on my hands and feet, hoping to restore them to the softness they'd had when he took me.

In one scene in the dream, we were sitting face to face as he tried to show me how weaving was done. He looked at the problem; from his position, it was upside down. He took it from me, turned it around toward himself, then back toward me. He turned himself around one way then another, in order to look at it from my perspective. Twisting this way, then that, he finally crawled over me and got behind me to view the project from my side. Fitting me comfortably between his legs, he encircled me with his arms, took my hands in his, along with the project, and we continued.

Seen wearing buckskin, my clothes were outgrown, worn out, and remade into garments for our children. I pieced together the scraps from my dress into a vest for him. In the dream, he wore this vest over his buckskin, as he mounted a pony. He spoke to me with his eyes, and I to him. I learned the power of a glance. Wearing moccasins and leggings decorated

*with tiny beads, amulets at his waist, his bow and arrows on
his back, he departed quickly without emotion. I was standing
there with our two children.*

As I read this dream journal, entry dated months earlier, I was
shocked by the information it contained and oh so glad I had written it. My heart was beating rapidly. I was struck with the thought
that the pottery in the dream was identical to the pottery with the
incised feather design the elderly Native American woman contributed to the museum. The similarity to the woman in the dream
was shocking, and I was sure, no coincidence. I was overwhelmed.

10
The Water Castle

THERE IS A PLACE like no other—sacred—magical and spirit charged. Listen and look carefully, or you will miss it. This is a space—in between—where spirit meets earth, and reality blends ever so slightly with the spirit world. If you allow, it can be felt.

Here the Hindu Goddess, Saraswati, Goddess of Knowledge and the Arts—of Creative Expression—is at her best. Here she conspires with nature to manifest beauty in its purest form, through creative expression. This is a place where an elixir of the mist of time transpires, in which water vapor drips and drops continually to form never ending trickles and rivulets until runnels tumble down. Then joined together as streams, they mingle and coalesce, and spill into water traps that over flow, and run down and somehow in this magical chaos there foments the divine music of the *gamelan*.

It is then that a conglomeration of metal percussion instruments, an ensemble of metallophones and wooden bar xylophone-like instruments, drum-shaped, hanging and cradled gongs transform nature into rhythm and melodies, creating a heavenly stream of sound that mimics swells and surges, torrents and cascades, inundation and waterfalls. Here music is divine, celestial, and splendidly made.

In this realm of poignant lush jungle and perfume-drenched air, Saraswati enlivens the world as she consorts with mist-kissed nature to create a playground. Her fine hand can be seen with artists' brushes and *batik tjanting* tools lightly touching plants, and vines, and flowers, transforming nature through the divine creative force into superb and unsurpassed textile design. Here the flow of the moving spirit inspires all who seek her. Her reality is gripped and embraced by nature's bounty; nature yields and delivers its divine essence, as plant dye is extracted; and a fusion of color, wax, and line is captured in *batik tulus*.

Here a vibrant, pulsating, yet ill-defined energy stirs the imagination, if you let it. Here the flow of Saraswati's magical river of consciousness creates the dance, as she blends grace and movement into lifeform. In this place, where life is merged into one with creative expression, stories and tales of living tradition are spoken and acted out behind the shadow screen of *warang puppetry*.

Here behind delicate features and flawless skin, moisturized by nature, the people are light, refined, languid, and flowing—their spiritual countenance prevails—and creative expression is clearly fundamental to existence. As we see an elaborate, complex, yet simple, *puja* (worship) ceremony lived out—where small gifts of *pusham* (flowers), *phalam* (fruit), *jolam* (water), or *dhupam* (incense) are offered—the ongoing cycle of sacred vibration is a conduit of communication between the community and the Divine.

Thus, the universe is dreamed into being. Here the grand wheel of life turns, and volcanic mist circles, then serenely settles on an ancient culture. This is Java.

We were children—brothers, four and five years of age, five and six, then six and seven. Not older than that. And this was what I remember. Our small bodies were lean, our skin mocha colored. Constantly exposed to the sun, we were bronze all over and glistened from the jungle humidity. If allowed to grow, our hair would be black and straight, but it was shaved off close to the scalp. This avoided head lice.

We were genetically coded not to reach two meters in height when fully grown. Our diet assured that. It was composed of rice gruel and rice, bananas, some other fruits, peanuts, and vegetable broth with an occasional vegetable or fragment of shrimp or chicken. Our daily fare.

On special holidays things changed radically; we had a scrumptious feast. Fruits and melons were luscious and plentiful. Food was served on large, lightweight monkey pod and heavy teak wood platters; it was all artistically decorated with flowers—live flowers, paper flowers, and fanciful colored wooden cut out flowers. Elaborately arranged fruits were offered first to the gods in ritual ceremonies. After the gods took the essence from the fruit, the fruits were returned for us to eat. Sometimes chicken satay was served; it was my favorite. I wanted to eat the small pieces of chicken fitted together on thin bamboo skewers in a fiery spicy peanut sauce everyday.

During those times of celebration, a wild boar was roasted underground or set to burn on a spit. Served whole, elaborately dressed with fruits and vegetables, leaves and roots—with its head on, the sight of its snout made me sick. I really didn't like to look at it or the people eating it. I couldn't understand how they could enjoy this. They seemed to relish the grease it as dripped from their fingers and ran down their chins. I thought it was gross to look at them. Just the thought of people devouring a pig made me sick enough to puke.

I was certain someone on the palace grounds ate satay everyday. My brother said no, but I often smelled it cooking. When I napped, the aroma of the spicy dish wafted by on a breeze or in a dream. While at my lessons, the pungent essence seeped into my space and hung around me. I salivated, remembering the savory tang, and my stomach got noisy. My brother says was my "e-magination."

We were barefoot and naked, except for an amulet, which we wore around our waists to protect us from harm and assure our future reproductive potency. My brother wore an identical amulet, except that each talisman was inscribed with our name, a date, and the carved seal of the Sultan. I couldn't read, but I had been told that the other markings and symbols had been made by the priest, who documented incantations specific to the wearer. My mother told me. She could read.

We belonged to the Sultan because our mother belonged to the Sultan. At an early age, she came to his palace to study music and dance. She was a gifted dancer, known for her unforgettable large brown eyes and the message in her fingers and hands. She was exqui-sitely graceful and beautiful. It was said she was the Sultan's favorite.

Except for the incident of our birth, she had no bearing on our lives. We saw little of her. She had separate living quarters within the palace, not in the women's quarters. She was pampered, in-dulged, and profusely cared for by servant girls; her every whim was immediately addressed. She focused solely on her dance, was self-centered and self-involved. She performed at court functions and privately for the Sultan. She had no interest in us and rarely called for us.

If we were brought to see her, she was practicing her dance on the many terraces in her gardens. Sometimes she was waiting alone in her private garden, surrounded by huge potted plants and fine woven and teak furniture with colorful cushions. Her garden was very special, with several water features—including two waterfalls that spill over large rocks and emptied into pools deep enough to swim or bathe in. Another pond had water lilies and large golden carp.

If she was dancing, we were admonished to sit as quietly as a mouse so as not to disrupt her. Other dancers performed the tradi-tional dances, but my mother created new dances, telling new stories with her eyes and hands and body movements. I was told she inter-preted nature, the movement of the butterflies or the winds, gentle winds or the turbulent wind before a storm. I could see that. She was, as they said, exquisite, superior in every way to other dancers.

Her living quarters were open to the air, and from every di-rection she looked out on the lush gardens. The interior was lav-ishly decorated, with carved screens and divans with silken pillows. Playfully colored silk batik paintings were hung throughout the living areas. They moved whenever she walked by or there was the slightest breeze. Her bed was a raised platform of carved rosewood, inlayed with mother-of-pearl and draped with a gossamer fabric held with golden ribbons at the ceiling by carved, painted but-terflies and phantasmagorical plants.

My mother's body had the scent of flowers; a light fragrance of gardenia surrounded and followed her. Everything smells like gardenia, except of course the orchids. She had orchids of every color imaginable, kept both inside and out, sitting, hanging, climbing, crawling, and cascading everywhere. It looked to me like she floated through this space, barely touching the floor, like the petals of a bougainvillea dancing on a light breeze.

On one rare visit, we were admiring the many different birds she kept in an odd assortment of ornamental bamboo cages. In a generous moment, she gave us a little olive colored parrot with red and gray markings that talked. A visiting Maori chief, who admired her dancing, gave it to her. We named him Kaka because he was a Kaka brought from Aotearoa. Over time he mimicked our voices, copying our words and laughter, exactly.

During State affairs, we dressed in finery befitting the Sultan himself. We paraded forth in splendid costume, regal, yes very splendid and very royal but very stiff. Except for bare feet, we were totally and uncomfortably covered and instructed to sit erect, stay quiet, and very still. This was very difficult because the outfit poked and scratched me everywhere. The headdress was most difficult to endure. I suffered as I waited to take it off and be free.

The *gamelan* drew my attention at these events. From where I sat, I couldn't see the many instruments, which included gongs and drums, metallophones, xylophones, bamboo flutes, and stringed instruments. Twenty or more men, mostly seated on the floor at one end of the pavilion, struck bars of xylophone-type instruments, like the *saron* and *gangsa*, which had metal bars, and the *gambang*, which had wooden bars. The cradle gongs were called *kenong* and *bonang*. They were large sets of gongs laid out horizontally in front of the musicians, unlike the *kempul* gongs, which hung. Together they played the most heavenly music. Sometimes the *gamelan* accompanied the girls as they sang and danced.

If I closed my eyes, which I may not, it sounded exactly like a real waterfall. If I got too enthralled with the music and began to dream, the head master seemed to know because he poked me in my back with his pointer stick. My brother never got jabbed. He told me to pay attention. I said to him, "Pay attention to what?" He ignored me.

I wished they wouldn't disturb me. I was listening intently to the notes and rhythm, and I was thinking about the ancient Javanese god, Sang Hyang Guru, who ruled all of Java. He needed a signal to summon the gods, and so he created the gong. Then he invented two more gongs, just because he had a more complex message to send. I was trying to imagine what Sang was saying, when I got poked.

There was no doubt that we are brothers. The resemblance was abundantly clear, and we were inseparable. Our features were identical, close in age, less than a year apart. From our sizes, it wasn't readily apparent who was the older. We were nearly the same height and there was never more than one kilogram of difference in our weight. I was the younger, but it really didn't matter in the grand scheme of things.

As issue of the Sultan, my brother and I were raised with utmost care—along with the rest of his children—of which there were many. The girls were in separate quarters from the boys, and the two groups were schooled and trained differently, so we had no occasions to know one another. There was great emphasis on music, dance, and social graces for the girls. Sometimes we heard them practice their music or caught a glimpse of them practicing movement and dance positions in the gardens. I thought it peculiar that no girls play in the gamelan.

There were other lessons about numbers and letters for the boys. We we sat cross-legged, toes curled back, dreaming in the heat and humidity with some vague hope that the teacher would soon stop talking. Exercise period would come next, and we could then get up and play.

Despite our mother's favored position and reputation with the Sultan, life was no different for us than for any of the other boys. The best we expected from life was a position as an administrator, an army official, an engineer, or for the least ambitious, an assignment as the Sultan's representative in some jungle outpost. My brother said I had better pay attention or that's where I'd be going.

Aside from the fact that my brother, Melongyazi, and I took our lessons together with the youngest boys, Yazi and I created our own games and played together. We were constant companions; seldom separated. We shared everything and looked out for one another; no one came between us. We were like the two peas in one seedpod. My name was Melongeidori, Dori for short.

During the heat of the day, we rested and slept together with about fifteen other boys near our age. At night, Yazi and I lay naked, curled up together, overlapping like puppies on the grass mat. Fresh woven grass mat was replaced and installed on our sleeping platform regularly by the servants. The sleeping platform was raised a full meter above ground level, designed this way to protect us at night from rodents and other animals. We slept unmolested, as nocturnal animals roamed easily under the platform.

Occasionally, one or more wild boar mistakenly wandered on to the palace grounds; this caused a great commotion. If at night, guards brought out torches and weapons, and a frightening rampage ensued. I witnessed a boar, quite unexpectedly, charge out of a jungle ravine, and I looked at the bloody stinking head of a dead boar, closely. To be totally realistic, there was a food chain in the jungle and somehow I knew it. Given the right circumstances, I could be eaten by a wild boar or another animal. I told myself, *If I don't eat the boar, maybe the boar will not eat me.*

In case the talisman around my waist failed, I called on every Javanese spirit and Goddess I knew of to protect my brother and me from wild boar. I had nightmares about a stampeding wild boar. Terrified and shaken, I cried out loud and my brother tried to calm me. When I was younger, the headmaster took me to the women's quarters several times because he could not settle me. I'd sob until I collapsed, whimpering and exhausted.

During the day, we were observed by an assortment of guards and servants and the Sultan's administrators. There were a numbers of watchtowers. Yazi and I made a game of slipping out of the guards' sight. Although strictly forbidden, we cleverly outwitted the guards many times, so we could explore the palace grounds on our own.

The best time to slip away was when we all went to the Water Castle to play and have our afternoon swim. We did this every day. The Sultan created the Water Castle as a dual pool for his young children. One pool was created for the boys only. The girls had theirs. The girls' pool was adjacent to ours but separated by a wall. Yazi and I called this the pool of the nymphs or the pool of the water sprites, for reasons I will tell later. We boys heard the girls squealing like piglets while playing in the water, their keepers frequently hushing their shrill voices. Then peals of laughter bubbled up and their snickering and giggling commenced.

The trick was to escape precisely at this time while everyone, including the guards and our caretakers, were distracted by some commotions caused by the silly girls. When their boisterous effervescence jumped the wall separating the two pools, that was the moment to act. Yaz and I bolted out of the pool and took cover in the shrubbery. This was an interim position directly under the guardhouse, where they couldn't see us. From here, we climbed the berm, then under cover of dense vegetation we disappeared into the gardens.

We learned by experience that the Sultans' landscapers and gardeners worked mostly in the early morning, not in the midday heat. However, Yazi and I had the misfortune of encountering gardeners while out on an escapade. If we were lucky, some raised an eyebrow, indicating they saw us; others looked away, ignored us, and continued trimming. They always seemed as surprised to see us, as we were to see them. They never said anything to us. The gardeners and workers were not likely to report us, primarily because we were children of the Sultan. But administrators might.

On one of our forays, we darted off our hidden pathway and did not notice a ladder leaning against immense garuda topiary. We blundered into the base of the ladder, tripping and almost knocking an old fellow in a crusty old batik *tulis* sarong and dusty bare feet off his perch. Startled and floating for a moment in midair, the old codger almost toppled off but managed to grab the scaffolding and regain his balance. He shook his fist at us as we dashed back into the cover of foliage. He was a funny sight, clinging to the bosom of an immense garuda, the Javanese mythological creature with outstretched wings.

Frankly, it was really not very difficult to elude our caretakers, to escape our keepers. They were inattentive, bored, and apathetic, at best. They used this time at the pool to visit and gossip with one another. The oppressive Javanese jungle heat had dulled their senses to a state of stupefaction. They mastered the art of looking alert while being at some level of sleep.

The condition of the watchmen was similar, but they were lethargic and had no compunction about dozing in the heat. One simply covered for his snoozing fellow worker. They took turns watching each other's back. Another difference was that the watchmen were ensconced behind walls or hidden by the watchtower. If one observed them closely, as Yazi and I had done in order to pull off our caper, one soon noticed they rarely, if ever, watch the boys' pool. They watched the girls' pool. We reasoned that the girls could not swim and therefore had a higher need for closer monitoring than the boys, who all swam well. Until one day, when we brazenly crept very near the girls' pool. We followed the wall around, hid in the dense foliage, and peeped in the girls' bathing area. They swam and sunned stark naked; we could not believe our eyes. No wonder the watchmens' eyes were always averted to the girls' pool!

Somehow, it didn't seem proper to spy on the Sultan's daughters, and we didn't go back again. It never occurred to us that if we saw the guards through the shrubbery, the guards could see us.

It was a lot easier to get back into the pool than it was to get out. It took a bit of acting to carry it off. The game was to quickly roll out of the shrubbery, pop to your feet at the edge of the pool, raise your right arm high in the air, pinch your nose shut with your left hand, and leap out into mid-air with your knees tucked up to your chest. We did this swiftly, did not fumble, and made a big splash.

At this, of course, we were expert.

We found that the children's pools were but a small part of a grand design. The Water Castle and pleasure gardens were vast, with fanciful gazebos, teahouses, waterfalls, and other water features, holding many secrets. When we eluded our caretakers, we enjoyed exploring the gardens.

It had taken many years, many engineers, and many laborers to construct the Water Castle. There was a most elaborate series of pools. Some were fresh water and some were seawater. Some were for bathing. Some were for pleasure. The Water Castle covered many kilometers of lush tropical gardens. Exotic plants and flowers were selected to add fragrance to the days and nights at particular locations. I heard that a great deal of study and consideration had been given to the color of the blooms. At a precise time of day or night, each emitted its unique perfume. Nothing was done by happenstance, and everything was artfully cared for.

The Sultan himself had designed the Water Castle and the entire palace complex, which included the women's quarters, the Sultan's quarters, and office and administration buildings. These were places Yazi and I avoided. Although, eventually we were known to the weavers and food handlers, keepers of the vineyards and arboretum, vegetable gardens and gardeners and grounds keepers, all of whom were generally careful not to acknowledge our presence if our curiosity happened to draw us too close, or we unintentionally crossed paths.

Not far from the women's quarters were the artists' studios and artisans' workshops. Some craftsmen made baskets; fabric weavers and potters who created things for the household worked there. Lamp work bead makers, the silver and goldsmiths worked over an open flame, and like the young girls and older women who applied wax on fabric for batik, they didn't seem to mind the intense heat.

I don't want to bore you, but I want you to know that the doing of batik was very important in my culture. It was every bit as important as eating and sleeping. It was an intrinsic part of who we were. *Batik is* the *essence of Java.*

Many people were involved in the process. Young girls sat in a circle, front to back, front to back, front to back. Their right hand held a brass and bamboo *tjanting* tool, which they dipped into the pot of hot wax in the center of the circle. They applied the wax to the fabric, under the instruction of older, experienced women.

Once waxed, the fabric was taken to the dyers. After being dyed and dried, the old wax was removed from the fabric by women. And then it was ready for the next step, back to the waxers. The process was repeated over an over again until the design was completed. Sometimes the designs were applied with copper stamps. There were stamps of garudas and Javanese puppets stamps, which were dipped in hot wax and laid on the cloth. It was quicker than the work the girls did with the tjanting tools.

The dyers were separated from the waxers. Their building was full of vats of dye, big enough and deep enough for the dyer to wade around in and stomp on the fabric. His feet, up to his knees and his hands, up to his elbows, were dark blue. That dyers' building was almost two stories high; the ceiling was high and open. Many rods held the fabrics, which were secured in position to make a vast drying rack. The workers walked on a scaffolding to tend the length of fabric. The dyed fabric hung there until it was ready for the next step in the process. There were many waxing and dying steps in the process, and it took time to finish one meter of cloth.

The artists who designed the batik were never seen. I knew of one who lived with his wife in an enchanted cottage. He was very much revered, not as much as the Sultan, of course, but workers came to tend the flowers and vegetables in their gardens. I heard that he looked at the plants and flowers in the garden to create the designs for the batik. I could see that when I looked at the thirty or more fabrics hanging like banners on the rods in the dyer's shed.

The puppet master and designer of the *warang* puppets was also very much revered. He was a very old man and nearly blind. He, too, had his own cottage constructed with bamboo and woven mats. There were many gourds and flowering vines on his thatched roof. He sat outside on the narrow, shaded veranda, covered, and cocooned by the vines and his eager protégés. It seemed he didn't have a wife. The boys there made him cups of tea and took care of his needs. He taught them the traditional stories and the craft. They constructed the sets and performed with the shadow puppets at his cottage. Some boys carved the puppet heads and hands, other painted the faces, and still others made the puppet costumes.

Because batik tulus used only natural dyes, all the plant materials was gathered and simmered to extract the dye. Different plants yielded different colors. It was very interesting. Once Yazi and I followed the plant gatherers a long distance into the mountains. There we discovered a village of stone carvers. We heard them long before we approached their village. Alas, before we had a good look around, we were found out and two very concerned women ushered us back home.

Yazi and I climbed trees very fast. The soles of our feet were rough and calloused from grabbing the tree with our bare feet to pull ourselves forward and upward. We learned this from watching monkeys. Whenever there were breadfruits and coconuts to be gathered, the servants let us climb up and toss them down. Tree climbing was strictly forbidden for us, but the servants were old, tired, and lazy from the heat, so they let us climb up and collect the fruits for them.

Our parrot, Kaka, was allowed to fly in and out of her cage at will. One day, Kaka inexplicably vanished. She flew away and did not return. We searched for her, day after day. All the boys joined in the search, but we could not find her.

There had been rumors and signs of earthquakes. We were too young to understand about omens, but Kaka leaving surely was one. The old people knew that birds and animals were messengers, harbingers of things to come. But everyone was too busy and nobody paid attention to the words and warnings of the old people. Anyway, on an island there weren't many ways to escape from an earthquake and erupting volcano lava flows.

If it were not for earthquakes and volcanoes, this would have been paradise. We had many. They were continuous, you could say. When you were born in Java, where the earth shakes dramatically without any warning, we tend to ignore warnings. It was normal for us when smoke came out of the volcano and darkened the sky with ash for days. Fire shot out of the volcano, then stuff like stones and molten rock spewed out. It was a fact of life here, and life either simply went on, or was abruptly cut short.

Earthquakes routinely shook the palace grounds, the wooden buildings swayed, construction on the water castle was disrupted, and waterways were blocked. When this happened, the Sultan's engineers gathered around the caved in place, a crack or a fissure, and assessed the situation. Squatting motionless, sarongs stretched taut around their legs; quietly they pondered the problem for hours.

During my early childhood, there were ever-increasing concerns in hushed tones about the disruption of the fisheries. It seemed the sea lanes had been changing over time as the sea-mount continued to rise up from the deep sea floor. Old men said it was different in their youth.

Yazi and I hadn't yet reached the age to prepare for our life's work. We were in the innocence of childhood. One night, as we slept, the earth shook more violently than usual. Timbers fell, rocks rained down, and molten lava spread across the land in many directions. There was great chaos in the palace complex that night—and for years thereafter. The Sultan, some members of his family, and the court, including my mother, managed to escape.

As for me, Yazi and I lay curled together. Gasses from the pyroclastic flows killed us in our sleep. Everything was destroyed. Nothing could be done. The boys' sleeping pavilion collapsed, along with most other buildings, which were buried under lava and debris. Not much remained of the Water Castle.

This was yet another story, lost in the mist of time. I told it to you to make a point, not to make you sad. Do not be sad. We were born and lived a short, but meaningful, storybook life. In truth, our mother never cared about us until we were gone. We brothers lived together in love and companionship. We created a bond that will carry through eternity—a bond that can never be broken. Most importantly, we accomplished our mission. We came as a gift to our mother; because we lived and because of our deaths, she was given a significant opportunity to learn about love and the importance of human relationships.

Our mother survived, and she lived into old age, giving her many years. Like every other person who miraculously survived, she was dramatically changed forever. She did not return to the palace. She never danced again. She worked with the many children who were orphaned and would have starved in the aftermath. She never returned to the village of her childhood because it no longer existed.

Kaka returned to her when the earth stopped shaking and the ash cleared from the sky.

11
Moving Forward

LITERALLY AND FIGURATIVELY, I was putting my life in storage. The opportunity to work and study in Japan for a year was a dream come true. But there was a lot holding me fast. The planned museum projects might never happen, and despite my attempts to tie up loose ends, I was leaving much unfinished. The Board of Directors graciously assured me they would welcome me back—but I never backtracked in my life. It was a good option to have, but it was doubtful I'd return. That's just me.

I had mixed feelings about leaving friends and family—particularly family. Brad was the most supportive; Becka fumed, making an already emotional situation more difficult; Stan was behind the scenes but not involved. I felt this move might be best for both of us. Jake seemed confused, acting strangely distant and withdrawn.

Brad was helping me with the packing, deciding what would go in the garage sale and what would go into storage. I was taking very little—clothing and professional materials, some personal items, that's all. A letter from my English-speaking sponsor said that getting books in English was a problem. She gave me tips on what to bring and cautioned that my room was quite small. Everything I was taking would be locked in the guest bathroom so the packers couldn't mistakenly carry it off. I was reminded of a friend whose purse had gotten packed during a move, and so it went into storage.

Brad, working from the kitchen, shouted, "Mom, what's this pile of stuff here on the island with my name on it? It's a grey box with other stuff stacked on it."

"Yes honey, that's not to be packed. That pile is all for you. Put it in your car. The grey box is full of old family photos. The other stuff is some of my personal papers you might need, genealogy research I've accumulated, and miscellaneous stuff I don't feel comfortable putting in storage. Please hang on to it. Some day when I retire, I may write the family history. And there's a bigger box sitting on the floor right next to the counter with your name on it. Do you see it? That's silverware and other valuables I couldn't fit in the safety deposit box. There's also a signature card for the bank. You need to sign it so you can get into the safety deposit, if necessary," I said.

"Okay, Mom, I see all that, but what's this manila folder marked 'Saraswati,' that has my name on it? That's not family history." He came into the den where I was working, waving the folder of short stories.

"No, Brad, not exactly. Those are stories I finished recently; they're based on our trip to the Far East. I'd be interested to know what you think of it. It's about reincarnation. There's another story entitled 'Lavender Jade' in there, too. It happened around 650 AD."

He shook his head, saying, "Mom, I don't know how you have time to write a story in the midst of all this—this upheaval."

"To tell you the truth, I don't know either, Brad. When an idea comes to me now, I just sit right down and get it on paper. It's really quite strange. I have learned somehow to just go with this. I'm embarrassed to admit it, but now I simply overlook chores and things I used to think important. I've noticed that in some weird way, it's the mundane, run of the mill details of living that takes over a person's life. These things are still important, but my priorities have changed, or maybe I should say evolved. And, too, I suppose its sounds cold but for the first time in my life, I have time for myself. You know, Brad, a professional woman, with a husband and children, has little or no time for herself—at least that's the way I've lived my life up until now. I don't have any regrets, and I love you all. Despite my interlude for writing a poem or two, it seems everything is getting done. Thanks for your help, honey. I can't believe that in less than a week, I'm off to Japan. I hope I'm ready. I hope I'll have all this mess sorted out by then," I said.

"Oh, you're going to be ready—or not. I'm taking you to the airport!" he said.

I gave him a kiss on the check, as he said, "All the kitchen cabinets and drawers are empty and clean."

"You're a peach, Brad. I don't know what I would do without you. You're gonna make some lucky girl a good husband," I teased.

12
Japan

I EXITED NARITA CUSTOMS into a sea of Japanese people. Two diminutive Japanese women approached me. I was honored but awkward when they introduced themselves and graciously bowed deeply. I returned a feeble bow. Exhausted and overwhelmed, my eyes burned from lack of sleep, the time change, and the mid-afternoon sunlight. They took over pushing the cart laden with my heavy luggage with ease. Admiring the stunning bouquet of flowers they'd presented to me when I got off the plane, I followed them on the marked sidewalk across the busy street to a parking lot and the awaiting driver.

Usually only a two-hour drive, they said, "It will take longer because today is Respect for the Aged Day, a national holiday." They tell me, "Traffic is very heavy because everyone in Japan is visiting parents and grandparents." Three hours later, we were still on the downtown Tokyo expressway in unbelievable backup traffic—inching along, then coming to a total stop. I was fascinated by the cityscape but regretfully; jet lag caused me to doze off. I woke up embarrassed, apologized, and fought to stay awake before I dozed off again. They smiled, said they understood, and again apologized for the traffic.

Conversation was limited because I spoke no Japanese. I saw no signs in English, only Japanese characters. Now I wondered how I would manage. I had a moment of sheer panic. Why hadn't I thought about this before? This was folly. How would I teach? How would I make myself understood? All of a sudden, there was something almost incongruous about American Indian Art and Japan, and I wondered how I could make it relevant. My escorts said it wasn't a problem. "*Daijobu*," no problem, they said.

It was 11 p.m. when I finally settled into my dormitory room. More than thirty-five hours of travel door to door. If my escorts were tired, too, they didn't acknowledge it. They were very kind. They helped me with the luggage. They provided a packet with essential toiletries, a caddy with loose green tea, a petite china cup, lidded with a filter, and a basket with individually wrapped biscuits and sesame seed crackers, bananas, and persimmons. The older of the two left two triangular shaped, seaweed-wrapped rice cakes with bits of mushroom she'd prepared for the trip, but which we had not eaten. She tied them in a neat bundle with a lovely piece of silk.

Before leaving, they wrote their phone numbers down and showed me the lavatory and a miniscule kitchenette near my room. On the way into the building, they had pointed out the pay phone. They told me my sponsor would come and take me to lunch at noon the next day.

I was awakened out of a deep sleep by a tapping on the door. Confused for the moment by my surroundings, I realized that it was noon in Japan. Groggy and in my pajamas, I went to the door and apologized for not being ready. My sponsor, a British lady, brought hot coffee in little cans, some sausages, and fried egg sandwiches she'd made, along with clothes hangers. I apologized again.

She said, "No apologies are necessary. It's perfectly understandable." She helped me unpack and sat with me as I fumbled around organizing my personal belongings.

I was thinking, *She's been through this before.*

She suggested I relax and just take it easy, reminding me that it was Sunday and there was nothing that had to be done.

I'd lost a day.

I needed to shower, and wanted to call home, but it was after midnight at home.

My sponsor said, "I'll come back for you around five o'clock. We'll have an early supper at a little noodle shop nearby. By your bedtime, it will be early morning in Oklahoma. I'll show you how to use the pay phone then." When she was about to leave, she turned around and added, "As hard as it may be, try to stay awake all day. Your days and nights are going to be mixed up for quite a while. Do as you want, but you'll understand this when you wake up at 2 a.m. wanting a hamburger."

After she left, I cried. I really missed the kids and wanted to talk to Brad, and I wanted to talk to him now! It was beyond frustrating. It was maddening not having the convenience of a phone in my room. I felt ridiculous not knowing how to read or use the Japanese pay phone. Independent by nature, reality was beginning to set in—I was in Japan, and life was going to be different, very different.

I pulled myself together and went down the hall for a shower, all the while questioning why I would exchange my life of convenience for a dormitory situation, in which I was now wasting a lot of time just trying to figure out how to use hot and cold faucets. Habits and routines built in a lifetime were useless. I felt I was not functioning well, but fortunately there was no one around to watch me fumble.

When I got back to my room, without warning I cried again. I was way out of my comfort zone and all out of courage. How would I be able to live a year in this tiny space? Life for me had been very easy for a long time. Things had changed. I dismissed my tears as over tiredness; it was too soon to be homesick.

I looked at the coins on the little desk. Pushing them around and turning them over, I had no idea which or how many might be required for the pay phone. What an inconvenience not having a phone in my room! With consideration for the time change, I realized that calling home late at night or early in the morning while standing outside in public was going be a real bummer. How could I keep in contact?

I sat down and drained the can labeled "Royal Afternoon Milk Tea" my sponsor had left for me. Good stuff. I turned the can around to check the calories. Not a word in English. It was sinking in that rote, mundane tasks were going to be a learning experience.

Later in the dark, cozy ambiance of the noodle shop, a few tears leaked out. My sponsor reassured me, "You can expect more teary moments in the future. Don't worry about it. It happens to everyone. Consider it normal. Tears come out of the blue, apparently for no reason. I experienced it."

Things went surprisingly well. Everyone I met on campus was extremely gracious and courteous. They were patient with me and punctual. I realized I was dependent on the kindness of strangers. Therefore, Japan was a good place to be. There was a strong sense of order and decorum in this society. There was a protocol for everything, even for gift giving. Sometimes I missed these nuances. I saw that I had a lot to learn.

In our culture, we openly and easily express our disapproval or raise our voice in anger. That was okay there, but it would be rude in Japan. Rudeness and bad manners were unacceptable. Then there was the appropriateness of clothing relative to a woman's age. I chose the darker or somber colors in my wardrobe, now, leaving pink, pastels, and brightly colored clothes hanging in the closet. Those would be deemed not suitable for a person of my position and age. I felt the need to modify my behavior and speak softer, also. There were many adjustments to be made, but overall I was fascinated and keen to learn their ways.

The overwhelming numbers of people interested in the Native American Indian culture surprised me. In anticipation of unforeseen requirements, I brought hundreds of pottery, basketry, and textile slides with me, so I had plenty of resources to prepare or configure a class or seminar as needed. The evening lecture series was a huge success and was always filled to capacity with people coming from museums and other universities. At the request of the school, I added a presentation on "Painters of the American Southwest."

Communication was not easy; technical terms were a major source of frustration. Working with graduate students, we prepared bilingual handouts and viewgraphs, listing useful terms that supported classes and the lectures. Technical papers I had previously written were being translated. Esoteric terms were even more difficult. I was constantly researching or studying, looking for answers.

I concluded I needed another lifetime to gain an understanding of this culture and their language

Months passed and just as I was about to adjust to my Spartan, frustrating, and intolerable living situation, things improved. It was a mini-miracle. I had given up; I just ceased to struggle against the frustrations and accepted the language and cultural barriers as a test. Indeed, I was tested! Anyhow, I was notified that a suite with a private bath was available for me, if I wanted it. If I wanted it! Absolutely, I wanted it! After that move, things improved exponentially. I had telephone service in my room. I had more space to spread out. My contract had been extended.

Once the telephone was installed, although hampered by the time change, I was better able to keep in touch with Brad and Becka. When cut off and not hearing their voices, I had teary, depressed moments. I missed my former friends and co-workers.

I called Rae a few times to say "Hi." I asked her if she might be able to "pick up on" some of the people around me. I asked her about Jake.

Her words were, "It seems he's 'stuck' here. He came here for you, but now he's just 'stuck' here. He feels like you abandoned him."

Rae's information was disconcerting. For days, I pondered what she'd said and what she meant. I wrote Jake several letters and sent photos. He wrote once. Even if he and I were as close and compatible as "soul mates," what was I supposed to do about that? People came in and out of my life all the time; furthermore, I was here in Japan, and he was in the States. "He came here for you," she'd said. Why? What did that mean? Did he have some karmic obligation to me—or I to him? Often, I didn't understand what Rae had to say, but there was a karmic implication in her words.

For me, I was settled with the reincarnation theory. It explained our comfortable synergistic relationship in which I started a sentence and he finished it. Somehow this unusual compatibility triggered an awakening of sorts in me. Real life events and my dreams confirmed it. I had been given new knowledge, and I saw myself in a new light. I accepted the premise that I'd had various roles and relationships in the distant past with this stranger who had simply walked into my life—for a brief period of time.

I had no doubt the Ancient Echoes series of poems came out of my subconscious as a result of knowing Jake. The things that happened as a result of being around him somehow caused me to examine the meaning of life—and death—more closely. Even if there was no proof positive, I was certain that some part of Jake and I knew each other before.

I came back to Rae's puzzling words: "He came here for you." It provoked many question. Why? Who sent him? Why me? What had been accomplished? Why "here" and not someplace else? Why at that point in time?

Our meeting had not been happenstance; of that, I was certain. Indeed, it might well have been worked out somewhere as part of the grand scheme of things. Speaking for myself, a great deal of spiritual and mental growth took place. As a result of him coming there, I had a more creative approach to life. I'd venture to say, I was more creative. Coming there was a good thing for me because somehow Jake inspired me. He was my muse.

13
Enn

A DAY OFF TO just enjoy "being." I took my camera bag and water bottle and headed to one of my favorite shrines, a train ride and a long walk, about forty-five minutes away. I bought a snack when I got off the train and squeezed it into my camera bag. I was getting a late start.

I climbed a steep, paved road with a retaining wall on one side and a dangerous drop-off to the street on the other. I reached the very old and worn stone slab stairs, beyond which I passed through the *torii* gates. Probably no one would be there. I saw a priest sometimes and nodded to him. Sometimes I got a glimpse of his wife, but she scurried away. Rarely had I seen anyone else.

Today, as I was taking the dipper in my hand at the dragon spouting water, I noticed a man, in penny loafers, khaki pants, and a light blue shirt with a button down collar going into what I decided was the priest's home.

My eyes scanned the grounds. I had relatively no understanding of Shintoism or Buddhism, but I went to the shrine, dropped some coins in the box, and bowed my head in respect. I was certain they could use the money for upkeep. Then I took a photo of a large bronze bell and the statue of Ippen, nearby. The peace and quietude about this place spoke to me on a deep level. I was comfortable in this *wabi* space. I felt safe and at home walking here, alone.

Today, I wanted to take photos of the many lichen encrusted Buddhist statues of Jizo in the cemetery around back. They were o-*jizo-san* according to the woman who had first brought me here— that's all I knew, except that they were photo worthy. Why some of them had little red bibs I didn't understand yet, but I intended to find out.

I walked down a broad path bordering a section with newer "graves," which were small, crypt-like structures. An American would consider this the equivalent of a family plot. I walked among the sites, which likely held remains—ashes—not burials. I looked at the many items left for the deceased: withered flowers, silk flowers, a can of Asahi beer, a small sake bottle, burned incense, many sake cups, and some kind of "wooden sticks" left by the priest. Crowded together but well kept, I shot a few pictures and thought about the items people had left for their departed relatives. I walked back out to the main path and stopped to photograph a tidy "family plot," when the man in the blue shirt came in sight. Respectfully, I waited for him to pass before proceeding. He stopped next to me. Inquiringly, I looked up. He was handsome, well built. I judged him to be younger than myself. He said, "Aha, I see you have met my papa and grandpapa."

I said, "Oh, excuse me." I was flustered and somewhat embarrassed. I quickly snapped the lens cap on my camera and opened the camera bag to put it away. In order to make room for the camera, I pulled out the *mochi* I'd bought earlier.

"Oh, and I see you've brought my grandmother some *mochi*. However did you know it was her favorite? I should say, this is providence," he continued.

I wasn't sure what to say. It seemed he was joking with me.

"American?" he asked, raising his eyebrows.

"Yes," I replied.

Then he went on. "Seriously, my grandmother loved *mochi*. She made it herself. Well, I should say it was a family effort. You know, there is a great amount of pounding necessary to get rice into that gelatinous consistency. It brings back fond memories of my childhood. I should have thought to bring her some myself. As it is, I only brought this tiny bottle of scotch from the airline for my father. He did drink sake, but he and I had some interesting conversation over a scotch and soda. Next time, I will remember the *mochi*."

"Well, if you think it appropriate, I would be happy to share this *mochi* with your grandmother. I doubt it's up to her homemade standard, but maybe it would do." I volunteered the *mochi*.

He turned and walked to the other side of the path and searched among the fallen maple leaves. He came back with a large, leather-hard, bronze-colored leaf. He took one *mochi* politely from the package and placed it on the leaf. Then said, "Seeing we have none, this will be a perfect small plate." He carefully carried it over to a ledge of the marble marker and placed it there, saying to me, "Thank you very much."

"You are quite welcome," I said. "I enjoyed meeting you. I'll go on now and give you some privacy." We parted with a smile and deep nod. I continued on the path, thinking his English had been flawless.

I took a number of Jizo photos, as I had planned. Decent light for shooting was rapidly going, but I took my time shooting a half moon bridge at the back of the property. Then I decided to head back to the train station. In order not to retrace my steps, I continued around, passing the priest's house. I did not expect to see "button down collar guy" again.

Just past the Shrine, our paths nearly converged. We nodded and continued to walk. I was not far ahead of him, but when I came to some very old tombstones and markers, I stopped. I had been curious about this group of twenty or more stones, lined up in rows. Some were mossy; the three in the front were large, narrow, flat, and irregular in shape and about five feet tall. The words carved were still legible, despite their age.

When he reached me, I said, "*Sumimasen* (excuse me), I have been curious about these stones markers for some time. Could you read the inscription on this large one for me? I mean, could you translate it for me?"

His eyes scanned the calligraphic-like incising. Then he said, "No, I can't. Sorry. And, I am not sure there is anybody in all of Japan that could. These stones are very old. No, they are ancient. I can tell you, they were deliberately grouped together in rows like this. Some could be from these grounds we stand on, but they also could have been brought here from the surrounding area sometime in years past. You see how this section of ground is raised a foot or so higher than the path? I think you would say they were put here for safekeeping. But as to what they say, that would test the scholars. I can assure you they go back into antiquity. Hmm, lost in the mist of time."

I almost gasped when he said, "Lost in the mist of time." He'd blithely used the very words I had used as the title of my last story. I maintained my composure and didn't mention it, as we walked on. Was that a coincidence?

I said, "They are beautiful in and of themselves, works of art. I've photographed them several times, but you see how dense the foliage is here. The trees hardly let in any light. The dampness of the place is perfect for growing moss. I love moss, but it is hard to photograph. One photo I took here was rather eerie. When it was developed, there was a shadow of me on the stone, but I didn't notice the shadow when I took the photo."

We walked side by side, not conversing. When we got to the gates, he said, "Since you are interested in these matters, you will notice that we have here two *torii's*. The red one is Buddhist, the natural wooden one is Shinto." He went on to explain. "Shintoism goes back to ancient Japan, long before Buddhism arrived from China. Down through history, there have been many what could be called power struggles between the two, often connected to the leader of that generation. Making things more interesting, we also had Confucianism and Taoism issues in the mix. About the time of the Meiji Reformation, the politicians told them, to use your vernacular, to 'knock it off' and kindly 'get it together.' So here we have two *torii's*. This could be the idea of Ippen himself or the result of a compromise. I think you would find Ippen interesting reading."

On the way to the train station, we passed one of my favorite restaurants, where a good "set" meal cost about $10. I pointed it out and told him that I went there often. He said it was one of a chain and suggested we stop, if I was ready for dinner.

Our meals came. We both said, *itadakimasu*, which I understood to be the blessing. He repeated it again, saying, "I wonder if you know the full meaning of *itadakimas*? Literally it means 'I will receive.' More fully it means, I will accept with joy and gratitude your life, the life of each grain of rice we have here, or that mushroom, or each of those tiny shrimp on your plate. I will accept your life. I will have your life."

Obviously university educated and experienced by travel, his English was perfect. Our conversation flowed easily, except occasionally when one of us tripped over a word.

I had learned that the Japanese love to learn our slang or recently coined phrases. If I dropped one, it required a long explanation until they "got it."

We sat talking until many families had come and gone. If the waitress was disenchanted by the multiple times she warmed our tea, she didn't acknowledge it. Now it was dark outside, and two rows of large white lanterns hanging over the dark wooden booths were aglow. They were reflected in the windows that surrounded the restaurant on three sides, repeating over and over again into infinity. I thought there was something magical about it and pointed it out.

He said, "I never would have noticed. This has been a pleasant coincidence."

To which I instantly, but matter-of-factly replied, "I don't believe in coincidences."

He smiled and said, "Neither do I. This is *enn*."

To which I said, "I don't know the word *enn*."

He said, "I'll try to explain. *Enn* is an important esoteric concept in human relationships in our culture. Understand there is always the element of fate in *enn*. You could say that when the sleeves of two people brush together in the marketplace that is *enn*, and *enn* always has significance. It's true that some Japanese words have evolved over time, and some might translate *enn* to mean circle. Others might say it's how we are all connected."

He paused momentarily, and then he went on. "As I said, *enn* always involves fate. I'll give you an example. I have needed to come here for a long while, but couldn't get away from work. Then, on the spur of the moment, I chose today to take care of my overdue business with the priest. Then I meet an American woman, who just happens to have *mochi*, grandmother's favorite, photographing the family grave. This is *enn*."

164

When he finished, I said, "Thank you very much for explaining that. I will be grateful forever more."

He said, "Really?"

I said, "Yes, really. I'm thinking there is no such concept or word in English. I am happy to know this word. Aside from our *enn* meeting, today, *enn* explains a question about relationships that's been puzzling me for quite some time."

As we finished our meal, I was thinking, *Wow, this total stranger has just given me an answer I might never have found in life.*

He gave me his business card and told me that if I ever needed anything while in his country, to call him. "In consideration for you having brought *mochi* to my grandmother, it would be my *onn*, not to be confused with *enn*. *Onn* translates as 'my pleasure' or 'in repayment for a debt.' So, for you having given *mochi* to my grandmother, it would be my pleasure to assist you."

I wrote on the back of an old business card from the States the time, date, and lecture room for my next presentation. It was very bad form in Japan not to have a proper business card, but I held no expectation and considered it merely an exchange of pleasantries. When we said our goodbyes at the train station, I told him what a pleasure it was to have met him and how much I appreciated him for educating me. Five hours had passed quickly, and I felt a lifelong friend was walking away. For some inexplicable reason, I turned around to wave but he had vanished into the crowd.

On the evening of the Hopi Culture and Kachina Dolls presentation, every seat was filled and there were ten or more people standing at the back of the auditorium. One was my friend from the Ippen Shrine. I told my graduate assistant Shizuko that he was my guest and that I couldn't begin until he was seated.

After the event, Shizuko came to me, saying, "Your guest asked me to tell you he enjoyed the evening and learned a lot; and, *sensei*, he asked me to give you this note." She bowed slightly and presented the note to me with two hands. I thanked her and slipped it into my purse.

The note had been written neatly, earlier, and not on the spur of the moment; the fine parchment and envelope had a faint fragrance reminiscent of the temple. It said, "I must go to Kyoto on business for a few days later this month. I will be there from the 16 - 27. Do you have some time during that week? I would like to show you Kinkaku-ji Temple. This is the Golden Pavilion you see on travel posters, and the famous Ryoan-ji Temple. For a lady who loves gardens and temples as you do, Kyoto is not to be missed. For a lady enchanted by moss, I would like to take you to Saiho-ji Temple. Special permission is required there, but I will arrange it. The *sabi* Saihoji has more than 100 types of moss. Please call me at the office if you are available. If I am not there, ask for Michiko, my private secretary. Give her dates, and she will make your reservation. There is a *ryokan* I think you might like. If you prefer, there is a Holiday Inn. Michiko will also make a reservation for you on the Shinkansen. Bring your camera. Signed Takahashi."

14
Kunoichi - Ninja Girl

INSIDIOUSLY AND GHOSTLIKE, a stinking smoke was permeating the woods. Creeping into my woodland domain along the floor of the forest, I faintly smelled it; then I saw it, dropped my traps, and hurried home. A gang of filthy marauders was riding away fast. They were in high spirits, laughing and shouting and swinging many of my chickens by their legs. The vilest among them squeezed the neck of my pet duck in his filthy fists. I dropped into the brush at the tree line and froze, terrified and enraged all at once.

The renegades cut down my father and mother coming out of the rice fields, then burned our farmhouse and the out buildings. They destroyed the livestock and everything they couldn't carry away. I was nine years old at the time. Luckily, or unluckily, I had been playing, checking my traps, and snaring birds that morning. I'd escaped the slaughter, but my brother perished at their hands.

Maybe it was fright, or maybe something quite different that stopped me from running into the clearing, but to this day I carry the memory of my cowardice. Our house was on fire, rapidly burning to the ground, yet I cowered, shaking and sobbing, overcome by fear. Later that day, I found the remains of my little brother Kenji in the smoldering embers.

Drained of all inner and physical strength, and quivering uncontrollably, I stayed hidden there for hours. That evening, I saw a flock of ominous black birds circling in the sky. I went to my father and mother and attempted to move them. Overwrought, I was not sure what to do in this situation. My mother's body was partially in the paddy, sodden and too weighty, but I knew I must get her out.

I couldn't lift her fully, so I struggled to drag her on to the dike, pulling until I couldn't move her any further. Finally, I collapsed on her, sobbing and heaving.

I can't tell you in detail how they were murdered because the horror is blocked from my waking memory. However, I can tell you that I meticulously covered every part of their bodies and every drop of their blood with rocks, which I struggled to carry from a low wall near the house and stones from the stream. Only then did the crows stop screaming and circling.

I washed in the stream, and then fell upon the burial mounds that I'd created for the two who had created me and my beloved brother. I must have sat there next to them for several days, exposed to the night air, the rain, and the sun. It was the return of the birds that pulled me from the place where my mind had escaped. They circled and swooped above me. Weakened and overcome by it all, I gathered my strength and rose, and without looking back, I headed into the woods and away from the only place I had known as home. The darkness swallowed me.

It was a starless night. Two Shinto priests huddled against the cold inside a thatched wooden hut, talking quietly at the fireside and sipping the last vestiges of the green tea leaves. The glowing embers in the square fire pit cast light and shadow alternately around the space, against the walls and up into the rafters. An iron kettle of water hung from a hook above the fire. The moisture rising and swirling from the spout emitted steam that heated the cold air inside the room.

The moment was disturbed by the swoosh-of-a-sound as the worn and bedraggled youngster collapsed dully against the sliding door. The frail body was so light it barely moved the dust on the narrow porch of the hut at a small, secluded mountaintop Shinto Shrine that included several detached structures. The child lay unconscious in an unknown place, all alone in the world.

The priests, exchanging glances, remained perfectly still. When after a few minutes they heard nothing more, Yoshio, the younger of the two, set his teacup down and rose quietly. Hardly disturbing the air, he took several short steps to the door and listened. Nothing. He waited and listened for a while longer. Silence.

He slid the door open slowly but with difficulty as a small bundle of humanity slumped partially across the threshold and fell into the room. The young priest drew back in astonishment. Masaaki, the older of the two, quickly rose and came to his aid.

Visually they examined the lifeless body for injuries and signs of life. The body of a young child lay in the doorway. Looking at the emaciated form, Masaaki said, "Starved." He lifted the child gently, gathering the cold and soaking wet mass in his arms. With his right hand he unfastened his cloak, and with one motion took it off and wrapped it completely around the wet bundle. Coming across the small room, he carefully laid the child on the tatami close to the fire.

Yoshio's mind began to chatter; he scurried around, nervously rummaging among their meager belongings for a cup. He sprinkled a few dried herbs from a tiny canister into the cup. Carefully taking the water kettle from the hook over the fading embers, he glanced at his teacher, sensei Masaaki, who was cautiously peeling away the wet clothing from the child. Yoshio asked, "Sensei, I think we will need a greater fire for this night, don't you?"

Moments earlier, the two men had been about ready to retire for the night and the coals had been banked. A fire maintained like this would have retained sufficient heat for the small room, with some coals remaining alive until morning. Their futons had been laid out ready for sleep in opposite corners from where they had been sitting.

Masaaki was hardly aware of Yoshio's question, for a grave look had covered his already stoic face. Yoshio could not see it in the dim light. Under stress, Yoshio tended to scurry around and talk to himself, so Masaaki generally ignored him. Under normal circumstances, Masaaki and Yoshio did not verbally communicate about the mundane. In fact, Masaaki no longer dealt with the mundane. However, about spirit, about deities (*kami*), about the path, or about the way to the Godhead, they spent their days immersed in these thoughts.

Sensei Masaaki expected Yoshio to go about his day without much conversation. They had a routine, they had their rituals, and they had to attend to the deities of the shrine. They went through each day and every evening very much in silence—chanting and meditating were the ways of the sect.

The child Yoshio, an orphan, had entered the order. His dithering ways had never diminished or abated in the nearly twenty years that Masaaki had known him. At some point very early on, Masaaki recognized that appearing befuddled was simply a part of who Yoshio was. He realized that this would not be outgrown, and perhaps it was part of his charm. Yoshio's good qualities far outweighed the dithering aspect, and as Masaaki advanced in years, he realized that Yoshio was a blessing. In some ways, he had accepted him as the son he never had. Of course Masaaki was composed, practically to a fault. He would have retained his poise, dignity, and solemnity if a star had fallen from the sky and landed on the roof. Yoshio, being nonplussed, was no call to action on his part; Yoshio did not disturb his calm disposition in the least.

Ignored, Yoshio stood looking at the two. This event had thrown him out of kilter. His question had gone unanswered. He realized it was an unnecessary question, and he already knew the answer. His sensei looked up and absentmindedly said, "*Nani?*" (*What?*)

Masaaki gathered the child in his arms to give extra warmth. Yoshio found himself at his wits end, nervous, and distressed as he looked at the two. His uncertainty manifested as a quasi-agitated state. Not knowing how to proceed, he was almost unhinged, his mind sending him in too many directions at once. *I think we need more water and a greater fire for the night,* he thought, almost out loud. Then quickly and lightly he moved across the old, originally roughhewn wooden floorboards, now burnished and smooth, stepping outside into the crisp, cold night air.

First he went to get fuel. He located wood, dried animal dung, and miscellaneous pieces of coal; he selected a fairly substantial piece of hard wood. This piece was one he had been saving for the winter. It would burn hotter and longer that the others. It would have to be sacrificed in view of the circumstances. He sent out a prayer of thanks for the log, and a second prayer that another would be found to replace it before winter set in.

Laying this upon the *agarikamachi,* the large stone used as a stepping up place to the narrow porch on the hut, he picked up the largest water-carrying gourd and vanished along a trail that led into the woods. He knew the trail by heart, but it was tricky in the darkness. Moving swiftly but cautiously, questions formed in his mind. Where had this youngster come from, and how had he found his way to their hut? Was he alone? Were there others? Was he being pursued? Were he, Masaaki, and the child in danger? He struggled to push the questions out of his mind and focus his thoughts on prayers of protection.

Nonetheless, as he approached the water collecting pool, he advanced with extra caution. It was a secluded spot, but the moon had risen and the moonlight lit up the area like a beacon. Normally, the extra light would have been welcomed, but tonight was not an ordinary night.

There could be bandits in the woods. Although their hut was remote and secured from intruders by its design and choice of location, anything was possible. Someone could stumble upon their hut. Someone could detect the smell of smoke from their fire. Yes, it was certainly possible; after all, the boy had found them. It seemed wise to be extra careful, someone could have followed him.

A bamboo pipe jutted out over the pool, directing a steady stream of fresh water to gather into a shallow pool before falling below into a larger thermal pool, roughly eight feet in diameter. The lower pool was used for bathing and washing. Although it was a cold night, the water looked inviting in the moonlight as a nebulous mist hovered above it. Masaaki and an itinerant monk named Gao had built this watering place several years earlier. There was a mystical quality about it, enchantingly beautiful and refreshing in all seasons.

Masaaki himself had told him that Gao was not of the Shinto faith and that most likely he was a Taoist wizard, and Chinese at that. Masaaki also said that Gao had been with him for several years and that, just as suddenly as he had arrived—or materialized—in front of Masaaki while he was gathering roots and herbs in the forest one day, so, too he had vanished.

Masaaki said Gao had worked off and on, digging, rearranging vegetation, moving rocks and earth. Gao said there wasn't really much work to it. Just needed to rearrange "a few of earth's elements," as he put it. He had created a sylvan glade that was practical and pleasurable. It was nature at its best.

The place was well hidden, or disguised. It was only about 300 meters up a steep embankment above a seldom-used trail. Still further up the mountain was the original water source. There was not a clue to this water source, which might have attracted interest from those traveling the road. Gao had diverted and cleverly hidden the water source under ground and carefully dispersed the run off so that it was unlikely to be found by anyone. Furthermore, Masaaki and Yoshio were always careful to circumnavigate this area, leaving the dense vegetation undisturbed, primeval. Yoshio felt it was a magical place and whenever Masaaki talked about Gao and described how the place had been originally, it seemed to him that Gao had used magic to create it.

Masaaki said that he enjoyed Gao's company and their talks immensely, except when he played "the disappearing game." That's what he called it, for sometimes they would be walking and talking in the woods and the next thing you know, Gao had vanished. He would turn to say something but find himself alone. The illusive Gao was here one moment and gone the next. Later he would reappear further up the trail, or he'd be up in a tree with his legs and feet dangling from a branch. Masaaki said at first he thought Gao's disappearing act was amusing, but he later found it irritating—certainly not conducive to good conversation.

Sensei Masaaki said Gao was a very clever fellow—a wizard if ever there was one. He said Gao was no drain on food supplies; he ate little or nothing and frequently collected choice fruits and nuts from the treetops. Masaaki described him as sprightly, almost hairless except for a straggly little silvery-looking beard. Gao never divulged his age and given that he rarely ate food, he thought Gao might be able to survive on air. Although Masaaki said so that seemed absolutely impossible to me.

Masaaki said that Gao's tree climbing escapades were most unusual but even more fascinating was to observe him in meditation. He said it was most amazing how Gao would sit in profound silence outdoors for days on end. Dust and dirt would collect on him. All manner of small animals, squirrels, rabbits, mice, and chipmunks would simply gather round and watch him. Birds would light on his shoulders; little mice would walk across his bony legs as though they were sticks of dried wood. He sat through rain and snow unmoved, motionless, and unaffected.

Several times Yoshio thought sensei was playing a game with him. The stories of Gao were quite unbelievable. Yet there was this pool, and it was a magical pool, and it was unlikely that the hermit priest, his sensei, had built it himself. Masaaki had little physical strength. His strength was in spiritual matters. Of this Yoshio was quite sure. Indeed, this is why Yoshio followed Masaaki a year after he left the monastery.

Masaaki was a highly respected priest in Nara, when by choice he'd slipped from prominence. He was widely acclaimed as a highly disciplined and revered teacher. For more than forty years, he had built up a thriving monastery, which enjoyed the support of many prominent families, including royalty. He was renowned as a medium with great powers who had the ability to channel communication between the earthly and spiritual worlds. Many sought his guidance.

Over the years, as the monastery grew and prospered, conflicts and infighting increased among the various factions, creating disharmony, which eventually Masaaki could not abide. Perhaps, owing to his age, or simply because he grew tired of the politics, he laid aside his life's work and left in search of inner peace. It is taught that all things are temporary and everything changes. Indeed this is so.

By the time Yoshio followed him, the monastery was in the midst of turmoil and controversy. It became apparent that it was Masaaki, his work, and his character that had attracted resources to the monastery. When he left, major benefactors turned their backs with devastating results. The loss of support grew more evident as each day passed. The bickering grew worse. Yoshio could not thrive in the increasing political chaos. Eighteen months after Masaaki left, Yoshio went in search of him. He found the recluse in a stained, tattered robe in what one would clearly define as a hovel. Over time, the dilapidated shrine had been transformed into a hermitage.

Neglected, the single room shrine, called a *honden* in Japanese, the water basin, and the entrance to the shrine had fallen into ruin. Masaaki, with Yoshio's help, repaired the hut so they had a livable space. A new dipper was placed next to the ancient stone water basin and after several days of digging and channeling, the water was again redirected into the basin. Little by little, the formerly deserted, out-of-the-way Shinto Shrine was built up and when you walked through the *torii* gate, you knew at once you had crossed from the profane to the sacred.

This isolation was precisely what Masaaki wanted at this stage of life. Being a man of integrity he could easily have attracted money, even to this location, but desires and ambitions he had as a younger man had been overcome by wisdom and age. Here in this mountain dwelling, he practiced the Shinto rituals, offering the first fruits—though no one came. Here he was most touched by the spirit of the wind, the rain, the trees, and all of nature that he knew intimately in childhood. Here with few worldly distractions he was best in touch with the deities of heaven and earth, honored as *kami*.

Kami is inexplicable. It is the unknowable. Trying to explain it is like trying to explain the essence of a mystical or religious experience; it cannot be reduced to words. One can only try. So then, *kami* is the spiritual essence of all things created in the universe, a mountain, a human being, a tree, and a rock. Ancestors are *kami*; therefore, they are worshipped. In Japanese, *kami*, connotes spirit; *kokoro*, connotes soul. If it is awe-inspiring, it is *kami*. If it is outside the ordinary, possessing superior power, it is *kami*. At this particular Shinto Shrine, the mountain itself is *kami*, the mountain itself is the reason this shrine was established in ancient days.

Here Masaaki is the *kannushi*, a holy man considered to be the *kami*-master. Through purification rites he is an intermediary between *kami* and man. He is revered and referred to as *sensei*, teacher. The priest Yoshio is *shinshoku*, responsible for officiating ceremonies and overseeing shrine maintenance. Here in the peace of the *kami* grove, there is a very tangible silent and mystical connection to spirit.

In a relatively short time, Yoshio, Masaaki, and Gao had done much to restore the shrine. Although the roof of the *honden* had remained in tact over the years, water leaks had damaged some of the interior. By what means the roof repairs were accomplished is unclear.

Masaaki told Yoshio that Gao worked on the pool intensively day after day, abounding in energy and never tiring. Though extremely curious, Masaaki never, not once, witnessed how Gao moved the rocks and boulders into place, for they sort of appeared magically when he wasn't there or when his eyes were averted, and that puzzled him.

Nor had he ever witnessed how Gao got up in the trees, for it didn't seem he climbed the trees, as it happened too fast. How he was able to get there so quickly confounded Masaaki, who noted that Gao never had a skinned knee nor a scrape on his body. He told Yoshio he was so mystified by this that for a time he studied the forest looking for vines. He said he had learned a great deal from Gao—but not how to get up to or down from a high tree branch, nor how to move heavy rocks and live vegetation.

When truth was told, Gao fascinated Masaaki. In his heart of hearts, he knew that Gao had attained a degree of spirituality, knowledge, and skills far beyond his own. He felt embarrassed when Gao addressed him as *sensei*. Masaaki never thought of himself as sensei, a teacher, in Gao's presence. Gao's powers were incredible and somewhere beyond reality. Masaaki said he could sit in silence; go into deep meditation for days, even weeks, requiring no food or water, which seemed to make him beyond human.

In his free time, and particularly when Yoshio would go for water, or to bathe, he would wish that Gao would reappear. He imagined Sensei did, too, but time had passed and he never came back.

By the time Yoshio returned to the hut with the water, Masaaki had the child laid out on his cloak next to the fire. He was rubbing the child's hands and arms. "Near death. Near death, but living," sensei said, as he covered him gently.

The tea was still warm and mild. Yoshio handed it to his teacher, who raised the child's sweat-matted head slightly in an attempt to pour a few drops in his mouth. The child did not swallow and the tea, it slid out of his mouth and down the side of his face. His eyelids opened, his eyes rolled back and then closed. At first Yoshio thought the child had died, which caused him to drop to his knees, taking the tea bowl from Masaaki.

Masaaki cradled the youngster's head in his arms. Yoshio could not be sure whether the boy was alive or if he had slipped away. Masaaki was rocking back and forth and chanting. By his words, Yoshio knew that the little bag of bones was clinging to life.

Yoshio was at loose ends but he busied himself at the fire, placing the hard wood log carefully among the embers. He tucked a bit of tinder and some small sticks around it, causing a flurry of flames. It was good and dry and it would easily catch. This log would last the night and would provide more than enough heat for the hut, but given the unusual circumstances, it was needed.

The room grew hotter, even a bit too hot for comfort. He noticed that Masaaki had pulled off the boy's wet clothing and slung it out of his way. It lay in a heap. He had put a pair of two-toed woolen *tabi* on the small feet and wrapped a *hanten*, a quilted sleeping garment, around the little body, all much, much too big. Yoshio picked up the wet clothing and put it in a beat up metal washbasin; it was nasty and needed washing. He set it outside.

Yoshio watched as Masaaki knelt above the small head of the child prone before him. Having stopped chanting, he was now in deep meditation—his eyes closed, arms and hands outstretched over the forlorn little creature. Presently he began to circle the still form, his hands moving rhythmically, channeling healing energy over the length of the fragile body. Having completed his ministrations, he carefully drew the clothing up around the neck and shoulders, and then wrapped a woolen scarf around the tousled little head. Finally, spreading his own cloak over the silent form, he tucked it securely underneath.

Reflecting momentarily, Yoshio could think of nothing more to do. Warm water was in readiness. No need to prepare gruel; the mite couldn't even swallow water that he needed most. Thus, Yoshio picked up the pile of dirty, sodden clothing as he passed silently through the door and on down to the ever-waiting pool. Laundering and musing in the moonlight, Yoshio concluded this must be a rice farmer's child. Maybe a runaway, or perhaps one merely confused who had lost his way in the dense, dark woods. *These clothes are definitely in good condition, carefully and skillfully patched by loving hands, probably his mother. Oh! His parents must be frantic with worry. There is no telling how long he's been lost, nor from whence he came.* Yoshio's thoughts rambled and chattered in the silence. *Surely if there were farming families in this mountainous region their fields would have been visible in the distance,* he reasoned with himself. Then his thoughts leaped backward to his own childhood, orphaned and alone as a child at an early age, but no! He could not, would not dwell on such memories. So he pushed it aside. He could not endure the pain and great sadness upon which they touched, nor the veil of aloneness that haunted him still.

Thankfully, upon returning to the hut, he found the youngster sleeping, and Masaaki sensei, having assumed the lotus position, was meditating in silent transcendence beside the bundled form. Quietly hanging the clothes to dry over the fire pit, he glanced around for something, anything he might need to do, but seeing nothing he sank languidly onto his futon, directly opposite Masaaki sensei for their nightlong vigil.

Yoshio was not without healing powers of his own. He routinely visualized a ball of healing white light at his heart center. Focusing, he deftly moved the light throughout his own body to relieve pain and cure his infrequent illnesses; occasionally, he practiced this ancient healing art on others. Tonight, he had transferred the white ball of healing energy, visualizing its flow along the child's meridians; he sensed blockages and chi disturbances, before reclaiming the ball of light.

He went on, focused in silent prayer, visualizing the child surrounded by healing white light. His inner eye witnessed the light expand to include his beloved teacher—until all three were encircled in its brilliance. His spine straightened even more so, as his body searched for the softest spot on his straw-stuffed futon; and in his best lotus posture, his breathing eased into a rhythm that prepared him to embark on the long night of meditation they would travel. Especially now, he needed to quiet his mind in order to regain his composure, lost so swiftly and unwittingly by lurking memories that stirred unwantedly. Thus, like a river that cascades down a waterfall, he released himself into the engulfing flow of the cosmic consciousness.

The movement of his teacher, who was now kneeling over a convulsing child, whose eyes were wide open, disrupted Yoshio's meditation. Yoshio barely had time to unfold himself as he rose to his feet abruptly, somewhat light headed and befuddled from rising too fast. What to do? What to do? Yes, water for tea. Prepare rice gruel. Yoshio was in a quandary not knowing how to aid Masaaki, who had his hands full with the crisis.

Periodically, the child would shake uncontrollably. Masaaki rocked and calmly stroked the hair away from the comely face, murmuring quietly all the while. He asked Yoshio for a cool, damp cloth, which Yoshio dutifully prepared and wrung dry before handing it to Masaaki. He wiped the precious face and head repeatedly. The cloth picked up dirt and grime but a good long soak was needed. *Sensei* passed the cloth back to Yoshio and asked for another; bathing was accomplished in this manner. Afterward, Masaaki rolled the dear little soul into a tight bundle.

Yoshio began to brew green tea for himself and his teacher, and when the tea bowls and the water were ready, he took the tea to Masaaki, knelt down, and respectfully extended the tea bowl in both hands. Masaaki welcomed the tea. The warmth of the tea bowl radiated heat through his palms to all his fingers, up his arms, and down his spine. Only when Yoshio sat down with both hands cupped around the little hand wrought stoneware vessel did Masaaki take his first sip. He was grateful to Yoshio and slightly bowed his head, respectfully nodding approval.

Although not fully conscious, I began to come into some level of awareness. I had no idea where I was or with whom. I had no recall of time or the events of the past days. There was the sensation of warmth and security; I felt no pain. I think a conscious person would call this state bliss.

I was very warm, and an old man was wiping my face. I glistened in the low morning firelight. Then, turning his attention away from me for the first time, he touched Yoshio lightly on the knee and said, "Yoshio, please hand me that tea bowl. Perhaps she can take some of it." He held my head up and spoke reverently to me as he put it to my lips. I was not afraid of these strangers.

The younger man looked inquiringly at the other. "She? Did you say, she?" The older man, who was holding my head up, smiled at him and said, "Yes, yes I did. This is a girl child." He poured a little tea into my mouth, but again it dribbled down the side of my face. The younger one blotted my chin carefully with his shaking hand. The older one kept murmuring and talking to me so quietly I could not understand what seemed to be words of encouragement. After the third try, I swallowed some. The older one looked up at the younger hopefully and said, with a sigh of relief, "*Ne bashi.* We've crossed a bridge."

"Ah so, a bridge, yes a bridge, but a bridge to where?" said the younger. "A girl changes everything," he said, as he looked around at the austere, barely adequate hut.

I fell into deep sleep, dreams drifting through my mind. Sometimes I trembled uncontrollably. The elder kept watch and securely cradled me, rocking me like a baby. His ministrations permeated with physical and spiritual warmth. My body temperature had improved, yet the trembling continued throughout the morning. He gently coaxed some warm tea into me as the day progressed. Occasionally my eyes rolled open and closed involuntarily, without any sense of recognition.

At one point I peed. He said to the other, this was a good thing. The younger one had the mess to clean up. I soiled their *tatami.* The younger hurriedly fashioned a padded loincloth for me. The elder said, "Her urine is very strong. We have to get more fluids in her." The younger brought fresh water.

Normally the priests did not eat after the noonday meal, but tending to me was time consuming and upset the normal routine. It was late afternoon before the younger had time to prepare a frugal meal of miso, rice, and pickled vegetables. The familiar cooking aromas momentarily aroused my senses. My eyes flickered open in vague recognition. Then once again I lapsed into frightening dreams.

Perhaps the elder noticed a change in my condition. He suggested to the younger that I was nearly starved to death, and he needed to try to get some nourishment into me. He set aside his own meal and asked the younger to cook some rice to a very thin, smooth cream and then dilute it to a liquid.

He rolled a garment up into a neat ball and placed it under my neck. He dipped the end of a small bamboo spoon into the watery rice and barley gruel. Then gently, he pried my mouth open with the spoon. After dipping several times, I responded. Somehow I was able to swallow. It was very slow going, but he was able to get about two spoonfuls down my throat in an hour's time. After that I swallowed some weak tea.

I faded in and out but have a vague recollection that the younger frequently came in and out of the hut, tending the fire and fetching water, rolling up futons and laying them out in preparation for the night. I have a hazy remembrance that they discussed the necessity to maintain another all night's vigil. Delicately the younger one reminded his elder that he, too, needed sleep. He cautiously told him that he had had no sleep for more than twenty-four hours and for his own health, he needed some rest. He suggested that he take the first shift, so the older one could close his eyes first.

The dwelling grew still and silent, except for an occasional snap and spark from the fire and the old man snoring. My sleep was difficult and troubled throughout the night, but somehow in between bad dreams, I knew I had come to a secure place.

In the morning, there was a feather bundle found on the *agari-kamachi*. It was a packet of herbs. It looked like a fetish, wrapped in a fresh, bright green leaf and tied neatly with a vine, a feather tucked under the vine. Yoshio might have stepped on it as he left the hut, but there was an elaborate arrangement of smooth, flat pebbles surrounding it like a campfire. Yoshio called to Masaaki to have a look.

Coming out of the hut for the first time in almost two days, Masaaki looked down on the fetish-like packet and said intuitively, "Gao has been here." Yoshio was wide-eyed with childish delight and began glancing about, craning his neck to look far up into the trees, excited at the possibility of finally meeting Gao. Seeing no one, he asked, "Is this a game?"

"No," responded his teacher, "it's not a game."

Masaaki opened the packet, carefully untying the tidy little bundle. "Herbs for the child," he said.

"How do you know for sure?" Yoshio inquired. Then he wilted in embarrassment and was sorry he had asked because it was one of those questions his sensei would not and did not answer. However, he did give Yoshio precise instructions for handling these medicinal plants, which Yoshio had never seen before.

Although he was hopeful and expectant, Yoshio did not meet Gao, even though he left bundles on the *agarikamachi*, a large stone step up to the hut. Whenever Yoshio went for water, he carefully scanned the woods and tree limbs in hopes of catching a glimpse of him. Yoshio sensed Gao had been at the pool—and rightly so—but he never saw him. When Yoshio found a feather, he was not sure whether it was a coincidence or a playful message from Gao.

Slowly, slowly, day-by-day, I recovered some strength. I learned that I had come to the dwelling place of two Shinto priests. The elder was Masaaki, and the younger was Yoshio. Although from time to time I shook uncontrollably, it was not from fear of them. They were kindly, respectful, and caring.

I couldn't speak or didn't want to, or I'd forgotten how to, I'm not sure. My voice seemed locked in my mind. Sometimes, when the older priest asked me a question, such as where I lived, where I'd come from, or my name or about my family, I would begin to shudder uncontrollably. Eventually, he stopped asking me questions so as not to set off an episode. They didn't ask me, and I didn't speak.

The younger thought I was afraid of something, or possibly might be an abused runaway, however, Masaaki told Yoshio that the only marks on my body were scratches and scrapes from running

181

through the woods. Masaaki told Yoshio that there was no evidence of a beating or abuse, and that he believed I could speak, but that for some reason, because of whatever trauma I'd suffered, I just wouldn't or couldn't speak at this time.

As the days went by, my health began to improve. One day, in my weakened condition, they were supporting me as we walked to the bathing pool. They often spoke to one another as though I was not there. Thinking out loud, Masaaki said, "I wonder how she got here?" Without hesitation I responded, "I was carried over the trees. On the tree tops." Both were surprised at my first words.

"What is your name, child?" Masaaki asked.

"Yuki," I replied.

Masaaki realized immediately that Gao had brought me. Yoshio did not, nor did I.

Yoshio immediately thought I must have come from snow country north of here because "Yuki," means "snow." He questioned himself: *Did she say, "Yuuki," which means "courage?" Probably snow, he mused, but this child will need great courage to face the future.*

Positive glances were exchanged between Masaaki and Yoshio. No further questions were asked that day.

My health returned, and in the rhythm of life with the priests, I flourished. Thus, through childhood and youth, I remained with them and did my utmost to assist and be useful in the basic tasks of fetching water, cooking, and attending to other domestic chores. With simple ease, I roamed beyond the borders of the shrine, and despite my knowing that Masaaki and Yoshio followed a vegetarian diet, my old habit of trapping brought renewed pleasure. Masaaki's expansive heart understood my need for encouragement, and so he indulged me by saying I was clever and ingenious when I showed him the traps I fashioned from materials I found in the woods. And so these two otherwise religiously vegetarian priests partook of meals I prepared with the broth of small animals I caught in my snares, just as my dear family had done. In this way, Yoshio's household chores were lightened. With a heart of compassion, he understood the emotional needs of this little orphan. Thus our lives and dispositions blended well, and my gratitude increased towards these two quite different friends, whose perceptions and sensitivities encouraged my faithfulness to both study and prayer. Even my youthful energy and effervescence was quieted by patient meditation.

Throughout most of the year, I went gathering with Yoshio. He showed me how to identify edible wild mushrooms; dig *gobo*, which is burdock root, and wild potatoes; cut young bamboo shoots; pick wild berries and cherries; and where and when best to collect gingko, chestnuts, and other nuts. He had a small vegetable and herb garden in a clearing behind the shrine. He taught me how to cultivate some plants. We planted several kinds of greens, peas, and cabbages, sweet potatoes, and two types of squash. In late fall, I helped him store certain vegetables. He had dug deep holes angled down into an embankment, lined them with straw, and carefully layered in the root crops, placing straw between them. Some things we pickled in crocks. Whatever food we had, we ate some and we stored some for winter.

Ours was, of course, a meager diet, but we were mostly free of illness. Tracking and trapping rabbits was fun for me in the winter, and the nutrient rich broth fortified us as our food stores diminished.

Yoshio and I did our best to prepare the garden for winter, covering the live shoots with leaves and branches. Yoshio told me the snow was good insulation. During the long winter nights, as the snow piled deeper, my concerns for the garden plot grew until I could not keep my worries to myself, and so I'd ask him if he thought the plants would be okay. He always reassured me, re- minding me that we had done our very best. Despite doing our best, every year when we uncovered the garden in the spring, some things had frozen to death.

Whatever the weather—rain, snow, or sunshine—the priest went to the *honden*, the main hall that enshrined the *kami*, without fail. They had various ceremonies to perform and purification rituals. Wooden plaques called *ema*, bearing wishes and prayers were sometimes posted along with the old, weather-beaten, illegible ones. They chanted mantras there and around the grounds. Along with the priests, in my own way, I assisted them, as they reverently executed the practice of *harai*, airing out the shrine and sweeping away evil spirits.

The grounds were always presentable, should any pilgrims ever come up the mountain, but rarely did they. Sweeping the stone steps at the entrance by the *torii* became my duty. Except during inclement weather, I swept them everyday. When I was given this assignment, the steps were narrow, only about a meter wide. One person at a time could climb them. However, the more I swept, the wider they got. I swept and swept and little by little more of the stone was revealed. Over the passage of time, dirt and gravel and silt had built up at the edges and weeds had taken roots, until the entrance had dwindled to not much more than a footpath. I kept sweeping and clearing and uncovering until a fine natural stairway of flat rocks was unearthed, and the ancient grand entrance to the shrine was revealed.

When I finished, I went to Masaaki and told him I had a surprise for him, but he had to close his eyes. I took his hand and led him down the familiar wooded path, passing the *toro*, an ancient stone lantern created from three rocks. The top rock was ovoid, with a natural hole in the middle for the candle. This was on top of a larger oval shaped rock, which sat upon a round but irregular shaped boulder, which quite probably had been there forever, a part of the mountain. We continued on toward the *torii*, passing the water basin, known as *chozuya* in Japan.

As we stood at the edge of the topmost step of the stone stairway, I told him to open his eyes, flung my arms wide open, and shouted, "Surprise." A broad smile came across his face; then, I thought I saw a tear in his eye because he saw how wide it was. After a moment, I thought he was unhappy with me, but then he said in a whisper, "This is how I remember it when I was a very little boy and my grandmother first brought me here." It seems he had known that the stone stairs were that wide all along. I think he was well pleased. As we walked back to the hut, I said, "I know rocks are inanimate. I know inanimate things, just like animate things, have a spirit. Like rocks can have a spirit, right? Do you think these large stones at the entrance have a spirit?"

He said, "What do you think?"

I thought for a moment, then replied, "I think they do—now. I think they did long ago, but then they got covered up with dirt and everything, and now that they are uncovered, we can feel their spirit again. I think they are every bit as sacred as everything else here."

Masaaki smiled.

The priests taught me that the shrine was a sacred place; that we were indeed fortunate to live in a sacred place such as this. I found it easy to accept the good deities, *kami*, but I felt we spent an inordinate amount of time concerned about sweeping away the bad spirits, also. I did not mention this concern to the priests.

From time to time, Yoshio scolded me when I forgot and broke the rules. For example, they had explained that the *torii* was the separation between the sacred and the profane. That when passing between the timber columns and under the massive beam of the *torii*, one left the worldly and entered the sacred space of the shrine, commonly called the *jinja*. I made a game of hopping and jumping or skipping back and forth at the *torii*, between the sacred and the profane. Profane, then sacred, sacred then profane, and then back to the sacred. When Yoshio saw me doing this, he raised his arm, his sign to me to quit.

I mimicked their chanting. I could tell Yoshio was not pleased about that, either, so I created my own songs or sang the songs my family always sang while we worked. One day, when I was sweeping and singing and Masaaki had finished chanting and chasing the evil spirits away, he commented favorably about my singing. I said to him, "If I had my *shakuhachi*, I would play it for you and Yoshio all the time."

"Oh, really?" he said. His eyebrows rose in surprise. Then he said, "I played, but poorly. I didn't practice. My parents were disappointed with me." He stopped, paused for a moment, as if listening, then continued. "I dearly love to hear the ethereal sound of a *shakuhachi* at dusk. The tone takes my thoughts to some rarified place. I'd say, otherworldly. Yes, the sound of the *shakuhachi* is definitely otherworldly. Some would say hauntingly beautiful." Then he turned to me and said, "So, Yuki, I know you can sing and repeat my chanting, but tell me about your *shakuhachi*."

The deep loss of my flute had been unexpressed, my feelings pent up for a year. My words simply burst forth, as I launched into the opening left by his silence. "My father said my flute playing is divine. He said I would master the *shakuhachi* in my lifetime, if I practiced. As you know, it's not easy to play, but I play quite well. Not as well as my brother or my father, but well. Everyone in my family played. My mother did, too. He started to teach me before I was five years old. Then, I practiced every day. In the evening after work we all played. It was what my family did. We each played alone and we also played together telling stories with the music. Just as a story is told by Noh players, except, there were no words, our notes and tones told the story." The thoughts of my family and the instruments that had been in the family for generations but were now consumed by fire saddened and overwhelmed me. I dropped my head and turned abruptly to leave, so he would not see me cry. "It was lost. My *shakuhachi* was lost. Everything was lost in the fire!" I said, as I hurried away. It was in this way that various elements of my life surfaced.

In the first year I was there, I was told what I could touch and what I could not touch. I learned that only the priests went into the *honden* itself; it was the holiest of holies. Visitors were not to enter, nor was I. They explained that we did not have a *haiden*, a hall of worship for pilgrims, as some Shinto Shrines do. They said the great mountain itself was a vast hall of worship.

In all honesty, I cannot tell you that I have never been inside our *honden*. I will tell you I slipped inside many times. This, for an otherwise timid child, was a brazen act. Fortunately for me, my escapades were never found out, as far as I knew. Frankly, I touched everything, every *shantai*, sacred object enshrined there. There was a sword that needed polishing on a stand and an unusual, very old bronze mirror, which was sometimes covered. If it was covered, I didn't tamper with it. There was also a very common-looking smooth rock like you would find in a streambed, which sat on an ornately carved wooden base. The base was made especially for it. When I picked up the stone and turned it over, I saw old character markings on the underside of it, then I realized that only this particular stone would fit the base and fit only one way in the concave space in the base.

All my life, I remained curious about the mirror, which I didn't dare ask Yoshio about, lest he would know I had been inside the *honden*. I did overhear the priest discuss "a mirror that reflects heaven" and "the precious mirror of the dark heaven." I concluded that this mirror had originally been from China, and maybe Massaki used it to see future events. When I looked into it, and I always did, I only saw myself. I looked over every thing in the *honden* until I was bored to pieces and went out to play in the woods.

About twice a year, in late spring and before winter, two young men, initiates from Masaaki's monastery near Nara, come up the sacred mountain. They brought candles, incense, rice, tea, *umeboshi*, pickled plum, arrowroot, and a few other necessities the priests probably requested. A cart could go only so far up the mountain, so everything had to be carried part way. They were young and strong, but it was still difficult to get everything up to the shrine. I always helped. After a while, I looked forward to their arrival and was glum when they had to leave. I walked with them as far as I could, until they sent me back.

On one visit, they brought something for me. I guess Masaaki asked them to bring it, because only he knew I wanted a *shakuhachi*. After that our lives changed because I played every evening. I never laid it down. I kept it with me always. I never left it in the hut. When I went to sleep it was in the futon with me. I strapped it on my back with a carrier I fashioned from split vines, woven and lined with rabbit fur. I was afraid I would lose it or have it taken from me.

It was a very beautiful instrument, exquisitely made, with a tone that was divine. I told Masaaki that someone had loved it for a long time. I showed him how it was worn. It was a far better instrument than those my family had. It was finely made. I told him I thought this *shakuhachi* might be sacred, so sacred it was *kami*. I suggested that maybe it should be in the *honden* with other *kami*. He smiled and said he would be proud if I always treasured it.

The initiates from Nara came and went for the spring. Then, about six weeks later, they reappeared with a plump matronly woman, who seemed very weary from her journey. Yoshio and I did our very best to make her comfortable, and as she said later, the bath must have been enchanted because it did so much to invigorate her. Later, she casually said that the bath must have had special powers and the bath alone was worth the hardship of the trip from Nara. She had obviously been captivated by Gao's ingenuity, but no one ever mentioned Gao to her. She was friendly to me, but I couldn't help noticing that she observed my every move and scrutinized my every action.

I was shocked when I realized that the day had come when Masaaki had arranged for me to join a household in the area of Nara-Kyoto. I gleaned this from overhearing parts of conversations she had with him. I was quite upset, near tears, so under the pretense of going for water, I vanished into the woods. I ran away. I hid out in the woods and did not come back until I was certain they had cleared the area, which was more than five days. I was resourceful and adaptive and had skills enough to survive in the woods by that time. I was eleven. It was because of this event that I learned I could survive in the wilderness on my own.

At twelve, I had to run away a second time—when a tiny, somber woman with heavily hooded dark eyes came with the men from Nara. She never smiled at me and had no inclination to befriend me. She took a shine to Yoshio and was excessively solicitous to Masaaki. I immediately sized up the situation and took off to the woods. The Nara people stayed only long enough to recover from their trip. After that, Masaaki finally gave up on that idea.

Although I was generally a shy child, I was inquisitive and had more than a fair amount of curiosity. I was old enough to realize I had been thrust into the orderly lives of these two recluse priests;

therefore, I did my best not to disturb them with my questions. When not sweeping or gardening with Yoshio, or doing lessons laid out for me by Masaaki, I went to the woods. I had always been quite content to occupy myself in nature, and I did. It was there I first encountered the enigmatic Gao. I immediately realized there was something vaguely familiar about him.

It was during my very first year at the shrine, he beguiled me with his wily ways and playful trickery. We played many games in the forest, including his variations of the game of hide and seek. If he wanted, he could disappear without a trace, and I would never find him. I was destined to lose; the game favored him. At first, he left a smidgeon of a clue to entice me, such as the light snap of a twig on the forest floor or a rustle or slight movement in the trees, which required acute hearing. To some extent I was a natural, having already acquired some of these skills from tracking and setting snares. Little by little, he increased my powers of perception by forcing me to look ever closer. The game grew harder over the years—until he left no clues at all. I had to ferret him out on my own.

Sometimes we played, "*being*." Yes, "*being*." *Being* rabbit, *being* mouse, *being* owl, *being* rock. Some were comparatively easy. *Being* mountain stream, *being* vine, *being* bamboo, *being* feather, *being* mountain potato—these things required more thought and perceptual awareness. Gao had a knack for the game; he knew the very "essence" of a mountain stream. I didn't.

He said, "Be rabbit, don't be *a* rabbit! Yuki, feel. How does the rabbit feel?"

"He is afraid. His heart is thumping rapidly," I answered. Eventually I got it, but it wasn't easy. The more we practiced and observed, the better I became. I gained success when I stopped trying to mimic the creature and had the inner understanding, knowledge of its essence. Ultimately I was a vigilant owl, a fleet-of-foot deer, a graceful fall leaf swirling to earth in the wind, which, I might add, is different from a dry leaf of winter tumbling to earth or one that eddies in a stream.

The clever, spry, and supple Gao was himself a master of focus, timing, acrobatics, and disguise, and he conveyed all that to me. He changed the awkward me into a nimble, sure-footed creature of the forest. Furthermore, he gently but relentlessly tested me. His games increased my flexibility and agility until I was artfully balanced in nature.

Oh, he had his expectations—be alert, be willing, and be eager! The challenge was everything and all of it was about incremental improvement. There was no such thing as failing. There was only building on previous lessons learned. There was no being a sore loser. If something went wrong, we analyzed the matter and learned from the experience. This is how I grew up.

A basic tenant of Taoism is the practice of *sitting silent*. At first we sat, observing without saying anything for short periods, then all day. He rarely explained what or why we were doing things because I think he believed lessons should be caught, not taught. Once he did explain what could be expected with well-developed senses, like if I sat alert and in silence for long periods – like days – as Taoist do. Sometimes we walked around blindfolded. He told me that in his youth, he once sat in total darkness for a month. He stressed the importance of meditating with the priests at every opportunity. Like *being* rabbit, we often *sat silently, being nature.* As he explained, observing nature, blending into nature, being a part of nature, or being one with nature is not the same as *being nature.* That is something quite different. I thought about that for many years and eventually realized this is a basic premise for becoming invisible.

Playing hide and seek, sitting silent, and meditating for long hours were all preparatory steps for my life. As I grew older and more serious, he increased my survival skills in very subtle ways and taught me many of his secrets. By the time I was fifteen, having spent hours gathering with Yoshio and hours experiencing Gao's high jinks, I knew my way around the woods, having walked every inch of the mountain. Eventually I was good enough to elude him, having learned to cover my trail by walking treetops.

One day after *being nature* all morning and tree walking in dense bamboo all afternoon, we sat eating the wild cherries we had picked. Juice was running down our chins, and our fingers were decidedly purple. After a while I asked him why he never introduced himself to Yoshio. He sat thinking and then said, "If he wanted to see me he could see me but he's mostly functioning in his own world." He went on in a singsong, and what I felt to be a rather belittling way, "Walking and meditating, gathering and meditating, gardening and meditating, that's his way. I see him frequently. He's not looking closely, or we would have met. I'm not hard to find."

"Well, that's a bit of an exaggeration," I said sarcastically. "I think you should reveal your wizardly countenance to him at least once in this lifetime. He is a very kind person, and he has had his share of difficulties to overcome in life. Why just be something more for him to worry about? I definitely feel you should rethink this!"

After an inordinate amount of time, he said, "Seeing you feel this way, I will do as you ask. I'll try to get his attention."

Gao said, "Since we are having a heart to heart here, today, would you mind telling me why you call me 'Ochi?'"

"I do not."

"Yes, you do."

"I do? When?"

"From time to time," he said.

"Hmmm. I don't know, maybe you just look like an 'Ochi.'"

One evening, Yoshio returned from bathing in a twitter, thrilled almost speechless as he told us he had met Gao. He said, "He just appeared before my eyes, just materialized. There he was sitting cross-legged on a boulder. Just a wisp of a fellow he is." He said they talked of many things as they soaked, but Yoshio couldn't seem to remember what exactly was said.

I realized years later that it was not Gao's way to be involved with people, and that somehow I, too, developed this characteristic from him and the priests who had consciously chosen to avoid interaction with people. At a very deep level, maybe innately, I understood aloneness is something quite different from loneliness.

Aloneness is essential to thought and creativity. Aloneness should not be confused with loneliness. The three who shaped my life were various manifestations of aloneness. I was quite another.

As an adult, when I reflected on the outcome after the fire, I realized life on the mountain was a blessing. Certainly it was a peculiar blessing but a better one than other scenarios that occurred to me. Through childhood and adolescence, my feelings and emotions might have been concealed on the surface but the fire that destroyed my family destroyed me, too. It left me with a profound emptiness that neither the Taoist wizard Gao, nor Masaaki with the ability to pierce the veil of human experience to see into the world of spirit, nor Yoshio, the embodiment of divine love and compassion, could repair. I later wondered whether Masaaki saw my future in his ancient Chinese mirror or if Gao, a master of reading nature, could also read my thoughts. If so, would he have walked away from me knowing I would use his secrets in the manner I did? The mystical-mountain, Gao, Masaaki, and Yoshio surrounded me, but even these powerful spiritual influences could not alter the course of my life. I was scared. I had a dark side, a duality that simply had to be lived out.

I am Yuki, deeply angry at the sudden death of my beloved parents and brother, I am resolved to avenge them at every opportunity. I will rid the world of evil in this lifetime, live by the sword, and confront evil with evil. Yes, this is my mantra.

Little by little, a plan for my life unfolded. It was my plan; it was not a moral plan. I consulted with no one. It was not a plan to be proud of, but it was one that would wreak havoc on evildoers, such as those who had killed my family and left me an orphan. When I lay dying, I realized that this was a sinful, heinous path concocted in my youth and that a more noble path probably would have accomplished the same results without leaving blood on my hands and a stain on my soul so large it would take many lifetimes to undo.

My first overt act of aggression was to take the swords from a *samurai* as he lay sleeping in the dark of the night in a valley less than two day's walk from our shrine in the Inga Province. This in your present day is known as the Mie Prefecture, the Kansai region of Honshu. I didn't know whether this samurai was evil or not—probably he was honorable, but I needed his swords for practice. I often wonder how he explained his missing swords to his fellow *samurai*.

As far as I know, the priests never knew of my errant behavior. After a while, they accepted that somewhat like Gao, I would go away for periods of time. On my own, I became an accomplished marksman, swords-person, and an expert in marshal arts—all arduous skills diligently practiced alone. My physical strength and proficiency grew as I trained myself with these weapons. When I applied and integrated Gao's wisdom to the task at hand, my ability increased exponentially. The considerable powers of focus, concentration, stealth, timing, and cunning gained with Gao, coupled with my dexterity with weapons, caused a transformation in me. In my mind I was unstoppable. If I could be rabbit, I could be sword.

After I opened Gao's dragon gate of the Tao, there was no turning back for me. By age nineteen, I had developed exceptional skills of invisibility and walking trees. I applied Gao's teaching to my agenda, but I never made him aware of my ultimate plan. Gao did not teach me the use of the sword and as far as I know he never used one, nor did he carry a weapon, except for a pole used ostensibly for balance and a knife for utilitarian needs.

It was natural for the secretive *ninja* to attract my interest. Although *ninja* powers were not equal to the powerful foundation and skills I had acquired from Gao, and through years of intense practice, there was something to be learned from them. They had been shadowing me for a few years, if I chose to allow them. On and off, we played a cat and mouse game, while I continued to pursue my objectives and to work my plan. They were of no threat to me, and I was no threat to them. It was fairly clear to my *ninja* stalkers who I was and what I was doing. Often we had a mutual target.

If I chose to, I spied on the *ninja* farming communities and their training schools, known as *ryu*. I was bold, practically under their noses, but invisible to them. Just as I had mastered the use of the sword by spying on the *samurai* training schools, I studied the techniques of the *ninja* masters as they put would-be-*ninjas* through their paces. I was keen to strengthen my position of superiority by learning their methods; thus, knowing what I knew and what they knew, too.

One day, not far from present day Ueno, I allowed them to waylay me. I was expecting their ambush; I knew where they were at all times, and by observing them over time, I knew what they were going to do before they did it. I was not in danger. Anyway, we needed an opportunity to talk. They proposed that I join them. I told them I was not for hire. They knew from observing me, when I permitted, that I had a mission, and I saw where joining forces with them, making use of their spies and scouts, might further my objectives.

Thus, I was accepted into this *ninja* community with the expressed agreement that I had free will and the liberty to leave if I wanted and whenever I wanted. This was a mutually beneficial arrangement. I sold the *samurai's* swords and took up the *ninja's* weapons, which were much better for my purposes. The *ninja* used a slightly shorter *shinobigatana* or the *kitana*. The samurai swords were extremely heavy and cumbersome by comparison. I learned to handle the useful *taibumi*—a collapsible, hinged bow, very light and very useful—when on a clandestine mission. The new weapons found a place next to my *shakuhachi*, which for years now had ridden lightly on my back.

I quickly adopted the *ninja* stance, which was somewhat of a variation on Gao's teaching, and to appease them I donned the black garb of the *ninja,* which is totally unnecessary when you know what I know, but they didn't. Respectfully, I honed my skills on their masters, who admired me, but who did not fully reveal their secrets to me, either.

So I became *kunoichi*, female *ninja*. My acts were ferocious, lightning fast; I was precise and accurate, never tortured or taunted. I was more courageous than any of the men I met, and I held my own among them. Unlike most *kunoichi*, I never trapped or lured my victim by use of my feminine wiles, nor did I ever pose as a servant girl to gain access. I will tell you that I lured them with the moving lamentations of my flute, and that I did disguise myself as a musician when appropriate, primarily because it gave me the opportunity to play my *shakuhachi*, which was my bliss, my one and only true joy. The soulful-sounds abide in my over soul, etched there for eternity.

I cannot begin to tell you how many evil people left this world at my hand. I stalked them and surprised them on the trail, in their cups, in their bath, on the toilet, at their desk, taking tea or with their lovers. I appeared in the bedchambers of malefactors and ended their wickedness. I brutally punished bandits, rapists, and other swine; it was rumored that I made the Tokaido route safer for travelers. Most especially, I unabashedly tracked marauders who murdered and took the property of others. I played out my dark side without remorse. After all, I still believed, as I had since I was nine, that vengeance belonged to me.

This is the life I created for myself. Somewhere in time, all my vile deeds and acts are written. It may take many lifetimes to expunge the *karma* from the record of this life, as I lived it.

15
Enchanted

BUSY DEVELOPING A NEW lecture series and doing guest lectures, I was totally immersed in meeting the needs of the students and establishing my new life. I was also eager to explore all things new. And it was all new. In the first year, I had periodic waves of homesickness and moments when I questioned my sanity in having uprooted my stable life in the States. I felt guilt for making demands on my son Brad's time in order to find and mail resources in English, but I had no recourse. Books in English, even travel books, were rare, and the references I needed were rarer still.

I found a routine that provided ample time for local travel and photography, and I settled into becoming accustomed to my new environment. I missed my friends, and long distance phone calls eventually proved inadequate to keep in touch with them.

I had written to Jake several times, but when he didn't reply I stopped writing. Then sometime later, a letter did come from him saying he'd gone back East and found a job. According to his brief note, in the wake of my sudden departure he had to rethink how he would proceed with his life. He said he didn't have a strong reason for staying in Oklahoma City if I wasn't there, that he had continued working at the museum for a few months after I left, but without me there the place just wasn't the same. He said he felt that when I was gone, it was like all the good stuff was gone and everything was over—forever.

I had been warned by Rae in a psychic reading that Jake felt abandoned when I left. His letter pretty much confirmed her words. Anyway, I was far away now, and there was nothing I could do to assuage his feelings. I did, however, dwell on his word, "*forever*" in my pensive moments. There had been so much that had transpired between us, so many unusual situations, and now there was so much that would forever go unsaid. I knew I would always wonder about the coincidence of our meeting and the coincidence of the timing of a job in Japan. Was it all predestined? Was it "fate?" Was it just a moment in time? For both of us life would go on, but in different directions. We were both already headed out into opposite orbits.

I was far too busy with lectures and developing a new teaching series. I was totally immersed in meeting the needs of the students and establishing a new life. The initial period of homesickness and frantic calling friends at home finally faded away in the smoke of ancient rituals along avenues of stone lanterns. I no longer questioned my sanity in uprooting my stable, albeit humdrum, life in the States. Here in this enchanting country, a weird mix of the exotic and mystical with the menagerie of Tokyo's advanced technology, I had much to learn, and I was eager to explore.

One weekend, I stumbled upon an antique market on the grounds of a shrine. I marveled at the exquisitely designed antique silk kimonos, now discarded. There were stacks and racks of them. I was instantly hooked and, thereafter, I never miss a shrine sale. And I found many! I was intoxicated by what I can only call the Japanese aesthetic. It was genius. It was brilliant. A feast for my eyes. Sometimes, I got overwhelmed by it all. Someone told me that if I couldn't afford to buy it, I should take a photo of it. So in the space of one day, I shot a hundred images.

There was a quirky creativity to this place that was beyond my grasp. Like a dignified black antique kimono, where only the wearer and his lover knew the shocking surprise of color or the unexpected images on the lining. Americans did exactly the reverse: putting a plain inside fabric as the lining and the bright colors and designs on the outside. Then there was the petite young woman white-gloved and in a suit and hat at the top of the escalator, welcoming customers to the department store. My purchases were wrapped in high quality designer paper once, twice, and then put in a petite shopping bag. The paper folds were delightful and far too intricate for me to replicate. Try as I might.

Everywhere I looked, there was yet another surprise. Take pizza for instance. Certainly it was not native to Japan, nor was spaghetti either, yet so many seemingly bizarre combinations appear on the menu. Their quirky, unexpected oddities made me smile. Food was an art, and there is no end to the gastronomical epicurean delicacies.

School kids with notebooks often approached me, very politely asking if they might interview me. They were serious minded in this endeavor and meticulously logged each of my responses. They appreciated when I obliged them, and I always do.

I saw an exceedingly high level of artistry everywhere. An understated branch, or tiny flower with a single plain leaf in a small vase in the ladies' lavatory, had the impact of a work of art. Japan was a country that designates potters and master craftsmen as National Treasures. This was my kind of place. Some faculty women took me to the kimono museum of the artist Itchiku Kubota near Mt. Fuji. His work was breathtaking. His masterful skill in textile dying and design were beyond exquisite. Enthralled by his genius, I wondered about the mind of a man who could create such beauty.

No doubt there was curiosity about this blonde person in their midst. People befriended me; many wanted an opportunity to practice English or wanted me, a stranger, in their group photo. Others sensed my genuine appreciation for their culture and my desire to understand. They were proud to show me the best of it and did their utmost to explain. Under a dark summer sky, I sat on my less than one square meter of the lawn with hundreds of people watching an ancient "*Noh*" play. We ate cold *soba* noodles in the summer and long, fat *udon* noodles in a rich broth in the winter. I was fascinated even with the grocery store. I was captivated with the place, enamored with the culture, and charmed by the people.

On cold and rainy nights, I sat in the noodle shop with both hands cupped around my tea bowl, copying the Japanese women who warmed their hands this way. I felt the heat from the cup radiating through my fingers, down my spine, slowly permeating my entire body. Sometimes in a small *tatami* room, sitting on the floor, warming myself with the tea bowl, I had the distinct feeling that I had done this before—in the ancient past.

I knew that the blind or deaf compensate in other ways from the loss of a sense. I think a variation of that is what was happening to me. Since I could hear but didn't understand the language, to some extent, I was deaf. In some ways, I was also blind because I couldn't read the signs. Being cut off like this, speaking little, I found myself alone with my thoughts much of the time. Like an illiterate, I resorted to my powers of observation to get me though the situations I encountered.

Whether it was the fan-shaped ginkgo leaves that piled up curbside in the fall, the masses of people that crowded into the train at rush hour, or the night-lights in Tokyo, I was enchanted by this culture and found myself falling in love with all that was Japan. I easily found temple gardens and shrines to explore. Mostly I went alone. They were beautiful in all seasons. I learned that meditation can be done while walking around, and the quiet, serenity of a Japanese garden was the perfect place to practice this.

The Japanese people knew the precise day, peak conditions for an event, such as the very best moment for cherry blossom viewing or visiting a village specializing in hydrangea. At that time, a faculty member often seized the moment to take me somewhere special. Whenever I look at the Toshi Yoshida woodblock print, "Half Moon Bridge," depicting wisteria, I will forever cherish the student who insisted I "drop everything" to go to the park to see wisteria in peak bloom.

As I got deeper and deeper into my new life situation, I found ample time away from interruptions of school and the usual distractions of life that allowed me to tap into a wellspring of information. This happened more and more frequently, in dreams, in deep relaxation, or simply walking in the many gardens and temples. I bought a book in order to learn the practice of meditation.

When information came to me, such as the tale of Yuki or others, I took time to write out the particulars. Unlike when I was home in the States, I was no longer confused by what I had there perceived as strange or bizarre. When this happened, I accepted it, and sort of examined it. I concluded I was learning something about myself.

Gradually, I began to compare and contrast my personal Christian beliefs with my growing awareness of Buddhism and Hinduism. My understanding increased as I delved into studies about reincarnation and how dreams foreshadow events. I thoughtfully considered my everyday actions and how today's thoughts and actions build *karma* for the next life. I realized that the word *karma* had slipped into the vocabulary of our culture but our casual, even flippant, use of the terms "good karma or bad karma" was poorly understood.

Still thinking about this, I kicked my shoes aside, put my sushi in the tiny refrigerator, and flopped my sweater and handbag on the desk chair. I had been at a shrine sale all day. I'd bought an *obi* with chrysanthemum pattern, a carved bone *netsuke* of a rabbit, a small *kokeshi* doll about seventy years old, two Kutani sake cups, and three pieces of antique silk with Edo period images of "the floating world." All that I saw stirred my imagination. Very satisfied, I tucked the packages under the bed and changed into pajamas. I pulled my armchair over to the bedside. No recliner or footstool here. Before I sat down, I picked up a pen and notebook, just in case a poem wanted to write itself.

It was late in the afternoon when I propped my feet up on the bed and put my head back. I was happy and totally content; students were gone for the weekend, so it was peaceful and quiet, except for one big black crow cawing in the distance. I closed my eyes and savored the day's adventure. A soft breeze blew over me. Images of the shrine grounds, the stone lanterns, the worn stone pathway, the ancient dragon pediment of the weathered wooden shrine, and the faces of the antique vendors were fresh in my mind. My last thought was that the crow had moved further from my window. I fell asleep and began to dream.

I was shown a country road reminiscent of secluded rural Alabama. The road was a wet, slick, muddy surface, of rich, dark reddish-brown clay. It was dark there, but it was not night. The darkness was from the overhanging trees and deep brush on the left side of the road. I was not shown the right side, but I knew there was a fallow, overgrown field there.

Water, muddy water, was collected in a shallow ditch along the left side of the road. Normally, pooled water meeting the muddy road would go unnoticed, and would be of no importance, but in this situation, I was looking at the line of separation. The line was precise and critical because in an instant, without any warning, there was a zoom out and up, just like the automatic zoom lens action on my camera.

Precisely along the line separating the muddy water and the muddy road, the scene had changed. A cut line appeared exactly where the muddy water was; a river was flowing far, far below—like a canyon. The muddy road zoomed upward separating the canyon river below from the high overlook.

At first I saw only two feet in a pair of old-fashioned boots. The person stood lightly but dangerously close to the precipice. It was not a good idea to stand this close to the edge of a cliff; the earth was loose and crumbly.

The person was lean and small in stature, British or French. He was well dressed, in custom-tailored lightweight tan or khaki twill pants and shirt with matching pointy-toed, laced up boots, dark brown belt, hatband, and trappings. The broad-brimmed felt hat cast a shadow over his face. Perfectly outfitted, all indications were that he was an explorer, a scientist, or a military person from another era—early to mid-19th century.

If he had climbed to this point, he hadn't broken a sweat. He stood neat and prim, looking out in the distance, calmly surveying the vista and the canyon river below. This fellow was in control of himself and the situation. Repetitively, he slapped his riding crop against his boot. There was another person with him, whom I couldn't see and couldn't identify. I just knew that he was a younger male, perhaps an assistant or aide de camp.

Before I opened my eyes the cliff and canyon had vanished, and I had the distinct feeling that this fellow, a British explorer and archeologist, was me. My boots were seen trudging through deep sand in an amorphous, wavy distortion that could be the Gobi or Egypt.

When I awakened it was dark outside. I listened for but didn't hear the crow. I thought to myself, *That dream was really weird.* I ate half of the sushi and two soft, sweet *mochi* rice balls I had in the fridge. While I had a soak in the deep Japanese tub, I considered whether that dream suggested the past or foretold a future. Relaxed and content, I slipped into bed with a book of *haiku* poems by Matsuo Basho.

16
Tokyo

WE WALKED ALONG THE Ginza, the glitz and glamour of the department store windows sparkled out of the darkness, while above us rows of vertical electronic lights receded in the distance as they heralded one business after another. It was late at night and few people passed us.

"Are you hungry? Had enough of this window shopping?" he asked.

"Japanese design and innovation feeds my soul," I said, as I drew his attention to a stunning display of Mikimoto pearls. Hundreds of splendid silvery fishhooks on glittering fishing line suspended over the "pearl catch" carried my eye along the entire store front. "Brilliant! And I'd say kudos to the window designer. This store front is a spectacle I will remember for a lifetime," I told him.

He said, "Do you like pearls?"

I replied, "No, not particularly, but I do like this window display. It's altogether stunning."

I was about to explain, but before I could go on about the aesthetics of the window treatment, explaining the use of repetition, color, line, and texture for impact, he took my elbow and led me away. "Window treatments may do it for you but not for me. I'm hungry. What would you say to a nice bowl of noodles? I know a place nearby."

We crossed the street, walked a block, then made a turn onto a narrow road. Two short blocks later, we reached a district of small restaurants on narrow, dimly lit lanes. Lanterns and banners clearly indicated what fare awaited a diner inside. Depending on the customer's choice of establishments, one might be welcomed at the doorway outside by a "hello kitty," a *kanuki*, or a large piece of museum quality pottery or plants with a mantle of fresh street dust.

A three-foot high hello kitty's up-reached paw waved "hello" as he slid the door open and ducked his head under the blue curtain. He held the door and the curtain back for me to enter, then led the way into the small space of a cozy eatery. The dark wood of the small, rectangular tables with four stools were mostly taken by couples talking intimately over their cups of barley tea or dealing with the noodles. The aroma of the broth and noodles reminded my stomach that I was hungry.

I followed Takahashi-san down a narrow aisle to the back, passing by ten tables on either side, which were lined up snuggly against the walls. He chose one of three vacant tables near the chef's miniscule cooking area and counter. The chef looked up from his work immediately when we entered and acknowledged him respectfully with a bow of his head. No words were exchanged, and the chef did not look at me. By the time we settled on the stools, he'd served barley tea from a little tray, exchanged a few words, probably confirming our choice, and went away to prepare it. This was, after all, an *udon* restaurant—not much need for discussion, just the ability to read the banner outside, which I could not do.

I tried not to smile at a man eating one of the long, fat, slippery noodles. One end of the *udon* noodle was in his mouth, the other end of the noodle held in his *hashi*, chop sticks. It was extended almost arm's length above his head. Here and there a slurp could be heard.

I looked at Takahashi-san and said, "I'll try not to embarrass you or myself, but you know these *udon* noodles slide right off my *hashi*. They're a real challenge."

He said, "*Hai* (yes), for everybody. Japanese, too. You'll have to learn the art of slurping—like the rest of us. Consider this a practice session. By next winter you'll be what you Americans call a pro." He went on to say, "That cook back there and his family make these noodles. They've been in business for at least three generations. The broth is the best. I used to come here with my grandfather."

The *udon* came quickly. It was steaming hot. It was excellent. The more I concentrated on the task, the more the noodles slipped back into the bowl. I realized tenacity would be required in order to master *udon* eating within my lifetime.

I was thinking that just like Cherry Blossom in the spring and Obon Festival in August, *udon* is to enjoy and "take the chill off" during the winter months. The colors in an *obi* or *kimono*; the symbols of the crane, maple leaf, and others; or a food, was seen and enjoyed only at its proper and peak moment. Like the barley tea we were drinking, it was available now but not in other seasons. Cold *soba* on a bamboo mat is served only in the summer, for instance. For me, they are smaller and more easily managed with chopsticks. Now was the time for enjoying this rich broth and these slippery *udon* noodles. Having been in Japan for more than a year, I was beginning to see their pattern for life emerge. I could see, too, that their regime was linked to health and well being.

It seemed to me from observation that Japanese did not converse when they ate. They were focused and ate rapidly. Perhaps the objective was to vacate the space for others.

The city population was dense, which gave rise to an unstated code of conduct—manners and courtesies and a people that generally respected the space of others. Unlike Americans, they do not interfere with or inject themselves into the business of others. Some foreigners on the faculty felt that Japanese customs were tedious or tiresome, but I sought to understand. In so doing, I came to appreciate their quiet demeanor and realized that their system allowed a very large number of people on a very small island to function in an orderly fashion.

Having finished the *udon*, the cook came to refresh the barley tea. Takahashi-san must have asked him for a pot of tea because he stopped pouring and returned with a pot. Takahashi-san filled my cup about two thirds full before pouring his own. Then he said, "You haven't told me much about your tour to the Mogao Caves with all those teachers. How did it go? Was it difficult being with all those ladies? How did you get along with all those Japanese speakers?"

"Well, in a word, it was incredible," I said. "Certainly, I was an oddity in the group. Mostly, I think it was hard for them—dealing with me. They wanted so much to help me understand; therefore, someone was constantly translating for me. After ten days, I think no one wanted an opportunity to 'practice' English. This had to be tiring for them. I'm forever grateful, indeed, indebted to them.

"Did I ever tell you how much I appreciate you taking time to explain words in your language and things about your culture?" I added. "Meeting you has made such a difference for me. Thank God you're fluent in English. Do you realize that if you had not applied yourself well in school, we could not communicate? Truly this world is a Tower of Babel," I said.

He replied, "I'm not so fluent—as you say. And what is 'Tower of Babel?'"

Our conversations always took a lot of time, were interrupted, delayed, or taken in another direction because one of us needed a definition and an explanation of a word. I explained the Tower of Babel. Then I said, "While I was in China, I had an epiphany." I knew he wanted me to define epiphany, but I went on, quickly. "I had no idea that the Japanese goddess Kannon and the Chinese goddess Quan Yin were one and the same. You know, the Buddhist goddess of mercy and compassion, the protector of women and children. I did some research when I got back to Japan and this goddess Quan Yin appears in Tibet as Tara, in Indonesia as Dewi or Devi Kwan Im, in India and in all Asian countries with various names. That is what I mean by a 'Tower of Babel.' Sometimes I get overwhelmed with all of it. For example, did you know that God Avalokitesvara, the 'Buddhist King,' the ones whose face is carved in fabulous stone towers in Cambodia, is actually the male aspect of Quan Yin?

"I've found it helps to know the origin of the word, which is usually Sanskrit. It helps me understand the images and the sculptures. Like, Quan Yin is loosely translated as 'She who hears the cries of the world.' I now have a better understanding of the Buddhist images and sculptures with multiple heads or faces or arms. That's Quan Yin reaching out to those suffering in the world. And, furthermore, I've come to realize that there are several types of Buddhism, similar to the various denominations of Christians. I didn't know that."

"I'm impressed with your willingness to sort it all out," he said. "Maybe you will become a religious scholar before you leave Japan. Promise me you won't go off to meditate in a Tibetan cave." He gave me a curious inquiring look, which said, "You wouldn't, would you?"

"I feel so vastly undereducated. I feel I am only muddling through," I said. "I'm so deficient in language skills I can't discuss religion, philosophy, not even the arts and my profession in any depth. I always felt I was well qualified and competent. Now I don't. All my life I felt I had it together, now I don't. Maybe I'll have to stay here forever."

"What is 'had it together'?" he inquired.

When the words slipped off my tongue, I knew immediately there would be a delay of sorts while I explained, 'had it together.' Like most Japanese, he was constantly increasing his vocabulary. American slang, an old adage, a maxim, or some colorful language always demanded a conversation in itself. He especially liked to learn American slang and wanted to know the origins of my many "off-the-cuff" remarks. Often he referred to his electronic dictionary, which I learned frequently was woefully misleading or required further discussion of the word usage.

"So to make a long story short," I resumed, "the Mogao Caves are splendid. You can just see the Buddhist history of the ages. Sometimes, I felt very much a part of it. I mean in one section it felt like I had been there before, like I'd go around the corner and know what was there. I was looking at some wall murals, and I knew what was on the ceiling before I looked up. It was weird. Maybe I'd seen a picture of that cave somewhere, but I don't think so. There are not many photographs of it available, and tourists are restricted from photographing for reasons of preservation. My feelings were strange. It was a wonderful trip. I think you should go. On one hand it was exotic, and on the other hand it was so familiar. The same group is planning a trip to Egypt next year. If I'm still in Japan at that time, I may go with them. Everyone was so nice to me."

I jumped up. "Oh my gosh. Look what time it is. I must go I'm going to miss the last train. Where did the time go? I was just yacking on and on," I said, as I started pulling my things together.

"Sit down, don't worry." He looked at his watch. "It's too late, even if you rush, you'll miss it. My driver can take you. I'll call him. *Daijobu* (it's no problem)."

"Are you sure?" Slowly, I sat back down.

"Yes, it's no problem. That's what drivers do," he said.

"You always have a ready answer."

He smiled. "Yes, well you're in my town. And whatever problems you have I've probably encountered them before."

Twenty minutes later, the driver arrived to pick me up and an hour and a half later, we arrived at the campus entrance. The driver refused any payment, bowed excessively, and extending his arm in the direction I should go, indicated that he would wait until I was in the building.

Maybe it was fate or destiny, or my career had miraculously placed me in a country with people who have a fundamental belief in reincarnation. I observed, how almost without exception, they treated others with respect. Except for a group called the Yakuza, a sort of Japanese Mafia who, from what I understand kept to themselves, this culture appeared almost entirely without crime, murder, rape, and child molestation. Even theft was almost non-existent. I felt safe in this country.

At one point, I forgot and left my fanny pack on a train, and within the day it was brought to me on campus. Another time, I found a wallet under a bench at a park near the train station. I took it to a police officer at a nearby *koban*, the neighborhood police station. He meticulously questioned me, documenting my name, address, and other personal information about me. I was taken back by all the information he wrote on a form about me. I only wanted to get the wallet to the owner. About a week later, I got a well-written thank you note in English from the man whose wallet I had found.

Coming from the US, where violent crime is accepted as a fact of life, I wondered whether things would be different for us if our society believed in reincarnation. What would happen if we truly believed, "we reap what we sow"—not only in this life but also in the next; would it deter crime and acts of violence against another person?

17
Montuulgyar

My family and I lived a harsh yet peaceful life on the Mongolian steppes. Our clan worked hard together. We had a diet of meat and mare's milk. Recognizing the importance of each other for survival, everyone contributed and everyone shared the material needed for daily living.

We were herdsmen and horse breeders. My extended family included two of my mother's sisters and their families, and all of my father's siblings—his three brothers and their families, his two sisters and two brothers-in-law, and their children. All were involved with my life in one way or another. An old shaman, a distant relative to my now deceased paternal grandfather, was also around.

We enjoyed pleasant summers despite the demanding tasks of nomadic life. Together we endured the winter snow and buffeting winds, and thrived on nature's eternally changing cycles. The smoky soot of indoor fires that blackens and greases our faces was all a part of the natural order of things by which our lives were influenced. This is the rhythm of the steppes.

After a hard winter, we looked forward to moving to spring pastures for the time of birthing baby animals. Spring renewed the herds; the excitement of shearing sheep and camels renewed our spirits. When we moved to summer pastures, these young animals grew and fattened up, and there was food aplenty. In the summer, there was much merriment, games, and holiday gatherings. Simultaneously, the work, underway in preparation for winter, was demanding. The wool shorn in the spring was felted; repairing and sewing clothes was accomplished. Ever mindful not to overgraze when the first cool days of fall begin, we moved to fall pastures; there, we prepared our winter food stores of meat and milk products for the winter, before moving to our winter lodging.

Life appeared simple on the surface, but this was a dynamic fusion of human energy. There was a moving, complicated synergy to our clan. The mixing and melding of skills and knowledge had been carried forward from previous generations. The invisible transfer of skills and knowledge between adults and from adult to children took place daily, and season after season. Parents understood the on-going need to teach the children survival skills and transfer the insights gained over successive generations. Here on the steppes, centuries of accumulated knowledge was bound together with the rhythm of nature.

I lived in a wool-covered, cylindrical-shaped house with a domed roof, called a *yurt*. There were eight yurts in all. The design and construction were based on the cosmos, the vertical axis linking heaven and earth, the smoke hole symbolizing the sun, and the hearth, the navel. It respected the cardinal directions; the door opened to the south. Our home was a sacred place. Along with our prayers, the cooking aromas of frying flat bread and sausage mingled, as they found a way through the smoke-hole to feed the spirits. Powerful, auspicious symbols decorated the interior of my home: long life and happiness symbols; the dragon; and the five elements of earth, water, fire, metals, and wind were all carefully embroidered around the top, where the walls met the roof.

We often changed location, so our dwellings were portable, although they were moved with great effort. It was customary for the women to disassemble them and pack the animals and the carts. I never saw live trees as big as the timbers in the support columns and the roof poles. They were old, well worn, and carefully handled, like the crown; the poles had been passed down through the generations. When it came to erecting the *yurt*, the uncles were involved. There was a sacredness about this process and, thus, the spirituality of the uncles was important.

We all worked together as a team. In daily life, my parents and the men and women of the clan faced the joys and hardships of the steppes on equal footing. They faced problems together, and together they made decisions to resolve them. While many chores and duties fall along male and female lines, this was not always the case. My aunties and their husbands best illustrate the exception.

I knew my father's sisters as the aunties. The aunties were superior handlers of animals—sheep, camels, yak, and other livestock. No one else could match their skills. I was told that my grandfather and his ancestors insisted that the female as well as the male children be schooled in the traditions of animal husbandry. The aunties had a natural inclination, and thus, in this generation they came to know more about breeding than others in the clan, except my father. My father conferred with and relied on the judgment of his sisters in these matters.

Due to years of herding in the distant pastures, braving the glaring sun and the elements in the most inhospitable weather imaginable, the aunties' faces were as dried and wrinkled as old boots. Though they hadn't reached thirty years of age, their hands were rough and calloused.

It was a coincidence that the aunties each found a husband. I was told that the uncles were part of a troupe of traveling musicians and entertainers, who happened to come through our lands one summer. My father's two sisters enchanted them, it was said; and, while the others of the group continued on their way, two left their group and stayed to marry the aunties.

My father was the leader of our group. This fact can be noticed but was not spoken. Being the oldest of the brothers, this responsibility was bestowed upon him by his father and the clan, before I was born. He was the eldest brother, and in every way, he was also the strongest, the most able, and the most skillful of all the men I knew. I was told that he singlehandedly won all contests of skill and daring as a child and, rightfully, he proved himself among the men, although he never took advantage of his position in the group, nor did he let me. He also held me to a high standard. I was not allowed to shirk my chores. I learned very early that there was a penalty to be paid for not doing my fair share.

My mother and father were a good balance for each other. A woman of the steppes could hardly be described as soft considering the rigors of this austere environment, where the climate tans your skin to leather hardness by the age of six; yet, my mother's temperament was as soft as a baby lamb. She was soft spoken and had an easy flowing demeanor that was pliable and yielding. When faced with resistance, she melted a cold heart with a few words, or dissolved the will of a stiff opponent. She was straightforward and uncomplicated. I witnessed her quite easily smooth out some serious difficulties between other people. She was like grease to friction.

She was also a skillful needle worker, and she worked leather of all sorts. She taught the younger girls traditional embroidery stitches. Sometimes when she made my clothes, she embellished my coat with animal images stitched with colorful threads.

My mother knew all the plants of the steppes and their usage. She dyed fibers by brewing a vat of grasses that smelled almost good enough to eat. She knew the dyer's art and which plants of the steppes could be used for medicinal purposes. She gathered natural materials at the most propitious time for extracting the dye, cooking and straining them for the colors they yield, or drying them for medicine. When someone was ill or hurt, my mother worked closely with the shaman.

Because she was kind and sensitive to the needs of others, she was greatly loved by the women and children who frequently came to her for comfort. Although she was always busy, she managed to help everybody. My mother was very resourceful. On winter evenings, while others sat idle, their thoughts drifting throughout the universe, my mother's hands remained busy until there was no light left in the embers. If not serving someone, she was sewing or embroidering.

With children, she made a playful game out of work. Sometimes she teased them, making them solve their own problems. I caught on to her ways. She had done the same to me when I was younger, but now I just go do the job, whatever it is. My mother believed lessons were better learned when they were caught, not taught.

My mother made tassels for my pony with colored sinew and fine strands of skiver. Each year she made tassels to award to the winners of the games. She encouraged all the children to do their best in the competitions. Somehow she found a way to make certain that even the least of us got a tassel. She praised all the kids, making a fuss over each one, even if he was late and last to arrive, even if he missed the mark entirely. I told my father I didn't think that was fair. He said, "Never you mind."

Each summer I watched the animals grazing under mostly cloudless skies. In this vast open country, I stood witness to alternately rapidly moving, then lazy skies. Tending the herds made possible long hours to dream, walking through a sea of wild iris and lying in verdant meadow grasses. Whenever clouds formed in the distance, I measured the shadows they cast. I predicted how long it would take for them to catch up to me, when they would cover me, if they would chill me. I watched them stretch across the pasturelands, climb the steppes, and vanish into some other distant, unknown meadow.

I learned from my father how to read the land. It was he who watched carefully for over grazing, which was vital to our survival. It was he who decided when the exact moment came to move camp. There was no calendar, and every year was somewhat different depending on what nature brings.

I had a pony. I had good riding skills, and each year my archery skills improved—both were duly tested during the games, and my father sedulously observed my progress. The games inevitably followed the summer—and foretold a long and severe winter to come, a winter that could likely catch up to and overcome the oldest or weakest of the family. It was said that spirits snatch sickly babies, and old folks left for greener pastures during the heaviest of snowstorms. Except for the stories and music of the *throat singers*, there was little to occupy children in winter. No riding, no bows, no arrows.

Although not readily apparent by material possessions or a wielding of power, it was apparent to me that my father was the leader. It was he who decided precisely when we would move the herds. He made the critical decisions. No one told me this; I simply came to this understanding. Except for the *throat singers*, all the men were related by blood and grew up together. From childhood they learned to value the strengths and overcome the weaknesses of one another. Survival of the unit was more important than the ego of any one person.

If a situation arose that required my fathers' decision on behalf of the group, it seemed to me he was wise and fair in his judgment. From time to time, there were disputes to resolve. The women trifled occasionally, but he didn't get involved in riffs among them. I noticed he never apologized, nor did he explain how he reached his decisions; his decisions were never questioned, either.

On one occasion, the young son of an uncle wanted to leave the family and travel along with a caravan passing through our lands. His mother and father were strongly opposed. My parents, too, were of the opinion that he should not go. The family fostered the opinion that he was needed here, for the future welfare of the family. Everyone implored my father not to permit the departure of such an able-bodied young man. My cousin's mother was tearful and uncharacteristically emotional.

In the end, he embarked with the caravan with my father's blessing, a good horse, and all the rations we could spare. His father was silent; his mother was sobbing and inconsolable. As her second son left the encampment, she fell to the ground sobbing. I did not understand my father's decision; it left me with many questions. I guess the confusion showed on my face. The next day, he privately offered me an explanation.

My father told me that the boy's spirit had already left the clan. He would be of little use to us. "Had I forced him to stay," he said, "his spirit surely would have died, along with his dreams. I did not want this for him. Also, he would have come to despise me. As the years go on, your cousin would not come into alignment and work for the good of the group. His spirit would be somewhere else, along with his dreams. Sometimes I must place nurturing the spirit of an individual above the needs of the group." He went on, "In this situation it had to take precedence. This is the best situation for your cousin. It is best for our family. We will survive and thrive without his efforts. Hopefully, he will survive and thrive, but of that we may never know."

Maybe my father saw a flicker of curiosity as momentarily I chased my thoughts beyond the family pastures. My father's next words were firmly and quietly stated to me, eyeball to eyeball. "Do not consider the way of your cousin. It is not for you."

As my cousin vanished in the distance along with his dreams and the caravan, my mother tried unsuccessfully to console his mother. But, like the caravan, life moved on, and the name of her second born was no longer mentioned among us.

The following year, a new baby was born to her, and it seemed she had forgiven my father. Maybe she was too busy to think about her second son. Privately, I wondered what became of him, and what lay in territories beyond our pasturelands. I had only a few traders and my musician uncles to tell me what happened in lands beyond our pastures.

The husbands of the aunties were *throat singers* from a northern region of Mongolia. As musicians, they were exceptionally talented. They were involved in the vast exploration of sounds and tones, telling stories in song, and enchanting us with tunes and words that poured effortlessly out of their reverie. Sometimes drums stretched with skins and rattles made from gourds accompanied them. The uncles painted pictures with words and sounds, often singing soft and soulful stories of pretty young girls and their travels before they met the aunties. It seemed to me they made up the story as they went along, rarely ever repeating exactly the same story or describing exactly the same girl. They knew the sound of a single horse, or many; the sound of ambling along slowly, or moving rapidly, as if giving chase. The subtleties of different birds and animal sounds kept the littlest children riveted. Their songs told of interesting characters they had encountered or imagined, I'm not sure which. But, I was fascinated.

While their ability to repair saddles and harnesses couldn't compare with my mother's, nor did their knowledge of animal husbandry ever approach that of their wives, I think perhaps the clan-folk indulged them because of the joy they brought. They used their time and creativity inventing bow-stringed instruments. Their passion was experimenting with sound. Many times others picked up their chores, but there was no resentment. They brought us joy.

And so, much to my delight, the long winter night's passed with the rhythms and deep guttural sounds of the throat singers with their musical instruments, occasionally accompanied by bone rattles. The youngsters fell asleep in the familial bed with a sip of warm mare's milk in their stomachs, surrounded by the songsters and our maudlin, giddy, hard-working families.

My mother had a scarf. It was made of the finest, precious and most luxurious natural woolen fibers known to man—*kiviot* of the great musk ox of the North Country. My father acquired it in trade from two Russian traders. They had no horses, and they were in dire straights according to my father.

In truth, their arrival was foreshadowed by a very bad omen. It caused a great amount of consternation when, one winter night unusually strong winds blew the smoke-hole flap shut. That was not a good sign! It was calamity. My mother and the aunties were very upset, and the old shaman was called. The uncles did their best to assuage everyone's concerns with song. Over time, things settled down, and for me the matter was soon forgotten.

Then the two traders wandered into our camp one day, barely alive. They had no provisions, only some traps and trapping paraphernalia. Their trapping gear was lashed on to the back of a very old wild camel. She had barely enough strength to walk and stay upright. Looking her over, I would say she would not last the winter.

The two tired, bedraggled men had journeyed on foot for more than a month. They said they crossed the steppes fleeing in fear for their lives. They told of the slaughter of their three companions, two Turks and a Siberian. They said that bandits had savagely murdered the three in their camp.

They had survived only by coincidence, having left camp a day earlier to check some traps. They returned to an encampment laid waste by the poachers, food and horses gone, blood, gore, and charred remnants were all that remained. It appeared to them that marauders had surprised the three, interrupting the tanning process. The camp was plundered and sacked. There was nothing left of the season's work. That which had not been commandeered had been burned. It seemed to them that more had been torched than had been carried off. The overnight rain had rendered the embers cold, but they determined the attack had taken place very soon after they left camp.

The sight of the incinerated body parts of their dismembered workfellows left them frightened and traumatized. Even for trappers, it was too gruesome to bury the dead. They told us they hastily gathered up what little they could recover and set out on foot. They dragged some traps on a crudely crafted, makeshift litter they made en route. They said that after many days of walking, they came upon a wobbly old near death camel, which although skittish, did not run. Seems the old camel was grateful for their company and the three formed a tenuous, mutual alliance.

These trappers had little to trade. Their traps were vital to their livelihood. The camel was useless and of no value in trade. One trapper produced the wad of kiviot from inside his cloak. He said it was priceless. Indeed, it was more than simply a commodity to him. It seemed it had some great personal or sentimental attachment. Nonetheless, in desperation, he handed it to my father to examine. Also, in the deal was a smooth piece of fossilized tree resin, amber, with a tiny mosquito trapped inside, several untanned hides, and the foretelling of the future—a warning of danger.

The trappers stayed with us long enough to recover their strength; then, they went on their way. My father generously traded them two horses, as he told me, not suitable for breeding. There was no further mention of them, and their ominous warning was soon forgotten. Gentle, carefree people, we understand death as a part of life and violence only as an accident or the result of a rare natural phenomenon. The trappers' caution of slayers en masse was unfathomable—interesting but incomprehensible to us, a people who lived unawares, naïvely and oblivious of man's evil to man.

The summer came and went. Winter settled in upon us once again, this time with a vengeance. Cut off by drifting snow, the livestock suffered more than we did. The trappers and the smokehole incident of the previous winter were linked together in adult conversation.

The musicians fiddled and plucked their strings impromptu, a mellifluous rhythm and rhyming verse, a spontaneous flow. Sometimes they sang a mournful verse, then, to our great joy they imitated every bird, animal, and insect on the steppes. The timbre of the throat singers' voices was sometimes soft and soulful. I waited in anticipation for them to sound like horses, clopping horses plodding along, galloping, prancing and cantering horses, horses with or without a rider. I saw it all in my mind's eye. Together the *throat singers* created a horse race. That was the very best of all, when they quickened the pace and the horses picked up speed. We laughed with rollicking glee until we tired out. They sang until the weather abated.

The steppes were always swept by changing weather—some savage, some threatening and fretful, a gust or a blast of warm or frigid air, occasionally benign. With the last of the snows, the steppes shimmered with fresh green grasses. Overnight, waves of poppies and wildflowers burst forth, covering vistas in yellow, then blue, then pink. Dainty flower heads shimmered and shook in the gentle winds until they could no longer hold. Then came little puffs, each carrying a tiny seed that wafts and drifts until dashed into the grasses, assuring us of flowers for next year. These were the steppes I know and remember.

They exploded upon us at midday under pleasant skies, specter-like, at an unfathomable speed. Seeming to come from nowhere and every whither, swirling in midair, they were ferocious riders astride horses whose hooves reached skyward but never touched the ground—supernatural beings on horseback out of another dimension.

They passed through us like an unimpeded comet in the night sky. My father was first to be struck down. He barely rose to his feet, when one assassin drove a sword through him. I saw the amber amulet with the captured insect tumble from my father's pocket to be trampled into the ground. As in a dream, I reached for the amulet, as I rose up to go to my father. Simultaneously, two arrows pierced my chest. Before the pain could reach my brain, before I could cry out in anguish, my head left my body. It flew in one direction, as I lurched in another.

Like in a whirlwind, my spirit roiled aloft, lifting me out of reach. I was caught up in some sort of cosmic time warp. Rising high above the grasslands, I had a panoramic view. Strangely, I was seeing in all directions, simultaneously. I watched a wind burst in slow motion from above. The assassins below slaughtered all my cousins, the uncles, and the aunties. They butchered every one. One after another, every one of my family members ascended to join and mingle with the other spirits of the plains. The upward gyre lifted them from a frenzy and carnage too ghastly to recount. The old camel wandered off confused but unmolested.

In about the same amount of time it would take for a shooting star to traverse the night sky, the deed was done, except for the frenzied plundering, looting, gathering of spoils, and torching the remains below. We survived by reaching a new dimension. I viewed our demise safely above the blood-soaked grasslands.

Inexplicably, I viewed this specter without any pain or anxiety. It appeared as a cyclorama of rapidly moving pictures, flitting and flickering, which collected me up, carrying me beyond the steppes. Depending on one's perspective, this was an important or not so important segment of a great continuum that ultimately carried me higher in an updraft. Swoosh, the person Montuulgyar ceased to be.

My ordinary mind dissolved into the oneness of total liberation. I entered the vast and boundless space of my "sky mind," the moment life becomes death. My vital essence was now traveling through a vast openness of time and space, free to enter the wonders of other realms.

This was a personal glimpse of the Mongol quest. It is not for me to know, or say, why my young life was taken before it had barely begun. Why good and decent people died at the hands of hate mongers. Why generations of knowledge amassed over centuries through my ancestors would be swept away by others. It appeared, at least on the surface, that evil triumphed over good.

We were merely people living in spiritual harmony with one another and nature.

We were only a few of the innocent victims of the despot, Genghis Khan, and his hordes, when he chose to cut a wide swathe through Mongol lands and beyond, seizing power and marking a place for himself in history.

I lived and observed that throughout the course of history, this sort of thing happened again and again. These were pivotal moments in time. Moments in history that disrupted and retarded the development of civilization, and shifted us a bit off course.

18
Kyoto

WHEN I RETURNED TO the room after dinner, it had been transformed. The futon was laid out for sleeping. The low table and two low armchairs previously in the center of the room had been moved near the balcony. Some packets of snacks, cups, and a thermos of hot water for tea and an ashtray were on the table. Everything else was stowed behind sliding doors. I bathed, then slipped the neatly folded cotton *yukata* the maid had provided over my night gown.

A *shoji* screen, the rice paper-covered wooden lattice outer door, had been slid back to frame the dark night, the bars, restaurants, and living quarters along the opposite side of the Kamo river. Down the river I saw the Gion Bridge and made out silhouettes of heavy pedestrian traffic. It was well after midnight, yet lights were still ablaze.

Still feeling the effects of rice wine, *saki*, and a warm bath, I sat mesmerized watching the lights reflected and shimmering on the water. From time to time, I became aware of the people in the next room and was reminded to be ultra quiet myself because of the paper-thin walls of the traditional Japanese inn. It was not uncommon to be awakened in the middle of the night by noisy snoring or coughing in the next room. I pulled the *kimono* tighter around my bare legs and sat thinking about the people on the bridge, the light on the water, and the nature of the relationship between me and Takeo Takahashi.

I harkened to what seemed to be a tap at the door. My door or on the room next door? Then I dismissed it, until I heard it again. It seemed to be my door. Maybe the maid. I took five steps across the room, negotiating my way around the futon in the dim light, and slid the door open a bit.

It was Takeo Takahashi, not in street clothes as I had seen him earlier, but wearing a black hip length *haroi* and dark pants. The formal silk *haori* had the *kamon*, or *mon*, symbol of his family name; I had seen this symbol before. Without saying a word, I invited him in while wondering where he had come from. I was rather certain he was not staying in this *ryokan*, traditional Japanese style inn.

He stepped in. We walked around the futon to the little table and sat down. Without conversing, he went about making green tea and we sat sipping and looking out across the glittering lights on the water, mindful of the people next door. He smoked a cigarette. There was no taboo on smoking in Japan. It seemed tobacco use had a deep cultural tradition, particularly for men.

We had exchanged no words since he had come into the room. It was pleasant sharing the easy quiet with him and watching the flow of the river. Eventually, he got up and came around behind my chair, bending low to breathe on and kiss the back of my neck. His hand gently on my throat, his fingers soon slipped in to the V-neckline of my *yukata* and found my breast. He kissed my ear and throat, feeling my response, then lightly moved his hands over my arms, encircling me. Eventually, he took my hands in his and drew me up to my feet and into his arms. His every touch and breath was sensuous. We hadn't been like this before.

Standing in his arms as he kissed my throat and neck, he pressed his hardness against me, untied the sash of my *yukata*, then loosened the tie of his *haori* and let it and his pants drop. He left me weak and lightheaded; I needed him to support me. His skin was smooth and his chest, hairless. His body was lithe, but he was very strong and firm, his muscles lean and undefined. He pushed away my *yukata*, and we eased onto the futon as he removed my gown, sensitively kissing my ears, my mouth, my breasts, as he proceeded. We lay there kissing and touching. He continued only when feeling stronger desire from me. Clearly an experienced lover, he was unhurried. I kissed his lips, moving over them lightly with my tongue and lips. Passion was taking us over.

Before he further heightened my arousal, he touched one finger to his lips and then lightly pressed it to mine, as if to remind me that the walls were paper thin. I wanted to speak to him, but English seemed wrong, and I had no Japanese language skills in love making. In a passionate whisper I asked, "What does this mean?" He murmured, "Whatever you like edolady. Let me be part of your fantasy, your floating world. We can have our own floating world."

His reference was to the Edo period in Japanese history, famous for woodbock prints of *samurai*, courtesans, and the *kabuki* theater. Until now there had been no suggestion of romance between us, everything was proper and professional, but then the Japanese people don't show affection in public, and we had always been among people when together. There had been a tension between us that could be acknowledged, or not. But now, intimate like this, the tension was acknowledged for what it was, and in his arms, I felt like I had known him for a hundred years. It was as if we were two mature adults enjoying one another at a preordained time and place. Time after time, we had sex, then lay there together, our hearts thumping wildly in the silence of the night. It was the perfect time, it was the perfect place, and ours was the perfect sexual union.

The lights across the river were going out one after another. He went to the bathroom and brought back two damp cloths. He handed one to me, lightly blotting my forehead, face, and neck, encouraging me to do the same. Intermittently he stopped to kiss me, to nuzzle or fondle me, as he gently wiped perspiration from my breast and torso, taking my breasts in his hands or mouth from time to time. The night breeze and the damp cloth was cooling and I lay back, lost in the pleasure of his touch until my passion caused me to pull him to me, hungrily kissing his throat and mouth over and over again.

I was eager to have him finish with the cloth, but he continued, playing lightly over my stomach and navel, pausing only for licking, kissing, and caressing. He continued his lovemaking purposefully, his passion controlled, mine out of control. If we weren't kissing, he was looking at my body; I was writhing in response. Seeing me like this he chose to kiss my toes and the arch of my foot, still watching me as he proceeded to gently touch the insides of my thighs. As I willingly yielded, he tossed the cloth aside. His fingers had a strong but tender erotic touch, and I found myself to be a fully willing participant, open and eager to have him excite me. He was a man who understood a woman's body. With a full erection, he controlled his passion, while using his tongue and fingers to excite me. He watched me as he brought me to the moment of climax. Then with perfect timing, consumed in the heat of our sexual desire, we climaxed together. Collapsing in exhaustion, I fell into a blissful sleep.

I was startled awake by a noise in the hallway. The piercing sunlight was forcing its way through the *shoji*; he wasn't there. I had no idea when he'd left, but he must have closed the *shoji* to the night air before leaving. Lying there on the tatami, I considered that this had all been a dream, until I saw the remains of partially smoked cigarettes in the ashtray. I closed my eyes so as not to fully awake. I turned over and felt around for my handbag. Without opening my eyes, I reached into the outside pocket and pulled out a pen and notebook and wrote:

The cool damp air
a partner to the morning breeze
blows over me in waft-like tufts.
Slid back, the shoji screen
provides no barrier.
Night noises have silenced
to a solitary stillness.
The night absorbed into the dampness
of woven tatami grasses
and nothing moves.
I come into this silence reluctantly
pushing away the futon.
I embrace the breeze.
Knowing that this space in time
is fleeting and will not last.

I inhaled, then exhaled deeply. Opening my eyes, I felt a new feeling of contentment. I wanted to luxuriate in the moment, but thoughts of my OKC poetry group came to mind. I smiled. I thought they would be proud of me, but they would never hear this one. This place—Japan—feeds my soul.

Another thump by the maid in the hallway jarred me back to reality. I had to hurry. Yesterday we'd agreed to meet for brunch before my train departure, and I assumed that the events of last night had not changed that. His driver was to pick me up.

Hurriedly, I stepped into the small square of a deep tub and managed a shower using the apparatus available. I had just gotten my things together when the housekeeper tapped on the door. She spoke no English, so in her way she told me the driver was downstairs. As I was about to pick up my bags, she communicated to me that I should go on, someone was coming for them.

His uniformed driver bowed and opened the door. I got in and a moment later, the houseboy came with my luggage. Once everything was loaded, we drove through Kyoto streets for twenty minutes, then along a roadway with fewer houses until we arrived at what appeared to be a private club or resort in dense woods. We passed by an area where several private cars waited, two with motors running, their drivers standing at the ready. Fastidious, uniformed, white-gloved drivers inspected and dusted their shining black vehicles. The landscaping was masterful, and I wanted to bask in the natural surroundings, the gigantic trees, the light, and the remembrance of the night before.

Perfectly situated in an idyllic landscape with water features was an ancient structure with a high and thick thatched roof. At the entrance, I saw Takeo standing at the top of the stairs speaking to a man.

As the driver opened the door and I stepped out, Takeo was there to take my hand. In Japan, everything was always perfectly timed, as if choreographed. Situations were never awkward or ruffled by missteps. With his hand lightly at my elbow, we walked across the stone path and up the few steps. There Takeo introduced me to the gentleman, who was the owner and manager.

Almost immediately a diminutive *kimono* clad young woman appeared, directed us to some garden stools in the pavilion, and poured *saki* from a piece of green bamboo into tiny lacquerware saucers. Takeo and the owner drank theirs in one swallow. I wet my lips and savored a bit in my mouth. The two spoke in Japanese, then enjoined me to discuss the piquant of *saki* served from bamboo. An experience to relish, I felt.

The lovely girl in *kimono* with an exquisite *obi* came back and collected our cups, then another one, who must have been waiting for us out of sight, appeared. Takeo and I followed her outside and along a path of stepping stones, off which private tea houses were secluded by the lush landscape. Shoes at the doorstep indicated whether the place was occupied, or not.

We left our shoes on the doorstep and stepped into a small tatami room closed to the world on two sides and open to the privacy of nature on the other. It included a table over a pit, two cushions, and an alcove large enough for a scroll appropriate to the season, and a stunning, jaw dropping ancient pot, a stem of blossoms seemingly transfixed, floated above it. It was picture perfect. The door slid closed behind us.

Except to say "good morning" and the brief exchange with the owner, Takeo and I had yet to converse. I expected some moment of intimacy with him; instead, we settled on cushions opposite each other. His eyes wandered over me, and he took my hand to his mouth, his lips kissing each finger, sliding sensuously from one to another. Melting into his eroticism, immersed in him, I would have missed the incoming *kimono* clad girl as she slid the door open. He did not. He anticipated her appearance and rather smoothly but abruptly placed my hand on the table, assuming an air of propriety and decorum. Attempting to regain my composure, I diverted my eyes to the view beyond.

The steady stream of cooking and serving people, which began with a young man bringing the hot coals, provided ample company throughout the various courses of the meal. And we kept the conversation to the food courses and events of the moment, making no reference to the night before. He told me that the ancient house with which I was enamored dated back several centuries and had been moved to this site.

After eating, we visited another ancient house, examining the construction, the heavy oak beams and the artifacts, including farm implements, antique armaments, *samurai* armor, and some pottery and blue and white textiles.

Afterward, his driver took the two of us to the train station for my departure on the Shinkansen to Tokyo. He helped me with my luggage. I knew that he had a business trip out of the country coming up. And he knew I was taking an excursion to Egypt with a group of teachers. So we made no plans for a future meeting.

19
Sara – The Girl from Galilee

YEARS PASSED, AND I came to realize that there was no such thing as a chance encounter, that there was no such thing as a co-incidence, and that all relationships, whether for a lifetime or for a brief moment, something as trivial as brushing the sleeve of a stranger by accident in the market place or our children, particularly our children, were all part of some great and grand scheme of things, a divine plan. For me, serendipitous meetings punctuated this lifetime, and by old age, I was firmly convinced that no matter how seemingly insignificant an encounter appeared, it had meaning. I wished I had known this when I was young. I passed by people and through events thoughtlessly. In this lifetime, some meetings, acts, and experiences were burned into my heart and soul, and indeed, they were so significant, they were destined to become a part of my over-soul.

One particular day, I had stopped at the marketplace to buy some fruit for my mother. Normally our household help would have made these purchases as part of her daily chores, but on this day I was on a self-appointed mission to select the fruit. It would be fair to say that I was not supposed to be there, that I led a life of relative privilege, and being alone in the marketplace was not where my mother and father would prefer me to spend my time. Upon reflection, I always had an insatiable, innate curiosity or perhaps because of the restrictions placed upon me since childhood, I had developed more than a natural inquisitiveness, a strong desire to investigate places, and was keen on meeting people beyond our family compound. It seemed the more barriers my parents erected to blunt my actions, the more I turned toward what they would term "inappropriateness." The more they thwarted my activities and attempted to rein me in, the more they sparked my curiosity.

My father was a rabbi but not opposed to the education of young women. He encouraged me in history and religious studies. He was, however, strongly opposed to my having interests outside the home and adamantly discouraged my familiarity "with strangers," as he put it. I took that to include peasants, servants, tradesmen, and the working class in general. I thought this was quite ridiculous, unfair, rude, and ill mannered. For a person of his religious stature, it was hypocritical. I found this especially restrictive, particularly because since childhood I easily launched into conversation with merchants and shop keepers, the clergy—in short, just about everybody I met. My mother said I had done so since I'd learned to talk and that as a child, I embarrassed her by smiling and waving enthusiastically to anybody and everybody.

It was a perfectly beautiful summer day. I was alone in the marketplace, having a look around—on the pretense of buying fruit—which I did do. The sack gave way, and several pieces fell to the ground. As I bent over to gather them up, more started to fall and a sort of catching and juggling act began. Another young woman, older than I, saw my dilemma and immediately came to my rescue. As together we scrambled to pick up my dropped fruit, several vegetables fell from her bundle to the ground, too. Simultaneously, we lifted our heads and our eyes met. We broke out in laughter from the calamitous situation. I helped her retrieve her vegetables, and she helped me put the fruit in another sack. We bonded in an instant—friends forever. Her name was Mary.

These were not normal times. The presence of the Roman soldiers in our land was uncomfortable for Jews, both male and female. Women had always led modest, circumspect lives, careful and cautious not to attract attention. During these days, there was a reluctance to walk in public or take care of necessary routine daily chores alone. There were incidents and there were rumors of ill-tempered soldiers thrashing innocent citizens. Such was life during these times.

From my point of view, life was even more complicated for me because I was the daughter of a prominent member of the Sanhedrin, the supreme council of the Jews, having religious, civil, and criminal jurisdiction over our society at the time. According to what I overheard from my father's conversations with my brothers, things were turbulent within the Sanhedrin. Political conflicts within the body were getting worse, and it was impossible to get consensus on any issue. Deception, maneuvering, and manipulation among the many factions made his life difficult and uncertain.

Now, more than ever, unity and stability in the Sanhedrin was needed in the face of the Roman threat. With Greeks against the Hebrews, the Sadducees, Pharisees, Chaldeans, Gentiles, and other miscellaneous sects all stirring things up, there wasn't much hope of harmony. Many times I felt that my father was exasperated with the confluence of political and religious matters.

I had my own conflicts and frustrations, torn between the rules and rituals of Jewish society and living in my father's household, along with my own evolving feelings and beliefs on what was fair, right, or wrong. My dilemma was largely self-inflicted because, increasingly, I was doing what I wanted and disregarding my parent's wishes. Unbeknown to my family, I enjoyed the companionship of Mary, whom I considered to be a friend. She would not have been acceptable to my family. Through her, I allowed myself to get drawn in with her friends and acquaintances. Thus, my life became further complicated by my fascination with her friend, Joshua-Ben Joseph, who we called Jeshua and who later came to be known as Jesus of Nazareth.

Since I was frequently seen in the company of Mary, the fact that I could be recognized by someone who knew my father weighed heavily on me. For me, there was nothing higher than truth, and being secretive was being less than truthful. This internal conflict did not sit well with me and, consequently, I was not at peace with myself.

Our family's social position and the requirements thereof caused within me increasing degrees of tension and rebellion. I knew that my father was under great strain because of the political situation, and I did not want to cause additional trouble. I lived in fear that my activities would be reported to him, yet I couldn't bring myself to talk to him. I rationalized that he was too busy, and I wouldn't be able to make myself understood. As the months wore on, I felt suffocated at home and resented being a young woman in this repressive environment. I felt that laws governing society and family only served to deprive me of my free will—divinely given liberties, divinely given freedom. I felt the rules of the religious community were arbitrary and man made, not logical and not in line with the natural order of things. The reasons for oppressing the population and encroaching on people's lives and subjugating the less fortunate were not entirely within my grasp. It seemed to me that some were controlling the many, through rules, the Law, and taxation, simply to gain power and wealth. In no way could I reconcile what I was living and seeing with the will of the Creator.

Furthermore, I found a particular Roman soldier attractive, and any relationship with a Roman soldier was totally unthinkable. Reflecting back on it, my life at this time was in a real turmoil caused, at least to some degree, by my inability to be forthright with my parents. That they would not be open to discussing my feelings and opinions was another factor.

I had been talking with Mary of Magdal and Jeshua. We were discussing a plan, Mary's idea, which came about when she learned I could write both Greek and Hebrew and some Latin. It was uncommon in these times for a woman to know how to write, much less admit she could. I developed this ability quite innocently, first by silently observing my brothers with their teachers, and later at ages three and four, I simply sat quietly playing, unobserved, listening to them studying with the rabbi. Apparently, I knew this was not appropriate for a girl because I practiced with a stick in the sandy soil when no one was looking, then wiped it out with my foot. So by the time I met Mary, I could write Hebrew and I also had more than a passing acquaintance with Greek and Latin gained from my father's library and overhearing my brothers' lessons. Later, my whole family was aghast when they found out what I had done.

Mary had a plan. She wanted a scribe of sorts, someone to document Jeshua's work, his teaching at the meetings and gatherings, the baptisms and healings; furthermore, Mary and Jeshua needed this record taken to the Essenes' for safekeeping. Since among all of us I was able to write, I was the only choice to write an eyewitness sort of account of his work. The major problem would be getting the written information to the Essenes. It was far too dangerous for Jeshua's trusted men followers to carry this information on their person. Men were frequently stopped, searched, and questioned by soldiers. The Nazarenes, who surrounded Jeshua, were probably under surveillance by the Romans. They could be stopped, maybe beaten, and would have been prosecuted. So they couldn't do this. On the other hand, a woman was not likely to be stopped or approached by a soldier. So, we reasoned this could best be done by a woman, specifically me, because all of my life I had been seen communicating and interacting with every strata of society and all backgrounds, comfortably moving amongst the diverse population. I agreed to write it the best I could, and I agreed to carry the parchment to someone who would deliver these "testimonials" to the Essenes.

Within and around the city there was a presence of Roman soldiers. As time advanced, increasingly more soldiers were among us. There was rarely a carefree moment and a sort of dis-ease or paranoia set in. I felt certain my father was to some extent aware of my activities. Although I would not wish ill fortune on my father, nor did I want to complicate his life, it was rather lucky for me that he was too caught up in his own work and the problems of the day to approach me. He had implored my mother to set more boundaries to "dampen my spirit."

I overheard mother one evening, saying, "You know she has had a natural curiosity since early childhood, and you said yourself she has a keen intellect. I'm not sure what I can do."

To which he replied, "Well, you're her mother, and I expect you to deal with this, we cannot have her traipsing about the countryside like a vagabond. You could keep her occupied at home, so that she is not out and about."

Every family member agreed that my behavior was "inappropriate" in these treacherous times. My father's concerns were valid, for both Jews and women were in real danger from Roman soldiers. Added to which my father, and therefore his family, had enemies within the religious community and among some socially prominent families. Tongues wagged. There were always gossipers looking to strengthen their own position by running down their neighbors. Politics was involved, to be sure. Actions of family members were always under scrutiny by Roman soldiers and by the Jewish citizenry.

It was our customary practice to take leave of our group one or two at a time, so as not to draw attention to our meeting place or ourselves. One particular afternoon, I was walking alone on a rather isolated but well-worn path that followed along the remains of a partially collapsed old stone wall. Enjoying the beauty of the day, I was deep in thought. I was excited about what I'd seen, what he'd said, and what I'd recorded.

I was engrossed in an inner dialog of thoughts rapidly flittering through my mind. *He teaches love. That is his message, teaching people to love one another, and that was his main theme again today. What harm is there in that? He is simply teaching love. Think of the good he brings. The message is simple: Love one another.* Then the crosscurrents came. *What is it about Jeshua that causes so much angst among the many religious factions, including my father and the Sanhedrin?* It was hard to explain how I felt at that moment. Confused? Angry?

Then, when I mused upon those things I had witnessed that day, I had more questions. I didn't understand how he could drive the evil spirits out of those troubled folks, and I didn't understand how the evil spirits had gotten into them in the first place. He'd healed the infirmities of a little girl. Knowing that child was whole and able to play with others uplifted me, and a sense of relief passed through me. I saw many things I did not understand, and my rational mind wanted to make sense of it.

I wanted to discuss this with my father and ask him just why Jeshua was so problematic for the Sanhedrin. How to approach the subject with him was beyond me. I'm sorry to say that, but my father, like other members of the Sanhedrin, was not open to new thinking. He was content to ignore contemporary issues to maintain the status quo. Jeshua's difficulties with the Romans was bad enough, but why the Sanhedrin? The Sanhedrin should embrace him, he was a Jew, and one of us, I thought.

I heard him speak, and saw with my own eyes some remarkable things he did. My father hadn't. I had been there. He hadn't. It would be very difficult to explain. Even I had many questions I couldn't resolve. One could say people do not like change, and one could also say he and his followers saw that change was needed. True, Jeshua was disrupting the status quo during times when people were already disturbed about taxes and threatened by Roman rule, but I'd seen with my own eyes what transpired. I believed in him, the goodness of his work, and I needed no further convincing about his worth. How could I approach my father? He was so set against Jeshua. True, he'd caused a ruckus in the temple several times, but he was right. Not only should the Sanhedrin take action against the corruption taking place in a holy place, but also by their silence, they condoned it. Thoughts turned to the contents of my pocket. Had I written all I'd observed that day?

As I walked home, I was pondering deeply the events I had seen and was in the moment, totally oblivious to danger, as I walked right past a soldier who was concealed by the piles of stone rubble and underbrush.

"You should be careful of the company you keep," were the words he used, jarring me out of my reverie, so close that I felt his breath on the back of my neck. He practically whispered in my ear. I froze in place and a shiver ran through my body. Startled at the appearance of a Roman soldier standing next to me, who seemed to show up from nowhere, my eyes flew wide open, jolting me back to reality.

In perfect Hebrew, he said, "My apologies, I didn't mean to frighten you." There was a deep resonance in his voice that much to my surprise rolled off his tongue as soft and smooth as honey in the summertime. His voice didn't match his size, which was threatening and intimidating. He towered over me, tall, with broad shoulders and a well-developed chest apparent under his tunic. He was muscular and his powerful forearms had been scraped, rubbed, and oiled. At first, he took a stance with his hands on his hips, at his belts and weapons. Then he relaxed his arms. His voice, engaging as it was, piqued my curiosity, and while I should have averted my eyes, I didn't.

His military comportment was formal, his brown eyes and soft smile juxtaposed his physical strength and power, unnerving me. I was shocked and startled by his appearance. I faked a feeling of fearlessness and looked directly into his eyes, as if to say, "How dare you?" But not defiant enough to stir his wrath.

He paused, looked at me, not quite smiling, and took a deep breath, audibly inhaling and exhaling through his nose. He blinked his dark brown eyes, stepped back, and quietly said, "You're free to go."

Heart pumping, I continued on my way, but the ease of the day was broken. I was overcome by this encounter. Everything in me was a quivering, fluttering mass, but I kept telling myself, "Keep your shoulders back and your chin up, and whatever you do, don't reach for your pocket!"

Upon reaching home, I felt a sense of relief. The soldier's words, "You should be careful about the company you keep," kept repeating in my mind throughout the evening. I was a bit feverish, and my ear seemed too hot to the touch. Did he know where I had been? Did he know whom I was with? Did he know what I was carrying? Did he know my father? I didn't dare mention this to anyone in the family. I didn't want to get in a conversation that might reveal where I had been and what I was carrying. When my mother asked me if I was feeling all right, I said my menstruation was coming, excused myself, and retired early. Having no one else with whom I could discuss my uneasiness, I decided to seek Mary out the very next day.

Several times I caught a glimpse of that soldier, twice in the marketplace and three times on my way to the synagogue. He was always with an entourage who seemed to be under his command. Once in the marketplace I was quite aware that he was looking at me, but I just went about my business and did not lift my eyes to meet his glance. After a while, it became abundantly clear to me that he had made it his business to know where I was. Why? Was it his duty to follow me? Did he know what I was doing, or was there some other explanation?

He was not like any other man I had ever been near. The men in my family were small-framed, slightly built, you might say diminutive in size, devout and scholarly. This man was handsome, with a physically authoritative bearing. Although I knew nothing about military ranks in the Roman Army, I was certain he was an officer, a person of senior rank. Several centurions walked in front of him, clearing the way, and there were others behind him. To add to this spectacle, I noticed there was often another person in a red toga walking and conversing with him, who didn't carry a weapon and didn't seem to be a soldier. About his intellectual capacity, I couldn't tell, but he seemed to be the leader, refined and well mannered, commanding the respect and admiration of those with him.

He was young, about twenty-five years of age, very attractive, and he stirred something in me I'd never felt before.

I tried to get beyond these feelings for several reasons. First, the "inappropriateness" of me talking to a Roman soldier would prove my family correct. Second, the "testimonials" I wrote might be looked at as a crime. I knew that to carry them and pass them to the Essenes was very dangerous.

I was not on secure ground with him, either, and had no idea what was running through his mind. I was relatively certain he was aware of most of my comings and goings. Some of the time, it seemed he was trifling with me. It crossed my mind he might be flirting with me. On the other hand, he could be pursuing me, just doing his job, shadowing me in order to catch me. I couldn't determine his intentions.

One particular day, I went to the home of our seamstress to pick up some things. I was carrying several parcels, which were awkward and almost too much to manage. I stopped to shift my armful when he appeared seemingly out of nowhere, escorted by several young Centurions. He offered to help, but I modestly declined. He insisted, took charge of the situation, and gently swept the bundles out of my arms. Somewhat shocked but with little recourse, I yielded.

He passed my belongings to two soldiers and dismissed the others, giving orders to a soldier who seemed to be the oldest. Then he escorted me down the street with the two others flanking but several paces behind. I knew then that he knew who I was, where I lived, and likely who my father was. Obviously this didn't seem to matter to him. He delivered me and the packages to our gate, placed them on the garden bench, then politely nodded, almost bowing, and said, "Good day," before leaving.

There would be no covering this. I had been seen in public with a Roman soldier, with Roman soldiers, by any number of people, who would, without a doubt, report this to my father. I was shaking and casting about for a plausible explanation.

When my father came home, earlier than usual, he could barely cover his rage. He called my mother to sit with us. His face was red. He started by looking piercingly at me, saying, "Esther Saravannah, woe be unto you." He let those words settle, then cleared his throat and continued. "I do not want to believe what I heard today, and from more than one source, I might add. Do you realize what you have done? How often have I cautioned you about strangers? Since you were a young child, I warned you about talking to strangers!"

"I didn't speak to him," I interjected. This was true.

My mother, who had seen the soldiers at the garden gate, quietly but firmly said, "Do not interrupt your father."

"Do you know who this Centurion is?"

Not sure whether he expected an answer or not, I timidly said, "No."

"Well, let me tell you Saravannah, you have put me in an extremely difficult position. Life is difficult enough without this public spectacle to deal with. I ask you again, do you know who this man is?" He didn't wait for an answer. His voice got louder as he continued. "He is the *tribunus laticlavus*, out there," waving his hand in the direction of the garrison. "That is the sort of person you have no business fraternizing with. Do you understand me, Sara?" He paused but was not expecting an answer from me.

When he paused, my mother said, "For heaven's sake, what is the *tribunus laticlavus*?"

He turned to her, dropped the emotion of the moment, and said, "The *tribunus laticlavus* is a senatorial rank, Esther. He's right up there with the legatus. He's probably some snot-nosed rich boy from Rome, who had some sort of government job there, and now he's here serving enough time to qualify himself for a higher political office. Two, three years and he'll be gone from here. He's not a professional soldier; he's just a politician in the making from a wealthy, land holding family, putting in his time." Then he added, "Probably."

My mother naïvely said, "That sounds like a good thing, Abraham. I mean not being a professional soldier."

Shaking his head, my father looked at my mother in disgust; his eyes dismissed her comment.

I was glad she'd asked because father's answer clarified some things for me, too.

He continued. "He probably doesn't do anything out there," he said, waving his hand toward the garrison again. "It's his first job away from home, and I can assure you he counts on the *prafectus castrorum* to do his job for him. Doesn't know a thing, just a snot-nosed young Roman on the fast track, if you ask me."

I'd never heard my father call anyone snot-nosed. Yes, I knew him to be hypocritical from time to time, but he was never rude, and always respectful, particularly of rank.

Directing his remarks to me, he said, "And, Sara, I do not want you to be seen in this or any other man's company again. Do you understand me? You will not defy me. You will not disobey me," he said, glaring at me. Then, with finality, he dismissed me with a wave, saying, "Go to your room; we are finished here."

Eventually I realized the *tribunus lacticlavus* knew exactly what he was doing. He knew where I was and what I was doing, much of the time. Possibly he understood there was a family fracas caused by his help with the packages, and he didn't want to cause me any further problems. Although he was frequently in the marketplace with his entourage, he never approached me in a public place again.

He did seek me out. Our next meeting was on the path where he'd first stepped into my life. This time, he said he wanted to talk with me. I told him politely, "I'm sorry, please don't be offended, but I can't talk to you. I must not talk to you."

He smiled mischievously and said, "Well, it's going to be difficult carrying on a conversation with you if you can't talk, but it can be done."

I said, "That's very funny, but I am serious. I must not be seen with you. Those are my father's orders, and that's not likely to change. You do understand orders, don't you?"

He replied, "Indeed I do understand orders. So, we would be wise not to be seen together." Lightly touching my elbow, he directed me off the path and behind the dilapidated, falling down, stone wall. To my surprise, I went with him!

We met on that pathway many times and talked about many things behind the wall. We were there so often he made us a sitting place in the rubble. We talked about the weather, social issues, political matters, his job, my life, our likes, and our dislikes, anything else that came to our minds. Very soon we knew a lot about each other and our respective family members. If he took my hand, I did not withdraw it from him. Sometimes he looked at my hands, not saying anything, just contemplatively examining my fingers, my face, and my hair. Strangely, when he stood next to me, I felt protected and safe.

Once, out of the clear blue, he surprised me by asking, "Who is the Nazarene, and what do you know of him?"

"Well," I started, hesitantly, "Jeshua? Yes, I do know him. Yes, but he's not really knowable. It's hard to explain, and I guess it sounds strange. He seems to be an ordinary man, but he's somehow marvelously mysterious or maybe I should say, wise beyond measure. I try to sort out what I see and hear, but he is unfathomable. I have seen him heal sick people. Really. It seems he can look straight into a person's eyes and know everything about them. Me, too, I swear to you, he looked right into my soul. Really. We were walking along, I was limping a bit, and he asked me what was the matter with my foot. It's nothing much, it's only a stone bruise, I said to him. In the next moment, he healed it. Really, it was in an instant. Then I was overcome, so I didn't see what happened but instantly I felt warmth radiate through my body and my foot was completely better. It's hard to explain, it's rather a mystery, I think. I have also seen him drive demons out of a deranged person. I can only tell you, he has wisdom that passes all understanding. I am fascinated by his words and deeds, and I love to listen to him, but he really is unknowable. Yes, really. He truly is a good person. Different, but a very good person."

He looked at me, skeptically, in disbelief like all the others. So I went on, as if my witness accounts might convince him. "Interestingly, when he healed my foot, he said, in a reassuring manner, 'You are worthy.' It was at that very moment I had been thinking, 'I am not worthy.' It was as if he knew what was in my mind, like he knew what I was thinking. This is too hard to explain. I know it sounds strange, but it seemed to me he can see into my soul."

Just as someone who had never been in Jeshua's presence would, just as an unbeliever would, he said, "Well, Sara, you're a very transparent person." As if that explained it!

I wanted to be understood, so I gave some other examples of what I had seen him do, until he stopped me. "Sara," he said, "I do believe you, but I don't think you should be so open about what you have seen and heard. These are dangerous times, and I worry that harm could come to you though your association with him and that woman. Does your father know you see them, the Nazarene and Mary, the woman from Magdal? I have often seen you walking with them. Others will have seen you, too."

"I have never spoken of them to my father, so, no, I expect he doesn't know. Neither he nor my mother knows about my friendship with Mary. They wouldn't approve. I'm almost bursting to tell my father what I have seen Jeshua do and say, and just what special friends both of them are to me."

He sighed deeply. "I wouldn't do that if I were you," he said, as he took me by the hand and pulled me to my feet. "You'd better hope your father never learns of it. He'd have you locked in the house until you are old and withered." We laughed, both knowing that wasn't far from the truth.

Most days when I came along the path, he was there. When he wasn't, I felt disappointed. It was like my day was not complete, like there was no joy in it.

One day we were standing behind the wall talking, and I could sense that his mood was pensive. I could tell he had something on his mind. Finally, he blurted out, "I'm leaving soon."

"Leaving to where?" I asked.

"Home, to Rome," he replied.

"Why? Couldn't you stay longer?" I inquired, searching his face for a positive answer.

"No, I can't. Replacements are coming and should be here soon. It's really out of my hands. I have a job waiting for me in Rome. I should have told you sooner. I guess you knew that eventually my time here would end." Then, taking both of my hands, he pulled me close to him. I thought I might cry.

He rested his chin lightly on the top of my head and rubbed his cheek against my hair. He whispered in the voice that always went to the core of me, "Come with me." He tightened his embrace, and for the moment I couldn't move.

"What do you mean?" I asked. When he released me, I drew away both surprised and confused.

"Exactly what I just said. Come away with me. Marry me and come away with me to Rome." He put his hand up as if to stop my reply. He went on. "Sara, it's not safe for you here, without me. You could be found out." This was the first time he'd acknowledged knowing about the parchment in my pocket. He said, "You know I admire your courage, but eventually you will be found out. That aside, let's stay on point," he said.

"I know this is sudden, but please don't refuse me. I've had time to think about this, and you haven't. I know we would have a good life together. Sara, we would have a wonderful life together, more than you know. I can't explain. I'd have to take you there, to show you. You will be happy in Rome with me. We can have a family. Tell me you will think about it. I'm sorry," he said. "I didn't mean to spring this on you. Saravannah, truly, I can't imagine life without you, and I can't go and leave you here." He was looking into my eyes, searching me for an answer. He wrapped his arms around me and said sincerely, "It is too dangerous for you to be here without me. Believe me, I expect things will get increasingly worse. I know that if your friend Mary and the Nazarene are around here, you will be with them. There are other factors that portend danger for you. Understand, there could be some incident, and you could be caught up in it. I could never rest knowing you were here without me. Come away with me."

I opened my mouth to say it was impossible, but he seemed to know what I was going to say, and he put his fingers up to my lips. "Hush," he said. "Sara, I love you, and I think you love me, too. Tell me you will come because I don't want to leave without you."

I don't know how it happened, but somehow, from the day we'd met, I felt he was in charge of me. It's just the way it was between us. My strength dissolved when confronted with his. I went limp. I simply melted, dissolved, and this moment was no different. When he kissed my mouth, he lifted me off the ground—I knew then that when the time came for him to leave, I would go with him.

"I thought a Centurion was not allowed to marry," I said.

He said, "Yes, that would be true; however, my status is somewhat different from that of a Centurion. If I choose to marry, I can and I will."

"You do realize I am a Jewess, don't you?" I asked.

"Yes," he replied, "but I believe our love can overcome all things."

"What about your parents?" I asked.

"What about them?" he said. Not waiting for an answer, he went on. "They will love you as their own. I already wrote to tell my mother. They'll be expecting us. Any more questions?"

I was silent.

So he said, "Well, hearing no further questions, I will speak to the *legatus* and very soon the *legatus* and I will take this up with your father. Arrangements for our travel will have to be made, and of course, you will want to arrange for the wedding."

My heart skipped a beat. I was in a daze when I left him, wondering how I could keep this all to myself throughout the evening.

I later came to the realization that in those few months, we had been captured in our own love story. His desire for me was as strong as mine was for him. Come what may, even for a Jewess and a Roman soldier, love could not be denied.

My nature is to be open and honest, sometimes being excessively direct. My increasing boldness was exacerbated by my frustrations; I didn't like secrets. I didn't want to keep secrets from my parents. Perhaps it could be excused as growing into womanhood. Clearly there was tension between my parents because of my attitude. My mother no longer supported me, and privately she reminded me that obedience was expected from my brothers and me.

My father was talking to my brothers when everything spilled out. My presence there was solely to bring whatever my father requested from the kitchen or his library. Of course I was not included in their conversation. However, for nearly an hour, I had been questioning the veracity of what was being exchanged. I well knew that my opinion was not wanted, no matter how enlightening my thoughts may have been. Further, my brothers, who had recently lapsed into a habit of not looking at me directly when we were speaking, irritated me. True, men do this to women, making them disappear, but for my brothers this was a change in demeanor that I strongly resented. It was as if they were turning a blind eye to me. I was becoming invisible to them; they were no longer interested in what I had to say. My gender did not permit me to contribute to the conversation. That my father did this to my mother and me, I had somehow accepted as normal. Now, seeing this change in my brothers, my anger bordered on rage. The indignity of it was simmering near the surface. I was seething. I could not let this stand. I thought, in the sight of God, men and women are of equal value. I thought to myself, clearly Jeshua does not value women less than men. Yet, here are three men of God, my own kin, who think I account for nothing.

"As I see it, he, Jeshua works against evil in the world. If that means he is working against the Sadducees, the Pharisees, or dare I say, against the wishes of the Sanhedrin, then so be it," I piped up.

My father was stung by my words. He looked up at me, shocked that I'd even dared interrupt, intruding into a conversation between men. My mother stopped her task of tidying up teacups, stood frozen in place, but did not look up.

I kept on. "Father, you cannot deny that corruption exists among the Scribes and in the religious community. I've heard you say it yourself, that here are plenty who accept bribes and others who are in cahoots with the Romans."

My father, usually slow to anger, was livid, either because of what I'd said or because I dared to speak up in such a manner when men were having a discussion. I wasn't sure which bothered him most, but he was struggling to regain his composure. My outspokenness stunned him and my brothers, too, who were now looking directly at me. So I went on. "I sometimes wonder what those of you in the Temple know about the Creator. It seems to me that what is done and said is solely designed to serve the pious themselves. Certainly, there is no sensitivity to the overall needs of humankind. Self-serving, I dare say."

Although I am certain he knew there was truth in what I was saying, sadly, he could not admit it. He was too indignant that I, a woman, and his daughter would be disrespectful—to confront him with the facts. He was mad as a wet hen. "Sara, you need to silence that tongue of yours. What you say could be viewed as heresy. You may not speak to me like this in my house. First we have this matter of that Centurion and now we have this matter of this Nazarene!"

He asked, "How do you know of him, this Jeshua person?"

"I have walked with him, and I have talked with him. That is, with him and my friend Mary," I replied.

"I should say not!" my father shouted.

I realized that I had spoken too much, and while I'd never intended to reveal all this to my father in a heated conversation, there it was. I was into it, and I couldn't stop. My mother, hearing my father's raised voice, took hold of my sleeve with a slight tug in warning. "He has far more knowledge of the divine forces and the secrets and mysteries of the universe than anyone I have ever heard speak," I said. "Furthermore, he uses his insight and power for the good of all. I do mean *all!*"

My father was alarmed. He raised his eyebrows and glared at me, and then his eyes flew wide open in astonishment. "Sara, are you quite finished!" he said. It was not a question; it was a command. My brothers seemed amazed and sat motionless, looking down. My mother let go of my sleeve and retreated a bit, her mouth open in disbelief.

"Please, Father, I do live here, and I am not deaf. You and my brothers discuss these matters daily," I said.

Not accustomed to being challenged, he replied, "You may not be deaf, but you are impertinent, and you should not be listening to our discussions."

Quietly but firmly, I said, "From Jeshua I have learned *truth*, and about the invisible world, and I know that everyone, both man and woman, has a Divine mission, a purpose. You have yours. I have mine.

"Oh, really? Pray tell me, what is yours?" he said, uncharacteristically sarcastic.

"I'm not certain. It's not abundantly clear to me at this time. I pray about it, and I am meditating on it. I will not have my purpose thwarted, trampled, or sullied by the self-serving, and as long as we are having this discussion, I will tell you 'this Nazarene' has the power to heal. I have seen it, and I have experienced it," I said. Finished saying what had gone unsaid for too long, I left the room, leaving them speechless and aghast.

I am certain that throughout my youth and childhood, my parents had been looking forward to my marriage and a happy wedding day, but a Roman in our family was never included in whatever they'd envisioned. Nonetheless, there was a wedding, and there was a Roman presence there. It was not a joyful one. It was complicated, unacceptable, because Marcus was not a Jew. It was uncomfortable for my family with Roman soldiers attending. It was sad because some of our relatives, my father's friends and their families, chose not to attend. Everyone's emotions were held in check, and the strain on everyone was palpable.

There was no rejoicing in our happiness. Almost every one of the family members and friends that I knew and loved, were cold and distant to me. Those who attended came to give moral support for my parents, or perhaps out of curiosity. Marcus and I did our best to overcome the undercurrent of rancor and ever present cloud of gloom. I felt my father had to force himself to wish us well. When the day finished, we were exhausted. Marcus did his best to console me, saying, "When we get to Rome, we will have a proper wedding celebration."

Preparation for the wedding had been hurried, but leaving home altogether was accompanied by crosscurrents of feelings, spoken but mostly unspoken. Avoidance would aptly describe the situation at home. My father was angry; he looked defeated and dark. This was a family crisis. There was the aspect of the religious and political situation surrounding the marriage, but his position among family members and friends was a crisis of another sort. It seemed to me he would be happy when we were gone, the sooner the better. His heart would not let him disown me, but he could barely contain his wrath. My mother's mixed feelings were kept contained, except for a few tears; she came down along side of my father. Comforting and protecting her husband was her role in the matter. Perhaps there was an element of shame in her feelings. Tempered with the fact that she might never see me again, her pain and sorrow was obvious, but went unspoken. That's where the tears came in. I told her Marcus had promised me that I could come home to visit, and I would.

It seems fair to say I was in love, and my good judgment and perspective on things had flown out the window. If I knew the future, I probably would have done things somewhat differently. While normally considerate and caring of others, I was, upon re-flection, so busy and wrapped up in our moment that certain things did not get done or said. I was much older when I realized that in life, there's rarely a chance for do-overs.

Of course, my friend Mary did not attend the wedding, nor did Jeshua, a rabbi himself. Maybe if there had been more time, maybe some of the problems could have been overcome, or maybe this is simply wishful thinking on my part. Some of those days were a blur because everything transpired rapidly, and everything is cloudy in my mind because of the many strong emotions, both positive and negative.

It was known to both Mary and Jeshua that I was to be married and would be going to Rome. Jeshua, Mary, Marcus, and I did meet in what appeared to be a coincidence. The meeting was on the very path where I'd first met Marcus. Also, surprising, much like when I'd first met Marcus. We were circumspect, and I was happy they'd had a chance to meet Marcus. Privately, I wished that he could have been baptized, but time and circumstances would not permit.

The last time I walked with Mary and Jeshua to the gathering place, I was elated and excited about the upcoming wedding and the trip to Rome. My happiness could hardly be contained, and I was so self-involved then I can hardly remember our conversation. I was far, far away from home by the time it occurred to me that I might never see them again, or that I might never know what the future would bring for us all. I was naive, innocent, and inexperienced then. I would give anything to have total recall of what he said during those last days. Fragments of those, and other conversations I had with him, have often come to me throughout my life—sometimes in dreams, other times clearly out of the blue, particularly when rearing my children or the many times it was necessary to give comfort or encouragement to someone. Ah! No do-overs, but what I would give to see them again, and to ask him questions about what life hurls at me.

While I had the benefit of his teaching, and much of what he taught sat so comfortably with me that it seemed like second nature, there were also many mysteries and things that I did not understand. For example, he always said, "The Kingdom of God is within you." I knew and accepted this on faith, on a spiritual basis, but there was a part of me, my rational mind, that wanted more explanation. How? Why?

On that final day, I recall two things he reiterated and emphasized to me. He said, "Attune yourself to God within and when you pray, pray directly to the Father, remembering that you and the Father are One." He also said, "Sara, you have seen and heard many things here; think on these things forevermore and wherever you go, be about our Father's business."

I know he said more, much more. I remember in our last private conversation he and Mary both thanked me profusely for recording his work at the gatherings. Of that he said, "Know that your witness is in the safe hands of the Essenes, and your actions will be remembered for all time."

Later, when Marcus and I were in rough waters and dense fog, I remembered on that last day, he told me, "It is your destiny to travel. Have no fear, you are in a protected space." I had to hold on to that thought then and many times throughout my life. I never shared these specific words with anybody, but I did consider them often.

I had not realized the duration or the difficulty of the journey, although I had been told.

I simply stepped out in faith. I concluded much later in life that if we'd known beforehand what might transpire, we might never have ventured forth. Marcus and I traveled first to Alexandria, then on to Rome. Sometimes by horse, sometimes by camel, sometimes on foot, sometimes by cart or boat. It was an adventure, an expedition of sorts. I had never ventured beyond the region around the Sea of Galilee and my home, which was eventually taken over by the Romans and renamed Tiberius. Furthermore, my life had done little to acquaint me with horses, camels, and burros; I had almost no experience handling animals, and little inclination to learn. Marcus did his best to help me, as did his soldiers, but most of the time I felt more comfortable walking. After a while, I did find a rhythm to riding a camel; that was after Marcus asked me if I was going to walk all the way to Rome.

Marcus travelled with five soldiers and the two who wore red togas, whom I had seen him with from time to time in the marketplace. All seven would continue on to Rome with us after he finished his business in Alexandria. Eight more Centurions, who seemed to be guards or protectors, accompanied us; they were expected to scout and mount a defense in case we were attacked, which wasn't likely according to Marcus. I determined they would remain in Alexandria and return later. There was one other young man, a prisoner, and a deserter who was being taken to Alexandria. Others in the caravan were foreigners, mostly traders, as I understood it. I took them to be Persians. There were no other women. It was not a large caravan, but it moved slowly, carrying me further and further from home.

Marcus tried to amuse me to keep my spirits up. "Just look at this as a forced march, he said. What doesn't kill you makes you stronger." He was inclined to use a joke to josh me through the difficulties, but he was sensitive also, and he knew when humor wouldn't work. Then he resorted to using his softer side to get me through the ordeal of the moment.

I asked Marcus what he talked about with the camel drivers. "Not much," he told me. "About trade goods, mostly," he added. I concluded from his remarks and made the observation that because he was a Roman soldier, these foreigners on the caravan were intimidated by the military and reluctant to discuss much of anything with him. In fairness, Marcus was good at building a rapport with strangers. There was, of course, the matter of language differences, but that alone did not account for their reticence. If given a chance, I would have been able to communicate with them, but Marcus and his men were very protective of me and allowed no one an opportunity for an exchange of any kind, not even a glance.

For the most part, Marcus rode with his men; sometimes he rode side by side with me and we talked. In rotation, two Centurions were with me at all other times. He did his best to distract me from the uncomfortable, arduous journey. We both talked freely, and I got to know more about my husband and experience the world as he knew it. I relished this time with him. He told me more about where he had been, and with his ever-present sense of humor, he described soldiering as "wandering with a purpose." He said Plato had joined the army to get away from his wife. He got a big laugh from his own joke. I didn't know if it was true or not. Privately, I wondered whether Marcus was laughing about Pluto or the irony of himself joining the army and finding a wife.

He said he would be happy to leave soldiering behind for a comfortable bed and his new work. He didn't say what his new work entailed. He was looking forward to seeing his father and his family again, and he was happy we were going to have a life together in Rome. He ribbed me about choosing a life with him over the life of a vagabond with my friends.

His jibes humored me. "You don't know how often it crossed my mind that you might just wander off with those friends of yours.

I lived in fear that you might just take off. I saw myself sending a patrol after you. On this, your father and I would have agreed. You could have been a gadabout nomad. I think you were born with wanderlust. As I told you before, you're really quite transparent, you know."

"If my father saw me at this moment," I said, "he would have me certified a 'gadabout nomad.' Yes, in all honesty, I'd thought about it. Seriously, I'd considered it, many times. Jeshua has many followers, but of course you know that. Then," I added, sighing, "you appeared on my pathway, both literally and figuratively." Looking knowingly into his eyes, I smiled.

"Lucky me," he said, holding my glance.

"If I had known I would get a bath so infrequently, it might have changed my thinking about this nomad thing," I said.

"When I get you to Rome, you can stay in the bath all day if you like. Could you really have lived the life of a wanderer?" he asked.

I smiled and said, "Consider the lilies of the field."

He said, "Yes, I know of your 'lilies of the field.' It's something to ponder, but for me, I need to know where my next meal is coming from."

I laughed at his joke but went on. "You know, I heard Jeshua tell John, 'My food is to do the will of Him who sent me and complete His work.'"

"Hmm. I don't know about that. I just have to think about my stomach."

"You know, I never told my father that I had been baptized," I said. "And I never could understand why the entire Sanhedrin disliked Jeshua so. I think they feared him."

"Well, Sara, for one thing, single-handedly he managed to get the entire establishment in an uproar. At the very least, he should have taken another approach," Marcus said.

"Like how? Truth is truth. It's as simple as that," I replied.

"Sara, things are not always as simple and straightforward as you seem to think. Admit it, they got in an uproar because he said your temple was no longer a house of prayer. If I've got my facts straight, he said it was a 'den of robbers.' Come now, Sara, you can see that's an unforgivable insult, and I dare say inflammatory to those in power."

"It's not an insult, it's the truth! I told you, Truth is Truth. What more can I tell you. Jeshua said, there is no religion higher that Truth. I heard Him say it more than once, and I have thought about it, and I know he's right. Members of the Sanhedrin could have done something about it; they should have done something before he had to point out their failures. Then when confronted with the Truth, what do they do? They attack Him instead of fixing the problem. Woe be unto them."

"Well, Sara, here is the truth. We live in turbulent times. As for your friend Jeshua, his message may resonate with you, but his message seems out of step with the times. I know he is a good man, but from my perspective, I fear he is creating a dangerous situation for himself and others."

I was silent.

Then he said, with a smile, "Sara, is this Jeshua going to be with us forever?"

"Probably," I said. "Of course. Yes," I said with finality.

Our journey was arduous. Although there was adequate water to drink, there was none for washing. The heat and the dust, combined with the scarcity of water, made the words "cleanliness is next to Godliness" reverberate in my mind. My natural curiosity and words of encouragement from my husband kept me going, and our conversations were always thought provoking. There was always something new an observer could see and learn from, and there were always challenges to deal with and overcome.

When we arrived in Alexandria, I was happy that we were going to have a respite from travel. As Marcus put it, this would be a chance for me to rest and recover before we travelled onward. A month or more, he said, depending on how things go. I didn't know much about his work, and the month became three, nearly four months. His work seemed twofold, one part army related, the other part maybe not. At least there were more women, and thereafter there was always someone new to talk with.

At the garrison, the legatus, a general, and his entourage met us. Several grabbed Marcus in the embrace of a long lost friend, back slapping and looking each other up and down admiringly, as men will. The general had arranged for our lodging, and I wanted to escape to my room, but two women came forth to greet me. I took them to be Roman because of their dress and because they were Latin-speakers. I felt uncomfortable with the dust and dirt and grit of travel as they invited me to sit.

The refreshing cup of tea they offered was infused with hibiscus. A dark-skinned slave girl served it. Several other slaves brought in nuts and fruits and small teacakes. I learned that the women were the wives of two senior officers; they were effusive in their attention to Marcus but made me feel less than welcome. Marcus laid a firm hand on my shoulder as if to say, "Be of courage" and send a subtle message of reassurance, as he walked past me off the portico to a party of men coming through the gates.

Within a short time, a rather portly mature man with a shining bald head arrived. He was not a military man but all knew him. He was Roman, and judging by everyone's demeanor, I deduced he was expected, significant, and important. Greetings were exchanged all around in Latin, and he launched into a conversation with Marcus. Continuously mopping the perspiration from his face and forehead, he ushered Marcus out of the sun and into the shade. Speaking excitedly, he seemed very enthusiastic to see Marcus. Going on rapidly, I could see they had much to say to one another and concluded that he was part of the business Marcus had come to do.

Their conversation was so fast I caught little of it. After a short while, Marcus raised his arm as if to silence him, but gracefully changed it to a sweeping gesture in my direction. The friendly fellow's eyes came to rest on me. Instantly, he launched into an excited conversation as the two men hastily approached the three of us women seated under the portico. Marcus introduced him as Titus Claudius. The two women did a slight curtsy, so I did the same.

As if knowing I was not a Latin-speaker, and wanting to be understood, he said more slowly, "You must stay with us. My home will be much more to your liking. Oh, you will be far more comfortable there, and my wife will enjoy your company." I looked to

Marcus for his reply, while the friendly gentleman, Titus Claudius, added, "She, Arria, has very few guests, as you might imagine, and she will be ecstatic to have you, and Marcus and I must be gone. Yes, it will be perfect for you both."

Looking to Marcus for an answer, I pictured his wife as a pleasant woman, probably older than my mother. I didn't know how that would work out. Then there were these two military wives, now wrapped in a private conversation of their own, who had done little to welcome me or bring me into their conversation. As I said, they were far more interested in Marcus than in me.

My mind was whirling as he and Marcus discussed business in rapid fire, concluding with agreement. They had another discussion, which appeared amicable, with the Legatus, and within the hour, we were whisked away to meet the friendly gentleman's wife. Several of the soldiers and the two in red togas, as well as those who had come with the friendly fellow, escorted us to his house. I was coming to believe that Titus was a gracious and truly hospitable person. He talked nonstop, extolling the virtues of the place, giving a running commentary on our surroundings, the buildings and the projects, the Romans and works in progress. Doing his best to impart all he knew, he was both a great ambassador and salesman. There was so much new and different to take in, and though I was exhausted, aching, and sore from traveling, I did my best. I was overtired and overwhelmed with it all. Tears slid down my dusty face. It was all too much.

His house was grand. I had never seen a house and gardens like this. Marcus told me it was "Roman in style." Raising his eyebrows and smiling, he added, "With some Greek and Egyptian influence." I felt uncomfortable in the opulence, until I saw his wife coming toward us. She was surprisingly young. Not much older that me, maybe twenty-five. Her husband was old enough to be her father. Her greeting was sincere, open, and unaffected, unlike the two military wives I'd met earlier. She smiled and acknowledged Marcus with two little curtsies, but her interest was clearly with me.

Her husband, speaking to her rapidly in Latin, little of which I caught, told her I had had a very long journey and that I needed rest. Her face reflected a genuine happiness to meet me, alternating with her eyes that occasionally showed concern as he spoke of the journey. I could tell she was pleased we were there. She listened intently as he instructed her to arrange for clothing, and more that was lost to me because of my inability to speak fluently and comprehend their language. Although my knowledge of written Latin was adequate, I realized in that moment that would not be enough. I was concerned about my inability to communicate with her, and with his family and others in Rome.

She led me to the quarters that Marcus and I would share, which was at once expansive and elegant, opened on three sides to gardens. The finest open-weave linen, sheer and floating, provided little privacy. Then calling forth servants with barely a gesture, she gave the slave girls specific directions for my bath and then assigned one of her personal servants from Roma to my care. Like her husband, Arria was a gracious person. She said that she was so very happy I was there, and then noticing I was much shorter than she, she grew very concerned.

Quickly, she excused herself, saying she had to take her leave to make some arrangements, but would return soon. "I am leaving you in the best of hands, you will see." She introduced her servant, saying she was from Roma. "Ask her if you want for anything. These other girls are Pharaonic people. They are the best of the best, I assure you. You will see they know more about massage and the body than the Romans," she whispered. "You should take one with you when you go on to Rome."

Frankly, I would not have known a Latin masseuse from an Egyptian one, but the thought that I, a person, would take someone from their home, appalled me. At that moment my main concern was bathing and sleeping. I knew I was quite capable of bathing without anyone's help.

I was so weary that I simply went with the flow of things. The two Pharaonic slave girls led me to the most luxuriant bathing pools I had ever seen. I did not protest as they easily disrobed me and let loose my hair, while another slave girl appeared, gathered my soiled garments, and carried them away, I presumed for washing. Two other slave girls were in the water. They took my hands as I stepped down into the pool. Then the other two slipped in and began by pouring water over my back and body, then my hair. When I submerged, melting into relaxation, they washed and rinsed my hair, then dried it and wrapped a linen towel around it. I was not accustomed to this sort of help in bathing, but I did not protest. I didn't have the strength, but then why would I? There I was, truly naked among strangers but comfortable and curious about this Roman bathing process.

I could tell the natural curl and my red hair was a curiosity for them, but once they satisfied their curiosity by handling it gingerly, they gently washed it, applying pressure here and there on my scalp. They then went to work scrubbing me. One worked exclusively on my feet—touching, washing, feeling for sores or corns and calluses, using pumice on the difficult places, carefully avoiding sore spots, then skillfully working the joints of each toe. No pressure point was missed. Nothing was overlooked. Fingernails and toenails were clipped and filed and, later, buffed to a high polish. The miles I had walked were washed and massaged away. Special soap was used on several bug bites and sores. I wanted to stay in that space forever, but I was soon led from the bathing pool to the fresh tepid water of another pool, where I languished undisturbed until I nearly fell asleep.

Out of that pool, they dried me, then dried, combed, and admired my hair. They were confused by how to handle it. After everyone seemed satisfied, I was wrapped in a very fine linen toga-like garment, which was a bit too long, so everyone was nodding an apology.

I was ready for sleep. I could barely keep my eyes open, but they had different ideas. They were not at all finished with me. Sitting comfortably, sipping a mandatory cup of blended fruit juices, with a selection of nuts and bite-sized pieces of fruit at the ready, I was in deep relaxation. They were determined I must eat and drink.

A slave girl, who I recognized as the one who had expertly worked on my feet, appeared behind Arria's Roman handmaiden. She was now dry, naked to the waist, and accompanied by three other nearly naked slave girls, whom I did not recognize. At this point their nudity, nor mine, no longer embarrassed me. They had washed, rubbed, and polished to a high shine my every nook and cranny. Periodically, the modesty of the women in the Rakkath bath at home, surrounded only by heaven and earth, came to mind. The contrast of the simplicity there and this luxury was too much to consider. This was indulgent.

I lay on a cool stone pedestal-table, partially draped with gossamer-like linen. The table was waist high for the girls, who seemed to surround me. Then I gave myself up to the moment and was not cognizant of the procedures. The one girl obviously knew something more about feet than the others. I learned later she had been trained in traditional pharaonic methods of healing at the temple complex in Luxor, and that Titus had brought her from there after giving a very generous gift to the priests. I recall she started by barely touching my feet with a cool, damp cloth. She applied pressure to the ball of my foot, the arch, and the heel; I think she used the palm of her hand. Then her fingers found every muscle, joint, and bone. They worked on my scalp, my neck, and shoulders, limbs, hands, and fingers. The aches and pains of the journey, and the stress of the past months, were released one touch at a time.

I have a vague recollection of getting off the stone table, but it was dusk before I woke in a mystical haze. There was netting covering my bed. They must have been watching me because a slave girl immediately pulled back the netting and assisted me from the bed to a divan. I felt languid, like I had no bones in my body. A slave girl brought water, infused with a flower essence I didn't recognize. I drank gratefully and somewhat perked up by the time she brought vegetables in an herb broth. After that came a message written in Hebrew from Marcus, which said, "Sara, I have gone with our host, Titus, on business and expect to return tomorrow evening. I feel confident you are in good hands. Relax, recover, and enjoy. I will see you on the morrow. Signed Marcus."

I rose from the divan. The slave girl pulled back the netting and, forgetting my prayers, I slipped into bed. Sated and undisturbed, I fell into a deep and dreamless sleep until early morning, when confusing images of the sky and overhanging trees of the Rakkath springs at home were jumbled with images of Arria's bathing pools. Studying hard, I recognized no one in the dream. A slave girl's gentle susurrations in the room roused me. It was Arria's slave girl from Roma, who announced that her mistress was coming.

We were in Alexandria for nearly four months. Our host and hostess indulged me. My body was skillfully pummeled and buffed to a supple, smooth, and highly polished state. There were no indications of the blisters and bites I had received on my journey.

I improved my Latin speaking skills. Because Arria was empathetic and understood the plight of not knowing a language from firsthand experience, she applied herself to my dilemma. I learned a lot in the short time I was with them.

During this time, I was subjected to a new and different lifestyle, which according to Marcus was a very good facsimile of Roman life. After all, they were Romans living in a foreign land and so had assimilated some local ways, but their lifestyle was significantly above the pharaonic people and the military. Apparently, they did very little socializing. I was not aware at the time that their privacy had a lot to do with class status.

I learned that Arria had lived in Alexandria for more than five years in what I would term isolation. The military wives rarely invited her to tea, nor did she extend the courtesy of an invite to them. It may have had to do with social class or the military culture. There was something about this I didn't understand, but it would have been intrusive to ask. It seemed she didn't have any outside interests and apparently had no interest in reading or studying, that I observed. She lived her life surrounded by her slave girls. She and Titus had no children. I found her life to be at once boring and indulgent, but upon reflection it benefited me because it was a perfect opportunity to rest and prepare me, to some extent, for my future in Rome.

She knew of Marcus's family, although she had never been introduced. She told me that Titus Claudius was a foundling, raised by a now aged but well-to-do merchant in Rome. He was in someway connected to Marcus's family. That was unclear. How, was not. The infant, who was named Titus Claudius, had been left at the doorway of this person of the merchant class who, having no male heir, raised him as his own. Little by little the picture became clearer. Titus was of the merchant class and in some way worked for

Marcus, or Marcus's father. My husband's family was of the upper class. In my mind, Marcus was a soldier, but some dual role was emerging.

Arria's husband had done much to bring enough of Rome to Alexandria to keep his wife content. Many of the household servants were brought from Rome, particularly the cooks and gardeners. The sculptures in the garden, the tapestries, and the home furnishings were all Roman. "But it isn't *Roma*," she would lament, and a sort of melancholy would seize her. She didn't mention missing her family, and I felt that in some way they might have been responsible for her being there. I tried to cheer her up at those times. She said she wished she could go with me to *Roma*, we would have such a wonderful time. On one occasion, she called for a scribe to write a letter that I would carry to her family in *Roma*. Eventually, she had three letters for me to deliver.

Marcus did not explain exactly what his business in Alexandria was, nor did I ask. He and I had very little time together there. I could see that he had a lot on his mind, and he got very little rest. I gleaned information from Arria's comments, conversations between him and Titus, and my own observations. It dawned on me that if he rode off with his Centurions, it was military business, and if he rode off with Titus, it wasn't. Was there some nexus, because sometimes Marcus, Titus, and the Centurions all left together?

Once Marcus was gone for several weeks with a military contingency. Other times, he and our host went off for several days. During that time, Arria had her seamstress make seven gowns and dresses for me. She generously used the finest fabrics she had brought with her from Rome. She said I would need these dresses more than she, and apologized repeatedly for not knowing for sure of the latest fashions.

She acquainted me with the use of scents, kohl for my eyes, and how to make my skin glow—all of which caused Marcus to raise his eyebrows in such a manner that I couldn't tell if he approved or disapproved. When asked, he declined to answer directly, except to say he felt it was not wise to comment on the ways of the woman's world. While the servant girls were expert in applying kohl and minerals, Arria insisted that I practice until I could apply it perfectly myself. She provided a goodly amount for me to take with me to Rome, confiding that this was the cosmetic of choice by Roman women and it must be imported to Rome.

Sometimes we went to the marketplace. It was Marcus' rule that anytime I left the house, two Centurions accompanied us. If it were not for me being there, she would not have had a military escort and would have gone alone, accompanied only by household help. On these days, we selected fresh fish and fruits and vegetables, but for the most part food was delivered daily to the house, and they had a pantry of food staples in storage from Rome.

Arria introduced me to a goldsmith who had a shop there. With great enthusiasm and spontaneity, she decided I should take a gift, an extravagant gift, to my new mother-in-law. One evening she discussed this with Marcus and Titus. Marcus readily agreed with her, saying to me that he felt it would be appropriate for, and greatly appreciated by his mother. So when Marcus and Titus were away, we went back to the goldsmith's shop. Thereafter, Arria consulted with the goldsmith almost daily. Mostly, he called at the house in the evening. He designed a gold collar with lapis lazuli and scarabs for my mother-in-law. I was at their mercy because I had no knowledge of such luxurious things, and although I am no judge of these things, the piece he created was to me certainly fabulous, certainly extravagant, overpowering but regal.

The first project was a great success, and the goldsmith's work greatly increased. Marcus commissioned other pieces to include gifts for other members of his family. It occurred to me that he might be doing this just to keep us busy because he was gone so much of the time. He would explain to Arria something about his sister's relative size, personality, age, and marital status. From this information, Arria seemed to know exactly what was appropriate. Jewelry and other appealing items from Egypt were all assembled by the time of our departure.

We had two sizable but smaller gold collars made for his sisters. Both had a center scarab, mounted in multicolored enamel work in intricate gold channels in a palm leaf motif. For his father, two very impressive gold rings, both with Egyptian gods, and a third ring for his father had a very large scarab carved from the heart of palm and set in a cloisonné mounting with a blue lotus design. It was exquisite. He and Arria both wanted me to have a collar made, but I declined. Marcus said I would regret not having one made. I didn't think so. However, Marcus and Arria connived in secret and the following year on the birth of our first child, Marcus gave me a gold ring—chased work with the symbol of Isis and the most splendid gold collar of them all.

I must say that after being in Rome for a year, I was regretting never having had anything made for myself. When we were in Alexandria, I couldn't foresee how different my life would be or indeed that I could be swept up into Roman society.

Somewhere between my birthplace and Rome, my name morphed from Sara into Vannah. It started changing in Alexandria. Privately, and only privately, Marcus called me Sara or Esther. I believe that the day we met the military wives in Alexandria was the last point where my so obviously Jewish name was used publicly. He and I did not discuss this. It simply happened. Saravannah, simply transitioned to Vannah.

This issue of names arose again with the birth of our children. With the two boys, Marcus followed tradition in choosing their names. I easily accepted that, since I had no particularly strong reason to bring my father or brothers' names into our life situation. When our daughter was born, that was a different matter. I wanted to name her Mary. Marcus was opposed, gently but rationally telling me it would constantly cast her in a bad light, giving her more to overcome. I could see his point, given all I had suffered in this society, but I was steadfast. Marcus knew I had few reminders of my Galilean home. A compromise was struck. She became Dara Maria—Dara to the public, Mary within our immediate family. Privately, I baptized all three of our children as infants in the manner I had witnessed Jeshua perform. Marcus was the only witness.

Marcus did his best to shield me from uncomfortable situations of prejudice and mean spiritedness, probably more than I know. But life cannot be avoided. For the most part, I somehow had the good sense to keep my mouth shut and observe, which harkened back to practicing my father's unspoken rules. I tried my best not to judge others, their morals, their evil ways, and the depravity around me. This was nearly impossible. They worshiped a wide number of gods of all sorts—Greek, Roman, animals—continuously changing their allegiances along with the political sway. If asked, they didn't seem to know what or why they believed and if a better god or idea came along, they dropped the previous one. It was silly, at best. With their plethora of gods, I ultimately concluded they were a godless people. Their worship of and sacrifice of animals, I found particularly abhorrent.

I was surrounded by what I perceived as the sickness of Roman society. Marcus could not protect me from all that happened during the course of a single day, nor was I able to dismiss it. I learned to contend with difficult situations. I had to control my emotions, disregard the hurts and slurs; over time, it got easier for me. I realized I would have to harden myself against their aspersions, without hardening my heart, simply to survive. Mostly, and above all, I reminded myself every day that only I could say—I AM. No one could define or redefine who I was unless I let them.

That my life would be so radically changed, I did not anticipate. To be sure, I saw and dealt with prejudice and discrimination, both openly and behind my back. I was born a Jewess, and I was living in Rome. That in itself brought about problems. I was a foreigner despite my marriage. At this point in history, the situation was complicated even more by the constantly changing politics, making it difficult for Roman aristocrats facing the increased challenges from the powerful merchant class. It seemed to me Marcus' family, although clearly aristocratic, were engaged at least to some extent as merchants, using a network of surrogates northward and throughout the Mediterranean. I came to realize that it was indeed difficult for Roman aristocrats to navigate this treacherous period in time, and I witnessed the rise of the merchant class that left a much diminished and confused lot of politicians and aristocrats in its wake.

My life was one of luxury and privilege, but I was tested in many ways. I was tested about truth. Frequently, I had to hide the truth or manipulate the truth to protect our children and myself. I carry some guilt from being less than forthright. I saw no other way. The vicissitudes of Roman politics and the intrigues of Roman society were for the most part dangerous, and the times were always turbulent, in one way or another. These were times when character assassination thrust good families into ruin overnight.

I had anticipated a mother-in-law who would love me as her own. This was not remotely possible. I came to believe my mother-in-law did not have the capacity to love. She didn't understand the concept of love. It was my mother-in-law who encouraged women of all ages who lusted after my husband. I could not believe what I was seeing, and while Marcus was nonplussed and withdrew; I was appalled. My mother-in-law and the behavior of these women sickened me. They apparently felt this was acceptable. Marcus simply dismissed it.

I had looked forward to the sisters I never had. The sisters I got were not as I hoped or expected. One was petty, jealous, and, I learned from experience, not to be trusted. The other was outright hostile, rude, ridiculed or ignored me in public, and believed that I was a detriment to the family's social status. She took every opportunity to say Marcus had no right to threaten the family's position. Some of her rhetoric changed when their father died and Marcus became head of the family. Then she became obsequious and disgustingly fawning when she needed a favor from Marcus. This was not because of Marcus—he never denied her anything. It was her own shame and guilt over her words and deeds. All that aside, during the intervening years, I suffered their insults.

My father-in-law was an interesting, brilliant, and important man. He spent most of his days in his private quarters immersed in his business affairs and interests. Except for occasional dinners with the extended family, he took his meals there. Several servants, who he obviously held dear, attended to his needs. I never heard him speak a harsh word to them, and I thought he might have cherished them more than his wife—although he was never rude to her, despite her vulgarities. He often worked late into the night, his light cast across the garden. He had a private, luxuriant bedchamber there. Except for his sons, he appeared to have little interest in family matters, particularly matters relating to women. His lavish quarters included a massive library, a hall, and conference space for visitors who came and went through a separate entrance. In his official position, Marcus was away from home much of the day, but he conferred with his father, daily. I remember my father-in-law fondly. To me he was very considerate and sensitive to my peculiar, if not awkward, presence in his household by way of marriage to his oldest son.

One day he called for me; his servant came and escorted me to his quarters. Scrolls were strewn about, and he was reading from one. He picked another one up and said he was puzzled over some words therein, and that Marcus had told him I could read Greek. He asked me to look at it. I read through the portion he pointed out. I studied it for a few moments and explained that it seemed to be about old trade routes and lists goods coming in and out of a particular region of Macedonian. I told him it seemed to be a mix of Arabic and Greek, so it was somewhat of a jumble. Possibly someone with limited writing skills had written it a hundred years or more ago. He pulled another off a shelf and handed it to me, pointing to a particular passage. "Oh," I said, smiling, "this is something quite different. It is Hebrew, and it is esoteric in nature." I paused.

"Yes, go on," he said, "what specifically does it say?"

Some of it I translated it into Latin, but owing to my limitations in Latin, I could not explain the concept. If indeed Romans had such words, to me they seemed woefully poor in matters of the Spirit.

I wondered whether he was testing me. After all, this was a highly intelligent man. It occurred to me he might already know what the documents said. Then calling me, "Sara," which he had never done before, he said, "I have many books here, which may be of interest to you. You are welcome to borrow any you would like." We walked around the library, and he kindly pointed out things that he felt would interest me, and those which probably would hold no interest. He was proud of his library, which he stated had been built over several generations. He told me he would be happy to have me use it.

Before I left, we had tea, and he asked me if I would like him to provide me with a tutor in Latin. He stressed the importance of the language throughout the Mediterranean, and since I was pregnant at the time, he thought it would be important for his grandchild's development. I told him that was a wonderful idea and would do my best. He had a way of anticipating my needs. I always felt he was keenly sensitive to the struggle, which he knew was mine to bear.

In their formative years and early childhood, I cloistered our children whenever possible. They played together, and Marcus was very selective about their teachers and contacts. Eventually they had to meet with people and find their place in society. It's difficult to explain away the pain of discrimination to a child, being shunned, excluded, and, yes, persecuted. Marcus dismissed it, saying it builds character. I wasn't so sure. I felt it was damaging and caused injury to the soul.

Although unspoken, it became clear to me that Marcus and his father had discussed the future of the children very early on, probably before their birth. Both were thoughtful and deliberative about family position. They were realistic about hate and evil in the world, and as Marcus once remarked, to those who hate Jews they will be perceived as Jews and to those who hate Romans they are Romans. They needed to determine the best course of action for the children to prepare them for success, while preserving and securing the family's future.

Marcus took a keen interest in the boys. The military aspect of him sensed subtle undercurrents of civil unrest, and he tracked the threats to Jews both in Rome and in Roman occupied territories. He felt the boys would not have successful careers in Roman politics—neither the law, nor the Senate—due in part to the inherent uncertainties there. For other reasons, military careers were rejected. Nevertheless, their grandfather wanted both boys to be tutored in the classical manner—law, languages, oratory, and so forth—and they were. Simultaneously, Marcus was grooming them to manage the family businesses and affairs, which had exponentially increased as the Roman Empire was expanding. He was involved with the boys, nurturing their interests in a wide variety of subjects, including animal husbandry, engineering, materials, numerals, map reading, agriculture, and geography. He creating complicated puzzles for them to solve and used maps to stimulate their interest in distant lands. He tested their riding skills. He taught them to track and snare. Both boys rose to the challenge and were ultimately well prepared to serve the family in foreign lands.

Neither son made a proper Roman marriage, nor did Dara Marie. The youngest son went to the Hispania Interior, the farthest westward reaches of the empire. There he met his uncle, Marcus' youngest brother, and his family. Unlike Marcus, who went to Egypt and expected to return home, our son went west and never felt a desire to return to Rome. He was embraced by his uncles and cousins and married and started a family there. His uncle successfully operated many silver mines and established other ore businesses in that region. He exported olive oil and a variety of foodstuffs.

Our oldest went first to Egypt; there he found that he was accepted neither as a Jew nor Roman, just as Marcus had predicted. He went on to Galilee with a mission to encourage my mother, now a widow, to return with him to Rome, but he found her living with my oldest brother, too frail to travel. He reported to his father that he was appalled at the actions of Roman soldiers in this area. He carried a letter and gifts to Arria, who, he reported, had adopted two dark-skinned children years earlier and now had grandchildren. Soon after he returned to Rome, he left again, traveling with the military to North Country—Germania. Within two years, he returned to Rome before going eastward with the military. There he married a woman and returned with her to Rome.

When the two boys were babies, word came of Jeshua's death. Marcus knew I would be devastated and chose a time when the rest of the family was away to tell me. If Marcus knew all the facts, he spared me and was vague about any details, but by that time I knew that Marcus was privileged to business reports and information from many foreign countries. Neither Marcus nor I had ever mentioned Jeshua or Mary to anyone in Rome. Family members noticed that I had withdrawn, and when tears inexplicably fell, and they questioned my state of mind, he simply told them that a close friend of mine had died.

Through all of it, my belief and faith in God, although tested, were never in jeopardy. With constant exposure to people drunken from too much wine or bowing before pagan gods, you would think I'd get carried along with it. It was quite to the contrary. I was like a passive observer. At my core I knew who I was. Yes, I was poorly treated and painfully buffeted around by the circumstances, but I never changed from who I was—a child grounded in Judaism, a life touched by the love of a person who later became known as Jesus the Christ.

There really wasn't much I could do about all the hedonistic Romans or indeed even the Romans in our circle. I came to believe that even seriously sinful, evil, and miserable people like themselves as they are. Initially, I tried in small ways to share my beliefs with others. I did so particularly when I perceived someone needed comforting. Often I was rebuffed. Mostly, I felt misunderstood in those early years in Rome. Later in life when our children were adults, I grew more outspoken, openly postulating my beliefs. If Marcus raised an eyebrow, I told him privately, "They need to learn Truth." I asked him, "Who else is there but me to tell them?" He said he understood. I was nearly a middle-aged woman before I overcame the prejudice I met with and regained the self-confidence I'd had in my youth.

I was never really assimilated in the culture. Except for my beloved Marcus, I didn't need or enjoy what Rome had to offer. One could say I lived in isolation to protect myself. Even so, I was never truly alone. Nor was I lonely. Somehow I knew the difference between loneliness and aloneness and used that to my advantage, enjoying my children and my father-in-law's library. Often I recalled one of the last things Jeshua said to me: "Sara, you have seen and recorded much that has happened here in Galilee. Take your light into the world, and know that all things are possible to those who believe." I did think about this, and I did meditate upon it, asking God to show me how. I was woefully slow to mature and slow to action. Just how exactly would a person such as me take her light among hedonistic idol worshipers? I think I fell short, and at my death I was still pondering whether I had done all I could do.

For some years after the death of Jeshua, I was concerned and troubled that all his great work would be lost. I thought about what I'd seen in Galilee, about my experience with Mary and Jeshua and how then I'd had the courage to conceal my written witness on my person, getting it into safe hands. I wondered whether it was still safe with the Essenes and what would become of it. Marcus told me that from what he could gather, some of His follows were continuing to teach His word. There was no information about Mary of Magdal.

By experience, I knew that Romans looked askance at people who believed in God—one God, that is. However, after the death of Jeshua that didn't matter. I concluded that those who had known him, those whose lives he had touched were called to be active servants of God. Who better was there to carry on his message than one who had witnessed His work? I reasoned that since I had walked and talked with him, and received instruction from him, and knew first hand his teachings, then perhaps a responsibility had been placed on me to speak what I knew. I considered that I had been blessed to be in the company of Jeshua and that this probably was more than a coincidence. I had an understanding of the religious mysteries of the day, and life was showing me I was gifted in the healing arts.

You might say his death inspired me to action. By thinking and praying about it, vivid images of the words I had written came to me in dreams, and as I went about my daily routine, I regained my lost strength. I thought back to the day I'd told Jeshua and Mary that I was marrying a Roman soldier and going with him to Rome. Jeshua commented, "Sara, it is your destiny to travel. You will certainly shake up the status quo." We laughed together about this at the time, but in due course I lived out the profundity of his words.

Marcus' family had several working farms near Rome. One was a particular favorite. The boys learned to ride there, as had Marcus and his father. His father had expanded the property into a vacation villa, investing mightily in it while retaining the farm. Several generations of a family had lived there, retained for life. Dara Marie loved these woodlands and as a little child went fishing and picking flowers there with her grandfather.

Dara Marie was a gentle child who became a graceful and beautiful woman. I think she was acutely aware of the prejudice I suffered and was empathetic. Perhaps because of that she was not a typical female of the day. For one thing, she had little interest in becoming a wife and mother. She was an accomplished writer and musician. Her grandfather wanted to arrange a marriage for her and found several suitors. She expressed no interest in them. Marcus and I both felt it unwise to marry her to someone for whom she had no feelings. Nevertheless, securing her future was a great concern. This was resolved upon her grandfather's death, when she inherited the farm and villa they both so dearly loved. Women in Rome could inherit and hold property, and she was capable of managing this place she loved. Should a change of fortune occur, she could prosper and be secure.

I baptized Marcus there with our Mary as a witness. Near his death, Mary assisted me in baptizing her grandfather there. Through the years, my father-in-law and I often discussed the scriptures; additions he acquired for his library, ostensibly for me, would have pleased my father. He read, pondered, and asked me questions. We prayed together. He asked many questions about my friend Jeshua. He was intrigued by "the power of God" and posed all sorts of questions. He like the idea of "grace" but had a bit more trouble with "faith." Explaining to him how God works in our lives and how he works through us helped me codify my thinking. Then, after many years, he told me he had made some sort of transformation and that he believed in the one true God.

Quietly and in the spirit of Jeshua, I began teaching the word of God. After the boys left Rome, I increased my activities. Mary was always with me. In the fullness of time, I became deeply aware of who I was in the sight of God and how I needed to apply myself; but, for Mary, it seemed she'd always known the task at hand and rose up to meet it. She was *Of the Spirit*, single-minded, committed, and she carried on my work with a passion. Mary found a greater purpose for the vacation villa. Foundlings and orphans were sheltered, elderly were cared for in their last stage of life, and she baptized many.

20
Carvers of the Bering Sea

THE FIVE SAT HUNCHED over, cross-legged, elders and young men indistinguishable from each other, covered as they were in skins. They were all the same blood. They had been carving for hours unaware of the time of day and oblivious to the snow blowing in gale force over their small lodging. The stone oil lamp with a moss wick created a great deal of soot but very little light. For the most part, they worked in silence, until one of them was moved to tell a story.

The oldest among them had already lived a long existence. He was toothless and nearly blind, but he continued to carve. His fingers knew what to do from years of carving. The Angulluaq, the old man, was the best storyteller, having lived so long he had much to tell. While he chronicled his experiences, he recalled the history of his people from listening to the previous generation; he was master of ghost stories, and he kept the men fascinated with stories he conjured of headless bodies that roamed the tundra and hovered with a phosphorescent glow by night.

His stories entertained the others, but now at this advance age and condition, they were often repeated. Not always, but more often at some point in the story he would nod off. The tool would slip from his hand as if too heavy, then a partially carved piece of bone would slip down, and finally Angulluaq slipped into another world. The others continued to carve in silence, respectfully waiting as the great hunter and master carver's chin incrementally slipped to his chest and his mouth fell open. Where he went and how long he would be there was not predictable, but his story would resume when he awakened. Remarkably, he always picked up in mid-sentence exactly where he had stopped.

It was rare to have a man of this advanced age who himself had successfully killed six polar bears. To him this was a mediocre accomplishment. His stories told of one great hunter who killed seven and another who killed eight during his lifetime. His long life had allowed him to transfer his skills in building skin boats, harpooning walrus, and carving. He was revered among these men.

Cinga, not walking yet, picked up, examined, and chewed at random from the pieces of both carved and uncarved bone and ivory. His teeth were coming in, and just about anything went into his mouth in a continual search for relief. He did have an ivory teething ring, which had been used by all his siblings and cousins of previous generations. Somewhere it had been lost, abandoned, or misplaced among the carvers' bow drills and tools or under a carver's knee. It was a wonderful relic carved by one of his ancestors, embellished with circles from his bow drill and images of a puffin, a seal, and a walrus. It was polished smooth by him and the many babies who found it soothing. At the moment, it was missing.

Besides their genetics, Cinga and Angulluaq had something in common—they both drooled, and they both wet themselves.

The mantle of leadership had come to Ciulista, father of Cinga, who was presently being drooled upon as the toddler crawled over his legs and pulled himself upright, tenuously clinging to the fur skin over his father's shoulder. It was no intrusion to his father, and for the moment they shared the same space. The leader continued carving, ignoring the little fellow, nonplussed even as he toppled over and fell into his lap. He made no effort to put him upright, and after a baby-like struggle, the child managed himself.

The leader Cuilista glanced at the heap of bone and ivory and driftwood that lay on the corner ready for carving. He thought about the last trip they'd made to Nanvalliq, the place that was once a lake, a bone yard of ancient, woolly beasts. He considered briefly the need to return in the summer to collect mastodon ivory. Accustomed to the dim light, he surveyed the quantity of walrus ivory, harder than mastodon. He considered whether they had enough of the vital long, harder walrus tusks necessary for harpoon handles and sled runners. Maybe, hopefully, they did. Theirs was a life of scarcity. Responsibilities weighed heavily upon him.

Comfortable and secure in a place he found in his father's arms, Cinga, which translates into "wants to be kissed," started to pat everything—pat pat his father's hands, pat pat his tools, the ivory he carved, the bow drill lying there and an adz, the knives. If he pleased, he tried to chew it. His father took the moment to rest his eyes. Cinga, coming to his feet, bobbled up and down until he spied something nearly hidden under the knee of the carver sitting next to his father. Pitching head forward, he toppled over and then scrambled away to investigate, his pudgy fingers finally finding the precious missing teething ring.

The winter passed in such a fashion, with the men fishing, hunting, and carving, and the women working together on their tasks—all requirements for survival. Little children snuggled next to the women or found a cozy place to slumber among the floor covering—furry skins, sinew, and parts of mukluks and mittens. Older ones were pressed into the daily chores according to their abilities. Here skills were caught instead of taught, and they communicated with rarely a word. In such a confined space, each instinctively respected the others' private reverie.

Among the group was Maurlu, a very old woman who was totally covered with tattoos; she had an ivory labret in her lip. She was a mystic; hence, her name was Maurlu, which means mystic. Over the last two seasons, two other elderly women, her peers, also heavily tattooed, hadn't survived the winter. So with the press of time and her years, Maurlu was feeling a great urgency to transfer her knowledge of the art of tattooing to me. Maurlu had taken a particular interest in me since birth, and so by age twelve, I was accomplished.

Today, Maurlu's attention was divided between women and tattooing and distractions by the elder Angulluaq. Throughout the day, she glanced in his direction and once she walked over to the men, observing the dozing Angulluaq more closely. Maurlu was very much attuned to the spirit and increasingly, I sensed the spirit world was becoming Angulluaq's world.

271

Strangely, she started talking about the two old women who had passed. Then she began talking to these women as if they were present. Eventually she told me the tale of their partners, who along with other men had perished. This happened before my birth. Looking at the circle of carvers today showed a gap in age from Angulluaq and Cuilista. It seems his peers went out fishing and never returned. That tragedy was compounded because winter preparations had yet to be made when they were lost. The woman and the young would not have survived if it hadn't been for Angulluaq, who by a fluke or rare coincidence was not out with his peers that day. The death of the men was a great loss and was taking years to repair; it fell to Angulluaq to bring the young boys along.

He was held in great respect. Now the others sat quietly carving, waiting for him to resume his story.

Among the men was my *aipaq*, meaning my companion, my life partner, who was a gifted and prolific carver named Janakta, meaning "carver of wood," although he carved all manner of materials. A number of projects lay in front of him. He had roughed out two ivory needles and a bone handle I wanted for the top of a basket. He was young but nonetheless a master carver; his ivory took on a life of its own. He found form in any raw material. Occasionally he looked away from the piece he was carving at several small pieces of partially carved mastodon ivory. Every so often he reached out and turned the piece over, or stood it up differently, or picked it up and peered at it closely as if looking for something.

Ultimately, with the help of his few rudimentary tools, the materials hinted at, then indicated, what was likely hidden there. It might be a seal, a walrus, or a whale. Sometimes days went by without revealing the form. Most often a knot or knurl or simply the natural shape of the driftwood showed him a mask or handle. The variations in color and grain of the outer layer of the ivory spoke to him as the many mammals and birds of the North.

We had a rich life of communal oneness. Each was valued and treasured for whatever he or she contributed because whatever it was, it was most assuredly needed. Certainly we were not all born equally and some had physical limitation; and, in this harsh environment, survival of the fittest was the obvious rule. Weakling babies, the elderly, and the infirm did not last.

Taken together we were a peculiar composite of individual strengths and limitations that engendered courage, balance, and perseverance against incredible odds. And the incredible odds were numerous. Among them were facing ferocious animals, dense fog in rough seas, change in the wind's direction, mistakenly reading the drift of the snow, failure to understand the ocean currents, a cousin's loss of footing at a critical moment, the failure of the leader's heart with the rigors of harpooning. In the blink of an eye, another must be prepared to step forward. It was our cohesiveness that made us whole and promised our continued survival.

21
Mountain Hideaway

As THE CAR CLIMBED higher, it seemed we were running out of road. Limbs and plant foliage brushed the car. We were on a seldom-used dirt road, practically a trail.

"All private property," Takeo declared, not specifying whose. He was looking out the window. "As Longfellow wrote, 'this is the forest primeval.'"

To which I continued, "With the murmuring pines and the hemlocks."

He looked at me and discreetly took my hand. Together we continued, "Bearded with moss, and in garments green, indistinct in the twilight."

"You know Longfellow?" I inquired. "Takeo, you never fail to amaze me. How do you know that poem? It is one of my all time favorites. When my daughter was born, I wanted to name her Evangeline, but my mother and husband voted me down. It was two against one. What meaning does it have to you?" I asked.

"Skylar, I went to a private middle school; one of the teachers there was really big on reciting poems and not just a short *haiku*. Would you like a few words from Shakespeare? His works were my least favorite." He put his hand on his chest and said, "I remember, 'It is a far far better thing I do than I have done.' I guess, 'it was the best of times, it was the worst of times' is a universal thought. Anyway, it was her way of teaching English. At the time I didn't much like the memorization, which required reciting it in front of my father until I got it right. I disliked that part even more. It's strange now that those verses we learned are all I remember about that teacher. I sometimes think to myself in English, 'These are the best of times, these are the worst of times.' But whenever I come up this mountain I always think, 'This is the forest primeval.'"

He hadn't said where we were going; only that we were taking a long weekend, and that it was a special surprise. His instructions were to bring comfortable clothes. I knew his business schedule would take him out of town for the next month, when I was scheduled to leave Japan and return to the States. Both of us were looking forward to this time together. It was unlikely we would see each other again before I left, and it wasn't at all clear when or if we would ever see each other again.

I said, "You never say anything about your father."

Immediately I wished I had not said that. His demeanor changed, as if a rod had been slid down his spine. He continued looking out of the window and responded, "Not much to tell. He was my father." He paused, and then continued. "He was a successful businessman, a very successful businessman. He set a standard of perfection for me. It didn't have to be that way. Americans would call it 'type A.' He died too young."

My question had changed the mood, and I regretted it. I rubbed the top of his hand to relax his tightened grip.

Then he quietly added, as if it to remind himself, "I should be more grateful."

The tension was broken when Itosan, the driver, slowed and came to a stop at a wide, naturalized lawn of sorts at the road's end. He got out and opened the door for Takeo, bowed to Takeo, then came around to open the door for me. Deep in the woods, we had arrived at an unforgettable *shabui* dwelling; it was a naturally weathered combination of roughhewn wooden boards, opaque white plaster, and transparent shoji doors nestled in the evergreen woodlands. It was like something out of an ancient text.

I knew from my studies that artists from Western and European schools were influenced by the aesthetics of the Japanese, including this simple but splendid use of large and small rectangles, as in the rectangles of *tatami* floor-mats and *shoji* paper screens, bordered by horizontal and vertical strips of unpainted wood and heavy beams.

Austere, rustic, open—the interior and the exterior space created a sense of peace and harmony.

He hadn't said where we were going, but he chose well. This was the *wabi-sabi* of places: idyllic, deep in the woods. I wondered at the age of the place. It was a feast for my sensibilities. It was a simple, elegant, one-story enchanting rectangular structure about 20 feet long, with wood lattice and paper sliding *shoji* doors situated about eighteen inches off the ground. At one end, the shoji doors were pulled back, and I could see straight through the small structure to the woods beyond. The choice and shape of the trees and shrubbery surrounding the structure indicated to me that the landscape had been perfected over time but was probably constantly, expertly, and meticulously manicured to control and retain it as picture perfect.

There is no English word for *wabi*, which is best described as a feeling of quietness, solitude, and simplicity. Attaining the aesthetic beauty of *wabi-sabi*, time, weathering, and aging has to work its magic. It is not manmade. There is profound meaning in *shabui*, which connotes beauty in imperfection, understated elegance, and pleasing subtleties. The word dates back to the Muromachi period of the 1300s. My mind had slipped into my art history books when I heard Takeo speak.

"Here we are," he said, as Itosan opened the car door. Takeo took my hand, and I stepped out. We walked among naturalized plants to a short garden pathway of flat steppingstones laid in moss. He helped me step up to the house by way of the largest stone, the *agarikamachi*. Halfway bowing, he motioned to me, saying, "Skylar, please go in and look around; I'll help Itosan." I left my shoes at the threshold and stepped on to the tatami. He went back to help the driver, who was taking luggage and coolers from the trunk.

The room was about 18 foot square. There was a small fire pit about a meter square bounded by a wooden frame with two brocade cushions in gold and earthy red tones placed opposite each other. There was no furniture except a low, highly polished burl table. My eyes were drawn to the wall of sliding silk panels, the color and texture aged to perfection—just a trace of watery, mirage-like images of painted lotus stems and buds remained. A grasshopper on a stem scroll, befitting the season, hung in the *to-*

konoma, a raised recessed alcove; beneath it was a stunning ancient jug with earloops. I recognized it as a Karatsu water jug from the Edo period. Another pot nearly two feet tall sat under the round, translucent *marushoji* window. From the heavy texture and deep cracks of the glaze, I judged it to be from the Momoyama Period, probably 300 years old.

In the natural beauty of the environment and this place, I felt overwhelmed and overjoyed. I thought I was going to be emotional and fought to hold back my tears. I walked barefooted to the opposite side of the room. Two indigo and blue cushions had been laid out on a narrow veranda, the wide planks protected by the roof overhang. I stood on the aged boards, which had been smoothly polished over time, peering into the water. I could see the house was built partly on stilts over the water. It reminded me of the famous Kenrokuen Gardens of Kanazawa, but much smaller and more intimate. Huge *koi* swam up, their mouths gaping. I stood there surrounded by the mountainous woodland, fascinated as the movement of the gold and orange fish, some mottled with white and black.

I heard Takeo say, "They felt your vibrations and they're probably hungry. There should be a jar of fish food there somewhere. Look around." I glanced around and saw a museum quality, Edo period, wide-mouthed, stoppered black raku jar. It was every bit of two hundred years old. I examined the color and texture of the glaze, then took an aged wooden paddle-like spoon from inside the jar. Someone had long ago created it from the knurled knot in a hardwood tree limb. It was smooth and perfected with age, very *wabi sabi*. I started to deliver food to a congregation of wildly pushy koi. Saying to them, "You all must be very special to eat from such an 'auspicious' pot and implement."

I heard the men exchange a few words, the car door shut, the car drove off, and then the shoji door slid closed. I called to Takeo, "What happens if someone drops this precious antique jar in the water?"

From across the room he said, "That's easy. Somebody's got to go in after it."

We were alone. He came from behind, wrapping his arms around my waist. We stood there just feeling the moment in the radiant, mid-afternoon sunshine.

I turned around in his arms, saying, "I think I have died and gone to heaven."

He said, "I knew you would love this place."

Pointing to the pot in the alcove, I asked, "Takeo, is that water jug from Momoyama period?"

He said, "Yes." Then he added, "Lady of the Kachina Dolls, I considered making a trip up here to hide the pots so I could have your undivided attention." Tenderly he rubbed my back. "Are they going to be a distraction?"

For a long while we stood there kissing, until he asked, "Are you hungry?"

"Only for you," I said, and kissed him again.

"I was hoping you'd say that," he murmured, as he slid open a lotus screen panel, pulled out a futon, and laid it down on the *tatami* floor.

We stayed there hour after hour making love until the darkness of night closed in around us. Lying there pleasantly exhausted, tenderly holding one another in the silence, we quite spontaneously and simultaneously broke up laughing as the night noises reached a deafening pitch and the activities of the *hotaru* (lightening bugs) got so sensational we moved to the veranda over the koi pond, watching and listening to the sounds of the night. In a sense, nature was partying all around us.

Presently Takeo unwound himself, got up, and shuffled over to light the candle in an iron pagoda-shaped candleholder, which hung suspended from the wide, overhanging eaves.

Now that he was up, he excused himself and disappeared behind the lotus-paneled wall. He soon returned bearing a stack of lacquer ware boxes, which to my delight were filled with an array of delicacies known worldwide as *sushi*. Then like a magician, he made two hot, small cans of "Georgia Coffee" appear. I had become addicted to this strong, sweet coffee made for the Japanese market, found in their many vending machines on every street corner, and even lonely roads. A moment of sadness hit me. This was a pleasure that would soon be left behind.

The unprecedented privacy afforded us a weekend of uninterrupted time together, a weekend about making love. Sometimes we sat over the *koi* pond watching the night settle around us; sometimes we watched the light creep into the sky at dawn, immersed in love and the sounds and feel of nature. Ours was both a physical and spiritual attraction. Mirrored in a glance, a thought, a word, a touch, we succumbed to the powerful attraction that took us back to the futon.

We had little need for spoken communication, although I did ask him about the house and he said that the property had always been in the family. "*Always*," as in forever. I sensed a hint of apology when he said, "I had to make some improvements just to keep it from further deterioration from the elements. I did my best to maintain the integral aspects of it. It was terribly neglected by the time it became my responsibility."

He went on to say he knew the "*spirit*" of the place. Then, laughing, he declared, "Skylar, there is only a smidgen of difference between your *shibui* and what is dilapidated. This *koi* pond was silt filled, and the structure over the pond needed to be reinforced, so that's were I began." He went on to explain that he had consulted with a friend, who happened to be a world-class engineer.

"It had to be dredged, the water that feeds the pond had changed course. That had to be corrected. All of that and underpinning the weakened structure, upon which we are sitting, got costly. I always loved the place and somehow as the work progressed it became a labor of love. I did research in my spare time. You probably noticed there are hidden high tech solutions here. Some are experimental, but all are environmentally friendly.

"This place has always been my escape. It's my place to be alone. I never bring anyone here. Well, until now. I do my best thinking here. Itosan drops me off and knows when to pick me up. My grandfather loved the place, too. My parents, not so much. Once I finished the foundation work, I began to see how I could put in some conveniences for myself. Technologies being what they are today, I improved the lavatory and then took up the matter of refrigeration and food prep. You know I came for here years and years before all that."

"You mean before the rustic bathroom with a tub that holds the water at the optimum temperature? You mean the warm toilet seat? You had to have all that?" I teased.

"Skylar, on a cold morning, it's a necessity. Furthermore, I'm not getting any younger, and it's really cold up here in the winter."

"You know, I was warned when I first came to Japan not to touch the buttons on the toilets at the risk of getting my clothes wet. Japanese advancement in toilet technology is unbelievable. Aren't you afraid to be alone here?"

"No, I've taken some precautions; there are high tech solutions for that, too. There are very few who know this place exists, and they're all a trusted part of my inner circle. I think they appreciate the place as much as I do, like the gardener, who doubles as caretaker. After all, someone has to tend the *koi*. I'm working on an automatic food dispersal system for that requirement. My gardener is getting up in years. Part of the high tech has to do with a security system on the property. It's a difficult issue because of small animals, but I would know immediately if security had been breached. It's more than just the house—there's something else I have to show you."

The next afternoon, he said we were going for a walk in the woods. I couldn't imagine where we could walk; it seemed we were surrounded by dense woods. We pulled on our jeans and sweatshirts, slipped into shoes, and started across the open space in front of the house to the tree line. There he pulled back some shrubbery, and I saw the hint of a trail. I followed him into the woods. He held back boughs and limbs and twice we crossed over a shallow stream of water that bubbled and tumbled over mossy rocks. It was beautiful woodland, populated with birds and little animals that went about their business oblivious to us. Sometimes we paused to examine the plants.

After a half-hour climb, we came to a manmade intrusion into nature, a boardwalk that spanned the stream and larger moss-covered boulders below. Shortly thereafter, the boardwalk widened into a platform for sitting about six inches above a geothermal pool. A light vapor hovered over the pool. We stood on the warm platform. Somehow, he and this place reminded me of something or somewhere just out of my reach, something gnawing at the back of my mind but out of my grasp. I asked him about the tiny, luminous, bright green plants crowding together on the opposite bank. He said they were rare, that they could only survive and thrive in this particular hothouse environment, which sees the extremes of the winter cold, too.

He was talking to me as he undressed me, and I undressed him. "You see how this boardwalk overhangs the flat rocks underneath?" I nodded my head yes. "You see how the rocks underneath continue along there?" He pointed out how they circled about a third of the pool. "I suggest we enter over there. It's very hot. If it were I, I'd just enter from the platform. It can be slippery. I'll take your hand. I suggest we walk in over there where we can get in slowly. I must caution you. It's very hot."

We made our way around and, stepping down, we slowly sank until we'd immersed ourselves. "Oh my God, this is hot as hades," I said.

I wasn't in five minutes when I said, "Takeo, please forgive me. I really must get out; I can't take it. I hate it when my face turns red, and I must have a second-degree burn."

He said, "Daijobu, it's no problem." He lifted me out of the water and put me up on the wooden platform. While he stayed in the water longer, I sat nude, with him rubbing my bright red feet and legs, hanging over the edge. He looked at me and said, "Are you hot?"

"Yes, are you?" I said.

"Yes, I'm glad because I am going to get out of here and ravish you right here in the middle of these splendid woods. It crossed my mind the first day I met you."

"No," I said, "that couldn't be. When you met me we were in the cemetery."

"Yes, I remember the place."

"That's the day you explained *enn* to me. You know, a coincidence in which destiny is a factor."

"I know *enn* and our meeting is truly *enn*."

"We were talking about *mochi* for your deceased grandmother."

He got a broad smile on his face. "Yes, we were, but I was thinking about something else."

By that time, he was out of the water and lying next to me. "Shame on you, Takeo Takahashi. You are a naughty boy. Come up here and I'll show you a thing or two." I could tell he didn't quite get what I meant, but he was more interested in sex and didn't want to take time for an interpretation.

Later, as we picked our way back down the mountain, I casually said, "Sometimes I think I was a *ninja*."

"You mean a *kunoichi*. A *ninja* girl," he corrected me.

We stopped talking while we negotiated a watery gulch with slippery, mossy rocks. When we were all clear of mud and obstacles, he continued. "Probably you were."

"Were what?"

"Like you said, a *ninja*."

"Oh, yes. I think so," I replied, rather preoccupied.

"You seem to know a great deal about the woods."

"I like the woods. I was a Girl Scout when I was a kid."

"Yeah, but this is Japan. I noticed you identified all the wild edibles in the forest. It seemed instinctual, not learned. It was as if you were drawn to them. When you pulled up that wild sweet potato, a plant native to Japan and not likely found elsewhere, I wondered whether you were going to eat it. Did you know what it was? It seemed you were actively searching for something all the way up through these woods. You visually surveyed every leaf, stem, limb, and branch. You were more sure-footed than I, and I've been up and down that trail hundreds of times. You seemed totally comfortable. These are dense woods, Skylar; most women would say, thank you very much but no, not my cup of tea."

When we got back, we stripped off our clothes and sat feeding the koi while drinking a Kirin beer and eating *sembei,* a jumble of peanuts, crackers of various sorts, and miniscule dried fish. Everything was served on exquisite pieces of *raku* pottery. If my museum director's instinct kicked in, I would use gloved hands for items so precious and rare.

We didn't talk much. He insisted on fixing me a tub so I could use the ultramodern conveniences of the bath while he prepared some food. When I finished soaking, I put on an antique silk *kimono* I had found at a shrine sale. The silk lavender and ivory iris design had a bright red lining—a striking lining of this color was used in Japan about a hundred years ago during the Meiji period.

In the outer room, he had laid out on the table a mat of cold soba, some *oshinko* (pickles), some fresh vegetables, and seafood with several spicy dipping sauces and raspberries. We both were in a wistful mood. Occasionally he selected a shrimp or other morsel he knew to be my favorite and used his *hashi*, chopsticks, to put it in my mouth. We sipped green tea.

To block a penetrating glare of sunlight, he got up and released five panels of hand-crafted bamboo blinds one at a time. They were inconspicuously mounted at the ceiling along one side of the room. At first I didn't notice, but then the subtle image was revealed. Each sliver of bamboo had been fitted together in such a way as to make use of its bamboo notches to create a panorama of wild geese in flight. A slight movement of air riffled them. We gravitated closer to one another.

Lying there in his arms in the silence, I was thinking our time together was ending. Maybe he was, too. I knew neither of us would mention that. He stubbed out his cigarette. I got up on my elbow and caressed his smooth, polished chest and his taut face, which held only a hint of beard and mustache stubble. Running my fingers through his dark, thick hair, I considered the differences of the color and texture of our skin. I kissed his heavily lidded eyes, another feature that defined our differences. Looking into his dark brown eyes, I said, "Sometimes I think I've known you a hundred years."

He said, "You have, but not a hundred. A thousand—or more."

I laid my head on his shoulder. He said, "Having you again in this life is more that I could have imagined. It's more than I would have expected."

"I'm listening," I said. "What do you mean?"

"I'm not exactly certain how it was in our previous life times, but I am sure we were together before, many times before. In Japan you were either my wife or a courtesan. I think it was my wife. My feeling is that I was gone a lot. It's likely I was a samurai. I'm sure I wasn't around as much for you as I should have been. It wasn't fair to you. It was the times."

Every word he was saying rang true, but I asked, "Are you sure?"

"I'm as sure about it as I am sure that we're lying here together like this." He paused and then added, "and you know it, too."

He smiled. "Come here, Edo Lady. We need to make up for all that lost time. I'm feeling guilty, and I want to show you just how guilty I feel." He pulled my hand down to his erection.

"Takeo, don't be silly. This is serious." I nudged him way. "You are giving me goose bumps. Yes, I know you're right. I think I could fill in some missing pieces for you. It was during the Edo Period. It just makes sense. Why else am I fascinated by the artifacts of that era and the *kimonos*? On some level I know it and love it so much I want to cry. When I went to the Edo Museum, I couldn't hold back the tears. They were tears of happiness, tears of joy. It must have been a wonderful time for me."

"I never told you about this, but around four years ago, before I even knew I would come to Japan, I was in a poetry group. Every month we meet and read the poems we wrote to each other. I wrote several poems, including one about a woman waiting for her secret samurai lover. He often met her in the woods. Oh my God, Takeo. I haven't thought about that for ages, but I'm thinking back on it right now. In that poem they have a secret place deep in the forest where they would go to bathe. The story told in the poem is that he didn't want to take her there on this particular day and she, being immature, not seeing the dangers he saw, acted like a petulant child and insisted he take her there. Against his better judgment but to placate her, he did. She went into the water; he waited on his horse under cover at the tree line. He watched over her as she waded in and began to bathe. She heard a snap on the forest floor and froze. It frightened her and in that moment, that instant, she realized how she had endangered him. He had not revealed his location, nor did she, and due to his cunning and wit they safely got out of there. Let's just say she realized in that instant, in a single moment in time, his commitment to her and how foolish she had been.

"Takeo, this is giving me goose bumps. This is incredible! The flat rocks up at your thermal pool are almost exactly as I describe the woodland area in the poem. I bet if the wooden boardwalk were stripped away, a broad area of flat rocks would be there, exactly as I saw it in my mind's eye when I wrote the poem. That's weird. That's totally weird. I mean, that's more than three years ago, before I had an inkling I'd come to Japan. I've always wondered how that poem came to me. This is interesting. I am going to find it when I get back to the States and send it to you."

"I can see all that and more," he said. "My feeling is that times were so dangerous I slept with my sword, often having to see you under cover of darkness. These were treacherous times, times of intrigue and betrayal, often within families."

"Takeo, how can you be sure?

"Well, there is no proof positive, but I am what you would call 'intuitive.' You would be, too, if you trusted your instincts more."

"I don't know about that."

"I'm certain we were not only in male and female relationships." He didn't say anything for a while. Then he began again. "I can see us in the distant past in a cave somewhere. It's cold and miserable. It's high up a mountain. Cold, hunger, and scarcity mark that time. I mean these are ancient times. It seems it's someplace like Nepal or Tibet, the Hindustan, that region of the world. Where exactly isn't that important. We were both men. It seems we have a major ongoing discussion, indeed an argument, over how to get to the Godhead. Hmmm, as I am seeing this, it seems we were there more than once."

He hugged me and pulled me closer. "I'm glad we finally figured out that there is more than one way to the Godhead. It seems that we took maybe three lifetimes on that issue. I'm seeing that we had at least one monastic life here in Japan, too."

He rubbed his hand over my arm and kissed me on the shoulder. "Hmmm. Too much thinking. I have a better idea."

I put my arms around his neck and for the longest time I kissed him, my lips searching his, gently sucking in his lips and tongue until we couldn't endure more foreplay. He whispered to me, "Skylar, I thought the days were over when I could do this all day and all night. Don't stop doing whatever it is you do to me."

"*Samurai*, the feeling is mutual," I teased. I knew he wanted to check the word "mutual" in his electronic dictionary, so I immediately clarified by telling him, "You know, we feel exactly the same."

"I'm so grateful I found you, again."

The next day, we sat warming in the early morning sun. Drinking hot green tea and sitting with our feet dangling over the *koi* pond, thoughts of he and I together in various roles in previous times swirled in my mind. I considered where all he might fit with what I knew of myself.

"Have you ever been to St. Louis?"

"No."

"Colorado?"

"No, why do you ask?"

"Oh, nothing. Nothing important. I was just thinking."

22
Lotte

"Lotte, stop dallying. You can look at that later. Go 'round back. Hamish has the buckboard ready with Mrs. Clowser's delivery. You take that out to her place and don't be too long about it. If she invites you to stay for lunch that is okay, but you watch your time and get back here," my mother hollered.

I continued to unwrap the packages of yarn and thread and notions that had just been delivered. There was lace and new bolts of fabric. "Can't Hamish take it?" I pleaded.

"No Lotte, he can't. Daddy needs him here today. Stop your dreamin' and get yourself agoin.' Lotte, times a-wastin'," she responded. Preoccupied with her chores, she added, "I know Mrs. Clowser doesn't get much company, Lotte, so she will enjoy seeing you, but we need you back here by mid-afternoon, so don't be takin' too much time about it."

Because I wanted to ruminate over the possibilities of a new frock, I reluctantly rolled up the bolts, stowed a bolt of blue gingham underneath the counter, and grabbed my shawl and bonnet off the hook. "Okay, Mama. I'll see you later," I said, kissing her on the cheek before I went out through to the storeroom.

"Oh, yes, and Lotte there are two of Mrs. Clowser's 'wax sealers' there by the back door. Carry those to her, and be sure to tell her how much we enjoyed the blackberry jam."

I had already anticipated her instructions, picked them up, and put them in my carryall. "Okay, Mama."

"Here you are, Miss Lotte," said Hamish, as he helped me up and handed me the reigns. "Looks like you'll have a nice day for the ride out to Clowser's place. The sun's jus' tryin' to break through now, and Buster is raring to go."

It didn't look it to me, but I said, "Thank you, Hamish." He nodded and touched his cap respectfully as he smacked Buster on the rump with his hand and off we rode.

As we were going along, I was thinking about the elder woman whose supplies I was delivering. I'd never known her husband; he died before I was born. Every once in a while, Mama or Daddy would comment about the many years she had been a widow and what a tribute it was to the husband who passed that she continued his dream. At about age seventy, she was spry and in good health. She kept a strict routine, up before dawn tending to her animals. To me it seemed her place was a labor of love. She rarely had need for a hired man; she did her own tilling and planting, and repaired her own fences.

I didn't particularly share her interest in animals, and as the sun rose higher, I found myself hoping she would not ask me to go in the chicken coop. I'm not fond of live chickens or chicken coops, nor barns. I didn't want to step in manure or chicken poop. Every two weeks, someone, usually Hamish, came out to her place with her delivery. She said she couldn't take time from her chores to go into town. She had a standing order with Daddy, which included feed for her animals, supplies for operating her place, and some staples. She would give me a list if there were something special she needed.

She had an orchard and a garden and she always had produce ready for the return trip. Whatever she grew, Daddy could sell it. It depended on the season, but there were always eggs. Probably there would be tomatoes and fresh vegetables. Maybe the peaches would be ripe.

I think she preferred outside work to inside work. Every woman in town quilted. Mrs. Clowser never ordered fabric and she didn't sew. She always wore men's work clothes. Daddy special ordered items for her because she wore a boy's size. Mama said the quilt in her parlor had been left unfinished - since her husband died. Mama was right. Whenever I went to her house, I looked to see if she had made any progress, and sure enough, not one stitch had been added.

I helped her unload the wagon and put things where they belonged. She was fastidious about where and how things were placed. More than once she told me, "Form good habits when you're young, Lotte, because you'll need them when you get old."

After we put everything in its proper place, she asked me to stay for lunch. She saw to it that my horse got water. Then we walked to the house. As we went through the back door into the kitchen, I noticed she had many baskets ready for Daddy, including black-berries. Mrs. Clowser was a good cook, and she had corn bread and butter beans warming on the stove. She ate quite a bit herself. She offered me more and added, "I hope you've saved room for strawberry shortcake." I said, "I always have room for strawberry shortcake."

Near the stove, I could see she had trays for the drying rack laid out with white kernel corn and butter beans. She said the corn was just coming in, and the berries were the first of the season. She had picked some just that morning for Mama and Daddy. She also had two small crocks of corn chowchow from her family recipe. All my life, we had been returning baskets, crocks, and tins to Mrs. Clowser. If it were fall, she would have had applesauce made up; maybe next month it would be pickled peaches. But she always had something separate from produce for the store especially for our family.

I was stuffed full by the time we loaded up the wagon and I got underway. It had turned out to be a beautiful day, and I was happy Mama had made me take the delivery. Mrs. Clowser really was a very nice lady, interesting, and I liked to talk to her. I noticed that she had not added a stitch to her quilt project and was thinking maybe I should volunteer to finish it for her. I didn't want to be so forward to ask her, but I decided I would ask Mama if there was some way we might get it finished for her, maybe including it in a quilting bee.

A rider interrupted my train of thought. He was some distance up the road, coming toward me at a fast clip. As he got closer, I noticed he was whipping the horse, riding fast. It was Hamish on Daddy's horse.

Hamish was a nice person, about ten years older than I. He had no family in town. He worked for my father but also at the livery stables. The owner let him sleep there. He didn't even have his own place. Sometimes in the winter, Daddy let him sleep in our storeroom, where it was warmer. Flagging me down, he took hold of the reigns saying, "Whoa" to stop Buster, then he went to the back of the wagon and tied up his horse. I wondered just what he thought he was doing. His face was red, his hair disheveled, his shirt was all sweated up, and his pants were nasty, too. He jumped up on the seat next to me and attempted to put his arms around me affectionately, but I pushed him away. Ugh, he was soaking wet and stunk from perspiration.

Indignantly I said, "Hamish, what has gotten into you! Unhand me. Let go of me."

He took the reigns from me and slapped Buster very hard. Buster was not accustomed to being treated like that, and he jumped forward. I reminded Hamish sternly about the eggs. I had not seen behavior like this from him before. I was shocked and intended to tell Daddy.

He was driving the wagon entirely too fast so that I had to hold on. His jaw was set with determination, his eyes fearful and fixed, looking straight ahead. While racing along, he finally looked at me and blurted. "Lotte, there's been an accident. A bad accident. A fire. Lotte, there's been a bad fire." It was about then that I got a whiff of burning and saw the haze of smoke in the distance over our town.

Hamish was urging Buster on hurriedly, but Buster was shying away from the smoke and confusion. We got down from the wagon and ran down the street, where groups of people were standing about gawking. Some were crying. The smoldering remains of the livery stable, the bathhouse, boardinghouse, Mr. Frankenthaler's tailor shop, and our general store was all there was to be seen. I was looking around calling out for Mama and Daddy. In the chaos, a friend of my mother put her arms around me and said, "Come, dear." I heard people saying that it began in the bathhouse and went to the livery stable on one side and the two-story boarding house on the other. Then sparks landed on the roof of the tailor shop. The fire raced across to Daddy's store. Then all the roofs collapsed. Someone told me Mama and Daddy had been trapped inside, an elderly boarder died, and so did Mr. Frankenthaler. I must have fainted. Someone carried me to the preacher's house nearby.

One of my best friends, Emmy Wilcox, and Mrs. Wilcox came for me and took me to their home. Mrs. Wilcox said I couldn't stay with the preacher—after all, he was a bachelor, and furthermore I shouldn't be alone at a time like this. I wanted to go home, but she insisted that I come back to their house. I was overcome with grief, crying uncontrollably, and not thinking at all. Emmy took my arm, and we walked a few yards to their house, passing many people on the streets that were saying, "I'm so sorry for your loss, Miss Lotte." Hamish came up, trying to be reassuring, saying, "We'll be all right, Lotte."

I stayed with the Wilcox's overnight, and on the day following, Ephraim and May Wilcox talked to me about burial plans for the remains of my parents. I remember very little of the discussion. Mrs. Wilcox found me a black dress and hat, and I remember they both took my arm as we walked to the cemetery. I was grateful for their support. I think all the town's people were there. Then we went back to the Wilcox house, where the woman's group from the church had brought food and refreshments for the preacher and others. Inconsolable, I stayed with them in a guest room for two more days. Twice I overheard Mr. Wilcox say to his wife, "Well, she can't stay here." Shortly thereafter, Mrs. Wilcox suggested that perhaps I needed to go over to my house.

For the next two weeks, people came by to express their condolences and say what wonderful people Mama and Daddy were. Hamish came everyday. He even suggested that we marry. I told him "No!" I thought I would have to hurt his feelings to make him stop coming by. Some ladies invited me to their houses for supper. Mostly I sat in the house until it grew dark, and I found myself the next morning curled up in Daddy's chair.

The horror of their death consumed me until finally I began to grope with the thought that I had no means of support and the store was gone. Since childhood, I'd spent most of my days there.

Mama kept just a little money in the house. I checked that and knew it would not last very long. I didn't know how much it would cost to buy food.

I went to Mama's piano and sat there for the longest time, considering that possibly I could give piano lessons, but I wasn't sure how much to charge and whether there were enough girls in the town wanting lessons to sustain me. I thought, too, that I could read and write and that I could cipher and make change at the cash drawer; I could work in a store.

Through the mental fog and tears, I wrote to my mother's sisters—one was in Philadelphia, the other, in Pittsburg. I got no reply from them or my father's sister, who was elderly; she, too, lived in Philadelphia. Everyday I waited and hoped a letter or a telegram would come asking me to come to them.

I gave no encouragement to several suitors who pressed me. I avoided Hamish, who was ever more insistent and aggressive. He had assumed some new role in relationship to me. I had to stay clear of him, at arm's length; if not, he would put his arm around me in a possessive way. Finally I insisted he stop coming by the house, and eventually he did. There were others, too.

Through my grief, I came to realize that my father had been my protector, and my situation had changed drastically. Men treated me differently. They made advances that made me feel awkward and uncomfortable. It seemed every widower in town, regardless of his age, sought me out, with eyes wandering all over me—at least that's how I felt.

Worse yet was that women friends of my mother, women I had known all my life, grew distant. Their husbands were too helpful, warmer than I remembered, and unexpectedly affectionate. I didn't understand. Within the month after my parent's death, much had changed. I couldn't grasp the meaning. Most hurtful was the relationship with the Wilcox family. They no longer invited me to supper, and Emmy and her mother, May, almost shunned me.

I found Daddy's Will and Testament among the papers in his desk. It said that Mama was his heir, but in the event of her demise, I was his heir. I decided I would go see Mr. Wilcox at his bank. He was a friend of Daddy's, and although there was some sort of awkwardness with Mrs. Wilcox, I felt sure he could help me. I slept better that night feeling I had a plan.

Late the next morning, there was a knock at the front door. When I answered it, I was surprised to see the teller from the bank standing there. He said that if I were free this afternoon, Mr. Ephraim Wilcox would like to see me at his office. I said yes, that would be wonderful, and that I had been thinking about coming by to see him. He said, "Well then, how about two o'clock?" We agreed on two.

I sat on the chair outside his office; several people went in and came out. I waited until nearly three o'clock. I was feeling overwrought and blinking back some tears when the woman who worked for him came out. She said, "Mr. Wilcox will see you now."

She ushered me in and told me to sit in one of the two plush chairs in front of his desk. He wasn't there. I waited longer; tears welled up in my eyes. I felt very alone and needed Daddy at that moment. I was about to leave when I heard the voice of Mr. Wilcox behind me saying, "Well then, Miss Lotte, how are you today?" It was a polite, perfunctory question, not a question of interest or concern for me. I replied, "Fine, thank you, Mr. Wilcox."

As he sat down at his desk, I collected myself and regained my composure. He cleared his throat and began by saying, "Lotte, I know this is a terribly difficult time for you, and I do not want to add to your burden, but there is business that, as a banker, I must attend to come rain or shine. Your father left no guardian for you that I know of, and being nearly fifteen and a smart girl at that, you can understand what I am about to explain."

When he paused, I stepped into the silence and said, "Thank you, Mr. Wilcox. I appreciate your help. In fact, I was going to come by to talk to you about getting some money for household expenses seeing that I have nearly used up what Mother kept at the house."

"Well then, Lotte, that is more or less exactly why I called for you." He pulled several ledgers and some papers out of his desk drawer. Without saying anything further, he turned the papers around toward me and pointed to my father's signature. I heard him say the bank would take the house and the contents for what was due on the personal and business loans.

There was a buzzing sound in my ears; everything seemed white and fuzzy. It felt like a tight cap was pressing my head. I thought I might faint but somehow stayed upright, held together in place by the fancy upholstered overstuffed chair with broad arms. I felt very young and very out of place in his grand office. Then strangely, in the middle of this time and circumstances, Emmy and Mrs. May Wilcox seemed somehow not what I had known them to be.

As if in some sort of bizarre, slow motion dream, he pushed a paper toward me and indicated where I was to sign. He handed me a pen, and I signed where he pointed. He pulled it back furtively and put it in his drawer. He said something about two hundred dollars, and he took money from his middle drawer. I saw him scoop up the bills and count out two hundred. He then tucked them into an envelope and pushed it toward me. I could barely hear what he was saying because of the rushing sound in my head. He cleared his desk, putting the documentation with my signature back in the drawer. "I'm sorry for your loss, Lotte," he said, as he stood up.

The woman who worked for him appeared simultaneously. I put the envelope in my carryall and rose from the chair. I said, "Thank you, Mr. Wilcox." The woman escorted me all the way to the front door and patted my arm, saying she was sure everything would work out all right.

Somewhere in the conversation he had said, "You have two weeks to vacate the property." Dazed, I walked back home and collapsed into Daddy's chair. As night fell, I went upstairs, got in Mama and Daddy's big bed, and covered myself with Mama's double wedding ring quilt. I fell asleep wondering for an instant whether this family quilt belonged to me or was part of the "contents," which now belonged to the bank.

I stayed in bed with the scent of my parents embracing me for two days, ignoring knocks at the door. I was weakened from not eating, but I got up and went to the telegraph office to send a wire to my aunt in Pittsburg and the one Philadelphia. Everyday I inquired, but there was no response.

Soon after my conversation with Mr. Wilcox, a sign that read "auction" and the date was nailed on the front of my house. Everyday I inquired at the telegraph office, but there was no response, and I had a growing feeling of desperation.

A little over two weeks after the funeral, Mrs. Clowser came to town and learned of the fire and of my parents' deaths. She had her wagon laden with eggs and vegetables. Seeing the destruction, she spoke to Hamish, who was helping to rebuild the livery stable, and then came directly to the house. She hugged me, saying, "Mercy. Mercy." I just can't believe this. I am so sorry about this. You are so young, and this bank auction, that just doesn't seem right. She kept shaking her head "no."

She reflected. "Something seems wrong about this, Mistress Lotte. Your daddy had his store when Chester and I came here, and he built this house for your mama. He's been very prosperous. I knew your daddy and mama all these years, and there is something about this auction business that seems wrong to me."

Among all the townspeople she was the only one who was seriously concerned about my welfare. She asked me to come live at her place. She said, "For a young girl, I know it's not much, and I am so isolated, but you would have a roof over your head and enough to eat." She said she would wait while I got my things together.

I told her I was waiting for a telegram from my aunt. She said she would love to have my company, and I should think it over; she would have a bed ready for me.

That night, I decided I would go to see Mr. Farnsworth at the Butterfield Overland. He could tell me which way to go and how much it would cost me to take the stagecoach to Philadelphia. From him I learned that stagecoaches were no longer operating back East and therefore at least some of the way I would have to take a train. I'd seen pictures of a steam engine before, and thought it was kind of scary. Furthermore, he didn't have the cost of the ticket or a train schedule but said they could help connect with the train where the Butterfield coach line ended. He said that he "heard tell" that it would not be long until the railroad reached us, but in the meantime, Butterfield was contracted to carry the mail.

It was at the Butterfield Overland and Stage Company that I met Madeline. Or rather she met me. As I finished talking to Mr. Farnsworth, I felt I might just break down and cry right there. I was overwhelmed with all of it and decided to hurry home; I had too much to work out. I'd had no response from my relatives, and everything about transportation was vague. The hardship of all of this was too much to bear.

As I went out side, I heard the voice of a woman, a stranger in town, say, "You seem like you're in a great deal of distress. Maybe I could be of help. I heard you inquire about a ticket to Philadelphia. I must tell you, I think you're headed in the wrong direction. Having just come from the East, maybe I can give you more information than he did. Would you like to sit a moment over a cup of tea and some biscuits? Maybe it would clear your head." She kept calling me "dear."

She introduced herself as Madeline. She was very well dressed and wore a big hat. Her horsehair stuff petticoats rustled when she walked. She introduced the young girl with her as Ada. Ada was about my age; she had dark hair and very dark eyes. She was thin and seemed nervous. I saw that they were not blood kin, but their relationship wasn't clarified. Ada didn't speak and did not look at me. Madeline said they were staying at the hotel resting a few days, waiting for the next day's stagecoach; she suggested we go to the tearoom there.

I remembered some of that conversation and realized years later that she'd cleverly established the fact that I was on my own, with no means of support. Maybe I was too eager to tell her my business. She said respectfully that she was sorry for my loss. She told me that the "future" was in the West, not back east. She said that because of the search for gold, towns grew up like spring flowers and there were plenty of opportunities for everyone who went west. She said she would give me a job, buy me a ticket, and pay my expenses— that I would have a very pleasant room and not have to pay room or board when we got there. She said it was something like a boarding house. Upon reflection, I didn't ask the right questions. I was young and too naive to even know the questions I should have asked; and she was such a generous person! She bought us dinner. I ate well for the first time since Mama last cooked.

She told me that if I wanted to go west, and she made a very convincing case for it, I should go home and pack some clothes and be at the Butterfield Overland tomorrow at noon. This allowed time to arrange my ticket before the stagecoach came through at one o'clock in the afternoon.

I found Daddy's old valise and filled it with some clothes and my Sunday shoes. She'd told me to bring a coat and a scarf and only take what I would be able to carry. I decided to take my mother's woolen cape, which had a hood and an attached scarf; and it was newer than my winter coat. I put the money, Daddy's stickpin, my mother's garnet birth stone ring, and a gold ring with a small lavender-colored quahog pearl into a little silk pouch that had belonged to my mother. Mama said the rare pearl had been handed down from her ancestors, who settled in New England and traded with the Indians. The Indians used these pearls and mollusk shell beads as wampum at the time. I flattened it all and attached it inside the bosom of my dress. The next day, I took my valise and stopped at the telegraph office, hoping there would be message for me, but there wasn't. I met Madeline and Ada for the trip west. When the stagecoach arrived, the driver took the mail sack into the station, came out with another, stowed it, and tied down most of Madeline's boxes and trunks on top. The horses were changed, and within fifteen minutes of his arrival we were on our way.

Madeline was honest about one thing, how difficult and long the journey would be. I thought it would go on forever. All day and night we were moving. I kept sliding off the seat. We were bounced and jolted over bumps and boulders. After I was lurched off the seat altogether, I hung on to a strap. Mostly the driver tossed the mail to an awaiting station attendant, who was ready with a fresh team. He seemed disgruntled when Madeline insisted he delay long enough to use the outhouse. At "home" stations, when we had a meal, I learned to take an apple or a biscuit for later. Mostly I was hungry and needed to go to the toilet.

The stagecoach moved on day and night; there were no overnight stops. We slept sitting up. My wrist, wrapped in the strap, went numb. Rarely was there space to stretch out. If it wasn't dust and dirt, it was rain and mud. It became clear to me why Madeline said they had stopped for a few days' rest in our town.

Eventually we ran out of towns altogether, and then we ran out of telegraph lines. However, before we did, we stopped in a very small, one dirt street town with a few stores, some sad looking dwellings, a saloon, and a church. We had a meal there, and afterward Ada said she was going to the outhouse. When it was time to get on board, Ada was nowhere to be found. She'd disappeared, vanished. We called and called. Finally, the driver rudely told Madeline he could not delay any longer, and he was going to depart with or without us. He said we could either go on with him or be left; it didn't matter to him. He had a schedule and was now late. He climbed up, we climbed in, and with that, we left Ada behind.

I was distraught about this. Madeline didn't seem to mind, except she said she should have known better and now she was "out all that money." She added that Ada had a bad attitude, and it probably would not have worked out anyway. I agreed that Ada did have a rather unpleasant attitude. She never spoke, didn't even respond to something I said to her. Nonetheless, I was shocked that we had just left her behind.

Madeline could tell the episode lingered with me. Maybe her conscience started to bother her, too, and so she related how she had met Ada early one morning in a train station back east. Ada had slept there over night, maybe for several nights, and she was hungry. Madeline said she had befriended her, buying her food and getting her cleaned up. So in some way, I couldn't determine how, but Ada was beholden to Madeline, who told me Ada had run away from her home in New Jersey because her father died and her mother had "taken up" with a new man who didn't treat Ada well and had put her to working long hours in a mill. She said Ada was destitute, but it was a "poor investment on her part." She said, "Pray she finds her way. I'm not out that much."

I didn't understand what she meant by "her investment," but as the coach continued westward, days and nights of sleeping and dozing blurred them together, and Ada ceased to matter. The further on we went, the more thoughts of my life seemed to dissolve behind me. My situation seemed unreal, and I had some nebulous thought that maybe I was in a dream and would wake up and find myself at home in my bed. It came to me then that I would be more kind to Hamish, and if Mrs. Clowser ever wanted me to collect eggs from the coop again, I would go willingly. I would be grateful for and helpful to my mother and daddy, and I would love them much better than I had.

It wasn't a dream, and the stagecoach rolled on and on, taking me, I am not sure where. We ran out of telegraph lines, and ran out of taverns—everything was dwindling down to nothing, and when the driver stopped at a "swing" station for ten minutes to change the animals, sometimes there was hardly a dwelling, just a dugout in the side of a hill. The driver expected a meal at the "home," station but we often didn't get much. The further west we went, the worse it got. The single person at the rest stop was eager to talk, and sometimes he had something hot for us to eat. Sometimes we picked up a rifleman, who rode with the driver. It seemed we were picking up men or dropping them off into the nothingness. The men who got on and off mostly had little to say to us, hardly acknowledging we were there. Sometimes they spoke to each other, and from what I could gather, they were all relay drivers or company men, surveyors, linemen, businessmen. One from the East spoke about St Louis and how the population there was now over 100,000, and just a hundred years ago, St Louis was but a trading post on the Mississippi River catering to fur traders. I learned we were traveling across the Kansas Territory. One talked about how the Butterfield Overland and Stage had the mail contract from Kansas to Denver.

Another, I took for a railroad employee, said the railroads back East had made stagecoaches obsolete and that he was sure this would happen in the Kansas Territory, too. He couldn't say just how long that might take to happen, but he was certain it wouldn't be long.

One was an inspector who worked for Butterfield or the U.S. government, I couldn't tell which, but he walked around every station and kept writing notes in a book. There was a newspaperman who tried to engage Madeline in conversation; she ignored him and told me to do the same. Another person worked for Western Union, and the excited conversation was about how Western Union would soon tie the east coast to San Francisco. They talked about changes coming to the Kansas Territory. Several described things in San Francisco, methods for panning for gold, the gold rush towns of California, Indian Territory, different rivers and trails, but mostly telegraph and railroad lines. I learned a lot by eavesdropping, but all I could see were vast expanses of plains and wide open spaces with no people, which was sometimes splendid to look at but mostly endless.

We went for days and days in the same sweaty, grimy clothes, surviving mostly on hardtack and bison jerky. The dust and heat, combined with no place to bathe, was the worst part of it. I stunk so bad I couldn't stand myself. Madeline said, "Forget it, don't worry about it, we all do." It seemed the men could manage, but this was no place for a woman—and there were no women. In one place, the stagecoach line worker took us to the back room, where he had laid out basins and buckets of water for us. Hurriedly we washed up. Madeline gave him a few coins in appreciation.

Another time, a pleasant considerate older driver stopped by a lake and told us where we could easily get down the embankment if we wanted to wash our feet. He said we should hurry so he wasn't behind schedule but that he would wait for us. We clamored down taking off our shoes and stockings. Madeline pulled off her underwear and waded in, pulling up her skirt as the water got deeper. I followed her example. She washed her stockings and bloomers and since we were the only passengers at the time, she hung them out the window to dry. We were refreshed as we moved on.

Drinking alcohol, talking about Indians or stagecoach robberies, and falling asleep on a fellow passenger were among the things discouraged on the stagecoach, but it did happen. After all, we were traveling through Indian country. Some buckskin-clad men who travelled with us for a while commented "things were peaceful with the Indians—for the moment." The other said that "if the government keeps messing with the bison, it won't be peaceful for long." I drew from his remarks that the government was killing off the buffalo so the Indians would go somewhere else. I didn't say anything, but it didn't seem right to me. Off and on soldiers travelled with us; they were respectful but said little.

The landscape changed, and high mountain ranges could be seen in the distance. This caused one male passenger going to Carson City for the first time to say to the other, "What are the odds of snow up ahead?" "Not too likely," said the other. "Too early, if any, it probably won't be deep." However, the higher elevations were cold, and I found myself shivering uncontrollably at night. The foot warmers were of little use.

We came to a station that was run by a man and a woman who I took to be his wife. They had things to sell. Hardtack, knives, tin cups, enamel pans, camping implements, axe handles, and so forth. There were heaps of buffalo hides, pelts, and furs of different animals. Also there was a banjo and a violin and a small cabinet with a number of gold rings, several pocket watches, lockets, pieces of Indian beadwork, and small items that seemed out of place in this wild country. Madeline said, "Well, sometimes it comes to that," and I thought about Mama's garnet ring on my person. The driver told Madeline it would be wise to buy a buffalo rug for each of us because it was going to get colder. She did, but I heard her tell him, for the cost of the ticket, you should provide buffalo robes. He replied, "Sell them for a profit where you're going." She agreed.

A prosperous looking male passenger with the Union Pacific Railroad, who was with a botanist and geologist, bought a fur hat, and when we got back in the coach, he handed it to me saying, "You'll be needing this." I did and was grateful. When they left us, I was going to return it to him, but he said, "You keep it. It could come in useful again."

Madeline told me that she had had to travel back East to settle some family business, but she never told me that years earlier, she first went to California from New York on a steamer through Panama and that she had traveled back East on a stagecoach route that went from San Francisco through New Mexico, Texas, and

Arkansas. Nor that she had knowledge about the gold fields of California. I knew she was listening intently, often with her eyes closed, to what passengers said of business developments in the East and in the West, but she never commented or asked questions of them.

The flat lands changed to rough mountain passes. Several times the coach nearly toppled over. More than once we had to walk. Only when we were nearly out of the Kansas Territory did Madeline say, "It won't be much longer now." I had stopped asking. There were more settlements and more people to be seen. There were a few women, dressed in men's pants and heavy laced up boots. She told me our destination was—Cherry Creek.

Madeline told me to wait as she went in to the "home" station to arrange for delivery of her trunks and boxes. She came out and ordered me to follow her, saying, "Pick up your valise and come with me." When we got out of the coach, her demeanor had somehow changed from cool but pleasant to abrupt and bossy. I followed her through the wide, open, dusty street, passing through several blocks of livery and wagon storage or terminus. She picked up her skirt and slips to avoid the dirt and animal droppings. I did the same. After a while, she chose to cross the street and get up on the wooden plank walkway. I followed her, shifting my valise back and forth from one hand to the other, as we passed a number of storefronts, bars, outfitters, and gambling houses. Hearing our foot falls, men peered out the windows. Some women stopped to talk and look at us. By looking down the alleyways between buildings, I could see shanties and tents and shabby houses and storage sheds. There were quite a few men I took to be miners standing outside a building marked Assay Office; they stepped aside as we passed.

The saloons were active and noisy for early afternoon. Someone was pounding out "Wait for the Wagon" on a twangy piano as we came to a large, two-storied building with a big front window where the word "Saloon" had been carefully painted in fancy script and outlined in gold. This seemed to be the biggest saloon, and men's loud voices and laughter spilled out.

We walked past the saloon, went down the steps, and turned back into an alleyway that smelled like urine and where cats skittered. Near the end of the building at the back of the saloon, Madeline walked up a wooden step and let us in through the door. A wooden staircase was in front of us. Music came from down the hall to the left, and I got a glimpse of men playing cards, drinking, and the sounds of gambling. Madeline ushered me straight up the stairs to a hallway that was lined with closed doors. It appeared to lead to a balcony at the end.

A fancily dressed girl came out of a room and nearly bumped into us, crying out in surprise, "Madeline, you're back." Before she could say hello or anything more, Madeline told her to go find Victoria. The girl looked down, apologetically. "Oh, Madeline, I'm sorry but Victoria got married and went to California."

"When?" Madeline barked at her.

"She's been gone now for about two months."

About that time, two more girls appeared in the hallway. They attempted to greet and fawn over Madeline. Madeline said, "Look here, I'm tired and hungry, we'll talk later." As a way of introducing us, she said, "This here is Lotte. Well, then, Lilly put Lotte in Victoria's room. Cora, you go find Ella and have her bring up some food for Lotte and have a washbasin brought up to her. If you're not working, you girls help her get settled in. Clara, you collect up her clothes and bring them down for washing. Help her get cleaned up, and bring her something more suitable to wear."

The girls were Cora, Lilly, and Clara. Edwina, nicknamed "Winnie," was busy working at the time, and I met her the next day. Madeline had initiated a lot of activity, and the girls obediently followed her instructions without any hesitation. At first glance, Victoria's room was inviting but with an overabundance of frippery and frills, which was unlike me. Still, after the stagecoach, it was most welcome. All I wanted to do was collapse on to the iron bed.

Cora came back with Ella and a water pitcher; she first filled a glass for drinking and then poured water in to the china basin on the washstand. There was no chair, so I sat down on the edge of the bed. My head started buzzing with the storm of questions the girls asked of me as they came and went. All around me, the young women arranged the curtains and drapery, the room, and then me. They attempted to remove my clothing; their intent was to help me wash up. One lathered up a washcloth with soap. Interrupting the process, Clara came in with clean underwear and a colorful dressing gown; she laid that on the bed. Ella stood near the open door waiting for me to remove my soiled travel clothes so she could take them.

Rejecting their help in the process, Clara said with a snicker, "I think she's modest."

Lilly turned to look at me frankly, asking, "Are you?"

Overwrought and overtired, I nodded my head "yes." Then tears welled up in my eyes.

Lilly, seeing my distress, said, "Wait Clara, maybe she just needs some time alone. Do you want to be alone, Lotte? Come on, Cora." She gathered the girls together. "She's had a very long trip. Would you like us to leave you for a while, Lotte?"

I said, "Yes, please."

"Do you want us to help you wash up?" Lilly asked.

"No thank you," I said.

Cora rolled her eyes and said, "I think she's shy. Does Madeline know that?"

Lilly said, "Never mind, Cora."

Motioning for the other two to go in front of her, Lilly said, "Okay then, Lotte, we'll be back after a while. Put that dirty petticoat and your nasty travel clothes here by the door. Ella will come back for them. She will bring your supper. You must be hungry." She ushered everyone out and down the hall.

She left the door open behind them. I got up and went over to close it. Standing there with my back to the door, I realized I was in a desperate situation—the gravity and magnitude of which I was not certain. I did know they would soon be back, expecting to take the clothes I was wearing. They had taken Daddy's valise with all my worldly possessions, and I had a moment only to figure out where I was going to hide Mama's silk pouch, which had been tucked in the bosom of my dress. I was frantic—under the bed or in the bureau or washstand seemed out of the question. The heavily lined drapery seemed the only answer. I pulled at the hem and loosened it just enough to slip the pouch in. I smoothed it so it was not discernible to someone coming into the room.

Knowing they would soon return, I quickly removed my clothes and washed my hands and face. Then, from my head down, I began washing my body free of the filth and grit from the dangerous overland journey. Embarrassing scum collected in a ring around the bowl. I threw my dirty clothes in a heap on the floor where they'd directed and picked up the rather fancy but impractical underwear provided. It was not new; it had been worn before, but the fine cotton had been washed and ironed—every ruffle. It was not plain, but I put it on, grateful to be out of my soiled clothing. The flimsy dressing gown was another matter. It was of a colorful floral pattern on a light material that was practically see-through. Unlike the clean underwear, there was a faint scent of someone else on it. The married Victoria came to mind. I didn't put it on.

I took the dirty water basin and put it on the floor next to the bed, then washed one foot at a time. There I was when Clara and Lilly came back with Ella. Lilly laid some garments on the top of the bureau. Clara set to drying my feet, while Ella carried the dirty water and my soiled clothes to the hallway. Then she came back with my supper. It was the first home cooked meal I could remember in quite some time, and the aroma of food caused a ravenous appetite. Ella went to the bureau and put in two pairs of drawers and two chemises, then opened the bottom drawer and took out a quilt, which she laid on the bed. She arranged the comb, brush, somebody's hair pins, a hand mirror, candlestick holder, and an oil lamp on the top of the bureau, then waited quietly in the background while I finished the food. She then took my tray and left us. I think she was not accustomed to people thanking her because when I did, she looked up, confused as to what to say in reply. No words came from her lips, and she put her head down and scurried out.

I thought Lilly and Clara would never stop talking and asking me questions, but finally Lilly said, "I think Lotte would like to go to sleep, and we should probably be getting ready. So, Lotte, we'll say goodnight to you, and we'll see you in the morning."

I heard a key turn in the lock of the door soon after they went out. From the options given to me, I chose a muslin chemise along with some drawers with an open crotch joined at the waist by a silken ribbon, put it on, threw the quilt over the coverlet, and got into bed. I fell immediately into a deep sleep.

Intermittently, my dreams were disturbed by a heavy thump on the wall or a door being slammed in the hallway. Startled awake, I lay in the darkness of my room, my heart beating rapidly with fear. In order to calm myself, I said my prayers until exhaustion pulled me once again back into anguished dreams of unknown faces mixed with dangers that I couldn't quite define or grasp but were related to my journey to this place.

For three days and nights, things were much the same. The girls came to visit and talk during the day. They showed off several gifts Madeline had brought for them, including what they called a "cage crinoline," the whole affair made up of cane hoops and tapes. They were delighted with this contraption—a "new fashion." Each tried it on and pranced around, remarking how cool it was compared with regular petticoats. Several times I asked to see Madeline but was told she was tired or she was trying to get caught up because she had been gone so long.

At night I fell asleep with a false sense of safety because my door was locked. I came to realize that the thumps were of drunken men falling against the wall, followed by snickers and giggling from Cora or Clara. Usually the piano player downstairs in the saloon was at the keyboard, playing and singing. He had an interesting repertoire, and I wondered whether he was German or Italian when he sang "Die beiden Grenandiere," "The Two Grenadieres," in perfect German, or "Come, Oh Come with Me, the Moon Light is Beaming," in Italian.

Always as the night progressed, loud male voices downstairs frequently awakened me; but I was settling in to a new norm, and the music from the saloon put me to sleep as I sang along to "Rosaline, The Prairie Flower," and "Jeanie With the Light Brown Hair." Other times it pulled me from my dreams, particularly late at night or early in the morning when loud male voices joined the piano player, singing "Old Dan Tucker," "Oh! Suzanna," or a raucous version of "Columbia, The Gem of the Oceans."

One night I got up to pee. My preference would have been to go to the outhouse, but I had been furnished with a chamber pot commode chair. As I sat there doing my business, I heard a disturbance below my window. Without moving the curtains, I peered out to see three inebriated men laughing, singing, and holding each other upright. One collapsed to the ground in a pile, unmoving, and the other two ambled on. Things in the saloon were winding down in the early morning hours. I could faintly hear the piano player singing "Widow Machree." I got back in bed and fell into a deep sleep until Ella brought my breakfast tray.

I asked for my dress back, but they didn't bring it, and I sat in the room wearing only the underwear they provided. On the third day, my shoes were returned, but I had no shoehorn or button hook. The shoes, my best, had been muddied and dirty when they were taken but were now clean and polished. My other pair was in my valise, which had not yet been returned. Ella eventually brought a shoehorn and buttonhook; she placed them with the comb and brush—a matching set.

One evening after supper, I stood brushing my hair while looking through the curtains at men as they passed along the back ally down below. They were pretty much a sorry looking lot, who appeared to be miners. Some I judged to be carrying everything they owned. I was thinking back to the odd assortment of items in the display case at the last "home" station, wondering whether they had traded their gold rings for the gear they were carrying. I was about to conclude that everybody in the town was involved in mining when I heard the key in the lock. I continued brushing my hair, and didn't turn around, assuming it was Ella returning for the supper tray.

A gravelly, phlegmy male with rotten teeth said, "Come here, girlie." I turned, shocked and horrified to see a grubby man peal off his clothes down to his one piece long underwear, which he was now unbuttoning from the neck to the crotch. Being in my underwear, I grabbed for the curtain. I realized that was no cover.

I then jumped on the far corner of the bed and pulled the quilt up to my neck. I started yelling, "No, no, stop, stop!" But he didn't. He pulled his boots off and kicked them aside. As I was all the time telling him to get out, he was saying, "Now, now, girlie."

He pulled his underwear off one shoulder, then the other arm, and the repulsive, stained suit dropped to the floor. He stood there, bare naked; his big, crooked "thing" poked out of the hairy mass between his scrawny legs, pointing directly at me. I threw the hairbrush at him. It hit the oil lamp and shattered the globe. He lunged at me on the bed; when he did I jumped off, but the weight of his body on the quilt pulled it from me. He threw himself over the bed toward me, grabbing my top and ripping it from my shoulder. He was tipsy and not too agile as he lurched forward. With both hands, I pushed him with all my strength. As he fell back against the washstand, the ceramic pitcher and basin crashed to the floor. I had the advantage of adrenaline and shoes. He was bare footed and shocked. Shards were everywhere, but he pursued me as I ran out into the hallway in my torn underwear, exposed to all who came running to find out what was happening.

Intent on escaping him, I pushed them aside and ran straight down the hallway, out on to the balcony. He came after me, shouting and half wrapped in the quilt. Edwina and a man were on the landing, and I nearly pushed them over the railing as I ran down the stairs. At some point, or when I was nearly half way down the stairs, the music stopped and every single man in the saloon looked up at me in surprise and awe.

I froze, pulling the torn top across my nearly bare breasts, hoping the blousy seat area in the split crotch underdrawers was full enough not to reveal my private parts. He slowed down but was on the stairs, his feet bleeding. I had nowhere to go. All the men were gawking, and the saloon was in total silence. There I was exposed in front of these gaping strangers.

Madeline and a person I took to be the bartender appeared below from behind the staircase. I was relieved to see her but confused by the question she directed sternly at me. "Are you causing all this commotion?" As she came toward me, I realized that she had no concern for me. I was petrified, couldn't retreat up the stairs, and felt I'd have to flee out the front door into the street.

I didn't know how to answer her because I guess you *could* say that I was the one causing all the commotion. In the dead silence of the saloon, all coins and cards were dropped. One man rose to his feet, pushing over his chair. As Madeline reached me on the stairs, he came forward and in a commanding voice said, "Madeline, unhand her!" As Madeline was telling him to mind his own business, he rushed past her and came to my defense, trying to conceal my nakedness by taking off his jacket and covering me with it.

As he half carried me, wrapped in his coat, back up the stairs and across the balcony, he warned the drunk, who was examining his cut up feet, and all who came to see the hubbub, to get out of the way. They backed off at his authoritarian tone, but followed as we went to Victoria's room. Madeline followed us into the room. The girls were curious and stood whispering in the hall. I was shaking uncontrollably. He asked me who I was, where I had come from, how old I was, and then told me to get my clothes on. I told him that they had taken away my clothes and all my belongings were in my valise. He looked at Madeline, who was dismayed as she surveyed the broken dishes, lamp, and washbasin.

He may have had differences with Madeline from the past, and he minced no words. He focused his pent up wrath on her, describing her in unspeakable terms and directing her to have my belongings returned. Madeline's protestations and attempts to defy him caused a major confrontation, but he would not be thwarted by her words. He spoke of her vileness. He threatened to call the sheriff. She said that if he intended to remove me from the premises, she demanded the cost of my stagecoach fare and meals and restitution for all the damage to the room. He said, "Get her valise and clothing!" One of the girls ran to get Ella. As the gambler peeled out money for the ticket, then more money for other things for which Madeline demanded payment, Clara brought in my dress and valise. He met Madeline's demands, but still she seemed unsettled and argumentative. He turned to me and told me to get dressed, saying, "I'll wait in the hallway." Pushing Madeline ahead of him, he closed the door.

Quickly I pulled off the underclothes that belonged to the establishment and put on mine. When I put on my petticoat and dress, I felt like myself. Somehow, my sense of self had been lost on the Overland and under the influence of Madeline. As I picked up my valise, I remembered Mama's silk pouch hidden in the drapery. Picking it up by the hem, I ripped it further. Retrieving the pouch, I stuffed it down the bodice of my dress, then opened the door and went out.

He took the valise and my elbow and ushered me down the back stairs as the girls and Madeline looked on in astonishment. Madeline hushed Lilly when she said, "Goodbye, Lotte." We continued down the lightly trafficked-by-miners alleyway for several blocks before we headed for the main street.

Eventually, we arrived at a hotel—a rather large and prosperous looking place. He marched me right past the check-in desk and the attendant into a dinning room off the reception area. He hadn't said a word. He was all action. The room was nearly vacant, but he selected a table in a remote corner away from other patrons. He pulled the chair out and seated me; putting my bag down, he excused himself, saying he had business to attend to. He asked me if I was hungry. When I replied "No," he said he'd have tea sent to the table. He said he might be gone fifteen minutes, and he advised me not to talk to anyone.

I grew increasingly uncomfortable with the people and surroundings. Sitting alone invited glances and whispers. When he returned I felt relief. He sat down across from me, ate a full meal the server brought him, and despite the lateness of the hour, drank several cups of black coffee. I realized that probably he had been drinking and gambling for hours before I burst into the saloon.

Satiated, he pushed away from the table and rolled a cigarette. After he took his first puff, he said, "Somehow or other I have allowed your situation to entangle me. So, let's begin at the beginning, and see if we can unravel it."

I nodded.

"I gather your name is Lotte. Lotte who?"

"Lotte MacKenzie."

"Okay, Lotte MacKenzie. Where is your home?"

When I paused, nearly tearing up, he said, "Where did you come from. How did you get here?"

I told him I was from east of St Louis.

He said, "You've had a long trip. I guess you realize how difficult and extremely dangerous it was. You do, don't you? " Then he asked, "How old are you?"

I told him nearly fifteen.

He asked if I would like to return home, saying, "As it turns out, I've paid your way here, and if you'd like to go home, I would be willing to pay for your return trip."

Seeing tears in my eyes, he asked, "How did you meet Madeline?"

He seemed like an earnest person, who genuinely wanted to help me, and at that moment I needed help, so I told him, "Well, you see there was this terrible fire, and my mother and my father perished in our burning store. The roof collapsed on them. Too bad for me, I was out in the country making a delivery when it happened." Then I added, "I wish I could have died with them."

He cleared his throat and rolled another cigarette. "That is tragic, but your life is important, and this having happened to you recently. Well, Lotte, you are still grieving; you're very young, and not yet mature in your thinking. Be assured, you were spared for a purpose. I'm sure time will prove that to you. So, how did you meet Madeline?"

"I had gone to the telegraph office hoping to get a message from one of my relatives back east, but nothing came. Madeline overheard my conversation with the agent and on the way out she saw that I was distraught. She told me that she and this other girl with her were going west, where there were many opportunities— not in Philadelphia. She said there were no opportunities back east. She was very nice to me and bought me supper. The girl with her ran off a few days after I joined them. Anyway, the worst of it was that Mr. Wilcox, the banker in our town, who was a friend of my father, called me to the bank soon after my parents were buried and told me our house and everything in it would be auctioned off in payment for my father's debt. He gave me $200."

He asked me questions about how long I had lived in this house and how long my father had been in business in our town. I told

311

him I didn't know how many years, just that Daddy had always been in business, and he built our house for my mother when they married. It was before I was born.

"Well, Lotte, first let me say, I doubt Mr. Wilcox gave you a damn thing and just like every double dealing banker, I venture to say he swindled you out of your property." He seemed irked at something and then asked, "Did you sign anything?"

I nodded my head yes.

He seemed dismayed over my response. Then he finished that conversation by saying, "I'm rather certain that if a bank examiner just walked into his bank, Mr. Wilcox's records wouldn't stand up to the scrutiny."

I'm sure I looked confused by what he said, but I answered "Ephraim," when he asked me Mr. Wilcox's first name.

"A perfect storm." He shook his head back and forth and continued. "The colossal merging of two evil forces, your Ephraim and our own Madeline—and you only fifteen. I am sorry you have had to suffer all that. May God arrange for them to meet in a bloody battle in the nether regions—or somewhere—for certainly it will be in a place of great darkness."

I was shocked when he said that, and I didn't exactly know what he meant, but I knew it wasn't nice.

"Well, all that can be rectified over time. But first, Lotte, let me explain my position. I am happy to help you. At this point I don't know how I can do this. Understand that I am a gambler. That is what I do. I play cards, and I am damned good at it. I don't live in this town, but I come through here off and on. I'm a professional gambler, and I gamble in a lot of towns. That's what I do, and that's what I intend to do until my dying day."

I didn't know how to reply to what he'd said, so I said nothing.

"Since you don't want to go back, or maybe more correctly there is nothing for you to go back to, maybe I can help you make a plan for your future. I think you need a plan. If you are to have a future, you will need a plan. What can you do?"

"I can play the piano," I ventured.

"That's not such a good idea, begging you pardon, but it would put you right back in the predicament it seems I just rescued you from."

I smiled at him then and said, "In all the fluster of the day, I don't think I thanked you. I'm embarrassed and muddleheaded, but I really so appreciate what you did for me. I shudder to think what might have happened to me if you hadn't intervened. I did cause quite a ruckus, didn't I?" I added.

"Maybe someday you will be able look back at it and laugh." A smile came to his face and he said, "It was quite a sight, I assure you." Sensing my embarrassment, he went on. "I'm sure we gave them something to talk about for a good long while. It's possible to become famous for an incident like that out here."

He rolled another cigarette, lit it, and pulled on it until it burned bright. He looked at the burning end, then turned it around and drew in the smoke, blowing it up in the air slowly before he spoke again. "Well, Lotte, I am not a person to intervene in another person's affairs. I normally mind my own business, and gamble." He paused for a few moments, smoking and studying me. "Well, Lotte MacKenzie, maybe your luck has changed. Luck does that, you know—and seems to me you're overdue for some goodness in your life." After thinking a while more, he asked, "What kind of store did your family have?"

"It was a general store—food, groceries, shoes, boots, and all kind of things families needed. Supplies for farmers and feed for livestock. Tools," I told him. "Daddy ordered things specially needed, too. It was called 'MacKenzie's.'"

"I can see you were quite proud of it. And what did you do in it?" he asked.

"Yes, I was proud. I loved our store." I felt I might cry, so I further explained the types of things Daddy had for sale and how he'd worked with local farmers, like Mrs. Clowser. Then told him, "I did a lot of things. I used a wax marker and put the price on things. I made signs and sometimes made deliveries in the wagon. We had a horse. I helped the customers and did just about whatever Mama and Daddy needed me to do."

He asked, "Do you know your numbers, how to add, and how to make change?"

"Well, of course," I replied, a little indignant. "I often helped Mama count things so she could make up orders. Then when we got an overland shipment, I counted things to make sure we got every item that was ordered."

"I see," he said.

"And Daddy often asked me to add up or check his numbers column. Mama said I was faster than they were. My teachers said I was a very good student. I read, you know?"

"Well, I didn't know that, but I figured you did," he said with a little smile. "Thank you for telling me."

As we talked, I noticed that he was a very nicely dressed man; his nails were neatly manicured, and he had a good haircut. His dark hair stayed perfectly in place. There was just a very little gray at his temples. He was older than Hamish, younger than Daddy; I'd say about Mama's age. I liked the way he talked to me. He was direct, open, and forthright and spoke to me as though I were an adult.

He reached into his vest pocket and pulled out a gold watch, saying, "Lotte, maybe I will give some thought to your dilemma overnight; it's getting late. We can sort all this out in the morning. It's been a long day for me, and it certainly has been, shall I say, 'an interesting one' for you. I am staying here in this hotel if you should need me." He went on to say, "A lady friend of mine who does my laundry when I am in town owns her home and a laundry business; it's nearby. She is a very lovely woman, and no harm will come to you if you are with her. When I left you earlier, I went to ask her to take you in tonight. She is waiting for us, and if you are agreeable, I will walk you over there. We can resume this conversation tomorrow."

Miss Martha was a very sturdy woman. She was also generous. With the exception that she was husky and much younger, she reminded me somehow of Mrs. Clowser. She gave me a glass of milk and some sweet cakes in the kitchen. She had freshly made pans of lye soap lined up on the stove. While I drank the milk, she cut the lye soap into bars. She said we would visit more in the morning.

We walked out back and down to the outhouse. I could see by the light of the moon a number of overturned zinc washtubs and heavy wooden stirring sticks and clothes props leaning against a shanty and the ashen places where she built her fires.

She showed me to a small, plain bedroom at the back of her house. The wallboards were white washed; a framed picture of a Madonna and infant were nailed above a narrow iron bed. The other furniture in the room was a fragile looking, spindle-leg bedside table with a candle and a quilt rack at the foot of the bed and a straight back cane-seated chair like those in the kitchen. Miss Martha asked me if I needed anything, but everything was all laid out for me.

When I awoke and dressed, I went to the kitchen. I could see her out back; her days' work was well under way. Laundry was already hung and drying on the line, and washtubs over the coals and wood fires were full. Another woman was helping her stir a pot full of laundry. I went to the outhouse, and when I returned, Miss Martha said, "There is breakfast for you on the back of the stove. The blue enameled cup and pan are yours. William came by, said you should come to the hotel at noon for lunch."

And so, I found out that his name was William. I'd failed to ask, and he hadn't told me. As I bit into a large slab of homemade bread and butter, and ate the bacon and two fried eggs, cooked heavily in the bacon grease, I thought about what a strange turn of events this was. I tried to push away thoughts of the naked man in the saloon and the chaos that had ensued. I did my best to hold back my tears, but I wanted to go someplace alone and just cry. I wondered what my future held. I wondered just what a "future" meant.

We had lunch, and then we had tea. He talked. He had even more questions for me. At some point, he said maybe there was an opportunity in this town for me. He said that in his opinion, if you had to be somewhere in this territory, this might be the best of places. Several times he offered to pay my way back to St. Louis or send a telegram to my relatives. He said that if I wanted, he would take me to San Francisco and book passage on the ship—it would take me to Philadelphia.

"Okay then," he said. "There is a situation here that might work. I went down the street to casually inquire about work for you. I spoke to a widow, whose husband passed away this year. She owns an outfitters store that primarily caters to miners' needs. I'm casually acquainted with them, both nice people. I learned a lot over the years by engaging her husband in conversation. She's getting up in years, and I thought a young woman like yourself might be of help to her. However, she told me that with the loss of her husband, she doesn't want to stay here. She was firm about that. She said it was his, her husband's business, and although she was his helpmate, without him, she not only is not able to do it alone but she would rather be elsewhere. I took it from her that she always wanted to be elsewhere and couldn't wait to leave. Hmmm, that is too bad for her—living your life in a situation not to your liking. I sometimes think of women and their...circumstances. She has already made plans to go back East to live with a younger sister."

"On one hand, Lotte, we could look at this as a dead end, no job. Or, maybe it could be an opportunity. As I said yesterday, luck changes, and her situation just may be a lucky opportunity for you."

I said, "I'm not sure what you mean."

"Well, first, I want to make sure you want to be here. I wouldn't want you to spend your life like she did. Life is about choices."

I interrupted him to say, "So far, I haven't made very good ones."

"Just be aware of it, and don't be too hard on yourself. Life is about learning, and you have a long way to go. That's a good thing. So, let's continue. Lotte, I get around and I observe well. Cherry Creek is a pretty good town, but what is best about it is its location. I am quite certain this town is going to grow and those in it will prosper. Furthermore, if one of these miners you see walking around here strikes it big, there will be a repeat of the California gold rush. There is a lot of speculation about claims on the South Platte (River). Rumors are that it is likely to happen."

"I see, but I don't understand what that has to do with me."

"Okay, Lotte. First, you have to dream a little. As I've always said, if you *kick a small pebble you can affect the farthest star.* Can

316

you envision—can you see—a 'MacKenzie's' right here in Cherry Creek? Yes, I can see by the look on your face you can. You smiled for the first time since you crossed my path yesterday. So, okay, let's call that a yes. I will help you buy the Compton's store. I know you are smart enough to run it, so it would be only for me to arrange with Mrs. Compton. No one wants to buy it from her; they want to strike it rich. Oh, they want to buy things, they need things, but a store keeps you in one place, and folks out here don't want that life, for the most part."

He stopped, then asked, "How about you, Lotte? What do you think?"

I said, "Well, I don't think I have enough money. I only have $200."

"Lotte, Lotte, Lotte, don't ever tell anyone how much money you have! Promise me that you won't ever do that again. Even me. Even if I ask." I nodded my head, and he went on. "I will arrange it for you, as I said. I think that over time you will make a great deal of money, and you can pay me back and after that you can pay me 20% of your profits as long as you own the store. I have faith in your abilities. You have only to supply the 'dream' to make it work. If you have the 'dream,' I will handle the arrangements. We will draw up an agreement. I don't want to make this too complicated. I think you can manage all this, if I didn't we wouldn't be having this discussion. I think Miss Martha would be available to talk things over with you. Remember I won't be here. I make a circuit, and I am only in Cherry Creek from time to time. I suggest you board with Miss Martha for now; it would be safer than living in the Compton's quarters at the store." He paused. "This is a lot to think about. You go on back to Miss Martha's and think about this proposition overnight. I will meet you here for lunch tomorrow. Talk to Martha—she has a good business head, too."

And so it was that with William's help I established "MacKenzie's" in Cherry Creek. My store grew exponentially and I accumulated a fair amount of wealth. Whenever William came to gamble in Cherry Creek, I had ideas and he had suggestions. He encouraged me to take calculated risks and branch out. I followed his guidance. He was always supportive. He said, "Lotte, you have a natural instinct for business. You were born with it."

But I am getting ahead of myself. Two years after "MacKenzie's of Cherry Creek" was established, William stopped by the store, as he always did. He asked me to meet him at the hotel for dinner after I closed up.

He was sitting in the same corner of the dining room that was always available for us. He had a sheaf of legal looking papers. After we ate, he ordered coffee for himself and tea and desert for me; he didn't eat sweets, said it made his brain fuzzy. He said he had something to discuss with me. He patted on the papers and said, "This is for you. It's old business that has recently been resolved." He went on to say, "We were sitting right here when I mentioned to you that I didn't think Mr. Ephraim Wilcox's books would stand up to scrutiny if a bank examiner looked at them, and Miss Lotte, that is exactly what happened.

"Mr. Wilcox was quite unscrupulous. Your father's debt was negligible. He had more than enough in saving to pay the little he owed with much to spare. Furthermore, your father owned the house. It was clear of all debt. Wilcox, for some nefarious reason, held the deed, supposedly for collateral for two small business loans. Feed shipments and something else; it's all in here. Basically your dad didn't owe the bank anything. Wilcox was not only unethical but he was also dishonest. When the audit exposed his misdeeds, he was only too willing to own up to this swindle in exchange for not going to prison. It appears he swindled many, and he may yet go to prison. For sure he will be finding a new career, with any luck not on a chain gang. Although, in my opinion that's what he deserves."

"Oh, William, what about Emmy and Mrs. Wilcox?"

"I wouldn't give them another thought. They benefited mightily while he took unfair advantage of your family, many of the people in your town, and farmers in your region."

"Oh William, I feel so bad for Emmy. They have such a beautiful brick house, the only one in town."

"You should say, they *had*. Not anymore. Wilcox was, or is, a crook. But speaking of houses, let's talk about yours. I'm sorry to say it was sold. There are records documenting the sale in here.

Documents of the contents that were sold, that part is not as clear. Probably stolen, I'm sorry to say. But this," he patted on the papers, "is a pretty good accounting of what happened to your father's estate, including the insurance claims for the store fire, which Mr. Wilcox submitted in your absence and was clever enough to justify to the insurance as his, the bank's, entitlement to it. Without getting too complicated let me sum this up—bank fraud, insurance fraud!

"After paying some fees to attorneys, you have a substantial settlement. It has been deposited in your name with Wells Fargo. It's the safest place I know of. Also, I know you have great sorrow about the loss of your mother's piano, and I can tell you it was found in the Wilcox home. The sheriff confiscated it as stolen property once the situation became known. He asked Mrs. Clowser to help him identify other personal items belonging to the family, and they confiscated three boxes of family papers, books, and your mother's music sheets. They are coming here to you. It could take a while—they are shipped through Panama and San Francisco, but they will reach you."

It was my very good fortune to meet "William, the Gambler." I would say our meeting was providence. Soon after I opened "MacKensie's," as he had predicted, prosperity came to the region with the Colorado Gold Rush. Cherry Creek was renamed Denver. William was always a faithful friend and advisor. He never ceased to remind me to dream and he helped me dream into being other stores in the Kansas Territory. Our part of the Territory became known as Colorado.

Years later, William Sterling Davis revealed to me confidentially that he was a Federal Agent. All those years, he worked for the United States Government. He retired in San Francisco but often came to Denver to gamble. Much to my embarrassment, he occasionally reminded me of how we'd met.

23
The Lotus and the *Koi* Pond

WE WERE TOTALLY ABSORBED in one another. If we weren't wrapped in each other's arms, we were immersed in deep, intense conversation. There was no idle chitchat between us. Our moments together were slipping away, and on some level we knew we wanted every moment to be meaningful.

It was quite apparent that we'd known each other before. The intimacy was too profound. There was a lot I could learn from him; he said that was reciprocal. Takeo was highly knowledgeable, with a considerable amount of wisdom of Buddhism and Hinduism. He was acquainted with Christian scriptures and asked me my understanding of certain passages. He wanted clarity about Christ as a personal Savior.

He particularly wanted to know how I came to believe in reincarnation. He said I was the first American he had ever met who did. I explained that I began an inquiry several years earlier because of certain events that occurred in my life. I told him my understanding of Biblical history is that in 380 AD, Justinian signed The Edict of Thessalonica and 15 Heretical Anathemas, expunging the word "reincarnation" from the Bible and making it heresy to use the word.

He asked, "Why ever would he do that?"

I told him, "It seems he did it at the behest of his wife, who it is said came from questionable lineage and didn't want her forbearers discussed. After I read this, I dug deeper and found many references in the Bible that would lead a thinking person to believe the people of the time did believe in reincarnation."

He quoted freely from The Bhagavad Gita. One conversation was about "the indestructible Self." He called it "Self," I called it "vital essence or soul." From the Gita he quoted, "'Realize that which pervades the universe and is indestructible; no power can change this unchanging, imperishable realty. The body is mortal, but he who dwells in the body is immortal and immeasurable. Unborn, eternal, immutable, immemorial, you do not die when the body dies. Realizing that which is indestructible, eternal, unborn, and unchanging…. The Self cannot be pierced by weapons or burned by fire; water cannot wet it, nor can the wind dry it. The Self cannot be pierced or burned, made wet or dry. It is everlasting and infinite, standing on the motionless foundation of eternity.'" He finished it by saying, "'Death is inevitable for the living, birth is inevitable for the dead.' Gita 2.27."

That's just how intense it was between us, but it was always a pleasant give and take conversation.

For both of us, meditation was part of the rhythm of our lives. Meditating in the predawn hours was our practice, and despite our avarice physical passions, we didn't break our resolve. It was a necessary part of our day. Sometimes, after intense discussions the previous day, we decided in advance what we would meditate upon the next morning. Often it was a passage from the Gita. So in the early morning hours, without eating, drinking, or speaking to each other, we went to our side-by-side cushions and sat in silence over the *koi* pond.

On one such morning, after having discussed *"suffering"* and *"enlightenment"* the previous day, we were seated in silence on the cushions overlooking the *koi* pond. All of nature was silent—the *koi* were in the depths, and tightly closed lotus buds could barely be seen in the darkness. My mediation drew me to the lowest, murky bottom of the pond to where an entanglement of lotus roots struggled to push up to the light through multiple layers of muck and mire.

There upon the cushion, eyes nearly closed, I vividly experienced the symbolism of the lotus flower and the enlightened Buddha seated upon the lotus flower. I saw the lotus as every human soul growing, strengthening, sometimes falling back, striving to reach the light, to bring itself out of the darkness of the marsh. It's a long and difficult endeavor to come into bloom, a lotus flower. Reaching for enlightenment is a journey.

The mist of the early morning dawn crept over our universe. The hovering vapor was displaced as light exploded through the leafy canopy, alighting on every reflective surface, and the buds began to open to the light.

That morning, we sat eating some sea vegetables and tiny shrimp, observing the lotus buds open to the light of the new day. We discussed my thoughts and feelings about the lotus. Takeo, always a wealth of information, further clarified my thoughts by saying, "Consider the lotus as the union of opposites. You have the darkness, the water, and the light, the sun. From your meditation, you see the lotus as a symbol of *spirit*, just like a human, continually struggling to reach the light. The lotus is a symbol of transformation."

Asking and answering questions, sharing what we knew, we exchanged information throughout the day. Once he slid back the silk lotus screen, retrieved some fragile old scrolls, and then read and translated parts of The Four Noble Truths to me. We compared many religions and philosophies, enhancing each other's perspectives. The conversation was fluid and open-ended, flowing easily from one topic to another. We tripped over words. Often there was no English or Japanese translation for words in the Sanskrit.

He wanted to go to Egypt and was eager to hear more about my trip. I told him what I knew of the importance of the sun in the ancient Egyptian culture, about Isis and Ra, the symbol of the beetle now symbolized as a scarab. I told him of my fascination with the "false doors" in Egyptian temples, hoping he might have insight to their meaning, but he couldn't add anything.

"Always there is something more to learn," he said. At one point he mentioned that we should go to Egypt together, perhaps meeting up there. We let that thought hang because we knew there was too much immediately ahead for both of us.

322

Despite our common interests in other cultures and a deep interest in one another, neither Takeo nor I were needy. Perhaps because of this, and the fullness of our experience, we felt no need to make demands upon one another. Our relationship was one without expectations, our time together valuable, and to be enjoyed in the moment. We were both well rooted in our respective lives and cultures, and had no desire to change or control the other.

In the twilight of that evening, we were lying together on the *tatami*. He was smoking. I was thinking about the wonder of this place when he said, "Why are you leaving Japan? You seem so happy here? What are you going to do when you get back to the States?"

His question interrupted my reverie. Inspired by my surroundings, I was composing a poem in my mind about the Floating World of the Edo period. "Red smoke, green smoke, blue smoke, haze." The words came to me.

"Hmmm. Well, first, my son has met a woman he loves, and they are planning a wedding. That's the first thing on the agenda. There are other things pulling me back, too. My parents are aging. Although they haven't said, they want me back. Probably they need me back, but they wouldn't tell me."

I sighed. "I took a leap of faith when I came to Japan." After explaining what I meant by "leap of faith," I told him, "It was risky not signing another contract with the university, but eventually I know I have to return to the States and get reestablished."

"Will you go back to the Oklahoma museum?"

"No, I don't think so. I tend not to 'go back.' I don't know why, but I have a real thing about 'going back.' Over the years, frequently I have been nudged out of my comfort zone. I mean circumstances connived against me—depending on your perspective, maybe they connived for me. In each situation, everything worked out well or better for me, so now I sort of look forward to new things and challenges."

"It seems to me you have a great deal of courage for a woman."

"What do you mean, 'for a woman?' That's really sexist, Takeo."

"Well, then for a man *or* a woman. Be honest, Skylar, most women wouldn't take the risks you have. I'd say you're adventurous. Maybe even fearless."

"That's probably true, Takeo. It seems I don't have what you would call normal fears. I wonder why. According to my father, I was like that in childhood, too. Anyway, at one point I thought I might reinvent myself and become a travel journalist. I wrote copy pieces for your paper, and I enjoyed that. Then I reconsidered, thinking why should I make work out of traveling, which I dearly love? So I'll continue on with what I know best but try not to get tied down to a nine to five job. I never want to get back to how I was before, you know, being totally committed to the job. Actually, after Japan, I will be a misfit in our society, I think. My thinking has changed a lot. I've changed a lot. You could say that like the lotus I've had a transformation. I intend to keep my calendar empty, unlike Americans who measure their worth by the number of events they pack into the day, the month. I don't want that again. I need time to think and study and particularly to reflect on the experience of these last years."

"But Skylar, if I might be so bold as to ask, how are you going to support yourself?"

"That's a good question. Some years ago, by invitation I went to speak on Kachina Dolls at the Institute of San Miguel Allende, an art school in Mexico. I loved that place. I'd consider living there, but that's a different story. On the flight back, I sat next to a woman who recognized me. Just by coincidence she had heard my presentation. I was impressed with her depth of knowledge on my subject. We hit it off and talked all the way back to Atlanta, where she continued on to New York City and I caught another flight.

"I took her to be wealthy, and as it turned out she is prominent in museums and the art scene there. She owns several galleries around the country, and she represents a number of artists. Clearly she was a woman of means and very well connected. Since that flight, we have always stayed in touch. From time to time she paid me for consultancy work. I could get a job with her; she's asked me several times.

"After living in Japan, I could never live in New York City. Finding silence and tranquility and maintaining my peace will be difficult enough anywhere in the U.S., but the rat race of New York City, no, I'm not up for that. Not to say that you don't have a rat race of your own right here in Tokyo. It still makes me laugh to think of the first time I found myself going against the masses of humanity pouring into Shibuya Station."

I smiled. "I feel certain that through her I can get work as a consultant to museums and as a lecturer in my field. I could live somewhere else and avoid the metropolitan areas. I can't abandon what I know best. Hopefully, I can work on my terms. If not, I guess I'll look for a full time job."

Thoughts and motion crowded in. I turned my face away and struggled to control my tears. I was separating myself from a place and a person I deeply loved. I was grateful the darkness had overtaken us and the night noises had increased. I slid my hand into his and his closed firmly around mine.

Quietly said, "As you well know, every beginning has an ending—and every ending is a beginning."

Touch Points in Time

EGYPT:

3200 BC Thebes was the capital of Egypt during the Middle and New Kingdom. (Thebes was known to the Greeks as Thebai, to the Romans as Diospolis Magna, and to the Hebrews as the City of Amon (Ezekiel 30:14). It is present day Luxor, meaning "city of palaces." It is the location of the temple complex of Karnak. Across the Nile from Luxor is the Valley of the Kings. Ancient Egyptians referred to the area between Karnk and present day Luxor as Waset.)

3000 BC Memphis was the capital of Egypt during the Old Kingdom. (Memphis was a thriving port and center for trade and religion, which lost prominence to Alexandria by 331 BC. Ruins of Memphis are located south of present day Cairo. The Sphinx, the Great Pyramids, and Saqquara are nearby.)

359 BC – 336 BC Philip II unified Macedonia and conquered Greece.

356 BC Alexander (the Great) was born to Olympias and Phillip II, 20 July.

343 BC Aristotle (b. 384 BC, d. 332 BC) went to Macedonia for three years to tutor Alexander.

332 BC Sidon surrendered in February.

332 BC The Siege of Tyre. (The Tyrians refused to sign a peace treaty and refused to allow Alexander to go to the Shrine of Heracles on a fortified island. Exacerbating the situation, they killed one of Alexander's ambassadors. The ten-month siege of Tyre ensued, requiring the building of a mile and a half causeway to gain access to the Shrine. In August, with 7,000 Tyrians killed, 400 Macedonians dead, 2000 crucified, and 30,000 sold into slavery, the Tyrians capitulated.)

332 BC Alexander entered Egypt at Pelusium (Autumn).

332 BC The City of Alexander was founded in Egypt. (Dinocrates of Rhodes, the great architect of the Temple of Artemis at Ephesus, designed the city. It remained the capital until the Muslim conquest of Egypt in 641 AD. Prior to the establishment of Alexandria, this deep water port city on the Mediterranean was known as Rhacotis.)

331 BC Alexander traveled two weeks to Siwah, Egypt, to consult the oracle of Ammon (Zeus in Greek).

331 BC The sanctuary in Thebes/Luxor was modified and Alexander was depicted on the walls as pharaoh in the ensuing years. (When Alexander left Egypt, he left Alexandria in the hands of an Egyptian Governor. However, Greeks and Macedonians had full military and economic control until the Macedonian General Ptolemy I Soler (Savior) was appointed Governor after Alexander's death.)

324 BC In July, Alexander's boyhood friend, Hephaestion, died.

323 BC In June, Alexander the Great died.

34 BC A great fire destroyed The Library of Alexandria and 532,000 documents.

BIBLICAL TIMES:

106 BC - 5th century AD Alexandria became a protectorate of Rome. Two Roman legions occupied Alexandria. Legio II Cyrenaica was garrisoned there until replaced by Legio II Traniana Fortis in 106 BC. Leigo XXII Deiotariana was garrisoned there until the 1st century AD. Legio II monitored Egypt until the 5th century AD.

37 BC – 4 BC The reign of the indefatigable builder, Herod the Great.

27 BC - 14 AD The reign of Augustus/Octavianus, Roman Emperor.

20 BC -19 BC Period of construction of Herod's Temple. It was under construction for 46 years, with 30 more years of work. It was built by 1,000 priests.

6 BC Jesus was born in Palestine.

4 BC Death of Herod (Idumean).

1 AD Population of Rome is 1 million.

6 AD Augustus expanded Roman borders to the Balkans.

6 AD A permanent Roman garrison was established in Jerusalem.

14 AD The Roman Empire was comprised of 5 million people.

14 AD Augustus dies, and Tiberius becomes Emperor.

16 - 22 AD Herod Antipas built the City of Tiberius on the western shore of the Sea of Galilee. It was built on the site of Rakkath, the old town of Naphthali. In Joshua 19:35, this fortified city was assigned to the tribe of Naphthali. Naphtali, son of Jacob, appears in Numbers 1:43 and 26:50. His tribe settled in Canaan, having received the next to the last division of the land (circa 733 BC).

Rakkath had a bath and hot springs, located south of Herod's Wall. The Tiberius city project was patronage to the Jews by Herod Antipas, "The Builder." It included a palace, a forum, and a great synagogue.

A coin from the era of Tiberius, which shows a figure of Hygeia (health) feeding a serpent (Asciepius, God of Healing) as he sits on a rock over the spring, was a recent archeological find.

26 AD - 36 AD Pilate was the 5th procurator of Imperial Rome in Palestine.

30 AD The crucifixion of Jesus.

41 AD Claudius wrote a long letter to the Jews of Alexandria, known as the Nazareth Decree. This imperial ruling forbid the disturbance of tombs and graves, subject to capital punishment.

44 AD The government took over the administration of Galilee after the death of Agripa.

49 AD Claudius expelled the Jews from Rome.

64 AD The year marks the completion of Herold's Temple. His palace was adjacent to the temple in Jerusalem.

66 AD -70 AD The Great Revolt. Pro-Roman policy postponed the inevitable.

70 AD Herold's Temple is burned when Jerusalem falls to the Roman armies, thus helping the establishment of the Christian Church. The west retaining wall, the Wailing Wall, remains.

70 AD The Sanhedrin was abolished after the destruction of Jerusalem. Jews are spread throughout the Mediterranean region.

70 AD Marks the end of the Sadducean Party. The Saduccean High Priests ignored Jesus, denied the resurrection, maintained the status quo, and were conservative aristocrats favorable to the Romans. The party included chief priests, scribes, and elders. The Pharisees were secular.

300 AD Roman soldiers were garrisoned in Luxor. From 300 - 600 CE, the entire Luxor temple was incorporated into a fortified Roman encampment.

ASIA AND CHINA:

3rd – 5th century AD Bamiyan was the site of many monasteries. (Two colossal Buddhas were carved out of the sandstone cliffs there by monks and artists traveling the Silk Road. Bamiyan is located in present day Afghanistan. The Islamic Taliban, under the orders of Mullah Mohammed Omar, destroyed the Buddhas with dynamite in March 2001. An international effort is being made to reconstruct them. The destruction revealed 50 caves and wall paintings dating from the 5th through the 9th century. Also discovered by archeologists is a 62' reclining Buddha.)

386 BC – 534 AD Marks the period of the Northern Wei Dynasty.

202 BC – 220 AD The Han Dynasty flourished, as did trade along the Silk Road.

200 BC – 50 AD The Western Han Dynasty was established, marking the end of the Warring States era.

111 BC The Dunhuang Prefecture was established by the Han Emperor Wu.

100 BC Around this time Buddhism arrived in China from Central Asia.

50 BC The approximate time the Silk Road opened to the west.

366 AD The monk Lo Tsun had a vision of a thousand Buddhas in a cloud of glory; this is said to be the origin of the *ming-oi*, a rock temple complex in the Gobi Desert near Dunhuang. (Caves of the Thousand Buddhas are located at present day Dunhuang, County of Gansu Providence on the eastern slope of Mingshashan, Rattling Sand Mountain. The system of nearly 500 caves and grottos and 2,400 painted statues was carved out and painted by artists and monks traveling the Silk Road over a period of time.)

618 – 906 AD Tang Dynasty.

781 AD For much of the 8th century, Tibetans protected the shrines and caves of Dunhuang.

906 -1279 AD Sung Dynasty.

1206 AD -1260 AD The Mongol Empire.

1207 AD Genghis Khan attacked the Chinese in northern China.

1214 AD – 1215 AD Genghis Khan's Seige of Peking.

1220 AD The Mongols captured Bukhara and Samarkand.

1221 AD The Mongols captured Kandahar.

1221 AD Is the estimated date of the Mongol's Seige of Bamiyan.

1227 AD This year marks the death of Genghis Khan, the phenomenon of the 13th century and ruler of the Mongolian steppe people, whose swift hordes of mounted archers wrecked havoc and conquered lands from the Mediterranean to the Pacific and Baltic regions.

1259 AD This year marks the death of Mongu, the son of Genghis Khan.

1260 AD – 1294 AD This is the era of Kublai Khan, grandson of Genghis Khan.

1274 AD Kublai Khan sent a fleet of 150 boats against Japan.

1368 AD – 1398 AD Chu Yuan Chang drove the Mongols back to the steppes.

1368 AD – 1644 AD The Yuan (Mongol) Dynasty.

1368 AD – 1644 AD The Ming (Chinese) Dynasty.

1644 AD -1912 AD The Ching Dynasty. The Manchu formed the Quing (Ching) Dynasty.

JAPAN:

Of ancient India origin *Jizo* (gee-zoh) in Japan, *Kshitgarbha* in Sanskrit, is a savior, who appears in many forms to relieve suffering. (In Japan, *Jizo* is the Bodhisattva who watches over miscarried, aborted fetuses, the stillborn, and children who died very young. *O-jizo-san*, using the honorific 'o' in Japanese, is the polite reference to *Jizo*. Seen as a stone Buddha in the shape of a child, *Jizo* sometimes wears a red bib or hat, red to block the path of evil and expel demons or illness.)

1239 -1289 Ippen (pronounced e-pen) believed the grace of Amida was present in Shinto shrines as well as Buddhist Temples and that followers could join together in praise to Amida through song and dance anytime and anywhere; it was not necessary to build new structures. The Followers of the Timely Teaching (Jishu) numbered in the trillions.

1339 The Saiho-ji Temple in Kyoto was designed by Muso Kokushi. (It is sometimes called Koke-dera, the moss temple, because it has 120 varieties of moss. To protect the delicate balance of nature, visitor reservations are required.)

1397 The Kinkaku-ji Temple in Kyoto, known as The Golden Pavilion, was built as the retirement villa for Shogun Ashikaga Yoshimitsu.

1415 The Ryoan-ji Temple in Kyoto is famous for the Zen *kareansui,* a dry landscape of 15 rocks in a sea of sand. Ryoan-ji belongs to the Rinzai school of Zen.

1600 -1867 The Edo Period is an era characterized by the perfection of the arts of *ikabana,* pottery, the tea ceremony, gardens, Kabuki theatre, *ukiyoe* woodblock printing of the Floating World, *sumie* ink painting, lacquer ware, *nishi jin* silk industry, calligraphy, painting, the sword, martial arts, *Haiku* poetry, the honor code of the *Samurai,* and the art of the *ninjitsu.* The fan shell, pine bough, ribbons, tortoise, lantern, Mount Fiji, the chrysanthemum, and cherry blossom where symbolized in the arts then and now.

1644 – 1694 The poet Matsuo Basho is famous for *haiku,* linked verse, and *hokku.* He began his life as a *samurai,* lived as a commoner, and avoided the court life of Edo and Kyoto. His advice to his students was, "Do not seek to follow the footsteps of the men of old, seek what they sought."

1872 The Meji Reformation marks the end of the Edo Period. (The *samurai* code of honor and a high level of artistic and cultural achievement characterized the Edo Period.)

Acknowledgements

I AM GRATEFUL TO the many people in this world who allowed me to experience and appreciate their culture, their crafts, and their arts. Thank you for a smile when we had no common language. Thank you for the help when I was lost. Thank you for proving that for all our seeming differences, we are much the same.

To my dear friend Gillian E. W. Shaw, who read every word and corrected my errors, understood me, and faithfully supported my cause. I am forever grateful you persevered with the *Ancient Echoes* manuscript and me.

To my dear sister Sallie, whose opinions I value, who gave me her support, as she has since my first day on earth.

To Ruthie, whose love of all thing Japanese was contagious; and her generous and lovable husband, Stuart, who indulged and tolerated our every whim. Ruthie, it makes me smile to know that somewhere there is a Buddhist priest telling a tale of two American ladies sitting in the middle of his cemetery eating lunch. It was my good fortune to find you two again in this life.

To my good friend Jan, only a phone call away, her support and encouragement never flagged.

To Tim Hoover and other American soldiers who inculcated the spirit of the warrior in me.

To Shinya Okada and Masaaki Tanaka, friends through eternity.

To Peter Seeganna (deceased) and King Island carvers Earl Mayac, Sylvester Ayac, John Penatac, and Bernard Katazak (deceased). Melvin Olanna of Shishmerif (deceased), John Kalukiak of Tooksok Bay, and Larry Avakana of Barrow. Knowing you all brought joy to my life and helped me understand who I am.

I am a product of my education and teachers, and influenced by several institutions of spiritual and higher learning, including the Association of Research and Enlightenment, the legacy of Edgar Cayce and the following persons whose work has touched me: Mark Thurston, PhD; Henry Reed, PhD; Kevin Todeschi; Mary Roach; Charles Thomas Cayce; Mary Elizabeth Lynch, JD; John Van Auken; David Childress; Christopher Dunn; Shelley Takai, PhD; and Peter Woodbury. Teachers, all. Their wisdom and knowledge may be expressed herein.

To Ronni Miller, an extraordinary writing coach, who can be found at Writeitout.com.

To Stephanee Killen and Integrative Ink for her guidance and conscientious and professional service, who can be found at IntegrativeInk.com.

I thank those I worked with every day, who gave me an appreciation for all things Japanese. Yoshiaki Kobayashi for his guidance. Noriyo Nakamura, who tolerated my lack of Japanese language skills and my never ending questions our visits to a shrine provoked. I know translating exhausted you. Hydrangeas remind me of you. Yukie "Kay" Tamaki, washi paper wizard. Yoshio Nodera, Tsuyoshi Yajima, Takeo Shinohara, Katosan, Jun Aota, and Yoshinori Kuriki. Yes, Kurikisan, Americans are noisy. Hiroko Ida, who taught me the intricacies of picking antique silk, and Ikebana Master, Kikouetsu Tanaka, who never met a flower, stem, or leaf she could not improve upon.

The Theosophical Society of America's Madame Helena Blavatsky (HPB), who searched the universe for ancient wisdom and set it down for us—for whatever we might do with it.

CPSIA information can be obtained at www.ICGtesting.com
Printed in the USA
LVOW13s1310130913

352330LV00001B/2/P